Leather to the Corinthians

Tom Lucas

Publisher's Note: This is a work of fiction. Names, characters, events and places are used fictitiously. Resemblance to actual events, locations, corporations, products, entities and or persons living or dead is purely coincidental.

Book Design & Layout: Interlinear Dynamics, LLC.
www.interlineardynamics.com

Cover Art: Sean Bieri ©2012
www.themanwhojaped.blogspot.com/

Photography: Erika Barker ©2012
www.erikabarker.com/

This has been a Room 1331 production.

ISBN: 0988526107

ISBN-13: 978-0988526105

LCCN: 2012919854

Printed and manufactured in the United States of America.

For my wife, friends, and family – and all of my other ardent supporters.

"Your gratitude should really begin now…"

Could It Be Evil?
(a checklist)

- ✓ FAMILY MEMBERS
- ✓ FRIENDS
- ✓ NON BELIEVERS
- ✓ THE POOR
- ✓ THOSE WHO DO NOT LISTEN TO THE WORD
- ✓ NON-SUBSCRIBERS
- ✓ THE INDECENT
- ✓ THE IGNORANT
- ✓ PEACE-LOVERS
- ✓ POTPOURRI

To learn more about how to avoid being evil be sure to thoroughly read the enclosed primer handbook and then submit your will by visiting our website:

www.churchofthebigredj.com

Visit now and become an Official Sidekick of the BIG RED J today!

Leather to the Corinthians

CONTENTS

fax transmission

12.2789/A/46.0-01

Dear Mother,

I know that you really didn't want me to get into the wage wars, but I really didn't have much choice. I was not born with a silver spork in my mouth and there is no denying otherwise. I was put on this green grocer to work. I know that now.

I have joined the General's Army. Now I know that we always went to the King for his Deals but I'm in it for the Perks and valuable Cash & Prizes. The bottom line is that there are two types of people in this world: Servers and Customers. You know what father taught was always right...if I work hard at the first, I might become the second.

Work on the General's line is difficult and I must still deal with the rush. However, I'm beginning to see the Lite. The rumors of continued outright aggression towards the King leak about, and I can't help but think that the General is thinking about closing up early for the King. This is known in industry lingo as Dis-His-Franchise. I am resolved and ready to fight. I will fax or e-mail you as often as possible.

Your son's name here,

a soldier.

......**end transmission**

1. Come a Little Closer

Exterior: You are in a bleak field, filled with weeds and trash.

A crowd gathers and you recognize many of your friends and co-workers among the strange faces. An older man appears on a soapbox. He wears a large top hat and a bright red tattered tuxedo. He raises a megaphone...

I know what ails you!

Gather round, all you tattooed, lost soul wandering, Wi-Fi/Lo-Fi mutants! Come!

Come over here, all you swollen pineal gland, third-eye having, genetically crossbred hybrid super-freaks! Get on with your bad selves!

Turn on, all you telepathic, degenerate, UFO subterranean gaping-mouthed, prehensile tailed monsters!

Come see the true reality! Come see the answer!

I know what ails you.

I know what troubles bring you forward in droves to stare at the mighty juice, the glorious oil that transforms the beaten into full-blown raving geniuses. What I offer will not only satisfy, it will fulfill. I know this because I have looked into your shallow eye sockets and have seen the blood-stained traumas and horrors of your ancient astronaut ancestors – ancestors whose bio-seeds gave birth to the many-armed succubae tormentors of your secret psychic souls. Your years of meta-body personal apocalypse, for which no self-help book can assuage, are nearing their end as you drop open drooling jaws to this ultimate, extreme wonder-product of the new and improved age!

A tonic to exhilarate! An oil to lubricate! A cure for all that ails you!

Yes, come closer. See the cure. Witness its power. See for yourself that which you have sought all along! For I alone, have the cure for all of your miseries, mysterious diagnosed conditions, typed and phenotyped.

A blitzkrieg of postmodern, avant-garde consumption is what stands before you, sporting a gleaming showcase and stellar package design. Know that great pains were taken by reality contest-winning champions of marketing and psychology to achieve such consumer-leeching greatness!

Admire its modern sleekness with a nod to past tradition. Absorb its glorious aura that speaks to a wisdom beyond your miniscule sensory abilities. A Holy Tribute to all concepts of mass marketing, it plunges bull's-eye darts into your dark demographic, laser-sighting all of your self-flagellating desires.

All your life you have wanted to know what could fill your personal void. What spackle could handle a hole that size? You always knew there was something missing, and you have paced trenches into your Astroturf trying to figure it out.

Well, by fucking golly, here it is! Here is the panacea for your stunted and lackluster existence.

Wait – before I show you, there is much, much more.

Oh, what's that? Do I hear moaning? Do I hear whining? Will the sound of a thousand bloggers flaming this humble salesman rock the night sky?

Please— I know you're excited, but you really need to swallow the instant-action medication of your choice and take a deep fucking breath.

I know that your vertebrae have strained and snapped under the wheel of the MAN. I know that your condemnation to LIVE BY THE SWEAT OF YOUR BROW has incarcerated you in the prison of your manual labors. Oh, how the blood and tears have dribbled off your skin and fallen to the ground only to evaporate without acknowledgment! No crime so great should go unpunished. Honestly, I know. It's really too much for anyone to bear.

That is why I am here.

You scream, "GIVE ME MY SALVATION!"

I hear you.

You scream, "I'M MAD TO SELL BECAUSE I CAN'T BUY ANYMORE!"

I hear you.

Leather to the Corinthians

I know what ails you.

You scream and pull your hair out and nothing seems right. No amount of manufactured content can satisfy that deep, dark hole that you possess. The more you consume, the more you have to demand. This is truly madness!

I won't toy with you for much longer, my fine multi-celled beastly brothers and sisters. Mark my words, you will dig deep for this key to tomorrow's satisfaction. Your excitement is palpable! Rejoice in finally knowing that there is a final destination for your carefully-monitored paycheck.

That is why I am here today with my powerhouse product.

I know that what I offer you will silence the screams. It will ease the suffering and bring peace and serenity to all. Yes, it will cost you.

But then again, my friend, what does not cost you?

I see your eyes darting about at the searingly, clear-coated, and vending-machine-ready collection of fine goodies I place before you. I know that you ache to reach out and have these all-fulfilling objects of Styrofoam, aerosol-inspired creation. But know that the one true human emotion, WANT, will not so easily be vanquished by a mere touch. The desire to possess is beyond measure, but remember, the chase is always better than the catch.

Always, always leave them wanting more.

Unlike this lifetime, this all-purpose product has a warranty and a guarantee! And coming soon? A 24-hour, online support chat-room. So come closer and I will show you more!

2. An Account of the Invasion of the Village by Hostile Corporate Forces

He pulled at his tight regulation uniform shirt. Its plastic/polyester mix molested his skin and its resistance to his sweat made the shirt sickly damp and nasty. They told him that the artificial fibers would make him feel eight percent more efficient. At best he felt thirty percent more irritated. He snorted in disgust.

He pulled at the shirt until it slipped free from the elastic waistband of his pants. It was a soldier's duty to keep neat and clean, but it had been a long morning, and he just didn't care anymore. Grease stains mottled his once pristine uniform shirt, and the collected grit and grime of the rush over the hill jammed deep and black under his fingernails. A stench of putrid fryer oil and fetid meat permeated every false fiber of his uniform. At one time, he may have, but now he certainly didn't look like the blotchy-faced teenager on the recruitment poster the General had stuck on every wall in town. His uniform had failed to seal in his freshness.

Giving up on one of the General's favorite slogans, "Neatness Counts!" he decided that it wouldn't hurt to look around. His crew was busy tending to the wounded, straightening their squashed clown noses and wiping off the offending mix of blood and makeup from their faces. The logistics of outfitting an army completely with clown costumes were staggering, and prolonged battles revealed certain flaws in such an aesthetic decision. The General's ego, however, had to be appeased.

He pulled a smoke from the pack he kept taped to the front of his visor. Placing it precariously on his lip, he bent in search of his lighter. Fumbling through his "Smoking Is FUNdamental" promotional fanny pack (obtained through redeeming a large number of empty cartons), his fingers eventually found their target, and he pulled it up, smiling in victory. He put the death stick up to his smudged lips and cracked a smirk only someone who has been to flavor country could appreciate. He took a long, slow drag holding it deeply inside his lungs. Exhaling, he knew this feeling of joy would not last.

In fact, it was over.

Standing in front of him was the General.

The General's permanent smile had turned into a frown. Veins popped in his white forehead.

"Soldier!" the General screamed, "Smoking while off duty is not allowed! Extinguish that cigarette and tuck in that shirt!"

Quick to obey, the cig dropped immediately from his lips and his hands rushed to stuff the offending shirttails into his striped stretch pants.

The General was not finished.

"Soldier, do you know why we don't smoke in this man's army? Because it's bad for the corporate image, son. We have licensing agreements to uphold," the General said matter-of-factly. "Look, it's been brutal today. We have pounded the Village below for hours, suffered three charges by the King's troops, and all our taps are out of soda. How long have we held this hill? How long with nothing but kid's meals for rations and no fucking prize inside?"

The General broke into an even wider grin than his perma-makeup would normally allow.

"Too long. I know the time of day is beer-thirty, but we must press on. We must take the Village and depose the King. His marketing strategies are starting to take hold, and if we don't crush him now, the Village may never be ours. This is why we fight, son. This is why I fight. The King is mad and his food is bad, and it's up to us to end his tyranny! I am counting on young men and women such as yourself, to get into the trenches for me and make all of this carnage worth a fucking damn."

The Soldier stood silently. This guy was pretty inspirational, now that he thought about it. He felt his spine straighten a bit.

"Why did you join my fight, son?" the General demanded.

The Soldier stammered. "Because life under the King was bullshit, sir. I...I wanted a better life. I wanted to make a difference... I...I wanted opportunity!"

"Fight hard, and you will have it!" The General boomed.

The General sashayed away, motioning the Soldier to follow. The General's charismatic grin killed any resistance. He followed. The General, majestic in his creamy orange jumper (which lent a pro-styled chic look that contrasted nicely with the chemical burst fade of his fiery engine-red hair) carried himself across the battlefield with a strut befitting Alexander. The Soldier found himself in complete and captivated awe.

Somewhere, in the back of his mind, bands played glorious marching music. Drumlines became white noise. Clearly, there was something in the secret sauce he was forced to add to every meal in the mess hall.

The General stopped in his tracks.

"You know, young man, there is something that I really like about you. I can see you going very far in this organization," assured the General.

The Soldier nodded. The General was most certainly right. In this moment, he felt like a real team player. He felt like a real people-person who could interface with key clients.

The General looked deep into the Soldier's eyes and barked his orders.

"Soldier, I want you to round up the troops and make a reassessment. Really think out of the box on this one! Write me a report using no less than four software suites. A report that dazzles the mind – the kind that everyone will download and share with friends and families. And, I want it printed out in triplicate. You hear me?" the General ordered.

"Yes sir!" the Soldier responded obediently.

$

Scratch Microphone looked out from a small grove of trees down toward the Village. There was not much movement in the smoky rubble. Perhaps the red-haired one had finally polished off the Village's inhabitants. It made no difference to Scratch. This fierce warrior, head of the Dodge Tribe, bowed to no one and would conduct business as usual with the final occupants. The Elders of the tribe had always preached that one shopping channel is as good as any other. Yea, verily.

Scratch pulled out his supercool infrared zoom lenses to take a better look at the carnage.

Wow, this place is pretty fucked up.

Many buildings were destroyed or on fire. Heavy smoke hung in the air. It blacked out the sky and choked all hopeful light into nothingness. The only evidence of the sun was a strange orange glow that made everything above the horizon a sea of fire.

It would make for a great scene in a movie, like that end-of-the-world flick with John Cusack.

The King's castle seemed intact, as was the highly protected corporate enclave known as the "Sell Inc. Executive Living Complex." Its sparkling glass towers and high concrete barricades were completely untouched. Surely, their higher-ups had made some kind of deal prior to the attack. Scratch could see sweating consumers on their treadmills in the gym on the eighty-eighth floor. It would appear that they were completely unfazed by the morning's events.

Scratch continued his voyeuristic recon.

He could see the church. In the distance, a dark-cloaked figure was practicing slam-dunks on the half-court behind it. The figure played in a clumsy and awkward manner. Whoever it was, they had no game. Scratch made a mental sticky note to school this person proper when he had more time.

Everything else he could see looked seriously trashed, and Scratch wondered if there would be much business out of the Village anytime soon. He reassured himself that even bad business is better than no business, attempted to wipe the smoke from his eyes, and took another look.

At first, it seemed that there was little movement. Scratch waited. Soon he could see a green glowing figure, courtesy of his awesome binocular device. He really loved his eyepiece. Soon the glow multiplied, and they were all over the place.

Shit, the media has arrived.

Scratch decided to head back to the tribe's encampment. There he would consult with the Elders and come up with a plan. His original thought to hit the Village for books of old Green Stamps and the random crate of Spa-ham Lite for the kids would simply have to wait.

$

The side door to the inner chamber flew open, and the King charged in with purpose. His sudden entrance caused his underlings much distress as they had been leaning instead of cleaning, and the King was not one to tolerate anyone fucking off while they were supposed to be at fucking work.

The Royal Announcer quickly grabbed his microphone, cleared his throat, and bellowed the King's introduction with the biggest big-boy voice he could muster.

"Hailing from the gated communities of Nowhereimportantsville, let's give a big welcome to the Master of Disaster, The Purple Monster, the Underpayer of Manual Labor, the Man with the Plan, the One, the Only, his Majesty...THE KING!"

There was brief, staccato applause – nervous and tentative – as the King looked over at his announcer and winced. The King slumped in his throne. His advisers continued to swarm the royal chamber, quietly chatting about their current favorite shows and arguing about the funniest home videos they had ever seen. Was it the one where the skater crunches his balls on a stairwell railing? Maybe the child vs. bear cub fighting video? It was truly a debate that had no objective conclusion.

"SILENCE!" the King shouted. "I can't believe I ate the whole thing. Somebody get me a Bromo."

The royal advisers scrambled. Sane was not a word that one would use to describe the monarch and he was clearly upset. As was his stomach. The problem was that the more upset the King would get, the less sense he would make until he spoke only in slogan, search engine results, pop-ups, and jingles. The King was not all that friendly in these times. Considering that half the Village lay in rubble and smoke, he had a perfectly good reason to be all worked up.

There once had been a time, one spoken about only in whispers, when the King had been young, kind, and mentally stable. As time passed however, either the power or the responsibilities of the job had caused him to slowly unravel, and now merely speaking ill of him could mean death or the third shift.

An aide dressed in the royal polyesters approached the throne with a tonic and lime. The King, in perhaps his frumpiest of bathrobes, sat slumped in a relatively unknown yoga position – the Lebowski.

"Your Grace—"

"Call me Ishmael!" insisted the King.

"Whatever. Lord, thou hast grown weary from stress of battle and the months of siege upon our Village and castle. I fear that your eye for battle wishes to close from its rotten vision. I suggest you confer with your military advisor."

"Huh? I wasn't really paying attention to you. Did you say confer? What is that? Person or place? Seems kinda familiar."

"Sir, your Commander of Armies is here," said the aide with a sigh.

"Send him in."

The great revolving doors of the chamber spun, and Commander Thighmaster came thundering in, his black armor greasy and caked in filth. His thick black beard contained smears of blood and gristle. He also had the unmistakable stench of death upon him. The King pulled his slumped form up in his chair.

"My Lord, I bring news from the front," boomed Thighmaster.

"And what is it?" enquired the King.

"All is lost. We are half past the monkey's ass and a quarter to its balls," whined Thighmaster.

"There, there, Boo-Boo. I'm not mad at you. Tell Daddy what happened," crooned the King in smooth, sounding tones, the kind you'd hear in a kid's TV show.

"We lost the Colonel and all his men today on the hill," Thighmaster sniffed. "He said he had the secret recipe for victory, but it turned out to be a big bucket of shit! Then the foul General let loose with viral attacks, sneaky pincher moves, and released his demonic Kroftian beasts! We were hit from all sides, and possibly even from within. By the time it was all over, our men lay dead or dying. But that wasn't enough for the evil General, no sir. He then whipped out his giant hose and sprayed us with his special sauce! It was a money shot no one walked away from!" It was clear that this brave and manly knight was about to cry like a big armored baby.

"You are right, it does seem that all is lost. Perhaps we should consult the Oracle," the King concluded. "Aide, hand me my phone. I think her number is 1-976...."

$

Father Everhard looked at his watch. It was almost time to finish up. Stuffing the last bites of an Aunty Nuke's Gourmet Microwave Burrito into his mouth, the lanky, grey-haired priest rose from the table. Wiping his mouth on his sleeve, Everhard smoothed down his tunic and pulled up his garters, as he wondered how long his freakish metabolism could handle the amount of crap food he consumed.

"Damn things always droop," he mumbled.

It had been a bloody morning. The incessant pounding of the enemy forces on the ridge had given him one helluva migraine. He saw light spots surround the periphery of his vision. It was a struggle to think.

Father Everhard left the kitchen and walked through the dark hall that joined the rectory with the church. Stopping midway, he scrounged for his Archangel Michael Jordan Official Reem Team Basketball. Gripping its synthesized rubber skin, he trotted out into the back half-courtyard. He performed a poor crossover dribble and took a quick shot.

He missed.

"Well, GODDAMN!" he shouted.

This vicious cycle of weak technical skills, poorly aimed shots, and Tourette's style cursing continued for about 15 minutes until Everhard felt fairly warmed up.

Everhard made his way into the church. Its high ceiling begged for a regulation hoop. He reminded himself to go shop for one tomorrow, if there was one. The war had ravaged the Village, and Everhard was not much of an optimist. Still, he did have the church. It was *his* parish, and he ran a tight ship. If parishioners came late to Mass, they would most definitely not receive their complimentary French chocolates (with the hand-applied gold filigree crosses) after the service.

"Got to stay hard!" he reminded himself.

The priest walked up to the altar, pausing to do a quick grin and shuffle for the Man. The Man loved the soft shoe, and Everhard had spent months when he first arrived to the church searching for priest shoes that didn't clomp on the hard wood. What was that move he had just looked up on the Internet? The "Two-Step Buck

Time Two Step?" He struggled to remember the moves as he quietly scatted.

"Da hip da do ha hip hip hop hop."

He looked up to the cross.

"Oh Lord, help me to divine one's wishes," he proclaimed. "What is your plan for us now?"

The Big Red J looked down at him. There he hung, same old dumb look on his face, his painted blue tights and red cape frozen in wood. He offered no helpful suggestions. In fact, the effigy sometimes seemed aggravated that people kept asking him for things.

"Lord, give me a new and improved recipe for survival," Everhard decreed.

Big J just looked down at him, with his painted white teeth grinding as always, his hands clenched fists over neon green radioactive nails embedded deep in his palms.

"Awww, phooey," the priest whined. Standing once more, Everhard made the sign of the cross, busted out a quick tap step, and belched three times for good luck.

$

The corporate boardroom of Sell Inc. was packed to its off-the-rack, ill-fitted, navy-blue-suit gills. Whether it was daytime or nighttime, peacetime or time of war, Sell Inc. was always in business. Time is always time, and Sell Inc. always sells. These complete bastards, these horrifically sociopathic creatures, sought only to pounce on the weak and suck them dry. This multi-national, multi-dimensional, cross-media conglomerate owned damn near everything and everyone in the Village. They were often thanked by those they victimized.

The CEO sat at the end of the table, his fat belly pushing his shirt's buttons to the limit. The gaps between them revealed soft, fatty tissues and stretch marks. He rolled his thick thumbs. Various small computer implants were mounted in strategic places on his head, neck, and shoulders. Their twinkling lights and chirping beeps turned his head into a miniature Las Vegas Strip.

"Good, good," he asserted, "can we hear from our Advance Reconstruction Team Representative?"

A young, slender man in a tight-cut Burberry suit rose to speak. His tense, taut million dollar smile displayed an eagerness and self-motivation greater than the sum of all previously known self-help books combined.

"Sir, our conclusion is that once the takeover is completed, the first thing we do is kill all the lawyers," the thin man reported with a toothy, gleaming grin.

The boardroom exploded. Papers were thrown about the room and threats were made. The CEO chuckled and waved his arm to calm the rabid throng of MBAs and CPAs. The lawyers were damn near inconsolable.

"A fine suggestion, but far too literary for my taste. We need something much more post-postmodern, more proactive, more deconstructionist, more turnkey," the CEO announced. "I have thought about this situation for some time now. It has never been enough for me or any of the other board members to merely own everything. I have spent countless nights watching graphs and charts broadcast across my eyelids. I have run laps in my lavish penthouse. I have snorted copious amounts of speed and written out proposals and plans, even while fucking every hot broad I could get my claws on," he grunted, as he tightly clenched his fists, "all I could do was think about our next move. I feel that although we have acquired so much, there is this intrinsic emptiness that must somehow be filled with an external source...what we do next is everything!"

"But sir, most of us are pretty happy," chimed another bright and shiny slender penny. He was as thin as a dime, his internal hunger having corporeal form.

Without even making eye contact with the young turk, the CEO suddenly batted the young executive down with an open bear paw slap. A sickening crack revealed a new job opening in his department.

No one moved. Not a blink. Not a breath.

A brave soul slowly stood.

"Okay..." pronounced a third gaunt young exec. "We do have Plan Extreme."

"Ah yes, Plan Extreme. I had forgotten about that. Please refresh my memory," the CEO said nodding his head.

$

Brad Perfect, Network One News Anchor, sat pensively at his faux-mahogany prop desk watching for the stage manager's cues. Today's news was probably the most important news he had delivered in his manufactured life. Brad's forehead would be sweating profusely at this moment if it weren't for the fact that he had no sweat glands above the waist. Brad was the result of many designs and mishaps and the Network One talent geneticists had figured out a way to keep the perspiration out of the camera's view. When you think about it, it makes a lot of sense, the enhancements made to his neoprene prepped flesh easily handled the hot Obilights which were mounted on top of the cameras to smooth out facial features.

However, underneath his desk, below the eye of the camera, Brad's pants were soaked with so much sweat one might think he had pissed his pants.

At least my hair looks good, Brad thought as he checked his appearance in the preview monitor. This was a redundant thought as Brad's hair always looked good. It was a silky nylon microfiber and was never out of place.

Brad heard movement from the crew as he waited to go to the live broadcast. He was nervous, not only because of the seriousness of the day's events, but the impending danger of the studio crew. One had to be careful with the Network One studio crew. They exist to fuck with you, especially on live, international, streaming video.

Brad knew to look for false cues. The crew loved it when you stumbled to a start. They especially loved the "deer in headlights" look, it was one of their favorites.

One by one, the crew members took their place on the sound stage. They were very quiet, and were certainly up to something. Their dark shapes, hidden by the bright lights, added to the foreboding nature of their presence.

The stage manager began a silent countdown with his fingers.

Five. Brad tightened his tie.

Four. Brad cleared his throat.

Three. Brad scratched his balls.

Two. Brad scrunched his shoulders.

One. The Stage Manager took his one finger and promptly flew Brad the bird.

"YOU LOUSY SONUVABITCH!" Brad screamed as the red light of Camera Two blinked on.

Brad was LIVE.

The teleprompter pushed Brad forward.

With the calm of a ninja, Brad morphed back to composure, and with even-toned, standard North American Broadcast English, he began the news.

"Early this morning, the Rebel General MacDonald engaged in what turned out to be his most devastating attack to date. Although his siege of the Village has gone on for several weeks now, his attacks had been minor in comparison to the damage he caused today. Half of the Village is in complete ruin, and all malls have been closed until further notice. Word from the King is that we are to expect another attack before nightfall. Authorities strongly suggest that you find shelter now or bend over and kiss your ass goodbye."

$

The sound of an armored car's engine growling to life woke the Soldier suddenly. Sleep was a precious commodity. The Soldier's drowsy eyes began to take in the picture before him: hundreds of men getting their weapons ready for battle, armored columns forming from previously disorganized swarms of tanks and cars, supplies being distributed among the troops. This army was a freak force of nature, a death clown-car, a disheveled mess. This army existed for the purpose of destroying the King and putting the General firmly in his place.

Once more, towering above him, was the General.

"Have you seen Network One?" asked the General, with a freakish smile stretching from ear to ear. (Of course, considering the thick red lipstick grin painted on his face already, he would have been smiling anyway.)

He continued.

"We were all over the news just a few minutes ago. We've got them on the ropes. Today is the day! Time to kick a little ground chuck, fella. Up and at 'em!" the General commanded.

The Soldier jumped to attention.

"Do you have that little report I asked you to put together? Is it printed out in triplicate?" the General demanded.

The Soldier patted his pockets. *Oh fuck! I plum forgot all about it. Better just wing it.*

"Sir, I have created an oral report," the Soldier countered. "It is this: all the King's horses and all the King's men couldn't put the Land of Candy back together again."

"A lovely rendition and appropriation of two classic children's references. When we get back, I'll talk to the Biggy Boy and see if we can't get you some sort of promotion," declared the General. "Now, listen up! We have a battle to win. I want you to go over to B+ Squad and make sure those bastards are ready."

The General handed the Soldier a Junior Death Squad Funtime Walkie Talkie. It was made of thick, bulky orange plastic and was covered with skulls and crossbones.

"When you are ready, flash three times with the Panic button. Rave on," the General asserted, patting the Solider on the back.

The Soldier was off and running. He felt excited to be a part of something, and his blood was pumping.

Hmm, maybe there is something to this Wage Warrior business? He thought. *Maybe being a mercenary is an excellent career choice after all.*

Soon he reached B+ Squad's artillery station. The catapults seemed to be in order. The five-man crew sat stoking a big fat joint. They hardly noticed him. The Soldier cleared his throat. One member of the group, a blonde-haired, blue-eyed, muscle beach type, looked up at him and said, "Whassup?"

"The General wanted me to see if your crew were ready for the final assault. Say, umm, do you think I could hit that?" asked the Soldier as he eagerly eyed the monstrous roach.

Nodding his head in stoner approval, the Aryan youth handed him the burning ganja stick. The Soldier took a deep drag and sniffed the burning end of the blunt for good luck.

Three minutes later the Soldier released his breath, "Thanks, man."

The crew seemed good and ready, so he pulled out the Junior Death Squad radio and hit the Panic Button on his walkie talkie three times.

A half mile away, the General peered through cartoonish, fire engine red binoculars. The specs were one of his most prized possessions, a replica of the same used by Zanaxe the Slow Explorer in the short-lived cartoon, *The Cartographer Lies Heavy.*

The Village looked decimated, but he knew that there was still some healthy resistance out there. This time, it would be quelled.

He put down the binoculars and picked up his radio as it went off. He turned it on and barked the order to begin the final attack. Whistling shells flew into the air, and row upon row of sweaty men flowed over the ridge and into the valley heading towards the Village. "Mmm...McWar sure is swell," the General hummed in satisfaction.

$

Scratch gunned his classic electric blue 1969 Charger down a hidden road behind the Village's garbage dump. The constant crunch of disposable living could be heard as the car's tires cut a path through the remains of the day. He was certainly taking the low road. As he neared the tribe's encampment, he prepped the car for a full 180 degree bootlegger reverse. With Scratch, it was always about the entrance and exit.

The car came roaring towards the nomadic enclave, and Scratch slammed it into a perfect reverse. It was a glorious approach representing the warrior's victorious mood as it slid to a stop. Scratch grabbed the day's booty and jumped out of the car.

Immediately upon exiting, Scratch was surrounded by all the tribe's screaming children. Rushing him, they pulled at his studded leather loincloth, fiercely grabbing at his sack of goodies. Flexing his well-developed arms, Scratch corralled the kiddies into a neat line. The kids began their litany of requests, begging, and complaints.

"Did you get a Playtime Station 5 this time?"

"Candy! I want lots of candy!"

"Botox?"

Pausing for a moment, Scratch took a quick look at the circular compound, taking a short inventory of the other adult members of the tribe who were present. Most of the tribe stood outside their vehicles, except, of course, the Elders, who were enshrined in a Whiney-bago. The Elders never left the Whiney-bago. Ever.

After getting an eyeful, Scratch returned to the task at hand.

"Ok, you little Mall Rats, let's see what Santa Scratch has brought for you today!" he proclaimed as he reached into the bag that was filled with new trade goods from the Village.

Today had been a real Scarlet Letter day. There were goodies of all sorts in the bag. The children clamored and climbed over one another as he pulled out various jars of petroleum byproducts, dirty needles, Toonka Trucks, canned salami-like meat, two rubber president masks, plush toupees, espresso makers, rat poison, and best of all, a vintage G.I Soldier with Kung-Fu Grip.

The kiddies were ecstatic. Scratch was happy, too. Somewhere, someone laughed. Things were good. Then, suddenly, the booming of artillery shells echoed in the distance. The explosions were getting closer.

Scratch knew that the tribe was going to have to get a move on in order to better their business strategy. This decision, although his privilege, would have to be run by the Elders first. They did have the right to veto.

Scratch dropped the bag, causing a near riot amongst the children, as he made his way to the Elders' RV. Scratch checked his fanny pack for coupons. The Elders always wanted coupons. If Scratch even tried talking to them without tribute, they would insist that they were napping and instruct him to go away. Fortunately, Scratch had plenty of coupons on him this day.

He rapped the secret knock on the trailer's door. He could hear all six of the Elders inside, talking about times long gone. It vaguely sounded like they were playing their usual game of bingo between long-winded stories. When they heard him knocking, the voices stopped. Then a single, withering voice mumbled something indiscernible.

"What?" asked Scratch

"Do you have any coupons?" screeched the voice.

"Yes"

"What?"

"YES! I HAVE YOUR GODDAMN COUPONS!" Scratch screamed.

"You have our permission to enter," uttered another straining voice.

Scratch opened the door and was immediately greeted by a putrid wall of old farts and cooking cabbage. He vomited slightly, but kept it in his mouth and managed to swallow it back down. This was never easy.

He went up the steps and there, at the sacred card table, sat six of the Village Elders. These old prunes were really in charge of everything. Scratch couldn't even remember how old they were.

The three men looked much older than the three women did, but they all possessed ratty, silver hair and skin so translucent you could watch the blood slowly creep throughout their veins. The fact that they had long ago refused to wear clothing could give a person irritable bowel syndrome just by looking at them.

How old were these fuckers? Why wouldn't they just die already so he wouldn't have to go through this every time he had to make the decision to move? It was as if they lived only to spite him.

Scratch began to speak but was interrupted.

"TRIBUTE!" the six demanded.

Scratch bit his tongue as he produced the necessary coupons. He slammed them on the table, trying desperately not to look at their terrible, hunched bodies.

"SPEAK!" the six commanded.

Quickly Scratch began his presentation, going over all the major events of the day and pointing out that artillery shells could be heard flying over their camp towards the Village. His speech was eloquent, colorful, and succinct. In fact, it went so well, that Scratch was granted his request to move the camp. Upon hearing the confirmation, Scratch flew out of the RV. He was happy not only to get the approval, but also for the breath of fresh air.

"Hey people! Listen up!" he declared to the tribe. "We're off like a prom dress!"

$

The King was on the phone making friends.

Nice friends.

Talking to girls.

Nice girls.

Girls who would be happy to talk to you about their innermost secrets. Life was just one big party line for the King. In a way, it was reassuring that he was keeping to old habits considering the way things were going for him. In another sense, it was pathetic. Thighmaster approached the throne.

Startled by the commander's sudden presence, the King jumped up and cupped a hand over the phone.

"Can't you see I'm busy?" the King hissed.

"But my Lord—" began Thighmaster.

The King interrupted Thighmaster's words by slamming the phone down.

"Well what IS it?" he groaned, rolling his eyes.

"Sir, we have captured an enemy agent. He was in the treasure room. We caught him knee-deep in the goods," said Thighmaster.

"Anybody I would know? The General likes to keep a number of characters by his side."

"Would you like to see him?"

The King nodded.

"Wonderful! Guards, send him in," boomed Thighmaster.

The guards wrestled in a squirmy, babbling, dark figure. As he was brought into the light, he began to look familiar. He wore a striped prison shirt, black hat and cape, and a black domino mask. The King perked up when he realized that he did indeed know the so-called agent.

"Hamm, it's good to see you. I hope the guards weren't too rough on you," cooed the King.

Hamm the Burglar spouted some unintelligible noises.

"Hamm, I know that you have very little allegiance to the General. I was wondering if you might be willing to reveal some information in return for your freedom," offered the King. "Of course, this is contingent on someone here being able to understand your bizarre muttering language."

Hamm refused. The burglar shook his head violently.

"Then you will face the Torturer's whims. I will find out the General's weaknesses!" shouted the King.

The King motioned for the guards to take the prisoner to the dungeons.

"Flame-broil him!" ordered the King.

As if on cue, the thud of incoming shells knocked on the castle wall.

"Nobody here but us chickens," mumbled the King.

The guards dragged off the odd criminal as he continued to babble and make strange noises. Thighmaster looked at the King and shrugged his shoulders. Even if this enemy agent was rattling off trade secrets, no one in the court could tell.

The King took a deep breath and spoke.

"Commander Thighmaster, I think we may have to come to the inevitable conclusion that we are not going to win this battle. I want you to gather my Imperial Guard and protect the castle at all costs.

We can probably broker some kind of deal between ourselves, the General, Sell Inc., and the Dodge Tribe."

"Yes, sir! I am off and running," proclaimed Thighmaster as he charged out of the chamber.

As am I, thought the King.

$

Father Everhard left the church through the front doors and headed out onto the grounds. He surveyed the damage. Not too bad, he thought. He had been happy that his half court was intact. This was just gravy now. For the most part, the church's yard was surprisingly untouched by the battle.

Maybe these guys have a bit of reverence? Maybe they couldn't hit the broad side of a recently remodeled loft space? Pondered Everhard.

Walking out towards the sidewalk, the priest pulled out a set of keys from his roomy pockets. He smiled to himself as he fondled the "51% Bitch/49% Sweetheart" keychain.

Approaching the Church of the Big Red J marquee, his fingers found the small, thin plastic key that opened the sign.

It was time to change the message board. Everhard opened the sign and rearranged the letters. When he finished, he took a step back to admire his work. The sign read:

THIS SUNDAY'S SERMON:

JESUS AND THE PROVERBIAL TWINKIE –"GODLEY & CREME"

Who knew what heathens these invaders might be? At least they would have some idea of what was going down with the Big J. Then the gentle silence was interrupted by the sound of explosions at the castle end of the Village.

"Clearly the work of Lex Lucifer," concluded Everhard as he scurried into the church for safety.

$

Electricity flowed through the boardroom of Sell Inc. A young and unpaid intern rushed into the room.

"I have news from the front! I have news from the front!" the intern shouted as he waved a stack of papers in front of the CEO's face.

"Wonderful, wonderful!" exclaimed the CEO. "I'll take those if you please."

The CEO grabbed the papers from the intern and deftly pushed him out the window.

"What tries to go up must come down. Now let's see what our projections look like."

The CEO scrutinized the reports. He made lots of hmmmmm-ing sounds. The anxious executives tested the maximum threshold of their various antiperspirant products as they silently sat around the oval table.

"It looks like the General will have the Village under his control by the evening," stated the CEO.

Only those young business types that were sure raised their arms in victory. The rest of the room politely clapped. One man got up and danced a jig, albeit a restrained jig.

"Ok, gentlemen. Let's get ready for takeover. All those integral to Plan Extreme, get outta here. All others bring me the following: I want three televisions, two tuned to the Network One Broadcast starring Brad Perfect, one with a media player and the full Adventures of Buttman series playing continuously. I also want my best pair of Birkenstocks buffed and polished and three chocolate rolls placed on a Wang Dynasty China Plate for my personal consumption. I think that I will also require three feet of dental floss and a rubber chicken, but check back with me after you get everything else first."

These were not unusual requests from the CEO. He loved junk food and pornography whenever a plan went into effect. This was a good sign and his cadre of fat cats began to move quickly from the room. The CEO tapped at one of his implants and smiled.

$

Brad Perfect was on the air. Brad was the best media anchor in the business. One would hope so as Brad was grown and harvested from a vat deep within the Network One complex, programmed biologically to be the finest newsman ever to grace a desk.

Flawless news delivery was as much a part of Brad as was any genetic aspect of his being, from his sandy brown, molded plasticized hair down to his ten-inch trouser snake. The boy was built.

Reading the news was as natural as breathing for Brad.

So was the slight smile (for light reports), the furrowing brow (for more serious reports), and the blank stare (for commercial breaks). When Brad read the teleprompter, the words went from his eyes to mouth, never stopping at his brain.

This was good, as it left Brad with all his facilities to watch the crew. Remember, the crew liked to fuck with Brad. Out of his peripheral vision, he spotted a grip loading an Uncle Loopey's Big Fun Paint pistol. Brad stayed cool.

"Blah blah blah," went Brad, endlessly streaming the news.

The grip lowered the pistol and took aim. Still, Brad kept calm.

The grip put his finger on the trigger. Brad kept on with the news.

The grip fired. In one quick move, Brad swung the newscast out to a reporter on location and managed to duck the offending projectile which whizzed over his head and hit the weatherman squarely on the neck.

"Ha!" laughed Brad. "Ha ha hahahahahahah!"

An intern rushed a report ripped off the wire to Brad. Snatching the thermal fax paper, Brad scanned the page for the quick facts. The shelling had started once more.

"Now this is some explosive stuff," he blurted.

$

The Soldier secured his helmet and loosened his rifle. A push of men carried him over the ridge and down into the valley. Although he was deep within the throng of men, he still had a clear view of the Village below. Only a few days ago, the Village had sparkled with life, its cozy All-American immigrant-built homes filled with happy families and productive citizens. Now it lay in ruin, grey and smoky, with piles of broken glass, steel girders, and RealLook Plastic siding sitting where dream-come-true homes once were. *It paid to play with the winning team.*

Soon the rabid troops reached the valley and swarmed the hamlet. Resistance was quite low, with the occasional loyalist fighter coming out of their trench, hands raised and unarmed.

They, of course, were shot on sight.

"War is hell, so let's send them to heaven," the General had once said. His troops were more than happy to oblige.

The troops passed by a church that burned from the recent arrival of an incendiary shell. He did not recognize the religious symbols that decorated the front door. It was not his denomination. *The Big Red J must be on our side,* the Soldier thought.

After the church, he came into the town square. The men stopped to pull down the commemorative statue of Elvis shaking hands with the King. As it fell to the ground, one man pissed on the sign which read: "THE KING MEETS THE KING."

From the town square, one could easily see the Royal Palace. The General rode up on a glorious multi-colored horse. He pointed in its direction.

"That, men, is the final goal of today's carnage. Now I want a clean fight with no punches below the belt. But, if that can't be accomplished, then no rules, no regulation. Just kill, kill, kill. Let's slay the King and dance on his pulpy remains. "Sex, Drugs, and Rock 'n' Roll!" shouted the General.

Rallied to the cause, the men echoed the battle cry and shot forward, sure to take the castle once and for all.

$

From his vantage point, Scratch could see the effects of the battle. The General's men were making quick work of the castle gate, turning proud oaken doors into fine toothpick candidates. Scratch shook his head in disgust. The King had been his best trading partner yet. Through the deals Scratch had made with the Royal One, the Dodge Tribe had flourished, and it was questionable as to whether the invaders would keep up the arrangement Scratch had made with the King or if they would just clown around. Scratch knew that this couldn't possibly be the true end of things. There was always a sequel. Surely, the people over at Sell Inc. would want to cut a deal between all interested parties. That's what they always did. For now, the tribe had to move to safety.

"Gentlemen, start your engines!" yelled Scratch.

The tribe responded by firing up their gas-guzzling, Dee-troit chariots. Scratch ran to his other preferred vehicle, a dark green '68 Dart Swinger with a brilliant yellow racing stripe on its hood. Its door swung open and Scratch jumped into the car.

Same time, different channel, shitheads...

$

The King looked over his Handy-Dandy Fallen Dictator Checklist:

1) Talk to pictures on wall

2) Convince Wife/Girlfriend/Significant Other to commit suicide

3) Put on fresh BVDs

4) Put your head between your legs and kiss your ass goodbye

5) Or, if you planned ahead, find escape vehicle and hit the road, Jack.

Four down and one to go. The King could hear the thundering footsteps of the General's troops in the far halls of the castle. Panic struck within him.

"What did I do wrong? he blubbered. "Not enough Special Meal Deals? Not enough attention given to modernizing the company image? Refusal to bathe for any reason?"

The King looked at his throne room. In one corner, a black rotary telephone flashed a red light. This was the direct line to the CEO of Sell Inc. That bastard was probably looking to make a deal. If he had only called earlier, they definitely could have done business. It was too late now.

The King untied his cheesy cape and removed his fake beard. Strangely, suspenseful music began playing through the castle's public address system. Stripping down to his fresh underwear, the King then bolted down the dimly lit hall to the escape pod at its end. Popping the pod's stay-fresh seal, the King snuggled into its cockpit. Years of preparation led him through the launch procedures and soon the pod was airborne, flying through the hazy sky. For a second the Village below was visible. The King looked down and waved.

"See you, suckers!" the King yelled as he flipped his burning village the bird. "I'm off to Eastern Europe where people like me are in great demand. And we make good money!"

$

Father Everhard's headache was back. A ground-zero explosion had loosened a few bones in his noggin. When he rubbed his temples he was convinced that the concussion of the blast had loosened the plate in his skull. He genu-flicked a chunk of plaster out of his hair and tried to orient himself. The church had just received a ten ton love note from the invaders. It was a complete sty. Luckily, the Church of The Big Red J was a pessimistic one, and they had put an emergency manual in every box of Saintly Sweet Communion Wafers.

Everhard combed the church for his copy. Finding the book under a pile of *Richie the Rich Boy* comics, he looked up "Bombings."

BOMBINGS:

In the event that your parish should find itself the target of bombings by land or air, you should do the following:

1) Stand under a doorway.

2) Wonder why you didn't listen to your mother and go to Law School, and...

3) Remember that the Big Red J could very well be watching you. He might even help you out. Maybe.

Should your church actually be bombed and you have somehow managed to survive, you should:

1) Gather all classified documents together.

2) Pour gasoline on them and throughout the church.

3) Set the whole mess on fire as we have a really swell insurance policy and this is the only way we can recoup our losses on this sorry state of affairs.

“If you join the club, then you have to follow the rules,” mumbled Everhard. In rapid and efficient fashion, the priest set the manual's instructions into effect, and soon the church was ablaze. He grabbed his favorite teddy bear and headed out the back door. *I guess you might say God is Pooh-Bah Bear, if you were on Benzedrine at the time....*

$

It was high fives all around Sell Inc. as news of the successful takeover began to trickle in. Although the King had not answered his phone, the General did, and a fairly good deal was negotiated by the two parties. This would leave the Dodge Tribe the last to round up, but that could wait. The CEO had a big smile on his face and the boys in blue suits shouted and laughed as big bottles of Extreme Bubbly Champagne were passed around the room. The CEO brought the volume down and stood to make a speech.

"Fellas, a good thing has happened here today. As a proud sponsor of this entertaining event, I can tell you that a real tear of joy comes to my eye when I think of all the hard work you have done for me for this day. I'm sure that you all are expecting hearty promotions for the tiring groundwork and research you killed yourselves to put together. Of course, you would be right to expect compensation, however, Sell Inc. has hit some hard times as of late, and we're only showing a profit margin of twenty-five percent this quarter. As you can imagine, this is a bit of a blow. Therefore, I'm afraid you all are being let go," the CEO announced with a sly grin.

The spirit of the room died. The CEO then pointed at a chubby, weak man.

"Except for you, Peter. We're promoting you. Come to the board meeting tomorrow for your special assignment."

$

"This is Brad Perfect with the Network One Early Evening Sometime After Our Five O'clock Early Worm Report. Our top story: The combined forces of the General and Sell Inc. have finally defeated the King, completing their hostile takeover of the Village. First-hand accounts of the invasion suggest that there were heavy casualties and word is that Sell Inc. is now accepting applications for new residents.

Sources close to the General stated that a silvery, UFO-like object was seen flying away from the castle, but don't worry -- those sources have been admitted to the mental health facility of their choice. For quotes from the front, we join Ace Reporter Steve Dictate live on site."

3. And Now, A Word From Our Sponsor

Interior: Movie Theatre

You sit in the front row. The room goes dark. The projector flickers light and a man in a top hat (so close up – you can see his nose hairs) fills the screen. His eyes penetrate you...

Well, well, well.

Can you smell what's cooking? Are those delicious smells wafting under your well-trimmed nostrils? Are you salivating, chomping at the bit?

A-N-T-I-C-I-P-A-T-I-O-N.

Let me ask you, what banner do you fly? What's your flag? Where do you place that salute? Who gets your pledge?

As a wise man once asked, "What's in your pipe?"

"Cuz baby, you gotta know. I got this gut feeling, this instinct about you. I know that you aren't some nameless drone in a herd of Sheeple. Just by looking at you, I can tell you are something special. Here, have a participation trophy on me.

I would never criticize you, or judge you. You are far too amazing. You know, if no one has ever told you, I will tell you now.

You have potential.

I just lied – not about you having potential – no way. I lied about never criticizing you. I do have a critique for you. You aren't doing enough with your amazing self. I'm serious here! You have massive amounts of untapped potential. You are overflowing.

Feeling a little bit better? Good.

You need a banner to fly, or one to ride under. I think you may even have one of your own, but for some reason, you are paying some Neanderthal to guard it as it sits in a pay-by-the-month storage facility.

I'm asking you, baby, "What's in your pipe?"

If you don't know, or you're just not sure, then you have to stick with me. I have the knowledge, the key, the philosophy, THE CAUSE for you to believe in. I know that life has a way of grinding you like fair trade coffee; it has a way of digitally chaining you in the corner, with nothing but cold gruel and flagellation to keep you going. All I know about cold gruel and flagellation is that two out of ten people like it.

Looking at your face, I don't think you're in that demographic. I think you want out of those chains, don't you? Well, guess what?

You have the KEY. You can unlock yourself at any time. You don't have to put baby in the corner. All I need you to do is believe in me. Join me, and together we will rule the universe.

Look at those ants, those worker drones sitting next to you, quietly dying in their personal cells. Suffering needlessly because someone, somewhere, told them that this was the road to happiness, the golden pathway to salvation. Work hard, and you'll be rewarded. Do as I say, follow the rules, and it will be a glorious life of rewards for you.

What a bunch of fucking fools, right?

I know that you are not one of them. You are no fool. You have just been waiting for your chance, your mission, your helicopter ride out of the shit. Maybe you have felt incapable, or scared. That's ok. That's normal. That's exactly how they want you to think.

I don't want you to think like they want you to. FUCK THAT. I want you to think as I do, because believe me, it's the best thing for you. I don't want to see someone as special as you wither on the vine, programmed for self-obsolescence. I want you to tap into that great potential of yours, and put it to use.

Do as I say, and trust me, you'll be happy. I am the man with the plan. I got the spreadsheets, the inside track, I KNOW what's going down. Let me plant these seeds, baby, so you can dig.

This ain't no joke, I am not fucking around. I got the golden ticket right here for you, you just gotta sign on the dotted line. I need your signature, or this motion is never going to pass.

I can tell that I've got your interest. Let me ask you, "Who loves you, baby?"

That's right. I do.

I love you and everything you stand for, because you stand for me and behind me. Look, I know it's sudden. Here you were, lost in the woods, shipwrecked, given the wrong food at the drive-thru.

Then suddenly, there I was, powerful and enticing and possessing a hell of a message.

I know, I get it a lot.

What I am telling you is that I will give you the reason to fight. You no longer have to figure it out for yourself. I am your friend, protector, and champion. I will right what is wrong and you will agree with me because you know I am the right man for the job, and that I stand for everything I believe in.

At this point, that needs to be enough. I can't have you questioning my moves, because everything that I will do from this point forward, I do for me, for you, for us.

Sure, there will be the doubters, the protesters, those who won't shut their FUCKING mouths and get on with it, but you are not going to be one of those morons. You are going to be one of those brilliant minds that FUCKING gets it, knows what's up, and sees the trees for the forest. There will be no stutter in your step, that is for damn sure.

Because my friend, I am going to take care of everything for you. Everything. Just fly my banner, fly my flag, salute me when I walk by, and do what I tell you to do. You have to know that you are one of the special ones, remember that. As I told you before, you have massive potential, what you have to say matters, and I will always respect your feelings. Your cause is my cause as long as your cause is my cause.

So worry no more, get back to what you were doing, move along nothing to see here. I got your back, I got you covered, and I got it taken care of. Just stay out of my way and nobody gets hurt.

Nobody that matters, that is.

4. Let's Get Ready to Rumble

SIX MONTHS EARLIER...

The King and his war chief, Commander Thighmaster, sat with the marketing weenies of Sell Inc. Their high concept: A neat name for the upcoming armed conflict.

One marketron spoke up. "I have a really nice slideshow presentation that I think you will enjoy, some really powerful points."

The King scowled. All those nights of watching Network One thinking, *I could do that! What is this, fucking amateur night?* had not been in error. These slick Adverclones couldn't put a simple slogan on a basic household toaster. So far, these soon-to-be-unemployed jerks had come up with a lackluster bunch of titles:

1) One for the Thumb!

2) War, What You've Been Missing.

3) Hasn't It Been Quiet Long Enough?

4) Increase Government Spending While Thinning Out The Population.

5) Bored? Try War!

These supposedly catchy slogans lacked the flash and bling that the King craved. This did not please him. In fact, he began to downright stew. Without a killer catchphrase, a good solid hook, the only thing on the citizens' minds would be strife and suffering. What about T-shirt sales? What about movie rights? Then, there were always the toys, the action figure merchandising, book adaptations, comic books, videos, trading cards, bumper stickers, and promo appearances. This was no time to stumble for words.

"So what do you think?" asked another marketing slug, all the while nervously smiling as the wolves around the table eyed him like he was tonight's dinner.

"OFF WITH THEIR HEADS!" the King declared with a subtle emotional cocktail of frustration and blind rage.

The marketing scum may have been without talent, but they weren't stupid. Having already cross-referenced a demographic on various age groups and income brackets often associated with spontaneous beheadings by authority figures, they knew damn well that they were a target audience. They had already begun to repel to the ground with ropes they had inconspicuously set up as the meeting went sour.

"Damn those little monkeys," the King cursed under his breath as his Swiss army knife refused to cut the ropes. "Now they'll get away and breed."

Commander Thighmaster moved across the conference room to console his liege. "Sire, these people turn around fast. If you come away from the window, you'll see that they have already been replaced."

Another shiny-ass smile greeted the despot. "We've been working all night just in case this happened. Now...do we have a look for you! " the adman assured.

$

The soon-to-be Soldier had long been tired of life in the Village. The King ruled viciously, rarely allowing anyone to make theirs a "Biggie." That was the problem with this place. Nowhere to run. Well, walk, actually. No one could really run around here since their arteries were clogged with partially hydrogenated plasma.

Seeking escape from his deep-fried destiny, he left in the night on a comfort bus bound for the outlying hills, where the rebels camped. He had already practiced proper application of makeup and had messed around with a unicycle. Just to be sure he would be admitted, he got drunk and fucked a juggler, HARD.

Sadly, he was not accepted right away. It was first assumed that he was a spy. After having quoted in detail what the rebel General's menu items were referred to in French, he was finally welcomed into the rebel army and trained to fry potatoes. "I'm gonna make a difference," he whispered during his first training shift, "and earn valuable college credit."

$

After many hours of brainstorming, THE SLOGAN had finally arrived. What a glorious thing it had become! It was one of the hottest topics trending on the web with millions of hits on Foolgle. THE SLOGAN was on the verge of evolving from a nifty buzzword into the ultimate catchphrase. There was a logo on the drawing boards as well.

What a grand thing it all was.

The King bounced with thoughts just like these as he meandered he way through the palace. As Commander Thighmaster trained the troops with such maneuvers as the "Tuck and Roll," "Using Your One Good Arm," and a personal favorite, "Surrender Is No Road to Success," the King was busy tweaking the knobs of the war machine. A quick look out of the King's penthouse window was enough to make any callous profiteer squeal. THE SLOGAN was everywhere. Yes, everyone was wearing commemorative T-shirts as they walked under huge billboards with THE SLOGAN in 40 foot tall letters, as commercials looped endlessly blaring THE SLOGAN out of wireless speakers. The team colors of the Village (red and white for those scoring at home) provided the motif for everything. Yes, this King was going to make up all the money he lost on professional soccer in the early '80s.

Joy!

There was absolutely no way this could not be a success. The shareholders were going to be very happy indeed. Hell, why wouldn't they be? After bombing the local Birkenstock and organic Hemp dealerships, there were something like 5 people left to protest the war. Most of them were masochistic actors who got paid to be beaten by out-of-work Teamsters (who when they worked, worked for defense contractors). Agitation always increased productivity. All that was left to do was to cast the role of the King in the made-for-tv-but-ended-upon-cable-then-rereleased-in-select-movie-theatres-to-cover-the-loss-movie. Hey, how about Adam Sandler?

$

Sitting from a hillside vantage point, road warrior and most eligible bachelor Scratch Microphone itched his head in a mid-80's action hero kind of way. *What the hell is going on?*

It was customary for Scratch to spend his evenings perched in his favorite spot, peeping the locals and scouring the land for good deals via his trusty binoculars. Lately there had been a lot of movement and rumblings from the Village and its' hilly outskirts. His sensitive social acumen had gone into overdrive, and he was convinced that something big was going on. The question was: *How do I cash in on this?*

Scratch surmised that what was going on in the Village had to be classic frothing at the mouth. He knew that none of the Village's professional sports teams were in any championships, so the advertisement saturation occurring was either war or the post-summer crap movie dump. Based on the level of panic, logic dictated that the adverts, plus the fact that it was October, meant that the spirit of war was what was descending upon them.

Another clue was the rebel army – those pesky armed clown mofos choking the hills with bright orange tents and burning effigies of the King. The rebels were far worse than enthusiastic militiamen. They were a corporation. A corporation with a master skill in matches and accelerants.

Scratch preferred his loincloth gearhead ways. Kill an antelope and rebuild a four barrel Hemi in the same afternoon....yes that was life. The 66 Gods of the Route, the mighty tome "On the Road," the smell of burnt rubber. That was life. Trade and barter. Assure each side that they have an exclusive contract. Fix prices. Violate all anti-trusts. Then pull up emergency brakes and hit the dotted yellow line. That was life.

This is what the tribe leader would dictate to his people. This could feasibly be the last rest area for several 100 miles. They would grab all they could from the opportunity and then CONVOY. It would be time for the invocation of ROAD TRIP. Scratch would now have to find a suitable vehicle.

"Let's jump that crick, Bo," he prayed aloud.

$

Accepted by the rebels, the nameless Soldier began to contribute to the glory of the rebel cause. This was the good fight. The General had a saying:

THE NEXT REVOLUTION WILL BE ADVERTISED.

It was not an easy life for a rebel Soldier. There were many casualty-ridden missions into the DMZ to liberate prizes for happy little kid's meals, consorting with the Necro-Krofts (the demonic visages the General kept as mascots), and of course, the menial mess of cleaning the grease traps. The General had another saying:

DO YOU WANT FRIES WITH THAT?

The rebel intention was Jihad. Ragnarok. Hostile takeover. The General's manifesto, "The Declaration of Takeover by Hostile Means" was the first and last word in warfare. It was even better than "liquidating assets" and worlds away from "merger" hell, it was even milder than "police action" but why?

The General's army was composed of fallen angels. The King and his jester once had a peaceful coexistence. Those salad days, now long since wilted after endless nights of the King's heaping helpings of psychological and physical abuse. Now the once meek jester was a ferocious monster warmonger, and the King must now endure his barbs and smart missiles. What happened? The foul clown had spoken as a heretic. He wanted more than a supporting role in the comic relief variety. He wanted SPINOFF. Blasphemy! The King looked to his own as he cast the clown off into the hills.

Ah, what days of legend. Now, no one knew the definition of peace. This rebel enclave was the sole result of the migration of demanders needing supply. The Soldier looked about the camp and thought about downsizing the Village below.

The King ruled in manic glee. A MADMAN. A GENIUS. This was no more evident than in his insistence that freestyle breakdancing be the national dance. Not to mention his legislation written in Esperanto rhymed in Iambic Pentameter, then suddenly veering off into Blank Verse! And, you can't top streets named for snack foods and athletes. How could anyone suffer such madness? How could one live without it?

This Soldier had lived long enough on a street named Pork Rind Drive. As he considered this and other bitches and moans, his thoughts were interrupted by a large, furry purple presence.

"Hell-o," said the Necro-Kroft in a deep and dopey voice that seemed to actually originate from a sound booth many feet away. The Soldier whipped his head around to engage the beast. Large, purple and made of some enchanted evil fuzzy foam, the cartoonish figure stood at least eight feet tall. These freak things, the Necro-

Krofts had bad karma all over them. From what Hensonian hell had these primary colored, wide-eyed demons been issued?

"Uh, hi," said the Soldier as he slowly took a step back and watched his corners.

"What fun should we have today?" it asked with a wide, toothless smile. Its frozen expression offered nothing, but the Soldier knew to fear it. He had not been a rebel for long, but he knew to avoid the Krofts whenever possible.

Quite frankly, the Necro-Krofts form of play would crush an unfortunate fucker to the consistency of baby food. They didn't know their own strength. They had twisted forms of entertainment, mainly due to the highly psychedelic properties of their blood. One drop of that shit would make a normal employee of the rebel army trip for weeks. The Soldier had contemplated capturing a small one and bleeding it for extra dough.

"Let's play a game," it suggested, leaning in with wild eyes.

Warning. Danger. Danger. The Krofts had only one game they ever played. "You Deserve A Break Today," is what it was known as in quiet circles. If the human contestant in this game was lucky, it would be a clean neck break. Quick death and game over. Otherwise, this was a game long and painful in duration. Escape prior to kickoff was crucial.

"Hey look," said the Soldier pointing to the remote reaches of the bivouac, "It's anthropomorphic fried food nubbings parachuting in and chanting jingles."

The large terrycloth-like textured demon before him whipped its no-necked body around to engage the attacking appetizers.

The Soldier ran for his life.

$

Father Everhard had thought long and hard about writing Auntie Nuke a letter. Her burritos were a staple of his diet and he thought he might like to meet her and show her a burrito of his own. Things were changing in the Village with the upcoming war season. This year's nemesis was the Rebel General, grotesque in appearance and general food quality. Between him and his abominable mascots, this was going to be a whopper of a war.

Everhard wheezed in sympathy of the inevitable marginal non-combatant adjacent casualties. *Truly a buried statistic*, he thought.

"And the band played on," Everhard whispered to himself as he ladled a bowl of Hamburger Hill Helper mix together for brief afternoon snack. While Everhard cooked, he looked at his *Big Red J Vs. The Mennonites* calendar tacked to the wall. It was only six months until Yeaster, the high holiday for the Red J and his sidekicks. Everhard hoped that the war wouldn't affect the annual passion play. The play was everything to him. It was a yearly affirmation of his faith. It was also highly profitable, and daddy definitely needed a new pair of high-tops.

Soon, Everhard would have to hit the media to promote his show. This caused him great excitement, but then again, he was so backed up from a lack of sex that just about anything excited him.

$

"My Lesion," Thighmaster heralded.

The flighty monarch flipped his floppy hat at his aide-de-camp's disrespectful comment.

"Just seeing if you cared," Thighmaster mumbled.

"Go on," said the King, waving his hand as if it had been deboned.

"The men are ready. We have drilled and pressed and drill pressed and lathed. I have carved men from fat! I have sculpted men from boys!"

"I carved a little squirrel in woodshop once," the King replied nonchalantly.

"Look," Thighmaster said. "Let's start this party!"

"OK, OK, OKAY!" the King snarled back. "Get the wagons in a circle. Round 'em up. Get the troops and citizens down in the town square. I will cut in live to address them in a quick twenty."

Getting the response he craved, Thighmaster offered a brief salute and exited the chamber.

The King stood in front of the mirror quoting lines from Liz Taylor movies. She was truly the mistress of the dramatic, and one of the King's favorite divas.

"Our son is dead!" he said with no evidence of irony. The King put on his designer George C. Scott War Ware pantsuit with a variety of accessories to remind everyone who was the Big Daddy. Based on current trends fostered by chic, intelligent foreign homosexuals, the King determined that a purple sash was crucial to the ensemble.

Fashion critics would write the next day:

"The King's war speech was made powerfully effective by his Patton meets Pro Wrestler look. Do we smell a trend? Yes! But now it's over. Thongs are in again. Sash-shay Passé. Tee-hee!"

Well, at least for one day, he was truly chic. He was living couture, for the moment, a breathing example of big league style. And the power of that fact was that clowns have never been fashionable. Clowns, by virtue of their nature, can't do couture. He was already ahead of the General and he hadn't even opened his mouth yet. The King headed off to his balcony to address the crowd.

$

A large pricker bush was the best defensively-minded hiding place the Soldier could muster. His staggered bleeding wounds from nestling inside it showed what great pains he had gone to hide from the Necro-Kroft purple wildebeest. But what our nameless rebel hero didn't know was that the scent of freshly spilled blood was an aphrodisiac to the Krofts. It was just like a shark reacting to chum in the water. It was like tartar sauce on the end of a fish stick.

"Boogedity boo!" the beast yelled as it pulled the bush apart with its enormous hands. "I found you!"

The Soldier shit his pants. He attempted to make a run for it, but the purple thing towering above him decided to grapple his head in one of its ham fists.

"Mmmffffphh!" the Soldier exclaimed.

"Oh goody! You rilly do wanna play!" it said with a grimace.

Again, the Soldier attempted to escape, but this time he was caught in the creature's nerf-like, cushiony, kung-fu grip. It was soft, but it still felt like murder. The following half-hour was a horrific display. Cats play with their prey with more mercy. The Soldier boy found himself tossed around, his screams heard by no one and escape nowhere in sight.

Suddenly the creature stopped. The Soldier, confused but relieved, took a moment to inventory his injuries. There were no actual breaks, but his body was one solid bruise. His skin was now the same color as the beast's.

"Methinks dat is enough for tooday," it said as it wandered off.

The Soldier decided that if the time should ever come, he would stuff a rocket launcher up its ass and pull the trigger.

$

Scratch Microphone, half out of curiosity and half out of a losing search for a cure for his crabs (the old hammer and lighter fluid trick becoming very old) stood in the frothing crowd beneath the King's speech nook. *What great empowering facilitation was that insane boy gonna lay on the people?* Personally, Scratch wanted to know that the war had been green-lighted. He was already making the necessary moves, but there was a lot of work ahead.

Still, a great profit margin was assured by the tribe's double-dipping. Private endorsements by both war parties were bringing in stacks of cash, putting new tires and parts on the tribe's vehicles. New paint and even super-rad racing stripes could finally be afforded. The way it was going, Scratch would soon be able to make the sacred jump of the Impala. This would fulfill tribal prophecy. Glorious swap meets awaited on the yellow dotted ribbon of nomadic life. The plush interior luxury of wealth – this promise excited Scratch. A new land of milk and honey awaited. It had been some time since his last Road Trip, the most important and meaningful event in the tribe.

He couldn't contain himself. Around him, consumers of all types had gathered. The old, the young, the balding, the hairy, the salary men, the whores of Babylon, doctors, lawyers, chiefs (Hey! That was him!) – all rub-a-dubbed elbows.

"Speak, Monarch, Speak!" Scratch yelled, knocking his cane-like slap-shift fetish (Scratch was rarely without his wooden staff. It often punctuated important speaking points upon ignorant skulls). His scream melted into the thunder of the crowd responding to the appearance of the King on his balcony. Banners waved. Mouths pursed and whistled. Big, fat, foam fingers were raised high in the air.

"Now this is a hoo-tan-anny!" The King proclaimed.

Father Everhard looked at his watch. A truly amazing watch it was, its face adorned with the smiling mug of the Big Red J. And if you tilted it just right, his teeth would catch the sun and gleam. Everhard pushed a fat button on the timepiece.

"Wasting time is evil, do-gooders!" chimed the watch. The watch had over 3000 encouraging phrases. It was a useful tool of inspiration for all men and women of the cloth. He pressed it again. "Time for a drink," it said. Yay! Everhard piously hit his pocket flask.

He stood just outside the church grounds. Although far from the King's ledge of wisdom, the sound system broadcasting his speech made every word clear.

"You with the beach ball, get off the buoy!" the King commanded. Everhard looked at his flask and his watch. Then he looked back at the King.

"Just a little sound check, folks," the King said to reassure those with chemical dependencies.

Everhard relaxed and took another swig. The King began to boom over the microphone.

"Ugly people keep quiet!" he yelled. All but one man (Peter was his name) screamed back with vigor. If you saw Peter, you'd know why.

I love that line, because it always gets the crowd going. He considered the zeal of his people and knew he would have to write in more "call and response" material into subsequent speeches. Now, he could get going....

"Hey folks, damn glad you could all make the trip! Have a seat and take a look at the shiny new brochures. I think we can get started. Let's all be on the same page here. We are, as you can tell by the marketing campaign that has carpet-bombed your waking hours, in a state of war. What busy beavers you all have been, what with your voracious consumer habits. You can't know what a proud poppa I am today to see you sporting our commemorative line of sports apparel for this grand event."

Suddenly, the King sneezed. "Dien Bien Fu," a crowd member offered.

"Thank you," gestured the king. "Fucking hay fever season. Now then, you all know THE SLOGAN. You all could trace the war logo blindfolded. There's a lot I want to say about this upcoming war season, but before I get to seriously blowing smoke up your collective asses, I would like to introduce a close friend of mine. It's time to meet the Director of Operations on this project. Let's welcome to the show...Commander Thighmaster!"

Always arriving on cue, the Commander ran out onto the balcony, blowing kisses, waving, moonwalking, body popping, and whatnot.

"Hey my main King, I am glad to be here," commented Thighmaster with a gleam. The big military man gave the audience a good once over. "Who's from out of town?" he asked.

A few people clapped with tourist enthusiasm.

"Execute them!" Thighmaster ordered. "They'll steal our secrets, or even worse, ask for souvenirs!"

The out-of-towners were Done Inn ("Rates So Much Cheaper If You're Dead"). It was a page that Thighmaster stole from a Soviet playbook— "Fear the Foreigner," or something like that. It had always worked in times on conflict, and today was no different. Confident that Village security was established, Thighmaster felt safe enough to go on.

"Now the King and I have been taking many a meeting over this and we feel that it is time we empowered you regular folks with some vital statements so that you know why we want to feed that no good, cocksucking piece of shit clown his own entrails. This is about family values goddammit!" he bellowed.

In response, the crowd roared back like rabid lions.

"And how about those stats, TM?" added the King.

"Thanks for asking, my liege. Let's look at the facts. In the red corner, wearing traditional purple trunks, representing all good, kind, moral, traditional, responsible and ethical folks, your King! He's fit and ready to fill all of the new world's orders. Hell, he'll even King-size 'em. He has run this place forever and wants to keep on running it. AND, he's one sharp dresser," bellowed Thighmaster with mucho gusto.

"Now then," he continued as the King's drum corps ripped in ominous thunder, "the despicable, evil clown leader who is a clear heretic/blasphemer/betrayer is attempting to create a leadership which is the moral equivalent of the long-defunct XFL!"

The crowd gasped without prompting.

"Now you're getting it! This nasty guy sports an orange jumpsuit, big hair, red nose and consorts with demons. He'd just love to sell ya a seaweed sandwich! Ugh! Like you heard in the King's opening monologue, we are at war! Why we've called you back to hear this rhetoric is not to enforce a rerun, but to announce a special offer!" Thighmaster roared.

The King strong-armed Thighmaster and snagged the microphone away from his military man. "How much would you pay to see that clown's head on a stick? Howzabout if it was batter-fried to perfection? Can you picture a tasty, clown corn dog?" the King asked.

The crowd's collective mouth pursed as it began to answer.

"But wait, there's more! I'll throw a turkey in every pot, and coupons for free food offers. There will be no expiration date on this offer! Actually, here's the deal. I'm gonna kill every last one of those fuckers, bury their wives, mothers, and children alive and feast on a massive pate' of their ground-up genitals! And you swell Tories will get a good bite of the sweet meat victory. Yea...I beat my chest proudly as the Alpha male of the Village and associated properties."

The King grabbed an aluminum baseball bat cleverly placed by a pack of union stewards (only after ten weeks of debate, five days of holdouts, seven hours of deep negotiations and a free pack of cigars as a bribe). He raised the bat past the homerun fence and pointed it at the hills dotted with circus tents. Thighmaster snagged the mic.

"Let's get ready to rumble!"

The King stole the mic back. "We attack at dawn!"

Once more, Thighmaster grabbed the mic. The King refused to let it go. A serious scuffle ensued. Soon, after breaking the microphone stand and giving each other small lacerations and bruises, the King and Thighmaster moved the fight inside. The crowd roared with excitement.

$

If the crowd was ground coffee, the King's hot water speech had gone right through them. Father Everhard stood addressing the three day old wet grounds in the filter that was his church-going flock. He was trying to make sense of the merger-ous mess of the war. There were serious spiritual repercussions to armed corporate conflict. It was assumed that his congregation would harbor serious doubts, shoulder worry, and question Everhard's odds on the Super-duper Bowl conflict. He shepherded his flock to a mobile altar he had placed off to the side. His faithful crowd followed him to his portable pulpit, murmuring concerns and backup plans.

A hand rose from the audience.

"Yes, my son?" Everhard said as he pointed to the desperately confused soul.

"How is this war thing going to affect my mutual funds?" he asked.

"See your accountant. Now then, I would like to turn your attention to Issue #48 of the collected *Battle of Belly Lint* issues of *The Mark of the Big Red J* limited series. In this issue, the Red J faces the editorial committee known as the Council of Nixema. It is at this council meeting where the Red J renounces his war crimes, fakes amnesia, and sings popular rock ballads. The council, aghast at his lack of proper skin care, sentences him to community service and ten days as a civilian. It is at this point that J realizes his vulnerability to the law of mortals and reassembles his priority list. What can we glean from this?" Everhard asked.

A thin arm raised. It was attached to an adolescent girl who was mentally approaching her thirtieth birthday. Her body was barely thirteen.

Everhard called upon her.

"That white lies could save your ass," the precocious know-it-all answered.

"Can I get a HELL, YEAH!" Everhard commanded.

"HELL YEAH," responded the flock.

"This lesson will make more sense in the upcoming months."

With that, his congregation slowly parted ways and moved along with the rest of the Villagers who had to return to their mundane duties and boring lives (even though they were hoping to see more of the fight between their King and Commander). It all sounded great really, this war, but aside from nifty t-shirts, most of the residents of the Village felt that the war would have little to no effect on their lives. Oh, if they only knew then what they know now.

5. We Will Be Right Back After This

Interior: Courtroom

You sit in the witness chair. The courtroom is filled with accusing faces. A man in a top hat interrogates you in front of a sleeping jury.

Ok, I want you to do something for me. I want you to do it right now. Don't give me any shit. Take a good look at the sign on the wall over there. You see it?

The sign reads: "THE RULES."

Got yer tired eyes looking at the thing? Good. Here's the deal, and it's non-negotiable.

If you join the club, you gotta follow the rules. Otherwise, don't join the club.

I know what you are going to do. You're one of the smart ones, or so you think. You're the kind of Jägermeister swilling hip-to-be-square types, too cool for school. Think the rules don't apply to you. Yeah, I get it.

I want you to do something for me. I want you to do it right now.

Brush that trendy hairdo back and read the rules carefully. I am telling you right now that if you join my club, you will have to follow the rules.

The first one is "No spitting." That should be easy enough.

I have seen your type a million times. I have rejected your friend request and I have sent your uploads spooling endlessly. I can spot your M.O. in my peripheral vision. I'm that good.

You don't think you have to follow the rules, do you? Don't deny it, you know that it is true. Your whole life you have defined yourself as someone not like everyone else. Not a joiner, that's for fail punks and mainstream douchebags. You ain't drinking the Too-Cool-aid.

Fair enough. I bow to your coolness. In fact, I admire it.

But rules are rules, and don't even think about joining the club if you aren't going to follow them.

So you say, "No worries, daddy-o. I can follow those rules." That's because you know I got the good cookies, and there's something awesome going on backstage. You want that pass, I see it in your eyes.

I want to believe you, but I know you can't go long without making a contrary statement, pressing the vanity button. Still....there is something there, some kind of potential, that makes me want to say yes.

I love your enthusiasm. I love your willingness. I love that fact that you are willing to put down those wrinkled, rollback beliefs and join a winning team. Happy to have you in line with these initiatives. Welcome aboard!

I don't think a special someone like you would want to sign up for this if everyone was doing it. You're an early adapter, I get that. I know that if this gets too, oh popular, you'll start trolling forums and stir up the pot. Not only do I get that, but I am counting on it.

'Cuz, you can't make an omelet if you don't break some eggs. Trite yes, but damn true. We're talking about creative destruction. Let's break it, smash it down, and build it from scratch. Let's fuck with it and see what comes out of it.

This initiative isn't for the weak and palsy. Hell no, you gotta be tough to play my game, you gotta have wits, you gotta have creativity.

And it's clear to me that you have all that.

We're about to embark on a New and Improved World Order, we are going to make changes. YES WE ARE. When we get done, you're not even going to recognize the place.

Still with me? Like I ever had a doubt.

Now this is going to have some sacrifice involved. You may have to cut those ties, be ready to walk away in an instant. People are going to get hurt. And there probably won't be much of a warning.

I want you to do something for me. I want you to do it right now.

Repeat after me:

"Life can change in an instant."

Very good. Now say:

"Shit happens."

Excellent. Now one more:

"Better to be pissed off then pissed on."

Perfect.

I am going to be honest with you, and the fact that I am being honest with you should be yet another affirmation that you have made an excellent choice by teaming up with me. It's always good to have a backup plan. So if you don't have one, I need you to get with it. Map out that plan B, and maybe a Plan C.

I would love to give you a guarantee that everything will work out to the last lettered detail, but I am only responsible for the effort, not the result. No matter how it goes, it will go.

So go do whatever prep you need to do and get back real quick. We are about to position our shields and lower our spears to throat level. We are going to stick some pigs, you and I. They got it coming, and we are just the people to do it.

Just remember that sign on the wall when you signed up.

If you join the club, you gotta play by the rules son. My rules.

6. Battle of the Networth Stars

BACK TO OUR REGULARLY SCHEDULED PROGRAM:

Reconstruction of the Village started almost immediately. The Soldier had been involved in the greasy task of collecting severed limbs and bits of other good citizens who had been tossed like confetti about the crippled structures that used to be homes, businesses, and most importantly, liquor stores. He had used shovels, tongs, as-seen-on-TV EZ Grabbers, and tweezers in his instructed mission to collect every morsel of "collateral damage" he could find. This had been grim business indeed, and up until the past week, he had served as a Garbage Man of Death for the General. If it wasn't for the high availability of quality prescription painkillers, he might never have made it through.

Sell Inc. was overseeing the reconstruction of the Village as a private contractor. Almost every profitable enterprise in the Village was somehow a tentacle of this megacorporation. It was unclear to the Soldier how anyone could call them "private," but who was he to say? Sell Inc. had moved very fast, almost as if they were acting on insider information. Sell Inc. bulldozers began to plow the streets. Construction workers promptly set up cones, and found good places in the shade to nap. Engineers conferred with Blue Suits, and a virus of signs in neon colors proclaiming new and exciting building projects spread across all the damaged areas. It seemed as if the Village, when it was all said and done, would definitely be "New and Improved."

As he shoved unrecognizable chunks of flesh into black trash bags, the Soldier pondered the General's need to destroy so much when it was only to be rebuilt. This is not why he had left the Village and its ways. He had joined the General and his idealistic rebel army because it had promised a better kind of life—one filled with smiling faces. All he saw as he looked across the broken ruins was a grey frown of smoke and death. Where was the glint in the smile of victory? He was beginning to feel that he had been sold a bill of goods. The General's moral check had bounced.

Now, if I were in charge....

$

In a sub-basement of the Network One Media Mahal, a thin, bird-like man (nicknamed "Worm" by his insensitive, macho coworkers) in a lab coat handled a jar containing a brain and pickle juice. He picked up the jar cautiously and placed it gently on a work table. Normally he would have slammed it down due to his passive-aggressive disgruntled nature, but this wasn't any old brain in a jar. This was the brain of Brad Perfect, Network One News Anchor. Worm removed the squishy grey matter from the jar, attached electrodes to the brain and then connected those electrodes to a car battery using jumper cables and some old chewing gum.

Worm was under explicit instructions to keep Brad's brain alive at all costs. You see, Brad was no ordinary news reader.

Brad was special, and that meant EXPENSIVE. He had set Network One back some smackers.

Brad had been genetically engineered in Network One's Celebrity Nutrient Vats by a bunch of outlaw geneticists jacked up on coke and snarling all the way – typical degenerate biologists. Although today Network One typically creates all of its major personalities in vats, it wasn't standard practice during Brad's conception. There were a few goof-ups along the way (namely the hosts of lesser game shows like Vomit For Dollars or Name that Skin Condition) but Brad was one of the first, and some dare say (in private), one of the best. He definitely represented the deep end of the talent pool for Network One.

The first thing Brad asked for on the day he was pulled out of that vat, was a teleprompter. It was at this point that one scientist exclaimed, "This is gonna be one helluva contract!" That declaration was followed by a brief cardiovascular exercise of some sort, but that's old news.

The new news was that Brad was currently a brain in a jar. Or had been in a jar and was now unceremoniously sitting on a work table. How Brad got to be nothing but a brain in pseudo electroshock is not really important right now, but figuring out how to get him on the 11 O'clock-Go-To-Bed-Dammit News Report was going to take a major understanding of Frankensteinian electrical engineering.

$

Andy, who has no need for a last name, sat in his assigned cubicle somewhere deep in the Sea of Partitions. Just another pitiful intern, Andy was clearly a grunt in the Wage Wars. As he sat in his bleak earth-tone cell, he pondered his lunch amidst stacks of things that needed copying and filing. Certainly, this internship with Network One was ripe with what was called "good experience" and "possible college credit." Mastering a photocopying machine is preparation for the future, but the job was painted the color of boredom.

Andy stuffed some brightly colored junk foodstuff in his mouth and considered today's Network One broadcast offerings. With 10,000 channels under its network umbrella, One was the only real entertainment in town. Programs of every type littered the air: Drama Game Shows (*The Wheel Runs Red*), Shitcoms (*Mel's Bidet*— now in its 15th year), Info-edu-commercials (*Mail Order Welding School*), Squawk Shows (*David Lettucehead*), Gore Sports (*Chainsaw for Dollars*), and many more to numb you. Yeah, *Mel's Bidet* – now that was a show!

Poor Andy was stuck interning on the Network One News Starring Brad Perfect— *Fuck, if there ever was a custom-built asshole.*

Clearly, Andy would not be able to stand being an intern for much longer. He began to wonder if the fortune of fame was truly what he wanted. He should have taken the internship over at Sell Inc. His uncle had offered a job many times, but Andy wanted to be famous, and not a corporate android. Still, this crap job left little hope. He would have to keep alert for opportunities that flew past his assigned photocopier.

$

As the rebuilding of the Village went on, Scratch found a nifty, hidden place for his tribe to take a load off. They had settled nicely near a water reservoir somewhere south and west of their last enclave. He had spent many hours consulting the monitor screens in a family SUV. He watched the news and many other channels carefully. He was pissed. The General was not returning his calls or emails. He felt screwed without lubrication. And although that was sometimes nice, it was not a good feeling on this particular day.

It occurred to Scratch that he and the Dodge Tribe may have just found themselves cut out of a deal. It probably had something to do with Sell Inc. What else could explain how their mega complex suffered no damage in the attack? So what would be the angle? How could he wedge in?

The monitors continued to spit carefully constructed half-truths about complete lies. Scratch always liked watching the news. Hell, he would love to be a featured story on the news. After careful consideration of this fact, he called for his best field agent, Carlos ConPollo. He would use ConPollo to gather a group of men and infiltrate the Network One buildings. Then they would kidnap Brad and use the instant media exposure to raise their public profile. Scratch would take that teledesk and talk up a blue streak. There was no such thing as bad publicity in the Village. The whole event would surely raise the Dodge Tribe's stock with future business partners.

ConPollo came running to the multi-media minivan. He would be an excellent choice for this mission because he was one of the few tribe members who maintained a level of personal hygiene surpassed only by the Metrosexuals of Village Sector 8. ConPollo was just one more Birken-jerkinstock-wearing jag off, but he fully admitted it. Scratch spent the next three hours working out his plot as ConPollo buffed his nails while silently translating his leader's yada, yada, yadas, and figuring out his almost profane hand gestures. When they both felt that they had designed a "plan" ConPollo left Scratch watching brutal cartoons as he spent the remainder of the day gathering choice draft picks for his infiltration team.

The next morning, ConPollo held a meeting with his new team. As he sat before his troops, he pondered the mission that they were about to undertake. *It'll be good for a laugh, at the very least.*

ConPollo briefed his people on the location of Brad Perfect in the bowels of the Network One World Headquarters. He had also told them where to get a mean Rueben, but that was for after the mission. The soldiers had been divided into three groups: Blue

Team, Red Team, and Yellow Team. Made up of spurned Network One celebrities, they all had a problem with the big ONE, and were ready to do something about it. They were armed and ready to go. All they needed was for ConPollo to give the word.

ConPollo turned to his people and said, "What, you're still here?"

The screaming throng of actors who, of course, really wanted to direct, stormed off towards their target. ConPollo sprinted after them to keep up. It was all he could do to follow his highly energized method actor army.

$

With the high holiday of Yeaster quickly approaching, Father Everhard contacted his publicist in order to promote his latest production of *The Passion Play of the Red J.* As the highest ranking local representative of the faith, it was Everhard's job to create big attendance numbers for a stellar performance. His publicist managed to get him a number of appearances on the endless list of squawk shows Network One had to offer. Today, he was doing five interviews in five different studios. This afternoon was to feature the first.

Father Everhard stood up in the green room of the Village's favorite religious squawk shows, *From Nuts to God.* Each week several handfuls of viewers tuned in for redemption and other valuable prizes. Father Everhard was this week's guest, intended to help people understand the first day of the passion, the glamour of the play, and the Church of the Big Red J's biggest holiday, Mall Sunday.

Trying to ease his stomach, Everhard fiddled through a dish of various amphetamines, settling on what around the rectory were known as Little Boy Blues. Cramming two (because they're small) Blues in his mouth, Everhard washed them down with a refreshing can of Breakfast Beer Lite, the great tasting way to get the whole day's nutrition and tie one on at the same time. Everhard could hear the crew of the show getting the set ready.

"Hey Al," yelled a voice.

"Yeah," shouted a voice that probably belonged to Al.

"Why don't you get your lazy ass away from those donuts and help me with the microphones?"

Father Everhard began to feel excited about his national television debut. He almost puked he was so damn excited. As he paced the room, he practiced the spontaneous, off-the-cuff remarks he was to let loose during the interview.

"But the rash went away soon enough! (Pause) But it's a dry heat. (Pause) Depends how much money you're REALLY talking, Bob," he read from a little blue file card. This was going to be great!

$

Brad Perfect floated in a mysterious and thick clear fluid. Being that Brad had no means of locomotion, he had plenty of time to think. *The problem with merely being a brain in a jar is the lack of freedom one experiences.* Brad searched for the origin of his unfortunate predicament, but whatever had happened eluded his mental grasp.

The problem was simple. Brad needed to get back into his stellar bod as quickly as possible. RATINGS were at stake, and at Network One, any loss of ratings was disastrous. Hell, it might even mean that someone was doing something besides watching TV. If Brad couldn't make the 11 O'clock News, there would most certainly be a crisis of epic mini-series proportions. (We're talking a week long mini-series here, buster.)

Now if Brad still had his eye-balls he might be able to see the drunken swine of Lab 312 busy at work on a host body for the star of our show. Having taken a cellular sampling, the Network One geneticists were growing a new body down in Vat 15.

One technician read the instructions out to the crowd of lab-coated freaks. One out of five of the doctors would actually carry out the process, while the rest would merely chew cinnamon flavored gum.

"Burn the hops until the scent resembles whale sweat," the technician recited.

The other white coats turned various knobs and pushed random buttons. They all looked very important as they did a number of scientific-looking tasks. They nodded and concurred, and overall they felt confident that as long as they rushed things and didn't pay attention to safety protocols, they would have a new Brad Perfect by quarter to 11. This was enough time to get him up to the studio and in his chair ready to go for the broadcast.

$

The Soldier had been swinging a shovel for the last three hours, lifting load after load of brick, garbage, and bone. He, along with other rebel grunts, managed to make quite a dent in the cleaning of the debris that had covered the Village. The collected wreckage was piled up into two solid mountains of shame at the southern edge of town. Eventually, these mountains would be covered with Astroturf and laminated. Their gleam would provide the Village with bright shiny mounds for years to come. But for now, they were the biggest burial mounds anyone had ever seen. For his day's labors, the Soldier was rewarded with solitary guard duty at a small gate in the back of Network One's parking lots.

It was a bit shady here, and the Soldier was finally able to sit down and take a break. He was exhausted, and had the salt stains on his shirt to provide evidence of the hard work he put in. Slowly smoking a cigarette, he pondered a bit and sort of spaced out. Before he knew it, there was the smell of burnt plastic and a painful poke in his thigh. He nodded off and would have set himself on fire if it hadn't been for the flame-retardant artificial fibers of his striped uniform pants. He winced and brushed the burn off, throwing the cigarette butt far in disgust.

Then he laughed. In his brief shutdown, he had a dream that he was on a game show. In the show, you borrowed favors and never returned them. You lied and stabbed good friends in the back. You were rewarded for being self-absorbed with vacations and expensive gifts. The game had been called "Congress" and he had been a big winner.

It was a nice dream, and the Soldier was anxious to get back to it. In that dream, he had as much power as he wanted. Knowing that very little could happen at this forgotten back gate, The Soldier pulled the brim of his hat over his eyes and quickly drifted off.

$

Andy waded through the swamp of documentation that the news department gathered due to numerous lawsuits and child molestation charges. He stumbled upon a third-string story that never made last week's news. As Andy perused the fate of twelve

Irish fishermen and a duck, his all-encompassing interest prevented him from recognizing the footsteps of his idiot superior.

"Oh Andy... I have a little job for you," a sing-songy voice cried out from behind the partition. Andy raised his head and dropped his jaw in horror. It was the boss. If only there was a place to hide. The boss stuck his fat bald head around the corner.

"Come out from under that desk!" he demanded.

Andy pulled himself out from under the space-efficient desk top and faced front.

"Andy, your lack of enthusiasm is not the way to move up the ladder here at the Network One," the boss said, shaking his shiny bald head in disapproval. "If you can't get into your job, then you better get into somebody's bed. Now then, like I said, I have a job for you."

Andy slowly nodded knowing that interns didn't get jobs, they got the passed buck.

"Andy, this is very important," the Boss hinted. "Brad isn't around to get his shit together for tonight's broadcast, and I need you to collect some stories. Follow me."

Brad wasn't around? How was that even possible? The man, if you could call him that, never left the Network One campus. He just got shoved in a drawer or sent to the gym. This was an interesting wrinkle, and Andy felt that momentary excitement that comes from possibilities. He thought he might actually like his job today.

The Boss charged across the room and Andy jumped to follow him through the maze of cubicles, windows, and shelves that was the 103rd floor. He led him to the "Writing Nook." This room was only supposed to be occupied by anchors, so Andy's excitement grew. The Boss pushed a series of buttons whose beeps sounded a bit like "Smoke on the Water" and the door slowly opened.

"Here ya go, Andy," declared the Boss. "This is where all the writing magic happens, so why don't you get in there and play with your wand? We're counting on you!"

Andy leaned into the room and looked over the many pieces of technological accomplishment that embodied the "Writing Nook." It was truly an impressive array of gadgets, and far from the rudimentary word processing tools he was used to working with. Maybe he could make some real news magic in here after all. How hard could it be if Brad did it every day? He was an idiot, and genetically pre-disposed to half-wit his way through his plastic life.

The door closed quietly and locked itself behind him. It was just Andy, the machines, and his wand. Something good was about to happen, and Andy could feel it down to his boner.

$

After carefully scanning the Network One complex for security weaknesses, ConPollo settled on a small gate at the far end of the complex's parking lots. There was only one soldier guarding it, and he was fast asleep. ConPollo and his men moved past the sleeping sentry, and by hugging the plastic and titanium walls of the building, found their way to a door marked "Tours." Carlos said a few encouraging words to his crew and yanked the door open.

His men filed in. Yellow team entered first. Their objective was to secure the point. Blue team was to secure the flanks, and ConPollo along with the Red team was going to bring in the rear. The plan was flawless.

Upon entering the complex all the heavily armed and dangerous men found themselves stopped dead by a small old lady with a clipboard.

"Are you here for a tour?" she asked in a high pitched nasally twang.

ConPollo looked at his men. There they stood, holding assault rifles and knives, with ski masks over their faces. The little old lady either didn't notice or care.

"Ummm, yeah?" answered ConPollo.

"Follow me. Please walk in an orderly fashion and buddy up in case you get lost. The first stop is a video kiosk that features a virtual tour of the lab where Brad Perfect, our current number one news star, was constructed."

ConPollo held a finger up to his mouth and motioned for his men to follow. Quietly, they walked behind the shuffling old lady until they reached a wall of video monitors. The old lady pressed a red button and walked away without saying a word.

A large face appeared on the wall. He was a cheerful fellow.

The face had a perky and unstoppable voice.

"Welcome to another edition of 'Live On Scene.' Today we're talking about Brad Perfect and the Nutrient Celebrity Vats."

ConPollo and his men looked at one another once more. He thought about it and told his men to play along. If no one had reacted to their appearance so far, and there had been a few people walking past them that did not seem bothered by their heavy ordinance, then acting as if they were on the tour might help them infiltrate the studios.

The voice continued.

"Yeah, let me tell you, Brad Perfect is no average talking asshole. No siree! Brad is a fine-tuned, well thought out talking asshole with so much money behind him, he could just shit. (He would too, and really enjoy it, if only he had been designed to do so.) Brad is a special news guy, indeed. Yes, the rumors are true! Brad is one hundred percent baloney, engineered right here, deep inside the mega complex of good old Network One. The white coat jerkoffs in sub-basement 312 thought this baby up, and it was most assuredly promotions for the whole crew if the experiment was a success and if they survived the auditions.

Brad is a genetic wonder, a prime product of the Brand New World. He's a lab rat, a test tube celebrity, one of the first of his kind.

Brad was created in a thick vat filled with the sickly sweat of someone's spring loin. They have a lot of things figured out when it comes to growing celebrity clones in a vat, but they still need that squirmy star of the Testes Tribe, the spermatozoa. With a Starter Jizz Set (Trademark Pending), the nefarious doctors of Gene Pool One set out to create a smooth talking newscaster of ultimate potential.

Of course, there had been a few mistakes and they ended up hosting game shows like *Bust a Ball* or *Vomit for Dollars*, but those didn't last long. The audience was summarily shot for not enjoying the particular sense of humor branded by such Brad Near-Perfects. Mistakes can and will be made, otherwise there would be no chance of promotion out of the cubicle cell of One. Then they built Brad. And although this all must seem pretty impressive so far, the basement is a complete cesspool, so most of you must feel right at home. Brad certainly does when he occasionally comes to visit his parents, Eyedropper #12 and Vat 342/*a. It brings a life-like tear to his eye whenever he takes a piss on the floor under the table on which they sit. Now don't get me wrong, they love Brad. It's just that Network One security sometimes forgets to unchain the help, and accidents will happen."

At this point, ConPollo and his men were practically hypnotized by the voice of the face. Although they knew that they really must be going (there was that, ahem, important mission), they found they couldn't move their feet. ConPollo, while struggling to free his lower extremities, was oblivious to the fact that what he was about to hear was most crucial in the completion of his mission. Of course, at this time, he had no idea that Brad was currently only a brain in a jar.

The smiling face continued to blather on.

"Now is the time you have been waiting for. An actual virtual peek at Lab 312."

The screen faded from the face to a point-of-view camera shot. It was sweeping down a chrome spiral staircase.

The narration continued.

"Here we are on the staircase that takes us down to the main floor of 312. A spacious lot, the room in question holds all sorts of technical stuff and jismagoos required for manufacturing personalities to populate the screens of Network One's 10,000 channels of daily programming -- "With 10,000 Channels, Why Lead Your Own Life? Tune In and Be ONE."

The POV camera rambled down the steps. A bunch of total geeks awaited below, squinting through smudged, thick-lensed glasses.

"Welcome to the sacred place for Those Who Have Been Designed," the scientists chimed in unison.

As they pointed to the incredibly expensive machinery made up of many a household item, a graphic map appeared on the right hand side of the monitor wall. It highlighted the various components of the lab as the scientists listed them. Carlos grabbed a brochure to try to keep up with it all. It also contained a map to the lab. It read:

Guide to Lab 312

This is a brief map of the laboratory that gave you America's Favorite TV Host/News Presenter Brad Perfect. We know you love him, so pay attention. The large box you see on the right (#1) is a box of Dookey Donuts. We eat these. Right next to it is the control panel for operation Brad One (#2) It is packed with all sorts of little buttons that do things so incredibly far above your wee noggin' that we'd best move on. It is connected to a boiling pot of Yak piss and Yogurt (#3) which is used in the early formation process. Next to the pot is the Genital Drawer (#4), where the prospective father can dump his healthy load. It is pumped into a series of connected drinking straws (#5) which terminate in a stretched piece of pantyhose used as a filter (#6) This, of course, is tied in with the Fetal couplet (#7), where the seed is recombined and "shaken, not stirred". Then the project zygote is put into a storing bin made of old litter boxes (#8), where it incubates. We can then plug the various Rubic Genetic Combinations into the growing human body, to orchestrate proper goal achievement through this CrapIntosh Computer Terminal and Really Cool Cybernetic NanoDoc Arm (#s 9-11). When the body is fully cooked, it is forced out of the vat by a pair of Gorrilla Hands with "Lifelike Fur" (#12) and the father, if present, is bitch-slapped by the Gorilla Hands. This concludes your virtual tour.

In the span of only minutes, ConPollo and his men now had a map and a visual memory of the celebrity vats that created Brad Perfect. ConPollo became very excited at the prospect of his future success, and slowly he and his men were set free from the mesmerizing spell the video wall had cast upon them. Taking inspiration from the brochure, ConPollo bitch-slapped his men into focus, and now having a precise destination in mind, led them charging down the hall.

$

Father Everhard stood on the sidelines of the sound stage waiting for his cue. The show's host babbled on endlessly about some naked Bingo Brawl controversy that had put several blue hairs in jail. The audience was eating it up, but that was to be expected. They were programmed to do so.

The floor manager looked over at Everhard and taunted him with a variety of hand gestures. Everhard remained calm and waited for his cue. He tried to hold back his nervousness by trying to remind himself of the importance of his divine publicity work. He was here to promote this year's Passion Play, and to remind everyone how important it was to worship by buying tickets and attending the performance. The religious passion sweeps week was everything to

Everhard and his church, with the priority of promoting its lucrative lead holiday, Mall Sunday. Ritual collections and double billing brought in the bucks, but Mall Sunday numbers were astronomical and proof of downright genius on behalf of the religion's founders.

The time had finally arrived for Everhard to take the stage, he felt his heart race and his manhood stiffen.

"And now it's time for that man that needs no introduction. Spiritual consumers everywhere, allow me to introduce, the one, the only, Father Everhard!" shouted the host.

Everhard ran for his seat as the crew swung tee-ball bats at his head. Suffering only a slight knock on his head, Everhard flew on the set and it was high fives for everyone.

"So how the hell, whoops... I mean how the heck are you doing, Father?" asked the host.

"Shit, I'm all right. I've been touring around the Village telling people about Mall Sunday. It's coming up really soon and I hope to get everyone out on that special day to find the best sales and the lowest prices that God intended," answered Everhard.

"So do men of the cloth really get babes or what?" asked the host with a tight, pasty lipstick smile.

Everhard pretended to ignore the host's question, although secretly he had an answer for it. Everhard pressed on.

"What's even better than Mall Sunday?" he asked the audience.

The audience replied with a unison, "We don't know. Why don't you tell us?"

"Why, the upcoming Passion Play performance. Right here in town on Yeaster Sunday," Everhard answered.

The crowd cheered and did the wave in reverence.

$

Life was nothing but a blank TV screen devoid of snow for Brad. Since his horrible accident, life had taken a new shape and context.

When I get out of this jar I'm gonna sell the rights to my story and make a bundle, I'm talking big bucks.

The clock was ticking away and poor Brad was still a brain in a jar. At least as far as he could tell. Thanks to a quick removal of basic nerve endings, Brad couldn't tell that the boys in the lab were using his brain for a quick game of dodge ball.

One scientist lobbed the brain into a gaggle of biologists in the far corner of the lab.

"Last guy out gets all the product endorsements!" he proclaimed as the brain sailed through the air.

Even though he threw like an old lady, he still managed to hit the weak and spindly man known as Worm. And because Worm was hit, he had to leave the game and continue to work on the new body for Brad Perfect. In short, he was a loser all around.

Worm looked at the marvelous body forming in the vat. His eyes opened with amazement as he noticed the large particulars of the chassis of Brad Perfect. As he spun the polyester fibers for Brad's hair, he pondered life in a body as well equipped as Brad's.

He would certainly be able to lose Worm as a nickname. He might even be able to pull off a nickname like "Giant Worm" and that would get him lots of chicks. He would be famous, and most importantly, he would not be the first guy out in a game of dodge ball played with a rubbery brain.

In short, it would be a hell of an improvement if he had Brad's body instead of his own.

$

Andy sat at the News-O-Matic and pushed the various buttons needed to create fantastic news stories at a touch. He glanced at the instructions for a few tips.

News-O-Matic Operation Made Easy

1) Be sure that your mind is fully focused on objectivity. Having done that, proceed to ignore all inclinations and go with raw self-indulgent opinion.

2) Stand carefully over the control panel and be sure that your fly is in an upright position.

3) Wait for news information to be gathered on the LCD screen.

4) When facts come up on the screen that could make for a decent story, wait until something truly questionable arrives and run with it.

5) Press Button 4 to put story in simple, 5th Grade English and then

6) Sit back and wait for those paychecks to keep rolling in.

Now Andy knew how Brad could keep up with Dan Blather and Tom Blahblah. It was just a matter of sitting back and letting other people do your work for you.

The stories began to spit out of the machine and as Andy prepared the pile of reports to be fed into the teleprompter for the upcoming broadcast, he heard a strange beep and realized that an email had been sent to his station. Even though he wasn't supposed to read it (it wasn't his normal work area), Andy couldn't help himself. Besides, the subject line read "I Love You" and when was he ever going to hear something like that?

Andy opened the message and it read:

DON'T CAUSE A PANIC, BUT BRAD IS CURRENTLY NOT FUNCTIONING. HE IS IN FACT, A DISEMBODIED HEAD IN A LAB DEEP DOWNSTAIRS. THERE WILL BE NO BRAD WHEN THE SHOW GOES LIVE. THIS COULD BE SOMEONE'S LUCKY BREAK.

P.S. BY THE WAY, YOU NOW HAVE A VIRUS.

Andy smiled. He always had a virus. And, now he had opportunity. This could be his big chance, and he knew that another moment like this would be rare indeed. He set the machine on auto and quickly moved to an elevator so that he could go back to his apartment and search for his official Brad Perfect Lifelike Mask and Business suit that he had ordered out of the back of some old porno magazine. Tonight was indeed going to be a Special Edition.

$

By this time, ConPollo and his men could have made it to Lab 312, setting it ablaze and causing chaos. If they could destroy Brad Perfect's birth factory, they could then destroy him and know he wasn't coming back. Instead, ConPollo found himself in the Network One commissary, staring at a bowl of pudding with a skin so thick you could make a wallet out of it.

"We're hungry," some of the men had whined. "When are we going to get there?"

ConPollo had decided to appease his troops with a brief visit to the kitchen, but now he was clearly being taken advantage of.

"Yay!" yelled one man as he snorted red jello up his nose with a straw. "This is way better than the food court!"

ConPollo winced as his other men danced on the tables and went up for seconds, and even thirds. Running his hands through quickly greying hair, ConPollo knew that his plans of social revolt were being thwarted by tins of day old powdered foodstuffs.

A man sitting next to ConPollo let out a belch so violent the table shook.

"The horror, the horror," ConPollo groaned. He shoved bits of an Auntie Nuke's Protein Banana in his mouth as he watched a live feed of Brad's news channel on a flat screen mounted in the corner near his table. He just might have to go on the rest of the mission alone.

His highly-trained men had begun a food fight. As they made an absolute holy hell for Network One's custodians, ConPollo consulted a building map on the wall near the main entrance to the commissary. Upon locating Brad's studio, he slinked off silently using the ninja training he had picked up from an online course he took three years ago. His men, busy staining the walls and each other with artificial colors and flavors, didn't notice his departure.

$

"So Father, the purpose of Mall Sunday is to celebrate economic growth traditional to our culture?" droned the bored TV host.

"Yes! You see, Mall Sunday was the day our Lord, the Big Red J, returned to the Village with the rest of the J-League to combat Lex Lucifer and his cronies. It was six days later that Lex crucified Red J with Green Craptonite nails and Ma Krist buried him in an unmarked tube," said Everhard with glee. "Interested viewers should come down to the church auditorium next week and see this whole tale enacted by real, home-grown actors."

The show's host shot Everhard a look of disgust.

From Nuts to God, was going off perfectly. Everhard had launched into his subject with great vigor, and the host of the program hadn't had a word to say for three to four hours. As Everhard blabbed and blathered, the host found himself lost in both of his thoughts.

Next door was the studio for the Network One News Starring Brad Perfect. He could quietly sneak off the set and grab a couple of donuts from Brad's commissary. Everhard might not even notice that he was gone. The host looked at his watch. It was 10:45. His guest, Everhard had been on the show for 5 hours now. The host was starving. He needed sustenance.

Deciding that it was his only salvation, the Host slowly pulled away from his desk, lowered himself to the floor and crawled away towards the doors of his perfect neighbor's studio.

$

While the boys of Lab 312 laughed and played with the brain, the Worm was at work transplanting himself into the now complete NEW AND IMPROVED body of Brad Perfect. Chuckling to himself, he wired the body to the machine that would make the glorious transfer. Plopping onto the table, the Worm made the final adjustments before pulling the switch. He had placed a blank brain into the EZ-open skull of the Brad clone. The transfer would copy Worm's consciousness onto the blank brain, effectively giving Worm the body of Brad Perfect. Worm knew he would have to practice his non-regional diction, but felt confident he could masquerade as Brad for his remaining years.

After making sure that he had a clean pair of No-Leek Rubber Undies, the Worm threw the switch.

One power surge later, the Worm found himself looking through the eyes of the man that the world adored. Leaping off the table, Worm Perfect ran into the game of "Kill the Guy with the Brain," snatching the organic ball and making a break for the news studio. He knew that he had to get rid of the brain. Brad's real brain must disappear.

Having acquired a gymnast's level of speed and athleticism, it was easy to blast past the lousy screen defense his fellow scientists patched together. They stood affixed in shock and awe over the performance of their latest Brad. By hiding the brain inside his lab coat, they had no idea that within the construct was not Brad, but their former scapegoat, the Worm.

Worm Perfect cut a corner and soon he found himself alone. He anxiously searched for a place to hide the brain. Looking around, he noticed a small messenger cybot. This stout box with knobby all-terrain tires served to run errands throughout the labs. It currently housed the brain of a former reality celebrity from the show *Escape From the Box*. This show had failed miserably and all its genetically mapped talent had been banished to low-level cybots and civil servant jobs. Their nutrient vats had been destroyed and the blueprints shredded. No one would miss this brain.

Worm Perfect kicked the top panel open on the cybot and deftly pulled out its substandard brain. He slammed in Brad's brain, spun the cybot around three times to confuse it even more, and dropped the old brain in the nearest waste basket.

Worm heard the running footsteps of his former lab mates and ran for the stairwell. The clock above the door read 10:47 pm. He might have just enough time to put on some clothes, hit hair and makeup, and get in Brad's chair for the nightly news. Hopefully, his pursuers would find the brain in the wastebasket and mistake it for Brad's. Nevertheless, Worm made a run for his future fame.

$

With only a cheap Brad Perfect Halloween mask to hide him, Andy sat at the most popular news desk in the known broadcast demographic for 11 O'clock News program watchers between the ages of 18 to 34. Confident in his Perfect disguise, Andy anxiously awaited for the show to begin.

The director approached the desk.

"Brad, I have to tell you that on behalf of the crew here at 11 o'clock, watch your back. I don't know how the hell you survived, but the next time, which is right around the corner, we plan to do a complete job. I doubt you'll even survive the program," whispered the director.

Wow! This disguise really works!

Soon the broadcast was under way. And as Andy suspected, it was easy. But what Andy didn't suspect was the naked, sweating body of Brad Perfect barreling through the doors of the studio.

"That man is an imposter!" screamed Worm Perfect, pointing to the desk.

"That man is an imposter!" yelled Andy Perfect, pointing to the naked man with a brain cradled in one arm.

Had there been a live studio audience, they would have dropped their mouths in abatement.

Father Everhard continued to talk to the now sleeping crew and audience. Taking his first breath in an hour, he turned to his left and noticed that the host was long gone. This did not please the Father, who began to shake down members of the crew for the host's location. One emotionally weak fellow pointed at the studio doors upon a threat of castration.

The priest headed out the doors and straight into the Network News studio, which at this point was in complete shambles. Everhard made a quick assessment of the grounds - two identical men wrestling on the floor (one was strangely naked), various crew members placing bets, broken lights and other production equipment, and the smiling host of *From Nuts to God* munching on a donut.

Everhard marched over to the host's position and proceeded to give him a piece of his mind.

As the Brads continued their struggle for dominance, ConPollo found himself at the sidelines just a bit confused. He was uncertain as to how there could be two versions of Brad in one place. This was against Network One's talent clone protocols and couldn't possibly be right. Still, he was going to go through with the kidnapping. ConPollo figured this could become a "buy one, get one free" sort of thing.

ConPollo locked and loaded his weapon. He was relieved to see that three of his men had escaped the cafeteria, and they looked ready to finish their business. They ran up to him as they dodged objects thrown in the frenzy on stage.

What an epic battle it turned out to be. The Brads had gone from a type of Greco-Roman wrestling to swinging large pieces of lumber at one another. They both looked bruised and broken, but neither would yield. As the men chased each other around the news desk, crew members took cheap shots at them with microphone stands and baseball bats.

This exercise in human napalm was live and televised. This was the kind of TV you just didn't cancel. Most watching that night thought at first they had bad reception or maybe a porno channel had crossed wires with their usual programming. Still, it ended up being the highest rated news show in a long time.

As the Brads body slammed, ConPollo and his men took a tight perimeter around the skirmish and held their weapons high.

"Nobody move!" ConPollo yelled.

For a moment, everyone including the Perfects held still. This was just enough time for ConPollo and his men to grab both Andy and the Worm. They then charged out of the studio and made their way back to the gate from which they had started.

Some of the crew chose to pursue the kidnappers and their valuable prizes. The Floor Manager took Brad's desk and attempted to read the news. He stumbled on several words, and his genetic inferiority was obvious to everyone watching. Upon his embarrassment, he swore in some lost language, pulled a Luger from his tool belt and blew his brains out.

ConPollo and his men found the exit much more quickly than they originally thought they would. Maybe it was the adrenaline. Maybe it was the copious amounts of trucker speed they gobbled as they ran. They found themselves alone at the gate, with only the still sleeping soldier to sneak past.

"Hey boss," said a member of ConPollo's crew.

"Yeah?" said ConPollo.

"Do you think this guy is going to get in trouble? You know, for sleeping on the job and letting us get by?"

ConPollo was quick to respond.

"Fuck 'em. Just leave one of our business cards in his front pocket. If he survives the punishment he's going to get, maybe he can give them notice and join us. We can always use an extra slacker or two around the camp."

So a card was placed gingerly in the Soldier's pocket. Carlos and crew took the slightly struggling Brads off into the dimming light, sure that their leader, Scratch, was going to be very pleased with their heist.

7. A Pause for Station Identification

Interior: Church

You sit in the front pew. The interior of the church seems strange to you, the images on the walls are very disconcerting. A man in a top hat stands at the pulpit, addressing the room although you are the only one there.

Welcome to my cult. I can see that you have been getting very comfortable here. I take one look at you and I think: *This kid is going places.*

Hey, I don't have to tell you that. I have no reason to flatter you. Still you can put that little baby in your pocket for one of those unhappy days when the world shits on you and then drops down for several teabags before calling your mom and asking her out on a date that will never happen. Your mother's self-esteem stock will drop value, but I digress.

This cult, it is like no other, and I know that you know that.

It is the true cult of obsession. And from where we sit, obsession is a good thing.

How do you spend your days? From the moment I rise, I start putting it out there. I have my multi-status updates to share with the world, my adoring followers. I use every media channel available, and I have recently started Mental Mind Blogging, which is a fantastic way to spread your awesomeness. People subscribe to your thoughts!

There are many who are obsessed with me. They post their comments, write about me, compose tribute videos, forge holographic slash fictions, and smother me with their buttery love.

You could have this.

You could join in the obsession. You could have pundits wax poetically about your lunchtime choices, be the feature of blurbs and cameos.

You could have this.

You could have the t-shirts and the posters. You could have the squawk show gigs and the book tours. You're going places, kid.

You have to foster the obsession. Right place, right time. Location, location, location! You have to pull the strings, push the buttons, walk the walk.

But most of all, you have to be seen.

Their cameras are waiting. Their recorders are on. The moment I walk out the door, every breath, every step, every nose pick is documented. It can be a bit jarring at first, but to have a complete tongue bath of attention for doing nothing but walking to your overpriced exotic motor vehicle is a reward beyond value.

The obsession is intoxicating.

Of course, those folks have a healthy obsession. Money and fame of their own. You are the meat that puts the meat on the table. It is the circle of life.

They are the conduit to those who will hang on every word and be mindlessly entertained by your trips to the grocery store and regular high colonics. Your shit is their salvation.

They have nothing to live for, they have no greatness to see in the mirror. So they live through you. They find their peace in their obsession with you. The folks outside your door are the vehicles that drive it all.

You will have many fans, many focal points of obsession if you follow my ways. You will have what I have, and maybe, just maybe... more.

Careful though, there have been a few that thought stabbing me with a screwdriver was the most appropriate way to display their devotion to me. You might have a sniper or two, so watch your interactions.

It's really just the cost of doing business, and believe me the business is good.

That look in your eye as I explain the virtues and pitfalls tells me all I need to know about you. You're hungry and you're on board. You need that love, you need that attention. You are starving for it. You have a big empty hole inside you and the only solution is the spackle of narcissistic fulfillment.

That's why you're here kid. That's why you found me.

You have that hole, and no matter what you have used: mind-altering substances, flesh trade volunteers, copious consumption.

No matter what you did, no matter what the solvent, the hole remained.

Hence, your obsession...this is why you are here.

Welcome to my cult. It's where you belong.

Here you will feed your obsession, and grow it to a healthy size. Here you will learn how to encourage the obsessions of others. You will learn how to trick the human mind into thinking that your mundane life is filled with profound moments that will fulfill them at the highest levels and fuel their obsession.

It takes time, care, and coordination, but once you get going it will be pretty easy to manage. Sheeple are Sheeple baby, and no offense, but they will get obsessed with just about any muthafucka that got a headline.

You should be that muthafucka. I think you have the right stuff kid. Follow my lead, remember that bad PR is good PR. Never let them see you sweat! Get in trouble now and again to keep them guessing, and work in a redemption story to really grab them.

Welcome to my cult.

Their obsession will be your obsession.

8. The Passion of the Sweeps Week

It was only one day since Father Everhard's publicity blitzkrieg had begun, and he was already a self-doubting wretch. He sat slumped in his kitchen beanbag as he forked into an Auntie Nuke's Microwave Diet Chocolate Marshmallow Burrito. With heavy eyes and drooping face, he decided that he was all washed up.

"Aw fuck, I coulda been somebody," he muttered, choking on the last bite of burrito.

Indeed, the battle of the Brads had stolen most of his thunder. His news of the upcoming Passion Play had found little buzz, and few were downloading or linking to his announcement. Everhard had always been the sensitive, jealous-of-the-world type, and he found himself going down the slippery slope of intrinsic loathing. Everhard found that no matter what he did to fill the growing void inside his chest, it would not fade. Even binge eating (usually an upbeat last resort for his blues) had done nothing for him. He found himself facing a loss of faith, and sadly this wasn't the first time.

It was nearly the end of the fasting period of the most important holiday of Lint and Everhard had decided to give up trying to like himself. This was typical for Everhard. One might say that he had wallowed in self-pity his whole life. That is, of course, if anyone really cared. But life still plods long after it seems completely dead. Father Everhard knew what ailed him.

In moments like these, he knew that he could not turn to his faith, as it preached what the church called "A Can-Do Attitude."

No, there was only one person he could turn to, Dr. Hung, his master of medications. Everhard flipped his phone on and speed-dialed Dr. Hung – his consultant, prescription pad, and personal life coach.

Luckily for Everhard, Dr. Hung answered after the third direct-to-voicemail cry for help. After listening Everhard's faltering prattle about luxury problems, he offered some advice.

"Father, the solution is simple. Take loads of dangerous mood-altering drugs, drop your vows, whore out, and party like Rick James. That'll put the spring back into your step."

"I tried that last night," said Everhard glumly. "I got a rash. And I ate a whole box of chocolate burritos."

"Oh, yeah. Forget what I said. What you need is to, is...well, let me ask you a question."

"Shoot."

"What big Church holiday is right around the corner?"

"Why, Yeaster, of course."

"And what is Yeaster all about? Didn't a certain focus of worship RISE up, you know, RESURRECT!"

"What are you getting at, Doc?"

"It's Spring, and it's time to rejuvenate! Why not take that resurrection and concentrate your energies on it? If it worked for God, it'll work for you! Get active with your community. You have that big passion play thingy coming up, you just need to really dive into the deep end of the pool with it."

Everhard considered what his shrink was getting at. As a child, the Passion Play and Yeaster were nearly an obsession. The colorful characters, the exciting action, the opportunity to destroy evil violently – what more could a kid wish for? His love for the story led him to the church, and his profession.

The worn priest suddenly shot out of his chair. Yes, Dr. Hung was right. And at $500.00 an hour of the church's money, he had better be right. Everhard thanked the doctor, assuring him that payment would indeed be in the mail by the afternoon, and set about making a few more phone calls to get a meeting going on.

The truth of the matter was, although Everhard had spent a lot of time getting the marketing and publicity together for the Passion Play, he really hadn't worked hard on the actual production. People in the Village rarely questioned the quality of content if it was well packaged and advertised. This year, though, the hype would equal the message.

$

How to Present a Passion Play for Profit, Both Monetary and Spiritual:

In a traditional rendition of the Passion Play, there are four basic sets: one of downtown Sweatropolis, one of the SuperMall USA, one building interior, one of the League Headquarters. Unorthodox stagings have portrayed the mall as a strip mall and some heretical versions have actually set the play in New York.

Everhard sighed heavily from premature exhaustion. If one were to take a cigarette butt census, one would find nearly forty in the ashtray in front of the clergyman. This was round ten of the third script meeting for the actual working script. The boardroom was long and narrow, not unlike a coffin. Sitting at the head of a long table, Everhard wearily observed that the beady eyes and sweaty lips of the bastard Committee For Putting On a Damn Good Passion Play (CFPODGPP) was in full effect. These murdering, ignorant swine were making a farce out of Everhard's script. Their revolting ideas for script changes caused the priest to cramp and ache. These cretins were breaking Everhard's balls.

Goddamn sixth-graders.

To speak like a child required a child, so Everhard gathered all the school children that had been transferred into the Village since the reconstruction had begun. It was good for him to work with new students as all the old ones had filed restraining orders against him. These kids, however, knew none the better. They were more creatively aggressive than he expected.

Everhard had picked the oldest students in the elementary school because he had thought it was what many would call "a good idea." The sixth-grade had the most social and religious study experience and should be able to pull it off. Instead, all he had to work with was a bunch of knee-high gangsters with their own agenda. Special needs, union breaks, expense accounts, it was all in the fucking contract. See what happens when you don't consult a lawyer?

In order to properly produce the Passion Play, all the involved students had to be deputized as Official Sidekicks of the Big Red J. Normally, this is quite an involved ceremony, but Everhard had no time for such ritual sodomy, so he printed out a brochure/contract and had them sign on the bottom. There was no time to process the mail-in applications.

As the mini-monsters poured over the script breakdowns for yet another tortuous set of changes, Everhard looked over his brochure and re-read it with pride.

A PRIMER HANDBOOK FOR ALL INSPIRING SIDEKICKS OF

THE BIG RED J

DO YOUR PART! USE THIS SPECIAL SECTION TO HELP OTHERS GET TO KNOW THE BIG RED J!

Hey Kids, it's a dark dangerous world out there, a world that's ready to eat you up whole, grind your bones to mash and feast on your blood.

This is your world. There is no hope, no resolution.

Do you find yourself agreeing with what you've just read?

Many, many people do too. It's not uncommon in our cruel existence to lose sight of what is possible. We would rather just submit with what is in front of us than try to change it.

But did you know that there is a road to happiness? There is a world of JOY and love and justice for you to invest your hard earned spiritual currency. A place where the flowers smile and you can talk to the animals. This world exists in the heart of the Big Red J and he wants to let YOU in!

Now this isn't a game, but a way of living. It means living by a heroic code, and proving yourself to be a worthy fighter of evil and a champion of good.

In Issue #12 of *The Cape of the Red J, Page 10, Panel 28*, the Good Lord says: "Only those who bide by my code shall prosper as budding heroes." This is right from the horse's mouth, kiddies!

The Code is the one thing that unifies all those who wish to change the balance in the fight of good vs. evil. With the Red J as your model, you can become an Official Sidekick of the Big Red J (the ultimate superhero),thus helping bring change into this dreary world you inherited.

KNOWING THE BIG RED J

An important part of being a good Official Sidekick is knowing the Big Red J as your personal superstar. To wonder that maybe he isn't #1 is a gross and unforgivable sin in his supervision. You must fully admit under any amount of duress that he is indeed the Master. When you recite the Sidekick's code, you do just that! You must get all of your friends to also concede to the Red J. Doing so gives you a better chance at a promotion. (Remember Issue #3, Page 4, Panel 3, where our lord states while pummeling a super villain by the name Evil Otter, "If you ain't with me, then you is against me, and I will therefore deliver a slow and painful death unto you.")

This is the absolute truth, and it is something to remember as many people will question your belief in the Red J. Anybody who doubts your faith, denies your savior, criticizes or opposes your opinions are on the side of evil— they should always be considered the enemy. Sock it to them!

THE OFFICIAL BIG RED J SIDEKICK'S CODE:

I, as an Official card carrying Sidekick to the Big Red J, Do hereby relinquish all rights to the superior judgments of The Church of The Big Red J and Government Authorities with confidence because my goals are:

To jump and fly & to throw fists blindly at those duly designated enemies for the betterment of society as deemed by the experts, because they know what's best for all of us.

I also swear that I will purchase all Official Red J collectibles and never tire in the fight against:

- Super Villians
- Alien Monsters
- The Masons
- The McMansion Dwellers
- The Homeless
- Drug Users
- Smokers
- People Who Crack Their Gum In A Manner Sure To Annoy

And all other offenders to be listed at a later date.

With a hand over my heart,
And my other covering my genitals,

I pledge to my dying breath my intense and unwavering loyalty to the Big Red J.
I will attend church every scheduled meeting, and give cash generously in the hopes of a better tomorrow.
Thanks and Goodnite.

KIDS -- say this Official Sidekick to the Big Red J code every night before crashing because the Red J is listening with his super hearing, and if you do not do as you are told, he will come and rip your heart out of your adolescent chest and eat it in front of your mother! (This will occur without warning and could happen at any place or time.)

THE MODEL SIDEKICK

Obviously, your goal is to become the model Official Sidekick. This can be achieved by acting as much like the Big Red J as possible. He is the ultimate hero, and he is your Lord.

Each day, from the moment you wake, until you fall asleep from the exhaustion of daily living, be sure to put the Red J firmly in the front of all your thoughts. Remember, what you think and do is under constant surveillance by the all-knowing J.

When you see injustice, act on it. Crush it in its tracks. Report all Un-American activities to the proper authorities. Trust no one. Evil lurks in every corner and shadow, and it is up to J's army of sidekicks to help eliminate pesky evildoers everywhere.

Now you might be asking yourself the all-important question, "What is Good, and what is Evil?" And to be honest, we're glad you have the brainpower to form such a question!

The Good Lord states in the ever-glorious Issue #1, Page 5, Panel 1: "What is Good? What is Evil? Let me tell ya, Good is whatever I say it is, and Evil is anything else!

Red J then goes on to slam his eternal nemesis, Lex Lucifer, straight in the teeth, causing the loss of two molars!

All you have to do is listen and obey the Red J and all of his duly appointed representatives. Unlike the false beliefs others may buy into, the Red J is an alive and kicking entity that will constantly spell out his beliefs and requirements for all sidekicks. You'll never be in the dark! He will always be here to tell you what to think! And even if he should snuff it, he always has a way of coming back around! Just read the fine print!

THE PURCHASING OF GOODS & SERVICES

The Big Red J is a man of God and Country, so you must be as well. One important element of this is the continual consumption of Goods and Services. It is against God's will to NOT circulate your money widely and often. Do not worry about price or taxes, just BUY, BUY, BUY!

Money is the blood of your nation, keep it flowing! There are so many things you must want, so feel free to go for it! There are also many things that you don't know that you want -- yet. It is important to realize this and maintain a constant lookout for goods that you might want. Pay attention to advertisements -- study them for your hidden desires! Gather every catalog, socially bookmark every website, email every link to wonderful life changing material possessions that you know you can't live without!

The Wallet of J, the Special One-Shot Collector's Edition offers this: The word advertisement means to express what you have for others! It is not a negative term in the least. Contribute to the cause by contributing to yourself through ownership of new and exciting items. Griping your wallet tightly when you could be paying for services is not good will --

keep our glorious economy going! (Inside Cover, Panel 2.)

Perhaps you are a modest Official Sidekick or you are a very busy person (unable to shop on a daily basis). You need not worry that you might not be able to fulfill the Red J's requirements. You see, the Church of the Big Red J offers many holidays for you to justify purchases that may drive you deep into a debt dumpster!

Mall Sunday is, of course the largest consumption holiday besides Kristmas. Yeaster and Slash Wednesday are also considered high volume holidays. Birthdays, traditionally a day of introspective depression for all followers of the Church, are really there so that your pagan friends can invariably support our faith through their gift purchases to you! Ultimately, we are always in the black. (Issue #34, Halls of J, Pg. 3)

THE FIGHT AGAINST EVIL

The fight against evil goes on every day, in the streets and in your very soul. All Official Sidekicks must remain vigilant AT ALL TIMES. Evil is an ever-present threat. From Book 3 of the max-series, "The Blood of J," page one: The Big Red J offers us this simple prayer for our fight:

Oh, in my fight against
All things evil
I know that the Big Red J
Has my back
Because many times evil
Is very strong
And I could die heinously
In a fight against it.
But let my eyes be open
And my Judgement focused
On the roots of evil
As they may sprout in any and every corner.
I know that I must scrutinize
Everything and everybody
But no one can really be trusted
Other than my beloved (and beyond reproach) Big Red J
As well as all other Big Red J, God-saluting, Authorities.

This prayer should be held close to your heart.

Now Official Sidekicks, this is an important checklist of where evil could lurk under your very noses:

Could It Be Evil?
(a checklist)

- ✓ FAMILY MEMBERS
- ✓ FRIENDS
- ✓ NON BELIEVERS
- ✓ THE POOR
- ✓ THOSE WHO DO NOT LISTEN TO THE WORD
- ✓ NON-SUBSCRIBERS
- ✓ THE INDECENT
- ✓ THE IGNORANT
- ✓ PEACE-LOVERS
- ✓ POTPOURRI

NOTE: Some things are not directly evil but rather, are conspirators of evil. There are spies in our holy home. All other religions fall into this category. The act of investing in another religion is sin (the sin of denial) but is not inherently evil. However, every activity a person performs armed with a false belief is evil. Get it? (Issue #76, Cape of J, Pg.6 Panel 10.)

Learn more about how to fight evil by visiting: www.churchofthebigredj.com

PAGAN BELIEFS INCLUDE:

- New Age Crap
- Horoscopes (including Boozology)
- Gambling
- Pro-Wrestling
- Buddhism
- Hinduism
- McCarthyism
- Voodoo Economics
- Tarot cards,
- The Way of the Warrior (an insidious and notorious enemy of the Church)
- Anything that does not directly tie in with the Church of the Big Red J.

Crossovers and conversions are acceptable at time of purchase, but there are no cash refunds.

ALL CONVERSIONS ARE FINAL.

(Issue #112, Red J Adv., pp. 5-9.)

THE PACKAGE DEAL!

By making it this far in our primer for all potential sidekicks, you have shown a great interest for the future of tomorrow. So to reward your selfless behavior, we have a special offer just for you!

If you join the Church of the Big Red J now, you'll get:

1) A glamorous, one-size-fits-all spandex-like Official Sidekick outfit with Breetheeze ™ fabric weaved into the areas that most often gather perspiration!
2) A smart-looking photo ID to impress your friends and loved ones!
3) A trial one-year subscription to the club newsletter! It's chock full of the latest Red-J gossip, tidbits on the hottest collectibles, spotlights on the perpetrators of evil, a neat pen-pal pool, and up-to-date statistics on a variety of disturbing evil trends! And there's always a supercool crossword puzzle! Be sure to check it out!
4) Full amnesty by any government should you need to perform quasi-illegal acts in the name of religious fervor!
5) $20,000 life insurance should you die in the name of the Church, provided that you have adequately posted your martyr status prior to snuffing it!
6) A small computer chip surgically bonded to the base of your skull so that the Church tracking satellite can keep tabs on you at all times! GPS for the win!

Besides all these great perks, there are always new freebies, services, and wearables coming up!

Send in your name, address, and other pertinent info along with the accompanying application and a SASE to:

THE CHURCH OF THE BIG RED J
SWEATROPOLIS, PLANET EARTH 66666

(The Postal Service will know where to forward your correspondence. Our secret sanctum is just that, secret. You should not worry about this.)

Upon arrival your application will be processed by a swarm of low-paid college graduates. A careful background check will be initiated and provided your money order for $400 clears, you'll be one of us! You'll be so proud, you'll drive your friends insane with all your boasting! And that stylish cape you'll be brandishing day in and day out won't help matters, either!

Don't waste another moment, become an Official Sidekick of the Big Red J today!

✓ **Yes! I Want to Be On the Winning Team!**
Make Me a Friend of the Big Red J Today!

Enclosed is my signed check or money order for $400* made out to the Big Red J along with a copy of my official government issued I.D. and my fingerprint in the lower right-hand corner of this form.

Name: ____

Address: ____

City:__________________ State:__________________ Zip:________

Current Religion: ___________________________________

Political Affiliation:_________________________________

Please allow 8-12 weeks for background check and delivery
*Sorry No C.O.D.s

Send To: **The Church Of the Big Red J**
Sweatropolis, Planet Earth 66666

☐ Please check here if you would like to receive a free trial subscription to *Ma Krist's Home Décor and Crafts.*

Right thumb print, black ink only.

TAKE IT TO THE PEOPLE! VIVA RED J!

Everhard smiled as he looked up from the brochure. His style of snappy writing had really brought the kids in. Even though the script meeting was painful, it was promising. They had mapped out the cast of characters and written a synopsis of the first scene.

Cast Of Characters:

The Big Red J, Our Savior, aka Clark Krist
Ma Krist, his Mother
Lois Lame, his "wife"
Lex Lucifer, his arch enemy
Brad Perfect, narrator

The Disciples (The Amazing J-League):
Angel - his dark and brooding wing man
Cupid - his cherubic teen sidekick
Zippy - the streaking speedster
Martian Manfisher - the green powerhouse
The Light - wielder of the all-powerful lantern of truth
Straight Arrow - playboy archer
The Patriot - flag-waving, self-righteous bully boy
Wonder Bimbo - the big-tittied, sexpot supermodel/ hero

Bit parts:
A handful of Lex's henchmen
Citizens of Sweatropolis

SCENE ONE SYNOPSIS
The play begins on Mall Sunday, the day when traditionally the citizens of Sweatropolis take advantage of the early spring sales. This glorious festival of commerce is unmatched in its annual excitement. The mere talk of the holiday brings the masses to absolute frothing. Children daydream of the incredible shiny things they might find in wrapping paper. Adults eagerly rework their credit lines in anticipation. It truly represents the glory of blind consumerism. This time, however, the citizens of Sweatropolis remain in their homes, fearful to head out to shop as Red J's arch-enemy, Lex Lucifer holds the city for ransom with his Doomsday Device.

The first scene begins with Brad Perfect reading a news report to this effect, thus setting up the story. In this scene, Red J and the rest of the Jesus League return to the city from a long campaign in outer space. The result of J's triumphant return causes much joy in the citizens of the great Sweatropolis. When learning of his return, the people of the city come out of their homes and greet their Savior with hope, nervousness, and crumpled coupons.

So far, the production looked good to Everhard. He pulled a collector's edition of Issue 12 of *The Passion of the Red J* from its Mylar sleeve and read the following panels and dialogue:

"And it was on that glorious Mall Sunday when The Big Red J flew into his own Sweatropolis, the rest of the J-League following in quick succession. With his potent eye he found the SuperMall and thereupon did descend upon it. And a crowd did wait. And a Newscaster did say: Yea, Lord, how do you plan to foil Lex Lucifer and his Doomsday Device?

And the Caped Crusatyr replied: "To everyone watching, a big hello. Boy, it's good to be back. I have to tell you, these are exciting times. Spring Break is in sight, and here we are on Mall Sunday. This is a day to reflect upon prices and sales and make proper shopping choices. And let me tell you, I'm as mad as a stuck pig when I think about how Lex Lucifer thinks he can just close the doors of a town obviously open 24-7 hours. Just look around you. This is a town Built to Last. Quantity is Job One, and I'm gonna do my job for you. Let it be known that I declare this city Open For Business and I dare Lex to say otherwise...."

$

SCENE ONE - Outside the SuperMall

Setting: A Painted backdrop depicting the entrance to the SuperMall. Fifteen citizens stand in front of the mall doors. Brad Perfect stands stage left. Fifteen other citizens wait in the aisles in the back of the auditorium.

BRAD PERFECT: (with microphone in hand) Hello people of all major marketing demographics! I stand outside the gleaming doors of the SuperMall, home of over 600 incredible stores to serve you on this most precious of holidays, Mall Sunday. Earlier today, I reported that the city was in the evil clutches of Lex Lucifer and his Doomsday device. Well, the before and after pictures are not much different, but I do have some hope to sell you – The Big Red J and the rest of the J-League have returned from their intergalactic tour and promise to cash in Lex's chips!

Onstage group cheers.

BRAD PERFECT: In fact, here comes the "Man" that needs no introduction -- The Big Red J!

Red J is lowered onto stage by means of a rope. As he is lowered, the gathered crowd showers him with adoration in the form of thrown glitter, coupons, and money, traditional symbols of Mall Sunday. Upon landing, the Red J grabs the microphone from Perfect's hand.

RED J: Hello, everyone out there in digitized media land! It sure is nice to be back in good old Sweatropolis, home to bargain prices far below wholesale. I'm really excited, because this is my favorite holiday, Mall Sunday! I hope you have your shopping impulses honed to react to the deals you are going to find today.

Now, I have heard a dirty little rumor, that is to say, that a certain arch-enemy of mine, Lex Lucifer is currently threatening the city on this most holy of days. Well, I am here to tell you that you are not to worry, for I and my League are on the case. So I want you to get out there and honor God's wishes: "SHOP 'TILL YOU DROP!"

BRAD PERFECT: So Lord, do you expect a rerun of your last meeting with Lex, then?

RED J: Back-to-back, baby. Lex has no doomsday device that can stop me, the Big Red J. But enough of the grandstanding, it's time to take in with the holiday. Folks, take off those salary caps, dig deep into your pockets, and BUY BUY BUY! It's Mall Sunday, by golly, and it's time to act like it!

The crowd erupts into happy cheers. The actors waiting in the aisles come running down to the front of the stage as they shower the audience with free t-shirts emblazoned with action pictures of the Big Red J.

BRAD PERFECT: There you have it folks, the day is on like Donkey Kong. And, as to how Lex Lucifer is going to take the news, well, you'll just have to STAY TUNED TO NETWORK ONE...

The day's production meeting had wrapped, and Everhard found himself cooling off with a quick round of shooting baskets behind the church. Even though he had found a secret stash of motivation deep within himself, he began to realize that this monstrous project was sapping all his strength. So far, he had combatted this with a regular diet of caffeine, sugar, and imported amphetamines. Regular trips to the can and the occasional game of hoops kept him going.

The exhaustion from putting together an epic production of the Lord's Last Days was taking its toll on the old man's bag of bones. But the reward of the play itself, the total immersion into the holy realm was mentally refreshing and inspirational. Why, on his walk back from the meeting, Everhard had found nearly five good sales in one shopping mall alone, and he wasn't looking all that hard at all!

The priest leaned back, let the ball gently fly from his arms, and caught nothing but net. He stretched and crossed his arms behind his head, smiling. While the deadline was quickly approaching, he felt that all the parts of production would fall into place and the work would mean something indeed. It was just too bad that he would have to work his little actors into the ground, but he knew that it would surely build character.

After his short game, Everhard fixed himself the finest meal a microwave could generate and set about his evening of note-taking and inspirational blogging. With his newfound energy, he also found time to read one of his daily meditations. Opening a small book, he closed his eyes and flipped through the pages. He stopped at a random page and read it aloud to himself.

"There is the possibility that J actually had a twin brother. In the script, there are twelve mentions of the League member D-Thomas,

who could very well be the brother of J-Thomas, mentioned thrice. Thomas is, of course, a nickname, meaning 'twin'. Twin J, or DTJ, as the logo on his cape reads, could have been, the twin brother of J.

There is also mention of additional room in the comet which brought J to Earth and issue #189 depicts a four-person Jacuzzi in Ma and Pa Krist's farmhouse. It is possible that this twin did survive and carry out the messianic work under the moniker of 'Doppelganger' (J-League International member issues #211-268. A mint edition of his so-called "origin issue," JLI #223, goes for $300.00), who has the ability to mimic the powers of any individual superbeing he beats in a game of Racquetball."

-- From The Historical Red.

Wow, he thought. There were always so many small things to think about when one wrapped themselves fully in the mythology of the J. This would be something to rest his mind with. It had gotten late, and there really was nothing to watch on TV. So, Everhard climbed into bed, turned off the light, and touched himself. Tomorrow was going to be a busy day, indeed.

$

The script was finished the next morning and only one writer had quit. It was a complete success. Everhard found himself deep in rehearsals. The kids had run through the Mall Sunday scene, and had even shown a bit of talent as they portrayed their roles with authenticity. There had been a good deal of energy amongst the cast, and they were only showing minor signs of fatigue and malnourishment towards the end of the second day of rehearsals.

Each scene was of great importance to Everhard, and he was currently trying to iron the wrinkles out of the key second scene, J's prayer in the food court. J's self-motivational speech in the face of betrayal was well known, and had been used by many a coach to win critical playoff games in a variety of sports. No passion play ever did well during sweeps week, but this year was going to be different.

Short, fat Bobby Seward had chosen the role of Zippy, the streaking speedster. Unfortunately for everyone involved, Bobby thought "streaking" meant nude. He had walked onto the stage naked. No one really wanted to see a naked fat kid. To want to see a naked child at all is what most would label deviant (and criminal), but if one must see a naked kid it might as well be a skinny kid. Try as he might, Everhard could not persuade the boy to put on his clothes. They were losing time, and as a stagehand went looking for something to cover the boy up with, the director-priest pushed on.

As Everhard directed the second scene, he tried to avoid looking at Bobby's stomach rolls. He felt like he was going to cough up a hairball.

"Ok boys, let's go through the scene one more time. Red J, Angel, and The Lantern are patrolling Sweatropolis for signs of Lex Lucifer's gang. They encounter some of Lex's henchmen, fight, and send the thugs running. At the very same time, Zippy is running back to regroup with the League, having sold out the location of Red J's Food Court of Solitude to Lex himself. Later in the scene, Lex's henchmen return and capture the Red J during his private meditations. Do you boys feel comfortable with the dialogue?"

Bobby ("Zippy") raised his hand. "Mmmmggghhhppppppffftttt!" he said.

"Bobby, finish the donut before you talk."

And a few minutes later, he did just that. Once again he raised his hand.

"Yes, Bobby?"

"Mmmmggghhhppppppffftttt!"

Even if the boy was mute and dumb, Everhard was gonna kick his ass.

"Say your lines as Zippy, you murdering swine!" Everhard screamed. Bobby and the other two boys jumped. Studly Stevie, who was playing the Red J, started the scene.

"Using my keen super vision, I detect four lousy goons directly below. Perhaps they know of Lex's hideaway for the Doomsday Device. Shall we?" proclaimed Stevie as the Red J.

"Yes, of course," said Ronny as the Angel.

"Mmmggghhhppppppffftttt," offered Bobby, unaware that he wasn't in the scene yet.

The stagehands swung the ropes that were connected to the cables that were connected to the harnesses that were used to make the young actors fly across the stage. The boys now appeared to make their descent.

Thank God that it was only rehearsal. It was going to take some time to truly practice out the story of the passion and get it right.

There were so many minute details of Red J's life on Earth. Watching the children act out the drama reminded Everhard of when he was only a young student at Funday School. The many layers of the Red J's story were taught to him in that school, and each lesson made him want to collect every issue of the Red J that was ever published. He thought back to when his Religious Studies teacher (a stout and blustery man whose fire for the material he taught was most likely the reason Everhard had followed into the faith) first covered the concept of the secret identity of the Big Red J.

"And so being that our Lord was posing as a news reporter so that he might know the dreary experience of life as a mortal man, so he did sit in a nameless and cold cubicle crafting a story of the previous day's battle with Lex Lucifer's minions. Wanting to prove himself the true journalist that he was, our Lord did include a modest amount of typographical errors, an assortment of ill-informed facts, and many prejudgments. And he did type heartily until finished. And so it was that he spent his third day in the holy city at the time of Yeaster."

Editor's note: There is also much debate within the religious industry about the actual status of Lois Lame. While it is never mentioned in any of the original Red J issues, Lois is labeled a slut and is considered of ill repute. This is a case of tradition over fact, as the script never makes mention of any type of promiscuity. It does, however, mention her marriage to a "great" but unnamed reporter. It is interesting to note that Red J is present (as well as the J-League and Red J's mother) at the wedding and he seems to have host duties -- when the reception runs low on food, he flies to a nearby 7-11 to purchase 100 bags of potato chips and French onion dip, which are given to him, along with several cases of low-calorie beer, in "good faith" by a pimply faced teenage cashier. Why would Red J do such a thing unless he wished to save his own face? Why does the script not mention the name of the "great" staff reporter? These questions are not easily answered. It is sure that on his fourth day in Sweatropolis, Red J did rescue his "wife" from the grip of Lex Lucifer's men in the confines of the Daily Bullshit building where a Clark Krist did work as a reporter for some time. On this we have documentation on.

It was these lessons that Everhard drew upon as they continued through the rehearsal process, changing and reworking the script as necessary. He looked down at his notes for the next scene, where the impending death of Red J is demanded by Lex and his minions.

Staging for the third scene should depict the complete inside of the J-League Headquarters. All members are present. A communication comes on the video screen and the League gathers around to watch the transmission. When the image becomes clear, it is the evil Lex Lucifer. The script reads:

LEX: Hello, ladies. By now it is obvious that I have the total population of the city in fear. They no longer believe that the Red J and his League can protect them. The Red J is dangerous to life here as we know it, and I am willing to risk the lives of every citizen to prove it. I have only one request. Deliver me the Red J for my personal disposal and I will release the city from the grip of my Doomsday Device.

The League members explode into vulgarities and threats. Red J calms them down.

RED J: I'm coming after you, baby. And you better believe that I'm going to take care of business. You can't threaten me or the fine citizens of Sweatropolis!

LEX: Ha Ha Ha Ha, you big fool! I would like nothing better. I await your royal pain in the ass! By the way, (I'd) watch your back!

The rest of this scene features a League private meeting and dinner. Red J instructs them in his tactics. Red J shows a bit of nervousness as he fumbles with the bread, ripping it into pieces. Straight Arrow sees the broken bread and whips up a nice fondue, which the League shares. Red J then excuses himself and retires to his Food Court of Solitude (Scene 4).

After reviewing his notes, Everhard continued to force the children through more daily rehearsals. All being told, his loyal sidekicks went through the full production over 30 times in the days that followed. Although they suffered from dehydration and malnutrition, he was relentless in his pursuit of a perfect performance. Bodies dropped in singles and in groups, and when this would happen, Everhard would simply yell his directions louder. There were no true casualties, and when it came time for the performance, they were very ready, indeed.

$

Father Everhard looked at his watch and gulped as he realized that there were scant minutes before the curtain would rise upon the small makeshift theatre. The old community auditorium was a solid venue, and the tickets had gone much faster than anticipated. Scalpers were selling them for $75 or more.

The children were excited as well. Bobby hadn't eaten anything for at least 20 minutes and various members of the cast wandered around the cramped confines of the backstage area, filling it with nervous laughter and occasional belches.

Father Everhard took a deep breath. Peeking around the curtains, he studied the full house. Aside from all the newly imported residents of the Village, there were many VIPs in the house. He looked to the balconies and was shocked to see the rebel General with a bodyguard. The painted man was talking away with the CEO of Sell Inc. His cybernetic implants were flashing wildly, and Everhard hoped that this would not be a distraction when the show began. The whole crowd was lively, filled with executives, soldiers, salesmen, robots, mutant animals, and what appeared to be a few members of the Dodge Tribe. Strangely, they looked like they had better hygiene than the rest of the crowd.

As he continued to survey the audience, he felt a sharp pain in his leg as the metal corner of robot suddenly bumped into his shin. He looked down to see a small box-shaped cybot. When he made eye contact with the red headlight that served as the cybot's sensor cluster, the machine spoke.

"I'm Brad Perfect!" it squealed.

"That's very nice, now move along," Everhard said as he punted it straight to the orchestra pit. Enough fooling around, he had to get the kids ready. He gathered them around for a prayer and to distribute low-grade amphetamines.

"Dear Lord, please bless this performance with great pride and profit. We, your humble servants, seek only to honor your name with a show worthy of excellent reviews and hopefully the request of a sequel. We are your numbers to crunch, dear Lord. Please see that our legs are broken and we hope that you smile down on us at the last curtain falls. Amen."

The children's eyes glowed with excitement as the performance-enhancing drugs they had been given by their parents took effect. Soon after, the show was on its way.

$

Editor's note: Although the scripture treats Zippy as a traitor to the cause, there is reasonable justification for his actions, and theological theory states that treachery was an essential part of Red J's plot to rescue Sweatropolis. The tradition holds that Red J goes to his Food Court of Solitude to meditate, while Angel and Straight Arrow keep watch. Both heroes grow tired and fall asleep. During their slumber, Zippy sneaks through the back entrance, along with a contingent of Lex's men, who are armed with Craptonite. They surprise the Red J and subdue him.

Many have wondered why the security systems were not in place at the time? How did both heroes fall asleep at the same time? And, most curiously, how did a band of thugs happen upon a chunk of one of the rarest elements in the known universe? Why does something so rare happen to be in abundance at the absolute worst time?

One of the most pivotal scenes in the passion was the capturing of Red J. Everhard's well-trained sidekicks blazed through their dialogue like future award-winning performers.

STRAIGHT ARROW: Once again, we have drawn watch. I'll never get any sleep at this rate.

ANGEL: I need very little sleep. As long as there are villians and criminals in the night, I am too busy to sleep.

ARROW (yawning) Well I'm missing some serious nightclub action sitting here. Maybe it's just as well. I'm beat.

ANGEL: You lack discipline. Do not fall asleep.

ARROW: (putting head down on table) Oh, don't worry. I just need to rest my eyes for a minute.

Lighting on Arrow and Angel fades. Off Stage left, a light is brought up on Red J, sitting cross-legged, facing the audience.

RED J: Father, I can't rest from worry. My arch-enemy Lex has the city in his greasy palms and I wonder if the League is up to the good fight. Will I put a one in the "Wins" column or will I get a big goose-egg? I guess that I will have to just tune in next time to find out.

Lighting fades on J. Bring lights up on Arrow and Angel.

ARROW: (Snoring) ZZZZZZZZZZZZZZZ.

ANGEL: Idiot. How can he sleep when Lex grips the city at...(yawns)...and of (yawns again)...when the cold hand of crime is on its neck? (Angel falls asleep.)

Lights out on Angel and Arrow. Lights up Stage Right, where Zippy and three of Lex's henchmen enter.

ZIPPY: (Looking over at his sleeping teammates) Ah, I see that my comrades have taken to the sedatives I placed in their no-calorie diet sodas! Ok guys, it should be safe to go grab the Big Red J.

HENCHMAN #1: Gosh, it must be really tough for you to sell the guy out.

ZIPPY: Uh, no. Not really.

HENCHMAN #2: It doesn't bother you that you're giving America's Number One Fighting Man over to the enemy?

ZIPPY: I said no, alright?

HENCHMAN #3: Boy, I'd feel bad if I did something like that.

ZIPPY: Look! He's got it coming! I've got it coming! My contract is up, I could get traded, I gotta look out for me. Besides, he's a real ball-breaker. Now come on.

Bring lights up on Red J.

RED J: My super hearing has picked up some voices that I do not know. I must remain alert.

Zippy and the henchmen cross the stage and walk up to the Red J.

REDJ: Huh? Oh, it's you Zippy. You surprised me.
ZIPPY: Yes, well I am very quick. But you already knew that. Do you know what I am going to do next?

Zippy pulls out a large green rock. The henchmen laugh.

RED J: No! Oh no! Not Craptonite. Not my one weakness! I can withstand anything but the power of Craptonite. Why?

ZIPPY: I can't stand you. You always get all the glory.

RED J: I know that. What I meant was why does it seem that every idiot on the block has a chunk of my home planet? Seriously, it's my greatest weakness. Seems kind of stupid.

ZIPPY: Never mind. Get him!

The henchmen subdue Red J, who puts up a weak and ineffective struggle. Lights fade to full black.

$

Everhard was very pleased. For one thing, Bobby had agreed to wear a nude body suit instead of running around the stage stark naked. All the other children had been even more cooperative, and Everhard knew that it was his firm adherence to the scripture along with a somewhat draconian attitude to stage management that was keeping the show on course.

As the stagehands performed a quick turn over, the priest stole another glance at the crowd. There were very few empty seats, and that was very reassuring. The audience seemed to be suspending their disbeliefs and allowing the story to unfold. Aside from a couple of fistfights in the back, they looked ready for more.

Now the play was getting to the meat of the story -- the scourging of Red J via the thirteen trials and tribulations. By the end of the following scenes, the stage would be covered in blood and gristle. From this point forward, it would be a Grand-Guignol. Everhard hoped the people in the first three rows had brought their ponchos as instructed.

$

The scourging of The Big Red J has been interpreted in a number of ways. Because of the short attention span of the audience (not to mention their bloodlust), Everhard's production performed the thirteen trials and tribulations as short, dialogue-free vignettes until the actual carnage of the crucifixion was to begin. Little Stevie, the brave boy portraying The Red J, had no idea how bad this was going to be. It was all very exciting, indeed.

Turning to the script:

OFFSTAGE ANNOUNCER: And it was with his capture into the hands of the evil one that the Big Red J did face a set of thirteen trials and tribulations. A vile chunk of Craptonite, secured by the soldiers of Lex Lucifer, was shaped into the form of a gag ball and stuffed into our Lord's mouth. He was drawn by electric locomotive to a construction site in the center of town, where he was verbally abused and degraded.

Then the evil minions did release the gag from his throat and said: "You got more than you bargained for buddy, now you're gonna get it!"

And the Lord did respond: "Go fuck yourself."

And so the trials did commence. The first took the form of a ferocious battle with the Pagan God of Non-Returnable Bottles who did thrash our Lord about and nearly brought him down with a carefully thrown brown glass projectile. All seemed lost until the Lord did ask him if his shoelaces were untied, to which the Pagan God did look down and Red J did disintegrate his jaw and teeth with a great smite upon the mouth.

Once this great battle had ended, Lex's men did allow him to take five before commencing with the remaining 12 trials. Being that they were evil, his break was actually only 3 minutes and 15 seconds.

Then they opened two gates, releasing the Pagan Beasts of Products Both Real and Imaginary. This was followed by the brutal game show where Red J blew his jackpot by guessing "Carp" when he meant to say, "Cod."

But nothing could match the temptations of the toothless five dollar hookers, the coupon cutting paper cuts, or the infomercial brainwashing session. Or so our Savior thought!

Because then came the ferocious reunion of Red J and his old ex-girlfriends. They did descend upon him without mercy and did prove that you can get blood from a stone. Then came the tax accountants and slip-and-fall lawyers. And while our Lord lay on the ground -- bloodied, battered, and near-broken -- he had to suffer a call from his agent. Through blood and stinging sweat, the Red J counted off the trials he had survived. The number was 10. It was at this point he did actually cry "Uncle," but it was to no avail.

Lex's fanatic followers heated up a Craptonite brand shaped like a large letter J. Our Lord was branded upon both buttocks as the men laughed and mocked him. Our Man did swing at them, but his now-weakened fists were ineffective, and this only caused more laughter and humiliation.

J's mother, Ma Krist had watched all the proceedings with terror in her heart, screaming all the while. She was consoled by Lois Lame, but the sheer brutality of the afternoon left her fully fixed with the thousand yard stare. It would take many years of therapy before she could move past the events that had transpired in front of her eyes. This was no made-for-TV movie, this was the impending, slow death of her son.

And her heart did sink deeper as the Red J tried to crawl his way to freedom. He was stopped as heavy boots stamped down on his hands. They were the boots of Lex Lucifer.

$

A tear came to the pious priest's eye when he realized just what his Lord God had endured. A single glorious tear, a masterful tear.

Little Stevie, the boy actor chosen to play the Big Red J, was about to endure the same punishment. This was a highly accurate production. Everhard was impressed with the boy's sacrifice for his art.

As the script reads:

Lex stands over the beaten body of Red J.

LEX: And so, Caped Loser, you have been forced to the ground. Admit defeat!

RED J: Never, you madman!

LEX: Mad or not, it is I who shall be named the victor. It is I who will rule Sweatropolis and eventually the world!
And you know what the best part is? It was all a bluff. I made up that whole "Doomsday Device" thing. Ha hahahah!

RED J: (burble...cough)

Several of Lex's henchmen wheel out a large cart. The cart is filled with a copious amount of shiny and sharp looking objects. They have strange shapes, and glint with menace.

LEX: Just say the word, J, and I will stop. Until then, taste the pain!

Lex begins to pull torturous tool after tool from the cart. He attacks Red J with a fury one might associate with complete and utter hate, the kind that one finds tattooed on fingers in prison. There is a shower of blood, and bits of flesh, bone, and hair fly about the stage.

Little Stevie bit down hard on his mouth guard and attempted to remain conscious. He had not expected to face such monstrous brutality, and he seriously wished he had not signed the waivers clearing Everhard and the Church of any possible wrongdoings. That had, as it turns out, been a bad choice.

The crowd gasped and sometimes cheered inappropriately as the boy/Red J was steadily covered in large bleeding gashes. They fell silent when they heard the sickening crack of bone. No passion play had ever taken the scourging of the Red J this far. It was both impressive and revolting. The crowd was astounded. While the whole play itself was charged with action and excitement, it was the gory last stand of the Savior that really got them salivating. They began to yell and scream, stomping their feet and foaming at the mouths.

LEX: Renounce it all, Fly Boy!

RED J: (strained) NEVER!

LEX: SO BE IT!

Lex pulls out his industrial nail gun, loaded with Craptonite nails. He positions the battered body of Red J over a cross section of steel girders. He begins to fire the nail gun into the palms of Red J, firmly mounting him to the girders.

LEX: How about them apples?

RED J: I forgive you Lex, even though you know very fucking well what you are doing.

LEX: Bah! Just die already.

The steel cross is raised and Red J looks to the sky, muttering something about how he "would rather be fishing," and then simply closes his eyes. There is complete silence, and then a very loud explosion off-stage.

LEX: Shit, maybe that doomsday device thing wasn't a bluff after all. I have so many plots to take over the world, I can never remember which is which.

Fade to black.

OFF-STAGE ANNOUNCER: We are not the first to suggest that the Big Red J was crucified. It is interesting to note that there are no photographic records of the event, but only the testimony of vested interests that formed the word of the script. And while this is the key moment and climax of the battle, it is not the end of the story.

The scripture says that the League defeated Lucifer immediately after Red J's death and saw that the fallen hero's body was properly buried. Three days later, a message by Red J appears on the League's TV, telling them that he has attained a higher form of existence and that they "shouldn't sweat it." Thus began the cult that begat the church we know today.

Still, why is it that no Leaguer or scientist knew of such a standard Craptonian evolutionary pattern? Why are there no forensic records of Red J's body? What about an autopsy? Why were there no bones or body? We uncovered serious evidence to suggest that Red J actually lived through the ordeal and moved to a trailer park in Houston. But tonight, we put those questions aside and simply marvel at the miracle we now know as Yeaster, the Rising of the Lord."

Lower curtain.

Everhard could hear the thunderous applause from behind the thick velvet curtain, and he felt great. Yes, this show was exactly what he needed. He felt a feeling of satisfaction rise up as he watched his wee actors rush out on stage to soak up the applause. With rediscovered confidence, he pulled the curtain back and stepped out to take his bows.

The crowd surged when the priest made himself visible. The applause rushed to the stage like waves hitting the beach, and Everhard soaked in it.

Yes, it was a good night. A fantastic night.

Long after the crowd left the auditorium, the spiritually recharged priest began to pry Little Stevie's collapsed body off the set piece. If only the young man knew how much he had done to raise the priest's spirits. Everhard would have to thank his parents.

9. An Important Message from the Management

Interior : Your Living Room

Your cell phone rings. You pick it up. The screen reads Blocked Number. You answer it anyway. A raspy voice speaks to you in a loud whisper.

These are dark days. I know it. You know it. These are dark days. The forces of evil surround us. Can you feel it? Can you feel the vibrations of negative energy pushing upon you? Like a sinister bubble, it encircles us, and it seeks to destroy us.

These are dark days, my friend. Won't someone please save us?

Won't someone fly in and make it right? Who will serve up the justice that is so desperately needed?

Who will save us?

Why is it, you and I, why is it that when the chips are down, when the dark clouds roll in, when the coupon expires, why is it that we take a quick look around the room and ask:

"Who is going to take care of this mess?"

We went to the restaurant, and made a big mess at the table! We like to think we can peel off a couple of bucks, throw it down, and let some mangy hippy busboy clean up the mess. Damage control through commerce.

So here we are, smoke plumes rising, water pipes ruptured, corpses in the street. Here we are, guns in our hands, bodies on the ground, powder burns on our fingers. We are the wardens of our darkness, and the co-signers of destruction. But yet we look to the sky for our great messiah to save us from, well...

Ourselves.

These are dark days, perhaps the darkest of all. What are we to do?

What would you say if I told you that I have the solution, I have the power, and I can deliver it unto you? Are you intrigued? Are you quickly flipping open your digital handheld to see when you can fit in a session with your doom trainer to figure this all out?

You better ink me into that calendar, you had better make the time.

You say, “Don't you worry, I am on board, I am on board one hundred percent.”

Good! Because I have the solution, I have a way out. I have a way that we can break through the clouds of pure evil that hover over our heads, ready to dump warm piss upon us. I want you here with me, because I believe that together, we are impossible to defeat. Invincible you might say.

Join me on the mystical road to victory! With great power comes an even greater responsibility, and rest assured we will be imbued with both! Join me, and the others who also look to the horizon and see the menace of the days to come.

You may have asked yourself, what is this evil, what is its essence? What is the definition of evil? Evil is the opposite of what we believe in, my friend. I ask you now, to put aside your childish ways and groove to this tune.

There will be those that look at you and say that you are brainwashed. Let them. They will not know what you know. They will not have the arcane knowledge from the many issues of grimoires, the premium collectors editions, the information encoded in the foil holograms, but you will. Let them judge you, for they know not.

There will be those who say that they don't understand what you have become. Let them, this is for their protection. The war against the dark days hides in the shadows of full light, and only the illuminated can fight, all others must move to the sidewalls. We too will hide in the full light, masking our true identities to fool the enemy and protect our allies.

We will use a language that sounds incredibly similar but encodes hidden meaning in every word. This will confuse our foes, and buff our victory. They will burn valuable cool downs in an attempt to glean understanding, but we will spec our trees in such a way that there will be no effective countermeasures.

You must be a true believer to fight the good fight. Do you believe?

I believe that you have the faith, you have stayed fast for this long, you would not listen to me with such an open mind if you did not.

We will go into battle with many weapons.

First, we will be united: me, you, all our brothers and sisters, field agents, sales agents, oracles, sellswords, minions, companions, mounts, pets, human shields, cannon fodder, and my uncle Frank, who is a complete badass.

Second, you will be anointed with the almighty light, oil, and flesh of the righteous messiah, for whom we fight. You will take your pound of flesh and utilize it as a stim-pak of vitality and mental vigor. You will have the power flow through your nervous system, and in your blood. One bite, that's all it will take.

Third, know that we employ the most innovative forms of kidnapping, extortion, mind-control, sharpshooting, psychological abuse, backstabbing, propaganda, sexual abuse, water boarding, tickling, mass suicide and phone calls to parents. We must be ruthless in our tactics, for our evil nemesis will spare no quarter.

In our days ahead, these dark days, we will uncover many conspiracies, plots, covert actions, and press events. There will be things so offensive to us that our disgust will seem unbearable, and it will only be the sweet release of cruelty to our enemies that will keep us in check.

Know this, your faith, your blind faith will be your shield against the darkness. You will need it, for we face the most super of villains, the most dastardly of individuals and groups who possess total opposition to our beliefs and a desire to undermine them.

Our problems have one simple solution, and I will repeatedly emphasize that solution in the dark days ahead. I will give you a new identity to work with, one that you will keep secret. I will give you unconditional love and attention if you devote yourself to the cause. I will control the flow of information you receive, and you will be grateful for it.

Because these are dark days.

I know it.

You know it.

10. All Things Be Going Down on Palatial Grounds

The weeks after the double-kidnapping of Brad Perfect had been very strange for the Soldier. He had fallen asleep while guarding the back gate of Network One's Media Mall, and as a result, allowed the brave and brilliant outlaws an easy escape. The General, who was known for cruel mercy, did not kill or punish him. No, he did the Soldier much worse. He promoted him. Now, the Soldier was known as the General's "Moral Advisor/Personal Assistant."

This new promotion did appear to be a fate much worse than a morning execution. The Soldier found himself deep inside the General's star chamber, surrounded by the architects of the revolution. The Soldier was assigned many duties such as setting up restaurant reservations, taking messages that would never be returned, and doing random repetitive movements. Whatever the General ordered, he made it happen. A side effect of this was that the Soldier found himself questioning the sanity of the General and his recent revolution. When the assignments became bizarre or top aides disappeared in the night, the Soldier would find himself fondling the strange business card he had found in his shirt pocket the day of the Brad-nappings. It simply read:

FOR A GOOD TIME, CALL CONPOLLO

THE DODGE TRIBE

The Soldier had thought about this card and this ConPollo. There was no number to call. He did know the Dodge Tribe, but he was not sure where to find them.

These were fleeting thoughts. For now, the Soldier was spending his days pissing on small fires started by the General. Today was one of those days.

The Soldier, recently alerted by an alarm, ran down the imposing halls of the palace's Far Right wing. Immediately following the revolution, the General had set up shop in the very home of the King he had just deposed. Sell Inc.'s outstanding reconstruction crews had worked triple shifts, and the palace had some new found glory. As he passed through room after spacious room, the General's security was all he could keep in his mind.

The General, the General.

Hallways turned into doorways, and doorways turned into rooms. Great tapestries adorned the walls before massive staircases, which led to hallways, which turned into doorways which led to rooms with huge paintings of the General. The Soldier craned his neck into every corner, in the vain hopes that he just might find the General to relay his crucial news.

But even in his valiant display of endurance and strength (he did run laps around the palace and its grounds at least five times, you know) the Soldier had to sit and catch his breath. The silence of the palace enveloped him, with only his panting smoker's wheeze to disrupt the calm. It had been exceptionally quiet all day as everyone from the palace was across town for Merlin's Magical Truck Pull and Necromantic Showdown at the Village Coliseum. That was always a big draw.

As the Soldier pondered how he, as Moral Advisor, had missed out on tickets for such a cool show, he heard electronic noises echoing out from a distant hall. Having rested enough, and stuffing a hi-NRG bar in his mouth, *for-a-quick-burst-of-NRG-when-he-needed-it-most*, the Soldier rose from the floor with a majesty usually reserved for royalty and Olympic gymnasts. Well, maybe it wasn't majesty...maybe it was purpose. Yes, purpose. After all, that's what the expression on the Soldier's face seemed to show. Hi brow turned down with purpose as he rolled up his sleeves and marched down the corridor to locate the source of the electro-beeps.

As the sound grew in volume, the Soldier scrolled through his options menu for deciphering the source of the noises.

Were they:

1) A time bomb?
2) A Cornish Hen?
3) A bizarre homing device?
4) An alarm clock somebody forgot to turn off?
5) A new weapons system of alien origin?
6) A lost cyberbot?

7) The desperate, futile cry of the sane in an insane world?

Ever tightening his grip on the obvious, the Soldier knew the only way to know was to find out. His search led him to the janitor's closet on the third floor. The noises that emitted from the closet were erratic and almost musical. They composed a strange, broken melody. Then the Soldier heard the voice of the perpetrator.

"Well, GOD DAMN!" the voice yelled.

The Soldier's face twisted into sheer fury as he burst down the door. His face then untwisted in surprise at what he had found. There sat the General, cross legged, with potato chip crumbs lining his bright red lips, his yellow and orange jumper stained the color of Berry Flavored Cools-Aide, playing his Super NoFunDoe electronic gaming system which he has recently received as a Yeaster present from a business associate.

"Sir!"

"Whaaaaaat?" wailed the General.

"Sir."

"Can't you see I'm busy?"

The Soldier began to feel anxious, as if his "interruption" might result in physical punishment. "Yes, your greatness. I would not bother you if I did not --"

"-- Bother me? Soldier, you kicked my door down with a force great enough to put splinters three inches long into my snack cakes. They're ruined," interrupted the General as he pointed to the plastic plate on which sat three delicious snack cakes unfortunately decorated with splinters.

"Sir, on my word, I assure you that I will replace those delicious snack cakes with ones even greater in taste. But now I have to make an important news break in your regular programming schedule."

"It's nooooot about the CEO, is it?" asked the General in a juvenile whine.

"No, it's not about the CEO. It's about..."

"Go on."

"It's about..."

"Yes?"

"Well, it's just that..."

"Uh huh."

"It seems...uhhhh, welL.. It"

"My God! What the HELL is it?"

"Sir, we have found a number of sensitive recording devices throughout the castle and its grounds."

"What are those?"

"Bugs, Sir. It seems that the castle has been under watch for some time now. Someone is recording our every word and every move."

"Soldier?"

"Yes, sir?"

"I set up that equipment, you DOLT! If you would ever come to a security meeting, which would be awfully nice, as you are my fucking Moral Advisor, you would know that we wired the place to hopefully find out who was delivering our secrets to the King's loyalist resistors! Ever since we got rid of that bearded bugger, they have been lighting up our troops and causing all kinds of disruptive mayhem. But because you constantly shirk your duties in this dump, you never know what the hell is going on. I never know when some sonuvabitch is going to frag my sorry ass. It's nice to know I have such a crack squad to protect what I have spent my whole life building."

"So you knew about the recording devices?" asked the Soldier.

"YES!"

"So I don't have to worry?"

"No, you don't have to worry."

This was a great relief to the Soldier. The whole conversation was not something he was comfortable with. In fact, since his promotion, he had been increasingly more uncomfortable. The General was a brilliant man, certainly. However, he could be cruel and did not tolerate slackers and the ignorant for long. Somewhere deep inside, the Soldier felt that he had been promoted only so that he might fail, and be used as an example. This overall feeling of discomfort was causing him to act, in his own words, like an idiot.

The Soldier was most definitely not an idiot. And he knew this. There were times, especially since he had moved into the palace, that he felt he was the only complete person in the General's posse. This promotion was looking more and more like a mistake as the days went on.

"Sir, as your MORAL ADVISOR, I think that you might want to look at this. It was enough for the security at the front gate to hit the alarm. It got me running," the Soldier said as he handed the General a most important fax.

SPECIAL REPORT
Re: The Filthy Loyalists
From: Forward Scout #34B, the General's Army
To: The General, His Advisors, and Other Applicable Lousy Bums

It's those pesky loyalists again. They have a way of getting into those hard-to-reach-places and causing a whole ball o' trouble. Lately, they have been a lot of trouble. Can anyone around here even remember the day when we didn't have the influence of the King to watch out for?

Anyhoo, why did I fax you this? Oh, I know. Let's face facts -- it would be a change of pace. The loyalist resistors, have swelled in numbers. Granted, they still grill their meat while we fry, but strangely enough, they have accumulated a large standing army. Why? Most likely it is that they always have a free prize or offer or some shit like that. Not to mention Olympic sponsorships!

If we are to truly take power in the Village against these beefy upstarts, we need to seriously review our PLAN.

We also suspect that Sell Inc. might be providing them weapons and supplies. If so, this represents a serious breach of contract on their behalf.

What this means is serious military action.

If we don't move first, forget Broadway and Park Place. We'll never get past Go and we'll be Sorry! Concentration is what is needed to save our Monopoly or the rest will merely be a Trivial Pursuit.

Let's crush the Loyalists! This is not a game!

End Report...

The General managed a frown under all of his makeup. "This is not good. I will be putting you on a special duty."

The Soldier winced. "Special Duty" was often times fatal.

"I cannot think of a young man better equipped to help me handle this," the General said as he looked the Soldier up and down. "But before I get you going on this, I need you to help me with this current distraction."

The Soldier and the General played a furious game of Chronic the Blunthog. Passing the controller back and forth, they both completely mesmerized themselves with the swirling colors and sounds the game's lifelike cartoon action delivered.

"Do you think that the loyalist resistors are as big a threat as that recent report suggested?" asked the Soldier, who was amazingly coherent.

"I don't know, man," offered the General.

"I mean, we've always been in a state of war. That is the natural state of things. The question, or the issue, is to maintain the advantage. The great strategist--"

"--You're not going to start with your 'Way of the Warrior' religious crap, are you?" grumbled the General.

As the General's Moral Advisor, the Soldier had been doing a bit of reading. He had stumbled upon an ancient tome which described a philosophy which combined Zen and combat. Since he had read the book, he had talked endlessly on its writings. The General, who did not have much time for Zen, could have really cared less.

The Soldier was persistent. "Let me finish. The great strategist, Sun Tzu, said that you never fight if you don't have an advantage."

"The great Sun Tzu has never seen a Manley Cup playoff round. Get a hot goalie, and it doesn't matter who you play against," retorted the General.

"—Now it's my turn to interrupt, sir. As Moral Advisor, of the General's Armed and Dangerous Forces, I have to consider your men and their valuable lives," said the Soldier, strangely without any hint of sarcasm (well, maybe a hint).

"Son, you've made a good point, and after I finish this level, it'll be your turn to play the Chronic."

"Cool. You bogart that game."

"But, besides all that, you've made me think. We've let those loyalists go unchecked. Now we really must act before they close the store. Immediately after this game of the Chronic, we will saunter over to the war room and plan out some strategies. By then, everyone will be back from the truck pull and we can brief the troops. Our need to remove the loyalist threat is now on the short list."

"Wow."

"What's that, soldier?"

"I never made it to the Dungeon Level on the Chronic before. What happens here?"

"Well, Chronic must play submissive to a gang of Rasta Dominatrices while Dancehall plays in the...hey, wait a minute. I have something to show you."

The General reached over to his left and presented a colorful box. It read "Hostile Takeover: The Game." The package design was upbeat, depicting the excitement of war. It was adorned with detailed portraits of all the major players: The King, his Commander Thighmaster, the General and his Rebel Army, etc. Exciting corporate logos were layered on silhouettes of soldiers, fighting in the muck.

"This is hitting all the stores next week. My consultants have suggested that we market our victory through a variety of interactive products, to help reinforce the new way of life in the Village. Remember, with the advent of online virtual reality, common video game systems, and quality hallucinogenic drugs, the video game is a must sell item. There are many old-time grand strategists out there who really enjoy a basic military simulation," said the General, clearly proud of the product.

He put the game into the console and got it going. The screen exploded with color and movement, as video captured from the actual battle played in quick cut scenes. The montage did not hold back, and by the time the General was ready to hit the start button, the Soldier counted 25 decapitations, 123 explosions, 52 severed limbs, 300 screams of terror, and what seemed to be an infinite number of gunshots. It ended on the General's perma-grin, and with a very happy jingle.

The General looked over at the Soldier. "Good stuff, huh?"

The Soldier couldn't form a response before the General continued with his virtual tour.

The main screen depicted the geography of the Village and its' surrounding areas in bold yet realistic colors. The actual makeup of the terrain was very realistic and lifelike in appearance. The General pointed to the screen.

"The Village, as we know, sits in a valley surrounded by a mountain range. The mountains to the north are the steepest, whereas the western and southern ranges are practically foothills. Of course, we both know that these mountains are massive piles of garbage. Three of the largest have somewhat returned to nature, with their thin covering of crabgrass and whatnot. The rest, well...they look like shit. There is a mountain pass to the east of the

Village which leads to another valley. There used to be another village over there, but no one has heard from them for some time. We're so self-absorbed over here that we don't really care how they're doing.

The Village is divided into five provinces, each with its own economic value point. The centermost province, where the palace lies, is the most valuable with 30,000 economic points. The Shopping District, directly north, where most of the Malls are located is worth a whopping 120,000 economic points. To the west of center is the Business District, where the world headquarters of Sell Inc. is located. It is worth 7,000,000 economic points. The district south of the capital is the Media District, where the broadcasting facilities of Network One and its subsidiaries is located. Its value is 20,000 economic points. And lastly, to the east, is the Residential District, which is worth 1500 economic points. I'll explain all this economic business later.

The surrounding mountains, with 25 separate districts, have a total economic value of 1000, with each district worth 4 economic points. The valley east of the Village, is divided into three districts, each with an economic value of 5. A river haphazardly runs from the northwestern corner of the board to the southeastern corner. It has no economic value. It does however have a strategic value. This completes the geographic makeup of the game board. Are you still with me?"

The Soldier's eyes were getting a bit blurry, but he was fascinated. "What the hell is that?" he said, putting his fingertip to the screen.

"C'mon son, it's a military simulation. What do you think it's supposed to be?"

"I don't know. Is it a pickle?"

"No! That's no goddamn pickle! It's a tank with a large cannon on top!"

The General was right, it was a tank, not a pickle.

"Now then, the General continued, "the great thing about the game is the realism. Why, they even have the weather programmed in. You get acid rain, and tornados, among other things. You know how bad the acid rain gets around here." The General picked up the game's jewel box, gently pulled out the game's instructions, and began to read aloud.

"Hostile Takeover is a game for two players. Player One is the Village, ruled by the King. Player Two commands the rebel forces, led by the General. In order to assure game balance, the King maintains an economic superiority, while the rebel army has the tactical edge of guerrilla warfare and the geographical advantage as they are occupying the mountains outside of the Village (which are notoriously difficult to take).

Each turn combines economic transactions, troop movement, and combat. Special turns for drug research and consumption are allowed in the advanced game. To win, Player One must kill every rebel, any relative or friend they might have, and do three flygirl dances in front of a panel made up of old Solid Gold Dancers. Player Two must take the palace and or/assassinate the King.

There are a ton of great characters in the game. For Player One, colorful tie-died animations represent important figures such as the King and his Commander-in-Chief, Thighmaster. Also represented are infantry and armor, artillery, broadcast news anchors, fire engines, submarine sandwiches, industrial buildings, homes, restaurants, and one wholesale lingerie dealer.

For Player Two, elegantly rendered characters in dirty orange and shit brown represent the rebel forces and their key figure, ME. There are icons which represent infantry and armor, cash registers, drive-thru turnstiles, Blastburger Attacks, tin can telephones, research laboratories, nutritional supplements and handy one-bite-fits-all snack pack ration containers.

In between the battles are great movie-quality animated scenes that depict all the fun of surgical strikes, population reduction, ethnic cleansing, post-combat syndrome, 'smart' weapons, etc." The General put the book down.

"Now then, shall we play a game?"

The Soldier nodded and grabbed a controller. The General started up the game, picking the King's army as his team. The Soldier was stuck playing the General's actual role in the battle. He was nervous, naturally. It didn't take much game play to raise the Soldier's blood.

In fact, he fumed. This computer battle simulation was kicking his ass straight to Idaho. How could he ever eliminate the King's army if he couldn't notice the difference between a tank and a pickle? Oh the tragedy that could spring from such a mistake -- thousands of computer animated men died for his failings.

In desperation, the Soldier entered a command which moved his electronic troops to the electronic front. They lined up on the opposite bank of the electronic river. On the other side, the King's troops seethed with bloodlust. The Soldier's lower lip trembled. His reluctant thumb hovered over the game controller's buttons, as he pondered the possible carnage that awaited his green light. A drop of sweat slowly rolled down his forehead, clinging precariously from his eyebrow.

Finally, he hit the button that would execute the charge. The little cartoonish soldiers began to bolt into the river, swimming fearlessly. The King's troops fired on them with large caliber automatic rifles. Soon the river was the deep red color of blood as fatherless limbs and decapitated heads floated whimsically in the gentle current.

The General let loose with a line of laughter. The Soldier threw his controller down with such force it smashed into uncomfortable chunks of black plastic.

"How the hell can you laugh at that?" boomed the Soldier. "Not one of my men survived."

The General continued spewing his guffaws. "Oh buddy, hee hee, don't, hah, worry--it's only a -- bwaa ha ha -- a game! And it's been great, but it’s time to get down to business and figure out how to deal with the loyalist scum. We'd better get our asses over to the War Room so we can smoke and drink a lot, develop weak strategies and stroke our cocks, er, I mean, egos, positive that what we think is right regardless of what the actual figures say."

"Good plan," said the Solider. "If we hurry, we can tie one on and rub one out before the others get back from the truck pull...."

$

The War Room was a wide, open oval-shaped room in the palace's sub-basement. Encased in concrete walls three feet thick, online with sophisticated military/information gathering satellites, equipped with hundreds of TV monitors, computer terminals, lube, and other neat-o stuff, this room provided its users with all the toys necessary for the uncompromising and complete destruction of the enemy, wherever or whoever they might be. In the middle of it all stood the General and the Soldier. They towered over the one original piece of equipment in the War Room. This artifact representing hundreds of years of military campaigns -- the victories and the defeats -- was a large oak table on which sat many small reproductions of infantry and tanks, along with realistic NoKare plastic reproductions of trees and shrubbery. The two men were clearly in the thick of planning out the crucial opening move in the forthcoming battle with the loyalists.

"I want to roll first," whined the General.

"But you always roll first," protested the Soldier.

"That's because I'm in charge, you moron. Now give me the dice before I cut off your head or something,"

The Soldier relinquished the dice. The General snatched the bones, shook them in his majestic hands for a brief movement, and let them roll.

"I win again!" celebrated the General.

"I didn't see what you rolled. I want to protest."

"I was only joking. Don't be so serious. After all, this is only --"

"If you say that one more time, I'm going to bust you up. Now sir, we must carefully plot our move using our expensive hi-tech equipment and these plastic models to assure our victory."

"Oh, I agree with that. Now as my Moral Advisor, what do you think our first move should be?"

The Soldier held up a finger, signifying to the General that he indeed had a finger up, his middle finger. After thinking for a moment, his eyes sparked and he shot over to the nearest computer terminal, typing furiously on its keyboard.

"Well?"

"Hang on."

"I will wait patiently for a moment and then I will wait impatiently."

"Great," said the Soldier, his mind clearly on other things. "One moment, please."

He struck a final key and then the computer whirled, clicked, and mumbled. Lights flashed on and off, and somewhere, a siren began to wail. Then, the computer's printer activated, printing with machine gun fury. He grabbed the pages as they flew out of the catch tray like paper bullets.

"This had better be good," said the General.

"Oh, it's going to be good," reassured the Soldier as he collated the pages.

Eventually the printer spat out the final page. He proudly handed over the hard copy to the General, who impetuously snagged the printout. His eyes buzzing at the computer's labor as he scanned the pages.

"What the HELL am I looking at?" asked the puzzled and frustrated General.

"That, my fearless leader, is a script for your state of the union address, which you will make tonight. We will attempt the hearts and minds scavenger hunt with the general public."

The General smiled. "This is good. What's this other stuff?"

"That other stuff, sir, is a small collection of articles printed from today's snoozepaper. Just wanted you to see what some people are talking about. I think it may indicate that the King is still alive."

The General looked down at the sheets and read carefully.

DEAR MISS MANNERS:

I'm throwing a war and I just don't know what to wear. I mean I've had successful wars before, and never have I sweated more blood over what to wear. Usually I'm considered quite the fashion combo plate. But this time, I don't know, I just want to do something outrageous, something different to really make an impact. Call it a fashion attack. My royal jumper just doesn't cut it anymore.

Signed,

The Man In The High Castle

Dear Man,

Miss Manners knows what it's like when dressing for a combat situation. You want something that's going to make an impression, but yet be flexible and easy to clean. The immediate question that comes to mind is: what are your men going to wear besides bandages and colostomy bags? Do they have simple, utilitarian outfits? Or are they bold and colorful? You do know that minimalism is the current trend in military fashion, I assume. Earth tones are out unless you are in a desert situation. Miss Manners suggests that you wear a deep and luxurious red velvet ensemble, with delicate purple accessories. Not only will it make a hell of an impact, but it will hide any bloodstains, and as everybody knows, freshly spilled blood (or brains) is not socially acceptable, barring a GOP convention.

Miss Manners

"Hmmmm. This could be serious. Let's get things ready for when the rest of my advisers arrive," said the General. He actually sounded concerned.

$

The palace was on fire with activity. Being that everyone had returned happily from the truck pull, most of its denizens were quite pleased at the prospects of a continuation of the war with the King.

Except the soldiers, but who the fuck asked them anyway?

The General, the Soldier, and the Secretary of State stood around the game table in the War Room. The Secretary of State began the tactical discussion with her usual aplomb.

"What gives you fucking morons the right to declare war without the proper permissions?" she inquired diplomatically.

"Howzabout these five stars on my chest, bitch? Besides, we haven't declared war. It's going to be a containment action," responded the General.

"Well, assholes, it's like this, neither of you are looking at the big picture. Video games and board games might be fun, but they cannot accurately depict the actuality of combat. Real combat is a lot more fun!" squealed the Secretary as she rubbed her hands vigorously. "Speaking of which, how goes the video game?"

The General spoke proudly, "In a typical game, based on our game testing experiences, the first round casualties are heavy on the Villagers side. The main cause of this would be the mountains they must attack. For the rebels, it's like fishing in a plastic non-recyclable bucket. However, one the Villagers manage to gain a foothold in the mountains, there are extreme losses to both sides, which of course, maximizes gaming satisfaction (which we all know means big fun). Big fun is what we're trying to sell here, so we are rather pleased at the game testing results.

Marketing has issued a report which essentially proves that the current package design also tested well. The attractive design truly sells the war-game, and the condescending rules booklet seems to really charm the players. Marketing has also tested a number of catch phrase/slogan type material to tack onto the package. We've got:

1) It's Wicky-Wacky-War!

2) Johnny Got His Fun!

3) We Want You -- to Have a Ball of Fun!

What do you think?"

The Secretary looked pleased. "I think we might have a big seller with this one!"

$

The General stood smiling in the mirror. Looking back at him was one dapper five-star kinda guy, appearing quite smart in a "Battle of The Village" T-shirt. He had them made to be distributed immediately after his victory, and although most of the new citizens of the Village had them, it wouldn't hurt to remind them who was in charge. Historically speaking, the victor always sells more t-shirts. On the shirt, there was a cute cartoon depiction of him and his adversary, the King, engaging in a tug-of-war with a hamburger.

"God, I feel all goosey. I had forgotten what a charge starting a containment action can be," he said aloud to himself in his dressing room.

"Sir, we are ready to record your streamcast," said the Secretary as she entered the room.

"Yes, yes. It's time for an invigorating speech to really get a rise out of the troops. I have to think of a good excuse. Just give me one second."

"Well, the video crew has assembled out in the courtyard, so when you're ready, just skip on out there," said the Secretary as she turned and left the General to his thoughts.

He shrugged his shoulders and straightened out his polyester jumper. He then pulled an ornate red handkerchief from his back pocket and coughed up one mean black phlegm ball, wrapping it up neatly. Bolting out into the courtyard, he bellowed:

"Who loves ya baby?"

The crew looked at him with the cynicism you find only with old media types. They simply stared and waited for make-up to make its final looks. The small team of artists circled the General quickly, making small adjustments to further redden his lips and powder off the sweat, they then disappeared as quickly as they appeared.

The General, not missing a beat, took his mark and waited for the red light to turn on. Once it flashed that the camera was recording, he began to spout out his speech.

"Good evening my fine soldiers and citizens. I am here to make an announcement."

He paused dramatically before continuing.

"I need to get very serious with you all now. To be frank, there is something threatening the quality of life here in the Village. And I think we all know what the cause of our problems is," proclaimed the General as he whipped out a life-size, cardboard stand-up of the King, resplendent in his historically vague royal robes. "It's the King's loyalist resistors and their need to cling to his nasty business practices.

Yes, we have developed a kind and decent way of operating our franchise here in the Village. We are accustomed to a particular style of service, management, and food preparation. But all that we have worked for could be pulled out from beneath us at the hands of this bearded devil's men! The threat is real, folks.

Being the industry leader that we are, we cannot stand by, content as number one, while upstarts undermine our status with terrorist activities, cute prizes, family style commercial announcements, and the blatant violation of anti-trust laws by offering more than three condiments at a salad bar. No, we must solidify our pole position by actively crushing our number two opponent!

By adhering to the rules and regulations of our Village, you have all made your corporate pledge to do or die for the revolution. And I assure you that I recognize your commitment -- however, at this time, I must also call upon it. I know many of you are still healing from our crushing and usurping attack not all that long ago. We cannot rest. Now it the time for a call of arms -- we need a full staff to handle this rush. We must force the going out of business sign on these deviants -- WE MUST GO TO WAR! However, as that word causes many of you to worry and protest, we will now refer to it as a 'Containment Action.' We cannot wait any longer. As you have seen in the various propaganda promo posters that we have decorated downtown with, the enemy is not human, but real-life plastic replicas -- automatons. Therefore, you should feel no guilt as our advanced weapons disembowel, decapitate, fatally wound, lacerate, puncture, puree, mangle, julienne fry, and amputate their bodies before your eyes and at your feet. Do not wince as there very life-blood spurts and shoots out of their near-corpses as their bodily functions let go and ooze out of various orifices. Their heads are made of material similar to jawbreaker candies, and when their brains leak from cracks in their head thanks to your bludgeoning and concussion-dealing weapons, rest assured that they are mere simulacrums without family, friends, or loved ones!

Now many, if not most of you will suffer fatal injuries, crippling attacks, and physical shock. Don't worry as combat-related hits to your personal zones are to be expected as a part of the sacrifice you all must make for me. You lucky dogs! You will each be assigned a large bag, made-to-fit, should you need to travel by post due to acquiring casualty status. We have been so thoughtful as to even pre-arrange COD to your next-of-kin! If any thoughts of the upcoming combat make you anxious, you can relax in knowing that I will never become a casualty!

I promise that I will minimize your future disappointment with me, or at the very least, distract your dismay at any high body counts we might endure with petty domestic or social issues. Men, report to your stations, I want a foul and dirty fight! Remember the Alamo! Here's a picture of an unborn fetus! Get your engines ready, on the count of three, get set, show 'em the tiger in you! Hut one, hut two, listen for the gun, here we go, one, two, three!"

With his speech completed, the General made a quick exit just as the red light faded from the camera.

He turned to the Soldier. "Just in case you were wondering, I'm putting you in charge of this mess."

The Soldier's stomach twisted like a drunk contortionist.

$

The following month proved to be very difficult for the Soldier. A "Containment Action," to say the very least, is an ugly affair that rarely meets its objectives. Most of the time, it becomes a grotesque parade of death and injustice. Every once in a while, it does stabilize the region. At least that's what Brad Perfect was saying on the news.

The Soldier had taken his job seriously. There was something about being in the General's presence that had a way of influencing his thinking. Back when he had let those maniacs slink past him when he was guarding the gates of Network One, the Soldier thought his days of serving the General were over. Strangely, he had been promoted. During that time, he had forgotten that at one time he was just a simple boy who had found himself unhappy with his quality of life. That boy had left the King and his ways for the General, in the hopes of making things better for himself and his community. That boy, when promoted instead of executed, had forgotten the reason for joining up in the first place. He found himself changed by power, acting a fool, and certainly not acting like himself.

Now the Soldier was maintaining a strategic office in a small strip mall northeast of the palace. Here he had directed the General's "Containment Action" now known as Operation Zip Lock. Since he had started up the office, there had been little containment but a lot of action. The King's loyalists had been making a destructive tear in the fragile fabric of the General's post-revolutionary Village. As the days and the bodies began to pile up, the Soldier found himself less of a believer. He now rarely spent any time with the General, the man's charisma could no longer compensate for the pure and utter bullshit that was happening in the street. That, and the fact that the Soldier had stopped reading the news or watching TV was helping him to realize that he was far from home -- and far from what he considered himself to be.

In the past week, he had buried twelve of his fellow men. There had been "a situation." The platoon of men had stopped what they thought was a press caravan chasing the hottest new slut-star from Network One, Jessica Vagina. In actuality, it was a loyalist trap. When the soldiers stopped the girl's vehicle in hopes of getting an autograph or a quick peek under her skirt when she exited the car, they were ambushed by the "paparazzi," who turned out to be carrying guns fashioned to look like cameras.

There had been no survivors.

The Soldier put his face in his hands as he sat in front of his computer. Toxic emails, sent by the loyalists had poured in. These emails contained viruses, and the Soldier watched his complete network crash before his very eyes. Then, the phone starting ringing. And ringing. And ringing.

About to cry, he picked up the phone.

"Sir, this is Codename Sealfresh," said a young male voice.

"Go."

"Sir, you need to get over to the Village Pointe Mall. There's a problem."

"What is it?"

"Well, sir — ahhh—the loyalists tainted the mall soda supply with some kind of drug. It's caused a riot."

The Soldier put his head on his desk.

"I'll be right there. Did you call Sarge yet?"

"Uhhhhh — he was off-duty shopping at the mall. He ate at the food court about an hour ago. He's as bad as the rest, pretty much trippin' balls. Every time we try to call him he responds, 'extra salty, extra salty.' I think we can count him out."

"Okay, I will be right there," the Soldier moaned.

He lit a cigarette and looked for his boots.

$

By the time the Soldier arrived at Village Pointe, it was neck deep in acid-drenched madness. People ran from invisible chickens, screamed for no reason, and jumped in the fountain found at the center of the mall. There were those that took repeated photos with their digital cameras just so that they could watch the trails of light streak across their retinas. About the only thing that wasn't alarming were the naked women dancing to jam band music in their heads. Otherwise, it was a mess.

The Soldier attempted to get his bearings. "Damage report!" he yelled.

A young, energetic private (who reminded the Soldier a bit of himself from six months ago) ran up to him.

"Well sir, not that good. There are three fires out of control, almost every sheet of glass and mirror have been shattered, and we are currently peeling a few dead bodies off of the floors."

"What's the deal with them? Why are they dead?"

"Sir, they thought they were the Big Red J and that they could fly. They all jumped from the upper level."

Suddenly, there was an explosion. The Soldier felt a great blast of heat and a scatter shot of debris hit him in the head and chest. He became disoriented as a high pitch whine filled his ears, and he fell to his knees. The young private who had started to brief him was lying next to him, and was now missing several key pieces of limb and lower torso.

The Soldier found himself grabbed by both arms as two other privates snatched him and dragged him to safety.

He watched in a daze as they fired their weapons at a small Auntie Nuke's delivery truck. The back gate was open and the Soldier could see several loyalist fighters attempting to dodge bullets as they reloaded a rocket launcher. Eventually the privates found their targets and the truck flipped over and caught fire. No one crawled out.

"Sir, are you okay?" one of the men asked him.

The Soldier wiggled all of his fingers and toes. It seemed like he was still in one piece. All he could manage was a nod.

"Good enough sir. We'll get you to a med-van and work on mopping this FUBAR mall for ya."

The Soldier smiled and managed a half-ass salute. Suddenly, it was lights out.

$

The Soldier awoke, strapped tightly to a hospital bed. Although the fog of sleep was still with him, he realized that he had been taken to the emergency medical tent set up at the far end of a used car dealership. Many of the other soldiers from his command lay in the beds next to them. They did not look good.

The only thing the Soldier could move was his head, and when he turned to the left, he saw a teenage boy in standard issue army uniform. *This couldn't be, he was far too young.*

"Sir? Are you conscious?" the boy said.

"Yes, I think so. I could still be dreaming. How old are you?"

"I'm thirteen sir. Just joined up."

"What are you doing here?"

"My orders were to keep you company and whisper ancient Polish jokes in your ear until you came out of your coma-like state."

"I WAS IN A COMA?"

"No, not really, but you have been out for a couple of days."

"Well, what the hell is going on?"

"Sir, in the time you've been out this dealership has sold out of every SUV they had. Many of them were sold to soldiers that don't even have legs to drive with anymore. The sales staff here is incredible."

"That's all fine and good, but I mean, what's the status of this sector's Containment Unit?"

"Oh that. We're not doing that great. A lot of shit has blown up since you have been strapped to that bed. Hey, would you like to have those straps removed?"

The Soldier nodded.

The boy in uniform began to undo the straps. "The doctors had to strap you in because you were flopping around and yelling things like 'do you want cheese on that' and 'that will be five-fifty.' It was terrible sir. It was as if you were still in combat. Anyway, a lot of shit has blown up and we don't have too many men walking around these days to contain anything. That's why they reduced the draft age to twelve, and here I am."

The Soldier sat up in bed. He was not happy.

"I've got to get out of this bed. I've got to go see the General. Help me stand up."

"Sir, you can't walk right now. Let me get the chair for you."

The Soldier looked down to his legs. There must have been 100 deep cuts where shrapnel had worked like a paper shredder before a legal inquest. These legs wouldn't work for a while. He could still wiggle his toes, though. That was a plus.

"I need a doctor. I need to know when I can walk."

"Sir, they are all out golfing. They told me to tell you that they don't know when and if you'll walk again. That's why they got you this chair."

The boy moved away from the bed and disappeared behind some large beeping piece of medical equipment. It sounded a bit like Frogger. He returned quickly, and with the most amazing wheelchair the Soldier had ever seen. It had large, off-road tires, heavy chrome accents, air-brushed flames, and a .50 caliber machine gun mounted on a swivel.

"It's self-powered. It'll go about 30 miles an hour. Makes me wish I was a paraplegic," the boy said proudly.

The Soldier hopped onto the chair. "Stick with me boy, and that wish will probably come true. For now, stay put. And give me your radio."

The boy handed over his walkie. "Where are you going?"

"I'm off to see the wizard."

The Soldier engaged the joystick on the chair and it rumbled into life. Pushing it forward, he bounced it off of several beds, knocked over a tray of food, and hit a nurse square in the ass.

Soon, he gained control of the chair and pointed it in the direction of the palace. He was going to take a meeting with the General.

11. Only the First Ten Callers Get the Deal

Interior: Video Arcade

You walk down aisles of video game machines, all of them loud and visually obtrusive. Some games you recognize, others seem dark and twisted. You find yourself compelled to put a token in a game that appears to have a circus theme. A large 8-bit man in a top hat comes on the screen.

The time has now come for the most glorious event in the life of any hero. It's the time when you approach your quest hub and start grinding for experience. I have a quest for you, and I know you can do it.

Life is a grind, and I don't want to add one more twist to your grueling, pathetic life. But I will.

Complete my quest, and you will not only earn valuable loot, but you'll be one step closer to that constant goal, the goal to level up.

C'mon! Who doesn't want to level up? Who doesn't want to chase the dragon?

Of course, we all do! My quest for you will send you to the far corners of the game map in the hopes that you will collect all the necessary components to build the great weapon, the weapon you will use to destroy the BIG BOSS.

Now, be aware that there's so much you need to master. There are the mechanics, you see, the mechanics of the fight that are unique but yet somehow familiar. There are really only so many ways to skin a cat, although I've personally never done so. Nevertheless, the mechanics remain to be mastered, and quite frankly, the mechanics are a bitch.

Perhaps the worst part of your quest will be the necessary evil of working with others to achieve you goal. There is only one true rule for working with people: You must realize that people will always disappoint you. And they will do so on a regular basis.

Taking one look at you I know that you're a lone wolf. You go solo or you don't go. Team player is not in your vocabulary. I can see how you are already formulating strategies that will minimize your contact with others. You have been so damaged by previous collaborations that the mere idea of having to form a party for your quest ahead forcibly empties your bowels. I get that, but I don't have an alternative for you.

People really do suck, it's true.

You have gotten so far in the game without them. It's been a pleasure to grind for gold, get your XP, and solo quests. It's your favorite part of the game, and I am taking it away from you.

Would it reassure you to know that this is a personal growth possibility? Would it help you to know that there is loot at the end of this quest that dwarfs all the loot you have managed to accumulate so far? What might I do or say that will entice you to accept my quest and seek the valor you crave so dearly?

Maybe if I gave you a public test realm walkthrough of said quest? Would that get your desire to clear mounds of trash to rise?

I can give you a bit of a preview, but mind you, there are patches and hotfixes ahead. Your results may vary. Make your savings throw versus massive disappointment now. Scratch your balls and pray you roll a twenty.

What if I told you that you would have the opportunity to eat mushrooms, grow large (or potentially small), get a second life, and valuable guild rep? What if I told you that the boss throws huge flaming barrels of fiery death? What if I told you that you could fill your belly with dots and run screaming from ghosts?

Starting to sound a bit more interesting? There are many phases to this quest; there will be much for you to study. There will be scrolls and lore, puzzles and traps. There will be many non-player characters to interact with. There will be cards to collect, and small creatures to match against your foes. It is key to know the abilities of these small creatures, for they will help you become a master.

So what say you? Will you help me with this quest? I am far too busy to undertake it myself?

What say you?

You say yes! This is good, I know that you will not regret the time invested, the ROI is quite high. There is much for you to do.

Update your add-ons, watch your videos, create a party, and go forth. You will have many obstacles to overcome, but with a solid vent connection and an attractive avatar, you are bound for glory. Go forth and conquer, the entire kingdom...maybe even the world, is relying on you.

12. The Dodge Tribe

It was in a wrapper-strewn field somewhere on the far outskirts of the Village that Scratch wandered looking for new transport. He had left his tribe a good half-day's drive behind in search of a good stock racer. Most of the day had proven fruitless, but Scratch was a man on a mission.

He had left his tribe without its competitively chosen leader -- yes, Scratch was the holder of The Belt (thanks to surviving a deadly cage match versus 11 other worthy candidates) -- and he carried its heavy weight well. In fact, he was so good that his tribe didn't even know he had left on a search. This was one of his classic moves, one of the Elders referred to as the QB Sneak. It was tough getting out without being noticed. Scratch had taken a hidden path to avoid the Paparazzi - those that would see his departure and whip up frenzy through creating hearsay. This was a secret mission that would grant Scratch some quiet time. This was known by the men of the tribe as a "business perk."

The Dodge Tribe had watched from a distance as the Village grew deeper and deeper into a violent spectacle. The Elders knew that what was being witnessed was no dramatic recreation, but that the violence was actually more real than what was being displayed.

There was no peace.

The General's revolution had caused more death after the fact than during the damn thing. Business was terrible for the tribe. It had been so much better when the King ran the show. Trade was good back then. There was always a sale in the Village, and you could always find what you wanted. It didn't help that somehow Sell Inc. had shut Scratch out. It made Scratch wish he had done more to keep the King around. He had been too cocky, and as a result, he couldn't even drum up a deal for some good two-ply toilet paper. The tribe had to settle for some scratchy brown bullshit that was tearing their assholes apart.

To make matters worse, the King's loyalists had caused so much damage to the Village morale that it looked as if that all-out civil war would resume a day from next Tuesday, at the very least. As a broker and practitioner of inside trading (known in the Dodge Tribe as the "Invoking the Boesky Ritual"), Scratch's instincts knew that it was really time to sell low and find better markets. The tribe's initial road trip -- that which took them to a safe grove - had been sufficient at the time, but now it was looking like they might need to find another city's teat from which to feed.

Morning would soon would bring red dawn, so Scratch was gathering every piece of Detroit muscle he could find. The tribe was going to have to move fast. They would need mass transport for the imminent migration to greener grass.

Scratch's mind raced as he walked across the trashed field. Years ago there had been a mega-concert here to save the environment. It had been quite successful as everyone who attended hauled their garbage out of the Village and left it there. People still talked about throwing another concert, but no musical act could stay popular long enough to bring a crowd. The field and all the garbage remained as a solemn monument to good plans forgotten. Like so many depressed urban circles, fields just like this one orbited the Village in a display of "future development here" opportunity. Scratch kicked old beer bottles across the field, keeping his head down in case there was some shiny valuable goodie to be discovered. He didn't look up until one of the bottles he kicked clunked instead of clinking.

What he saw was no race car, and it probably wouldn't go fast. But in some ways, it was better.

It was a bus -- not an average size bus -- but a pimped-out stretch. The bus was easily 90 feet long. A bus -- school, public, or transcontinental -- was rarely over 48 feet. This bus was far beyond any tractor-trailer as well. This bus was beyond the specifics of normal vehicular design. Somewhere deep in Scratch's memory banks a light went off. He knew this bus. This bus was history.

History, not the kind written by major wars or presidential assassinations or revolutions. This bus was the best kind of history. It was pop culture history. This bus in another time was known as the Eastwood. It had been made for the greatest widescreen, telepathic-interactive thought-flick of all time: *I Knew You Were Coming So I Baked A Cake.* The Eastwood was more super than Supertrain, more loved than the Love Boat, and it was not just a ride -- it was an adventure.

Now it was sitting in a filthy field rusting away.

Scratch knew that this monstrosity was worthy of the ritual.

In another time, ignorant masses performed the rite of public transport with little knowledge of its cosmic relevance. They would leave tribute to their vehicular idols so that they might be taken to their "point of destination." Their tribute was a broad gesture to the spirits of the inanimate and the grand worms of the underground. This was how Scratch knew the Old Ones had played the ritual out. Tribute and then travel. Above or below the ground.

Although the Old Ones were ignorant about the power behind their rituals, Scratch and his Dodge Tribe knew and respected the wheeled combustibles. They had no experience with the grand worms of the underground. Nor did they trust them. For one thing, you could not drive them. They drove you. The Dodge Tribe trusted nothing that would not let you control it. They did not put their faith in others when it came to travel.

With respect to things of this nature, Scratch began his ritual.

"So now the field," he began to chant. "So now the ritual."

He walked over and kicked one of the flat tires on the bus.

Scratch wondered if the Gods would let the tribe "keep on trucking." The painful slap of the wartime economy had caused the tribe to go from hunting, gathering, and trading to pawning and chop shopping. As the chant goes: "Wheels are a spinnin' - nowhere fast." It had been, as one of the Elders had said of a previous bad season, a real bitch of late.

Scratch gave the vehicle a quick look over. He made a momentary turn in the mythological direction of the Big Three and performed another ritual kick of the tires (which were flat and rotted cords of rubber shrink-wrapped around rusted rims). Looking at the bus, he imagined turning back the gauges of time and freeing the vehicle from the impound of aging. The ride had definitely been pimped in another time. It might even need Bondo to make it right.

Scratch looked skyward and spoke.

"Ancient and enigmatic Gods of the road, I beseech you. You know I search for a great deal with little to no money down. Quality wheels at an affordable price."

Scratch bowed to the bus, sweeping one arm and pounding his fist to his chest to punctuate the motion. Scratch knew that there were many trials and tribulations associated with the search for transport. This was feeling a bit easy. Finding a reliable used vehicle at a fair price was normally difficult. He would have to stay on his toes and wait for the other shoe to drop. Scratch dropped to his knees and held his hands out.

"Oh Gods, I know that there are many devils and deceits when seeking financing. I know of the lies of the odometer of life. I know that if something is probably too good to be true, it probably is."

Scratch jumped to his feet and began a slow jog around the rusting bus.

"I will perform a point by point inspection. I will ask for good value for my trade-in. I offer my soul in trade should this vehicle perform to basic standards."

Scratch began his inspection. The outlook was good. Most of the rust was surface, so a bit of the precious black tea would do the trick. The wiring looked almost new and Scratch felt as if he might be on some Network One hidden camera show. Could it be that this bus was nearly in running order? There would be one final bit of the ritual to perform in order to find out.

Scratch stretched his arms out to the sky.

"I thank you Gods of the flowing white lines. I will now engage the levers, switch on the lights, and honk the horn. If there is any juice left in this large vessel, I will perform the almighty Dee-Troit Hot-Wire."

Scratch smiled up to the open sky and then jumped into the bus. The interior of the bus was decked out in some kind of Mexican Day of the Dead motif. Bright obnoxious colors spoke of the wild times this bus must have hosted. Skeletons made of twigs and twine hung from various points throughout the interior, and it smelled vaguely of vomit.

Now, by the grace of the Gods, it could be salvation. Scratch sat down at the wheel and started to press on the horn. There was a weak sound, but it would be enough. He could hardly contain his excitement as he broke open the steering column and pulled out the wires that would fire "The Spark."

The engine complained at first, but turned over. Scratch laughed loudly, and found the lever to put it into gear. He happily sat in the epic swinging seat of the great bus. With the Gods as his copilots, he reined in the vehicle and invoked the spell that would make the bus move forward. He pushed the lever to the all-powerful "D" on the bus's dashboard. Yes, life breathed deep into this bringer of travel, this minion of freedom of movement. It roared with the power of the eight -- the pack of horse spirits which would lead this manufactured Detroit device.

Still giggling, Scratch knew that the vehicle appeared to "run good." Now it was time for the triumphant Drive Ritual.

$

Somewhere in a grassy patch sat a man who did not know who he was. The hard scrabble of moderate, unkempt beard molested his face with a painful itch. Scratching at it like a chimp, he stood slowly and began to shuffle along, making a wide circle through tall grass and garbage. This blank slate of a man stared at a stubby tree. He had been walking around this patch and others for some time now, trying to cross the oblivion of nothingness that was his mind. All he knew was that something had gone wrong, something very terrible indeed.

How much time had passed since whatever event had wiped the Etch-A-Sketch of his life's memory clean? He was clueless. All he knew is that he had a fire pit, a big dented metal egg to sleep in, and some ratty brown velour clothes. He stopped walking for a moment to consider the clothes. They looked as if at one time they had been nice. Like he had been somebody.

Now he was just a man in burnt and dirty clothing, eating random plants, and trying desperately to remember anything older than the morning.

"Did I owe anybody money?" he asked to the sky. "Am I in a Phillip K. Dick book here, or what?"

The sky offered nothing but dumb gray clouds and a merciless sun.

He picked a crappy looking piece of fruit off a tree and bit into it, knowing full well he would have the shits by lunch time. What else could he do? It wasn't like there was a 24-hour Dookey Donuts around. This thought crossed his mind every time he had to swallow some twisted vine or berry. Mother Nature really wasn't much of a cook, he decided.

It was madness, this blank existence. As he stood contemplating his navel for the millionth time, he heard a roar in the distance. It was a familiar sound. It was the sound of engines -- something man-made.

"Thank gods," he thought. "Maybe it's people. Maybe they can help me get something factory-processed to eat."

He began to run towards the sound. That delightful sound. He crashed through the brush and laughed and laughed and laughed. He almost began to feel like he was home, in some strange way.

The roar was louder now. He could hear the revving of a solid engine that was being throttled by a pro.

It wasn't much further through the brush. Past the leaves, he could make out the movement of something colorful and large racing back and forth in a clearing.

Losing breath but not anticipation, the unknown man broke through the last of the trees to find the dragon behind the roar.

It was beautiful.

$

The Drive Ritual was going well. Clearly blessed by the gods, Scratch performed a solid Rockford with the bus, flipping it 180 degrees at 55 mph. The bus rocked in the dust, but it remained standing. Scratch smiled, knowing that this four-wheeled salvation was a sign that his tribe could meet their current objectives and raise their survival quotient threefold.

All that remained was a couple of tight figure-eights, and he could keep on trucking back to the Tribe compound.

As he dropped the bus into gear, a sudden flash of movement caught his attention. Off to his left, he saw what he thought was a Bigfoot crashing through the trees at the edge of the clearing. Scratch stared at the thing, slowly reaching for a weapon out of his gunny sack.

The Bigfoot had stopped moving and was simply staring at the bus with a sloppy, mangy grin. Scratch paused his reach and carefully scrutinized the figure. This was no Bigfoot. This was simply a man. A man in need of ten showers and a body wax, but still just a man. What the hell was this about?

Scratch rolled down the window and yelled. "Ahoy, stranger!"

The man, startled out of his dreamy stupor, simply raised his hand. It was clenched in a fist, with the thumb extended.

Scratch let out a long breath. The guy only wanted a ride.

Scratch pulled the bus around to where he was standing. Pulling the door level, Scratch cracked a smile and said, "Alllllll Aboard!"

It had been a while since he had made a new friend.

$

The ride back to the Tribe's hideout had been trying for Scratch. The man asked a lot of questions, peppered with many *"Are we there yets?"* and *"I gotta go to the bathrooms!"* Still, it had been, as the Chinese might say, interesting. The man had no knowledge of who he was or where he had come from. All he could tell Scratch was that he thought he had been hatched from a "silver egg" and that he was dying for processed cheese slices. Strange. Scratch was puzzled by the unkempt man. The outskirts of the Village were his territory, and he always knew who was coming and going through them. Who could this man be? Scratch thought that maybe he was an escaped celebrity from Network One's vats. Or maybe he was a "retired" Sell Inc. executive that had been given The Long Walk.

The important thing now was to get back to his people. They could take the strange man in and clean him up like a proper savage. Scratch could always send a scout or two to investigate the "silver egg" at a later time. The main thing was to put up with the million-and-one questions that were flying at him.

"Where are we?" the man asked repeatedly.

Scratch's mouth was beginning to run dry from answering questions. "The Village," he replied.

"Who lives there?"

This was the third time they had gone around with this one. It was making the hour long drive back to the Tribe seem like days. Tired of the questions, Scratch suddenly remembered that he had a few rough drafts of press releases in his sack. The reading should keep the amnesiac preoccupied for the remainder of the trip home.

Driving with one hand, Scratch dug deep in his sack and found the press release for the Village his old buddy Jacob had whipped up about a year ago.

Without a word, Scratch shoved the piece of paper in the man's hand.

"What's this?" he asked.

Scratch just pointed to it and kept his eyes on the makeshift road ahead.

**FOR GENERAL MEDIA RELEASE* - VILLAGE PEOPLE*

I don't know how much you know about the world we're in, but...

Ya don't stop.

Ya can't stop.

The Go Blow Village is the end-all, be-all construction investor wet dream. Each and every aspect of it has been carefully researched, cross-referenced, and gone for broke. Every element of the Village is a societal integer in the sum chemistry of Village life. Each individual ultimately contributes to a town that never sleeps, always cheats, and beats Bangkok for night life.

You will see all types in this town. Sure, there are the beautiful people, the ones who define image, the holy ideal, the ones whose faces grace the glossy page in celebration of perfection. Oblivious to all but their minor woes, the beautiful people create the ultimate weapon -- HYPE -- which ultimately provides the Village with the extra resources even a seasoned ambassador could only kiss acres of asses to obtain.

There are the tech folk, the ones who have sacrificed years of well-rounding experience to study math, the religion of numbers. These priests and priestesses of engineering operate the gears of the Village that make it run. Their celebration of pagan Pythagoras and all his funky measures help maintain the techno-foundation of a town where a power switch summons the mysterious team synergy which run the precious labor saving fetishes of the masses. A tight, selecting and elite group, the electro-shamans represent all that runs without them, society is paused, with little chance of resuming game....

Manufacturing, the faceless brand-named, force the high concept of demand on the majority group, the consumers. We'll get to them in a bit. The manufacturers seek only to shit out that what careful study and manipulation prove to be the necessary objects of the Villagers monetary attention. Manufacturers ultimately live for the masses, consumed in their rites and drink. They self-perpetuate their sum existence. To be IN THE BLACK, not IN THE RED. The Consumer Being + Product = Manufacturer. Without the Buyer, they have no purpose or meaning and become worthless unto god. Go out of business, he proclaimed.

The Consumers, by far the largest social group inhabiting the Village stand ready to accept information and propaganda attacks formed from their darkest needs, and styled through the discount telepath of the Manufacturers. The Consumers are the blood of the Village, they make currency of all colors and creeds, move through their selfless incarnation of the spells of Purchase and Obtaining Services.

The army is a consumer, the residents are consumers, and in the schizophrenia of all in the Village, give thanks to high electromagnetic waves form formed by battery powered and electrical appliances. Eventually everyone consumes.

The sin and epiphany of consumption is what turns a tightwad into sophisticated customer and invokes the magical evolution of the low beings which inhabit all trenches of Go Blow society into career shoppers, or as known in the old tongue, They Who Look For Bargains. The Sale is the moment, the ritual of all religious consumers funded by the manufacturing and broadcast by the media slaves of all means. Life in the Village is simple if you are savvy. Maintain good credit, keep lots of spending cash around, and pay only your interest (never the balance), want what you can't have, always settle for less, never lose faith in availability, expect everything from those in the service industries, and never compare prices. Because, as the ancients proclaimed "THE CUSTOMER IS ALWAYS RIGHT," even in the face of florescent ignorance. Eat shit if you have to, strive to please, and never question or plagiarize consumer reports. God shines on our Village, but only if you play ball. Your subscription is mandatory and your conscience is past due. See you on Sunday for deep-down warehouse savings.

The man stared at the paper like the printed words were ants crawling about the page. Piloting the bus at high speed, Scratch looked over and noted the dumbfounded expression on his face.

"You look like none of that made any sense at all," Scratch said.

"No, it makes sense. It just feels like I have read this before."

The man put the paper on his lap and scratched manically at his beard. "This shit is killing me. I need a nice shave with five blades and an aloe moisturizing strip."

Scratch frowned. "It's been a while since we've had anything nice like that. The war just killed our supply. Shit's all fucked up right now."

The crusty man shook his head in disbelief.

"What war?" He asked.

"Well, there was a big civil war in the Village. Just kinda ended. Lot of people died. Hit us right where it really hurts. In the wallet."

"That's terrible. What started it?"

"That's a tale for another time."

"Fine. I feel like I might know it anyway." The man pinched his nose. "I fucking stink."

Scratch nodded violently. "We'll hose you down when we get back to the Tribe."

"So, are you somebody important?"

Scratch smiled. "Oh, I'm what you would call a big deal." Scratch fished around in his bag and pulled out another press release.

"Look, it won't be long before I get us home. Why don't you read this so you can act like you have a god-damned clue."

He handed the smelly, beard-scratching man the most wonderful piece of writing in the world.

Hey folks! Looky what we have here, another rattle and tattle report from Social Anthropologist and Pundit, Jacob P. Smorely! He tells us all about one of the most fascinating aboriginal celebrities of the last decade or so...

BORN FREE, WITH PROOF-OF-PURCHASE

Scratch Microphone, Tribal Stud, master planner, record Deal-A-Meal Poker $1,000,000 winnings holder, is a guy holding the reins of his people, yeah you know, THE DODGE TRIBE.

The Dodge Tribe consists of the basic inbred stock whitey ties into genetically. Heinz 57 Euro-modeled stock, with a bit of para-legal, para-social south of the equator flings -- Black, Hispanic, Asian or otherwise. Enough strains to the centric Go Blow historical make up to result in a decidedly nom-immediate yet curious cultural personality in the reference to the experts that be.

Scratch and his tribe (led by Scratch via a victorious fierce Mano-a-Mano, pay-per-view CAGE MATCH for the scepter of the Hetman Kingship, the All-Controlling REMOTE CONTROL. Only one man may possess this Magic Wand of Insistence, and Scratch just happened to be at the: RIGHT PLACE, RIGHT TIME. No nepotism, really. He did not drop an influential last name based on the ass-kissing of his patriarch so that he could earn things on his own merit. (That and the fact that Dad had been too busy on an Elderly Dragstrip Voguing Ritual World Tour, and kinda hated his SOB kid anyway.) Scratch is a self-made man, in the world of the Pre-Designed/Digested. Scratch, leader of the fetish-fueled, deconstructionist-but-not-academic members of THE DODGE TRIBE. He possesses the tribal savvy necessary to grab good PR but not ANGER the Gods. Elementals can get cranky, too. Being a pagan means being careful where you step.

For the Dodge Tribe, the purity of existence is to be in tune. Nomadic by nature, refusing to be forced to settle down by implications insisted by utilities or any other piece of paper requiring address change cards, they cannot dial CABLE ME, by ritual institution. They must act as individual antennas, Brave New Waves, and form themselves to the frequency of their chosen totem call letters.

The pursuit of identity is a constant debate among the DODGE TRIBE. The Elders, wise because they are old, stubborn and set in their ways also because they are old, have dialed many toll-free numbers in their search for personal satisfaction. They have RON-COed themselves by phone and have suffered the image/presentation vs. reality heavyweight-here-comes Don-King-to-bilk-us boxing match.

They have been ripped off and have engaged in the ritual of misrepresentation and at the same time have had a front row seat/backstage pass for the theatre of lies in the box. The Elders, in their archetypes, have lived through the times. Being free and constantly moving, they have settled on the fuel consuming, hell-in-the-old-days, fossil fuels were number one— the Whiney-bago. Glorious Whiney-bago, once a bunch of proud tribal fellas themselves, now immortalized in the ultimate symbol of Couch Potatoist of Dominance and Grotesque waste on the highway. An added M60 machine gun with armor piercing, energy eliminating, UN approved ammo doesn't hurt. Face it, people drive like they've been hit in the head with a hammer as it is— Drive to Kill.

Yet, the focus of this little highlight feature is Scratch Microphone. The aforementioned gent serves as the Mentor, symbolic royalty, Head Mechanic, or as you may have known such rank: Acne-scarred camp counselor. Scratch may listen, may obey, or may sneak out of the cabin at night. He has always acted on instinct. That is what has earned his tribe's respect for him. Also his high level weightlifting/gym sponsorship didn't hurt. The one guy who was up against Scratch had a similar machine/gym deal, but enjoyed the concepts of planning and scheduling more than actual exertion. This man, although highly regarded in his preservative dominated plastic wrapped communion consumption, ultimately proved himself beyond the common folk -- thus entering the Dodge Tribe Pagan Belief of the Spirit of the Screen.

A sudden rewind, a momentary flashback is all this stream of info is about. Golden Retrospective. Scratch, like any other leader wannabe, made himself what the tribe wanted, forged promises in the fire of aspiration, cashed bad checks, put it all on credit, with the offer to not have to pay interest for an entire era.

Sounds good for Scratch, bad for the tribe. But it was a good deal after all, as Scratch is a people person. Not content to merely file forms (such as the good 'ole A3609) and check off lists, Scratch used his Male Primal Football Death/Murder Dark Side to send his approval rating through the roof.

Scratch got down with his folks.

He had suffered the grass-roots origin. It was tough, but the Dodge Tribe, ultimate refuge for the undefinable, (if sheer accumulation and fetishization of material and engine-powered, horse-powered auto mayhem was not definable enough) the irrepressible, slippery due to quality legal representation, needed a person like Scratch. He could falsify emotion or integrity as well as any other Go Blow Royal family member or politician/publicist. He could swagger and scam for himself, his tribe, or his devious whims. He had his hands on the wheel of a Mopar/slapshift/four barrel/monster social collaboration.

He has dealt with the worst of anarchistic, nomadic political selfish attitudes. But he always asked his traveling Tribe, "Who will take care of the roads when the road commission is dissolved into Ancient Roman social semiotics?" No, he would respond (he did ask the question rhetorically, I mean c'mon, most of the tribe is so illiterate they get a rebate on multi-syllabic thought rubbings) No, he would say to all subscribers to magazines of extremist thought, our forwarding address is like the floating symbols that build meaning in our minds. We float like the signifiers that motivate, politicize, form identity, compete, destroy, mock, or preserve ignorance in those who embrace them thru reflex or inbred intention. The Dodge Tribe, free to vulturize, terrorize, and deconstruct the objects of human function and training -- consumption of the omnipotent (in the eyes of the tribe) PRODUCT.

The tribe, spiritual and on a mission related thru a timed-self-destructing media of the message, wanders, not to greener pastures (because they are already hip to the tragic irony that the grass is of course always greener where there are highly toxic chemicals non-conducive to human life), but is forever in the spiritual search for meaning and truly valuable coupons and/or rebates. Their rejection of organized religion with all its analysis and doubts in the face of the high precipice of waste of meaning has resulted in their group search and deconstruct mission. They rat pack, collect, barter, and attempt to own through transmission of value (thru ritual) or liberation. In short, they take all they can, they are impulse buyers of the trickle down culture of the Village, among other suspects.

Now back to Scratch.

No one knows when he was born. Some think he was the result of some trick of programming or glitch-bug in a modern entertainment technological interface priced competitively by the wise ancestors of the tribe. Scratch appeared as suddenly as a new guest right after the break. After the 5-second controversy celebrated in interpretive commercial break-dances, his unusual and tabloid-exaggerated entrance into the folk of the tribe caused him to consider the benefits of pursuing monogamous and fully clothed relationships with his co-workers.

In short, Scratch was busted.

Most of the controversy concerned young women, the need for speed, and narcotic waxings. The dissolving moralists preached that he should engage in a broadcast formation Pantheon -- a feel-good special with Special Guests In a Variety Format. Scratch was, as they say, a natural, whether it was a pretend circus of talents, cameo roles, or lead parts. The unseen forces of the Agented did proclaim -- you are beyond character roles -- SCRATCH MICROPHONE IS FULLY MARKETABLE, regardless of your prior hard copy segments.

The long process as a youth, the appearances, the gritted-teeth performances, the startled youth events that called the Camera's attention -- the "Commodification and Commercialization" as the over-

read theologists call it, was the necessary coming of age narrative that allowed his peers and members of other markets, to relate, identify, or buy into Scratch as front man for the band of merry currency mongers.

He was, as it turns out, perfect for the job.

They did want him to get experience elsewhere, but his full-length Virtua Production -- the resume -- forced them to deal with him right away. The ever so hip Go-to Guy did like Scratch's "style 'n' attitude" and pointed, motioning the career-minded, college prepped & conditioned wage warrior, to the front of the line for candidates. It is as the tabloid tablets say, Who You Know.

Of course, only the in-crowd is left in the temple to view the stone hot tips for those insecure in the definition. This area, in which the tablets are stored is known as the Cavern of Current Trends Accessible only by the annual demographic -- fueling revival to the pagan ritual known as Poll of our Readers. Poll, a devious hawker, seeks that cosmic awareness, that group consciousness that creates a consuming rush, whether the object of such religious piousness be food, electronic, or fabulous holiday shopping frenzy.

Scratch, proudly represented with the largest photo on the Post Office wall, is Most Wanted, Number One with a Bullet, on the Tribe's Best Top Ten List. Each and every moment is recorded by a specially trained Entertainment Shaman and the Brothers Paparazzo. So sure of his impending popularity, they fight each other in a distinct media savvy gymnastic discipline in an effort to capture Scratch in the embarrassing Right Now. It is a live-on-scene goose chase that most Brothers end in an early filmic seppuku -- develop negatives only, Double Prints next-of-kin, C.O.D. privilege. Scratch is the Big #1, as deemed by the people CEO (Chief Existing Officer), whose transition of power is limited, suffered to grenade-inspired change of officers.

Scratch is keenly aware of his people, thanks to the procedure of interactive applications, parallel-processed databases, and the marketing genius to know about designing the Product around the need, and the miracle entrance skill to create the need, around his personal holy of invention. Supply and Demand through social skullduggery.

He communicates to his people thru the simplest of all languages -- Rhetoric. Esperanto is a close diplomatic second. Another such channel of communication is known in the inner circles as Special Offers and Incentives or Discount Deals. This last option is reserved for when Scratch wants to really get to the soul of the people. Everything for a Dollar!

The sensibility and testosterone of the wage warrior is very prevalent in the mind of Scratch and all members of the Dodge Tribe. Many, if not all, have opposed the system, fought storm troopers, and the visceral cubicles of the magnitude of human violence. They have rebelled and incorporated by proper form-filing and they have battled the sins of accepting name brands without doubt, not price comparing in crisis, not signing with a particular telecommunications company, regardless of the fact that communication through copyright channels is preferred among these rhythmic primals. As mentioned earlier in the program, Scratch and his Tribe are in tune, in their self-enforced Motor Gang teamwork -- the complex even though Tome of the Month Chaos theory argues for heretical advertisements of Product, its omnipotent and web-like definition, its existence, the billions if not infinite faces of saturation marketing, the difficult and many recycled lifetime pursuit is in the much inked, very daily planner routine of the tribe. To invoke the spirit of the Dazerunner and organize down to the quarter hour. Scratch inks in just about every commitment with the tribe to meal, meet, or take a meeting. He listens to their hi-concepts and prepares to make executive decisions.

The sum of all this, the meaning ya dig, is the local news condensation and review of this leader -- this possible front for a true network of power. Only those who have been captured by UFOs and surround themselves with aluminum wrap -- the Raynolds gambit -- will tell you, the higher power has fallen into his capable hands.

He is the Quarterback.

The General.

He is Principal.

The General Manager.

Head Coach.

He, beyond his human existence walks the earth in Divine Rite TM sneakers, happy as avatar and supreme arena Rock God of the People.

And don't you forget it.

$

"Well," said the dazzled King, "that is one hell of a press release. This guy Jacob can spin with the best of them."

(Ok, there is really no sense in dodging this. This guy who can't remember who he is...he's the King. Surely you know this, a more perceptive reader would be hard to find. For the sake of things, just remember that you are the only one who knows this fact at this point.)

"No lie, Kemosabe. Jacob is the best. He spent some time with the tribe about a year ago. We have a tribal historian that wrote a little story about it. I will give it to you when we get back."

Scratch wrestled a bit with the large steering wheel. The bus seemed to seek out every chuckhole in the road, and its industrial suspension was unforgiving. Scratch could feel his bowels rattle.

"Look out!" Screamed the King.

Scratch was startled from a momentary round of groin scratching to look up just as the bus struck a slouching figure in the road. Somewhat panicked, he muscled the bus to a jarring stop. But not before he committed near vehicular manslaughter.

"What the hell was that?"

"Some guy who obviously doesn't know to look both ways. Let's go out and see if he's ok," replied the King.

Scratch looked at his watch and groaned. "I suppose we should check on the little bastard."

Jumping out the door of the bus, Scratch could hear the high pitched whines of a true sissy boy. It took a few tense moments for Scratch to make his way around the Day-Glo bus, he was in shock and awe by what he saw.

Lying in a baffling pile of flopping limbs and tears was a young man doing his best impression of a gnarled and knotted slinky. Scratch was pleased that he was able to identify the actual noise of a crying boy, but was a bit taken aback by the damage the bus had caused.

"Hey, come over here and help me!" The boy cried. "I can't do this myself! I can't do anything by myself!"

Scratch and the King ran over to him. Like a Stretch Armstrong toy that had been tortured by a post Ritalin bully, the young man was a mass of strange knots. How was this even possible?

"I know what you're thinking. I'm fine. I just need to be straightened out."

Scratch and the King began to work out the kinks and knots in the boy's limbs. They were quick to realize that the boy had no spine, and hardly any bones at all. Trading looks of disbelief, the two men managed to work over the whining and soon enough, had the boy all smoothed out.

In a manner that cannot be explained by science, the boy righted himself up and slowly stood.

"I didn't even see you guys coming. Sorry if I freaked you out. This kind of thing happens to me all the time."

"Excuse me," said the King, "Did you say this thing happens all the time?"

"Yeah, I was born with no backbone. Hardly any bone structure at all, actually. Whenever I get bumped or fall down, I sort of turn into a pile of mush. That's why I need help constantly."

"Uh, yeah," said Scratch. "What the hell are you doing out here, anyway?"

"I'm making my way to chiropractic school," said the boy with absolutely no sense of irony. "Say, have you seen my wife around here? I lost her somewhere on the path. She currently believes that she is a gooseberry bush and is hiding somewhere near by."

"Why don't you just call out her name?"

"Bushes don't talk, you idiot. That being said, I better get going. It's a long way to Connecticut."

Scratch and the King watched the strange boy slink off into the surrounding forest. Looking at each other, but not saying a word, the two made their way back onto the bus. Scratch gingerly started the bus back up, and without a word they continued their drive back to Scratch's camp.

$

The bus made its way home without any other incidents. As they pulled up, Scratch began to smile as his eyes took in the splendor of the Dodge Tribe camp. In his time away, the tribe had been busy stringing up novelty lights and connecting neon signs to generators. Scratch could hear the pounding beats of various boom boxes and stereos. It made him happy to know that regardless of how tough things seemed to be going, the Tribe was going full speed ahead with their lives.

It was also pleasing to the tribal leader to see that they had prepared for his arrival and had painted two parallel white lines approximately 10 feet apart. These two lines were intended to guide Scratch into the center of the camp and complete the transport ritual.

Scratch looked over at the King and smiled as he gunned the bus's throttle and bellowed a primal scream.

"Hold on pal, here comes the fun part!"

The King grabbed at an invisible seat belt as the bus began to speed up. The camp was coming up fast, and Scratch just seemed to pay no heed to the blurring landscape that flew past them. He seemed intent on rushing the bus into the growing group of waving, happy campers that was gathering directly in its path. Instead of running for their lives, they only jumped up and down while giving each other high-fives and belly bumps.

"You're going to kill those people!" The King screamed and covered his eyes.

"Nonsense, I know exactly what I am doing. Just sit back and shut up so I can concentrate."

Scratch leaned up on the steering wheel. The transport ritual required him to perform a perfect 360 degree maneuver within a circle of tribe members. He could not injure a single person or the vehicle would be cursed and it would be game over.

The bus bounced and rocked as it encountered every imperfection in the road. The camp and all that lived there, gathered and ready, filled the bus's windshield. It was time.

Scratch gritted his teeth and slammed on the brakes while performing a turn/counter-turn. The crowd opened up to accept the bus just as it began its spin. This was going to be close.

The bus swung its massive weight in a thundering counter-clockwise turn, screeching in complaint. Scratch fought the wheel as the King pissed his pants and babbled some generic prayer in tongues. The tribe cheered as the blur of color and steel that was their ride out of town tore huge trenches with its tires.

By some great miracle, the bus struck only two bystanders as it completed its 360. Just as suddenly as Scratch's trick driving had started, it was over. The bus rocked slowly back and forth, having created a perfect circle in the ground, which touched the white guiding lines perfectly. It had been a complete success.

Scratch jumped out of the bus with a shit-eating grin as he pulled the still crying King along with him. The tribe was buzzing with post-ritual orgasmic excitement. Just about everyone was smoking cigarettes and five dollar bottles of champagne and ripple were being cracked open throughout the crowd.

Scratch looked over the bodies of the two casualties to the ritual. It found that they were merely extras and didn't count towards the acceptable loss ratio that the gods specified for such things. Scratch regarded the torn corpses for a respectable moment and turned to the screaming crowd.

"It's on like Donkey Kong, muthafuckers!" he proclaimed.

The crowd responded by chanting Scratch's name. Truly pleased, Scratch turned to the King, who had calmed down a bit.

"These are my people, and they are good. Tonight we will celebrate our good fortune and get ready for THE ROADTRIP. You are now one of us, and tomorrow morning we will seal the deal."

"Really?" said the King. "You'll take me?"

"Yes, after the initiation. Right now though, let's get wasted!"

The King was down with that. It wasn't like his memory was going to get any worse. He found himself floating about the tribal party, dancing and basically acting the fool.

The Dodge Tribe party was definitely a place to get stupid. Handfuls of pills covering the full spectrum of mind-wrecking madness passed through the throbbing party, in sync with multiple varieties of techno music of a thousand sub-genres of beats and mixes. Booze flowed generously as charitable tribal women gave free lap dances and a few happy endings.

The King, guzzling a bottle of who knows what, stumbled about taking in the pure joy that was the Dodge Tribe. A small boy jumped up and down in some kind of spastic epilepsy-inspired dance. The King took him in with a strange fascination that he couldn't control. The boy wore a t-shirt with a familiar logo.

As the King walked over to the boy to get a better look, someone grabbed his arm and pulled him in the opposite direction. It was Scratch.

"My man, I got a couple of guys that I want you to meet. They're newbies -- just like you. They haven't been here long, and the funny thing is that originally we kidnapped them and brought them here. They loved it so much that they signed up for the long haul."

The King looked at the two men standing next to Scratch. They wore strategically cut up leather garments. One looked very familiar to the King. He was a muscular, good-looking guy with perfect hair. He had that feeling again, not quite deja-vu. It was more like a rerun. The other man was much thinner and nerdy in appearance. He had a mask hanging from a cord around his neck. The mask was of the face of the first man.

The King was overcome with feelings of nausea. Was he beginning to remember who he was, or was it just the peyote?

As he puked his guts out, the two men flanked him, rubbing his back and telling him it was going to be okay.

"Are you going to join up? This is the best thing going. I don't even miss my old life. I get a lot more blowjobs now," said the good-looking one.

"I hear that the initiation is kind of a bitch, but once it's over, it's all gravy," said the one with the mask.

Gravy was not a good word for the King to hear. He began to have a series of dry heaves that did not sound unlike the mating call of a sperm whale.

"Look dude, we'll let you be. I'm just gonna give you a little story to read that the tribal historian put together to describe the initiation ritual. Seems some guy came out here about a year ago and was the first in a long time to do it up," said Mr. Handsome as he shoved some pages in the King's dirty brown velour pants.

"Er, thanks," belched and hacked the King as he struggled with the final remains of his stomach. "I'll be sure to check it out."

With that, the King fell over in a heap as his two newbie friends held hands and skipped away. As he faded out, all he could hear was the sweet chorus of some random dance song that had somehow claimed victory over the cacophony of the party.

"Just put it all the way up there, up there, up there..."

$

A few hours later, the King cracked an eye open. Aside from a bit of murmur about him, the party seemed to have reached its logical conclusion. He could see a number of tribe members engage in various flesh carnivals, displaying a number of sexual options he had never even considered. Others lay either sleeping or dead. Scratch was nowhere in sight, but the fire that had been started when all the tribal women had burned their bras was still going nicely.

In the slow, calculated crawl of someone who has been shot by an unknown assassin, the King made his way to the warmth of the fire. Astonishingly, he felt well. All that vomiting must have cleared his system. He pulled up to the fire and sat like Buddha, pondering where his life was taking him.

Realizing that he had been given some kind of brochure or pamphlet, the King stuck his hand into his pocket greedily and pulled out what looked like a small book. What did that good-looking guy say? Something about a historian, something about some guy who came to the tribe and learned about them. Was it some kind of re-enactment tale? What was this story about, anyway?

Unfurling the pages, the King looked down at the neatly typed sheets. Someone had made some kind of effort here, so the King promised himself to concentrate as best as he could, and try not to listen to the sounds of sodomy that were only feet away from him.

The King began to read the strange story...

$

Forever cutting a dashing figure, Jacob P. Smorely (Esq.), Adventurer and Anthropologist, was dressed in his finest crisp white shirt and razor-creased chinos as he sat on a rare Persian rug ("Two-For-One at Bargain Larry's Rare Thingz 'N' Stuff) in the back room of the King's palace. Jacob was a recurring guest of the King's and always welcome, especially in the back room.

Jacob had helped himself to the King's vast collection of action figures and play sets. In this particular session, Jacob had selected the Jacob P. Smorely Adventure Series, featuring himself. Jacob admired the accuracy of the figure's design.

"Real coward-like underpants-dumping action," he whispered with astonishment.

Happy with his initial selection, Jacob pulled himself over to the Uncle Loopey's Playchest and began to select some other figures to adventure with. Jacob almost grabbed the Smellog's Cereal

Cannibals collector's series figures, but immediately thought the better.

"I barely made it through that ordeal the last time. FOR REAL," he muttered. "I'd be better off with something less dangerous. More of an anthropological exploration, like learning about some primitive backwards culture that could use redemption by the Great White Jake."

Giggling, Jacob selected the whole mess of Dodge Tribe figures and the Dodge Tribe Autoworld Playset. Working at a furious pace, Jacob soon had the whole camp set up: a full circle of full-size vans, cars, and assorted other vehicles. He set up the Elder's Whiney-bago off to the right, and made sure that there was life-like garbage and plant life strewn throughout the encampment.

Jacob looked upon the great array of fun and excitement and frowned. Something was missing. Jacob scratched his head and thought for a moment. Of course, no Dodge Tribe set could be complete without Scratch Microphone, Leader of the Dodge Tribe. Jacob looked for a bit, and found the action figure in the backseat of the "Leader's Car" toy (a fine dark green '68 Dart Swinger with yellow racing stripes) with one of the tribal women figures. Jacob put on their stonewashed loincloths and got down to business, placing the figure of himself next to the plastic tree line just left of the toy camp.

Jacob was a topnotch adventurer/explorer, travelogue writer, and most importantly, nondenominational. Soaking off an enormous trust fund, Jacob used his cultured status and big money to idle away in foreign lands drinking imported American beer and looking for a good hamburger. A seasoned diplomat, Jacob had sat in the highest courts of the most powerful leaders. What he was most proud of, however was his ability to seduce the wives, significant others, and discreet friends of the very leaders that had him as their guest. After one of these trips, he would write a book about his journey and hit the squawk show circuit.

It was these experiences and others that Jacob thought about as he sat in the NoKare Plastic Brush just outside the grounds of the Dodge Tribe Motor Village waiting for his contact. Jacob looked at his compass/watch/canteen. Whoever this guy was, he was late. To refresh his memory, Jacob looked at the tattered press release he had received a few months ago.

Press Release

Contact: Scratch Microphone

The Dodge Tribe is a free illiterate nomadic consumer party that is coming to a hamlet near you! Known for their wacky hijinks and near-naked, joke-filled, on-with-nature reputation, the Dodge Tribe is not to be missed! Always fresh and original, the Dodge Tribe seeks only to buy large amounts of "units" and move "product." Be a part of the excitement, and reserve your seats ahead of time by calling our 1-800-NUM-BERR now! Just ask for Scratch!

"Ahh, that's it! Scratch is his name!" Jacob blurted.

The brush rustled. A tanned, muscle-bound stud with long braided hair and a designer loincloth pushed through the realistic plastic foliage.

"Hey babe, that's me," Scratch announced as he grabbed Jacob's hand and shook it vigorously. "Damn glad to meet you."

Jacob managed a smile, attempting to cover for the deep pain Scratch's vital handshake had given him. Jacob soon had a sore arm as well, as Scratch grabbed the explorer and pulled him through the bushes into the Tribe's clearing. The majesty of the simple life of the nomad overwhelmed Jacob's cultured noggin. Scratched noticed the glazed look of wonder on Jacob's face and moved quickly to regain his attention.

"Hey big guy, come back," Scratch said snapping his fingers. "We're gonna have a ball of fun. First, we'll have a meet-and-greet with the Elder's , you'll probably need a shower after that, and we'll get you a low-fat shake for a quick burst of energy. Then, you'll get an overview and a guided tour of the campground, followed by another low-fat shake. Then, I'll sit down and give you an exclusive interview. We'll wrap up the official itinerary with a sensible dinner. After that it's free time, when we sit down around the fire and sing jingles and shit like that. It's lights out promptly at 1 o'clock. Tomorrow you'll get a continental breakfast and a chance to buy things in our gift shop."

Realizing that he may have said too much too fast, Scratch watched Jacob's face for any signs of life.

Merely astounded, Jacob turned to the tribal leader and said, "Such a simple life. What a treat it will be to get away from busy civilization and retreat back to simpler times. I relish my visit. Let it begin!"

And so the whirlwind day of big time public relations began. Scratch had so far proved to be a man of his word, as they had followed his itinerary perfectly, and the low-fat shakes had been delicious. The exclusive interview had been quite insightful, and Jacob was already daydreaming about the book he would write about the Tribe.

The day had faded into dusk, and Jacob found himself at one with the Tribe, sitting around the fire passing the crack peace pipe and reflecting on the nature of life and other bullshit the mind-altered prattle on about.

Scratch stood up under the clear night sky and the tribe's mutterings and utterings stopped.

"Tonight is one of those special nights, one of those nights when we have the privilege of having such an honored guest on the program. After having spent a killer day with a great guy, I would just like to properly introduce him to you. Everyone put your hands together for one helluva guy, JACOB P. SMORELY!"

Jacob stood up and spoke. "Thank you, thank you, thank you. Today has been FAN-TAS-TIC. I've gotten to know you, I've gotten to love you, and I must say that I am impressed by your streamlined nature-boy lifestyle and your great sense of humor. I would also like to say that it's rare that I really like new people. I'm pleased as punch that I came out her to meet you, and I assure you that this is the beginning of a lasting partnership that will yield substantial dividends for all."

The tribe clapped with enthusiasm. On that note, the tribe DJ threw on some vinyl and the tribe began to get down. Jacob got down with them. The throng of people partied until the early hours of morning, only stopping when they fell unconscious. Weary, Jacob crawled into a small compact car, leaned the seat back, and closed his eyes.

A day later, Jacob awoke to the beeping and booping of the native boys' handheld electronic games. Pulling himself out of his economy digs, he opened his tired eyes to the glory of a busy tribe at work with the daily chores. Jacob decided to walk over to Scratch's Dart Swinger and see what was shaking. As Jacob walked through the camp, various members of the tribe waved to him and exposed parts of their bodies.

"How utterly charming," Jacob pronounced.

Arriving at Scratch's car, Jacob was promptly greeted by the manly leader.

"How the hell are ya?" Scratch asked.

"Dandy, just dandy. What do we have in store for today?"

"Buddy, let me tell you, it's gonna be a great day. I'm going to have you come with me on a trading deal with the King, and then we might visit one of the other tribes that used to wander these parts. They have headed out of this area, in the great grass-is-greener sense. But first I have something important to say."

"What's that, Scratch?"

"Jake, you don't know how glad I am that you came out here. We sure had a blast the other night, and my people seem comfortable around you. The bottom line is that we would like you to become an honorary member of the Dodge Tribe."

If you have ever been an adventurer/explorer (WSM, A/E), or have ever known one, then you know this is an offer that makes their panties wet.

"Why, why it would be an honor, Scratch."

Exactly, what it boils down to Jake, is that we need more exposure. That's why I sent the release out. We need a man of your stature to do a nice glossy coffee table book about your visit with us and get us on the cultural radar. Think you can do it?"

"Consider it the next number one best seller."

"I like your attitude, Jake. You're going to have to stay longer, of course. This week we'll just get down to business and you can walk around and observe and write down what you see. I assure you that I'll have a Full Access Press Pass set up for you so you can do what you do best. At the end of the week I'll clue you into the final stage of your acceptance."

Scratch and Jacob bumped knuckles on the deal and so it went. The week that followed proved to be a highly educational and rewarding exchange of cultures that can be read about in the runaway bestseller *The Dodge and I: The Continuing Adventures of Jacob P. Smorely*, on sale now and soon to be a major motion picture. However, due to certain "Tribal Limitations," Jacob was not allowed to write about his final stage of acceptance. However, for the first time ever, we can offer exclusive details that have been pieced together for a dramatic recreation:

On that fateful morning, Scratch woke Jacob up early, so that they could leave the encampment without waking the tribe. Now friends, the two men walked in the early mist.

"Now is the time to conclude your greenhorn status. I will walk with you for many miles until we come to the warrior's grove. It is there that you will engage in the time release ritual."

Jacob nodded and attempted to conceal his nervousness.

"Of course, time honored, umm, release," he mumbled.

The invigorating preparatory hike was a good time for Jacob to gear up for the enigmatic ritual. As they walked through the wilderness, the serene environment calmed the adventurer down. However, time passed quickly and soon they had reached the grove.

It was a large circular clearing surrounded by ancient trees. In the dead center of a ring of old TV sets and garbage was a bean bag. Scratch motioned to it.

"Sit," he commanded.

Jacob plopped down into the cushy seat.

"Jake, this is the Warrior's Grove. All members of the tribe must come to this grove and commune with the Great One. You sit in the comfortable, form-fitting seat of time-honored tradition. Surrounding you is a circle of old TV sets which will be tuned in to a variety of entertaining channels. You are to sit here until you see a vision, a vision that will help the tribe in some way."

Jacob nodded, as if he knew what the hell Scratch was actually talking about.

"I understand. Piece of cake."

Scratch continued. "In order to help bring about your vision, you will consume various cherry-flavored cough syrups and high-caffeine energy drinks. Take these bottles and cans and consume them now."

Jacob took the cough syrups and with great bravado, threw away the dosage cups they came with. He guzzled the medicine down, following it by shot gunning four cans of energy drinks.

"It is with great admiration that I leave you to the Great One. May you score for our team," said Scratch. The mighty warrior chief then turned and left the grove.

Jacob's head began to swim. As he watched the TV monitors flicker with infomercials that became cartoons that became shouting preachers that became revolutionary new products, he felt his body weaken and he slumped deeply into the bean bag chair.

"Must remain vigilant...vigil rust memains," he slurred as he passed into blackness.

Day became night and it was the national anthem blaring on one of the TVs that brought Jacob back to consciousness. Trying to shake off the cough syrups' veil of obscurity, he looked around the grove. Off in the distance was a glimmer of light.

Or was there? Jacob thought.

Yes. There was a light. A flashing point of blue light. Knowing that it must be special, Jacob rose from his bedsore ass and ran for the light. Although it seemed far off, it was easy to get to and it was not long before he reached it.

And there it was, a glorious flashing blue light suspended in the air, and below it, were boxes and boxes of new and exciting hair care products that the tribe was sure to enjoy. This was it! This was the sign that would secure Jacob's entry position in the tribe.

"Hey." A disembodied voice boomed from above. "I thought you were gonna save some for me."

Jacob tried to shake off the ultra-strength cold medicine as he looked around the grove. It melted away, and soon he found himself in the back room of the King's palace, surrounded by toys.

"The Great One," was all Jacob could say.

"Is that all you have to say? Of course it is. You're all jacked up on the cough syrup we were supposed to share, and you've got all my toys spread across the room!"

Seriously pissed, the King stormed out of the room, his face twisted in a mean pout. Jacob cracked a smile.

Another adventure for the books.

$

The amnesiac King set the ratty pages down. His head was pounding, as if he had lived on Southern Comfort and Slim Jims for the last month. The story had proven disturbing. It was far too familiar. What was the real reason he had been given the story? What was he supposed to know?

The King didn't have much time to consider the bigger picture. The sun was coming up and he could hear footsteps behind him. The King rolled over and saw Scratch standing with the annoyingly familiar handsome guy and the one with the mask. He was wearing the mask now, and it looked like the face of the handsome guy. Was he dreaming?

The pain that raced through his bicep as Scratch grabbed him and pulled him up proved to him that it wasn't a dream.

"It's time," Scratch pronounced. "It's your time. Are you ready?"

The King now understood. He would have to have a vision as well if he was going to stay with the tribe. Considering that he had few if no other options, he decided to roll with it.

"We have an interesting situation here," Scratch said as he motioned for the three men to follow him. "I have three fairly solid guys here, and not a single one of them knows who the hell he really is. Due to time constraints, I really can't have each of you going out to the grove, so we are going to triple you up and do it wholesale."

The three men traded uneasy glances as they followed Scratch down a recently blazed trail.

"Another thing which is a real pain in the ass is that due to the war and moving and shit , we don't have a quality warrior's grove hooked up right now. However, ConPollo and some of my men worked all night to set this up, and I think it'll do."

Scratch led the men a little further down the path. It opened up into what looked like an old freeway service drive, with a steep hill and a flashing billboard at its peak. The cracked concrete road only seemed about 100 feet or so in length, as if it had been cut out from another place and dropped from the sky. The King noted three large telephone poles that had been planted roughly 20 feet away from the billboard.

"Ok guys, gather around," Scratch commanded as he placed handfuls of pills in each of their hands. "I don't have any cough syrup right now, and the tribe needs all their energy drinks for packing and staying productive. They need their wings right now. These assortments of assorted pharmaceuticals and street drugs should do the trick. Swallow these and then climb up the poles until you are at an even height with the billboard."

The three men gobbled up their pills and began to slowly climb their telephone poles. Handsome guy wasn't even halfway up before it was clear he was tripping balls. He was making monkey noises and scratching his groin. The King looked over in jealousy. Why was he having all the fun?

The King had very little to be jealous about as in moments he found himself extremely altered. He was feeling fine as he reached the top part of the pole. Stopping on a small platform, he stood directly across from the billboard.

Maybe the sign had taken drugs too. It was one of those video signs, and it seemed to be racing through still and moving advertisements.

The King settled in, and began to absorb the constant and frenetic message flow emanating from the billboard. It was a blur of ads for pawn shops, sex changes, kid's breakfast cereals, new movies, old movies made into new movies, crap TV, Sell Inc., chewing gum, fishing tackle, new age sex toys, video games, brain erasers, loaded dice, faulty contracts, pay-as-you-go elective surgeries, social networking websites, porn, porn, porn, frozen pizza, broken philosophies, club foot treatments, new diseases, old diseases made into new diseases, Halloween costumes, the Church of the Red J, head freezing services, prostitution rings, wedding rings, divorce rings, lemon cream pies, health shoes, diaper cleaning services, white slavery, scar removal, scar creation, dream vacations turned into nightmare vacations, mustache trimmers, donkey shows, hair restoration, juicy hamburgers, rat traps, man traps, speeding traps, trap door installation services, man bras....

The King felt a sudden thud in his subconscious. Juicy hamburgers? Juicy hamburgers? That was when everything fell into place and his damaged memory managed to struggle itself off the ropes and onto its feet.

"I know who I am! I remember everything! I know what to do!" exclaimed the King.

"Dude. We've only been up here for about 45 seconds," said Handsome Guy.

The King looked over at him in desperation.

"It doesn't matter. I know what's up."

"Well, you'll have plenty of time to think about it. There is no way that you are getting down from this pole in your condition."

"What are you talking about? I have complete clarity."

"Yeah, well if that's the case, why are you speaking Spanish to a squirrel on your shoulder? I'm not even talking to you. I'm pretty much in a Thorazine stupor," said Handsome Guy.

What? No way, that's a load of bullshit, the king thought. *This guy had no idea what he was saying...or did he?* The King squeezed his eyelids shut and took another look over. Sure as shit, Handsome Guy was drooling, the Mask Guy looked like he was doing 5 Gs standing still, and there, on his shoulder, was a proudly perched cartoon squirrel.

The King gazed at the squirrel. The squirrel gazed back with big Disney eyes.

"Que pasa?" it asked in a deep raspy Spanish accent.

The King felt completely fucked. He had little faith that he would remember anything by the time he finally made it down the pole. He was stuck and fucked. The squirrel sensed his dismay and stopped his current project, which was apparently trying to shove a fire engine red stick of dynamite up the King's ass.

"Hey man, I speak English and I can send text messages, too. I'll help you remember, so don't worry so much."

"Why would you even help me? You're trying to blast my ass open with explosives!"

"Ahh, I have my ways, señor. Cartoon dynamite can't even kill you. You wouldn't want me to go for your nuts, would you, esse? I mean, that would be so obvious, man. I don't even think I could do it without wanting to erase myself, man."

The King stopped to think about what the squirrel had to say. Strangely, it made sense. Although his head was a bubbling broth of uppers and downers, he did know who he was, why he was, and apparently was fluent in Spanish. That was unless the squirrel was speaking English as he had previously stated. Why did his head seem so clear in the middle of a mind-altering hurricane? Why did a hallucination make more sense to him than anything anyone had told him when he was still in power?

The King didn't have much more time to consider these things as he heard the spark and hiss of a lit fuse. While he had pondered the big picture, the squirrel had managed to plug his brown eye with the dynamite.

"Hey! What the fuck are you doing!?"

"Silencio," declared the squirrel solemnly.

$

The King felt his head. Yup, it felt like someone had played a drum solo on his dome with a pair of claw hammers. He didn't even want to open his eyes, knowing that it would make the pain seem even more real. He could hear the sounds of the Dodge Tribe's camp, and the growing volume of Scratch's voice.

"C'mon you slugs. Up and at 'em!" Scratch insisted.

The King managed to crack his eyes open. Although a hangover of a thousand parties torqued his temples, he managed a slight grin. He still knew who he was. Red J bless that fucking squirrel. He was right.

The King sat up, and saw that the Handsome Guy was really Brad Perfect. Brad was slurping something out of a bowl, looking content. There was another guy next to him, but he just looked pale and spineless. That must be the Mask Guy. He seemed to be enjoying a juice box.

Scratch stood over the King proudly.

"Sir, meet Worm and Andy."

"Worm? I thought he was Brad Perfect?" muttered the King.

"Yeah, so did he. Turns out he was wrong. Andy wanted to be Brad as well. Personally, I don't see the connection. Anyway, who might you be?"

The King stood up, and felt very solid on his feet.

"Why, I am the King! I am the sovereign ruler of this land, and the rightful owner of the throne. I have been removed without being given a receipt, and with your help, I will take my rightful place."

There was absolute silence. Then laughter in the distance. Soon, the King found himself standing alone as everyone that heard his proclamation convulsed in spastic amusement.

Scratch caught his breath.

"Well, two outta three ain't bad."

It took him a moment, but the King came to the conclusion that no one believed him. He decided it probably would be for the best if he didn't mention the squirrel.

"No really, I'm the King! I'm the guy! I'm the Big Cheese!"

Scratch looked at him sympathetically.

"I suppose anything is possible, but can we table this for now? We have a lot to do. The Tribe hits the pavement today. I need everyone to throw down so we can get the hell outta here?"

The King nodded sadly. It would take some time to convince these people. For all the trading and all the deals and late night phone calls, Scratch did not recognize him. Perhaps if he found a fake beard (his real beard being patchy and adolescent), he would be more convincing.

But it would have to wait.

"We have to find greener pastures, my confused friend. Greener pastures," Scratch said as he walked off, waving those flashlights the ground crew uses at the airport.

13. This is Only a Test

Exterior: Forest—Night

You are camping. You are alone. The sounds of the forest speak to you. Suddenly, you hear the beat of drums. You walk through the trees and find a group of strange tribesmen surrounding a fire pit. One of them, wearing a top hat, stands and proclaims to the group: "Minions! I will now teach you how to climb the ladder that is named Desire!"

Many, many commercial breaks ago, the great ones let loose with their fire arrows, laying waste to all. Not one Golden Arch was left standing, and no longer were the great gallerias open to the public. The Earth was left wanting -- no shirts, no shoes, no service. This was the great drought of consumption, and it is key to the ideologies of the Dodge Tribe.

The Dodge Tribe knows that death and destruction are open 24 hours. They seek purification through the rules of the road, keeping the pedal to the metal, and fighting the white line fever. Bathe in the black gold, consult the maps, and never miss an opportunity to stop at a rest area.

The Dodge Tribe recognizes the three major factors that lead to a positive exchange of goods and services. These are friendliness, atmosphere, and relaxation. When you create a world where these three factors are in full effect, you can change pushes into profits. This is strong medicine, and the Dodge Tribe nurtures it to perfection.

Pieces of the past seem strange to them, but yet the TV spirits give meaning to that which often has none. They invoke that spirit with dance, ritual, music, and cough syrup in order to commune with the Great Producers, and glean their insight. Remember, members of the Dodge Tribe consider themselves not just the client, but also the president. In this manner, along with getting back to basics, having a can-do spirit, and a bit of rough camping, the Dodge Tribe carves out their piece of the pie.

Although they may be allergic to modern technology, corporate culture, and small box living, the Dodge Tribe knows that in order to thrive, they must sink their fangs deep in the neck of what they disdain. It's a compromise in order to maintain their outlaw living. You need to make a deal with the devil to succeed, but you don't have to live with him.

They know that it is not just about making friends for your store. It's about knowing your market. The Dodge Tribe knows this. They also know that nothing makes a restaurant owner happier than having his place become popular with celebrities. A long waiting list is an assurance of quality. But how do you create exclusivity yet immediately service the customer?

Our natural needs and desires are always satisfied through the products and services that we purchase with our hard earned scheckles. We all want to be admired for our selection of fashionable clothing and elegant accessories. These can be outwardly expressed desires, or the result of deep psychological programming at a subatomic level. I ask you, did you buy your newest pair of slacks because you needed them, or because you wanted to look good and feel good?

The Dodge Tribe knows the answer. They know that our most primal needs -- protection, food, and sex -- line up with our emotions and personalities. They know that these base needs, along with love and affection, are easily solved with the proper purchase or trade for goods and services. There is that massive hole in our chest, and the Dodge Tribe knows how to fill it. This has been their key survival tool since the first days of the Gathering, and it is a crucial component of the Dodge Tribe's Mission Statement.

When Scratch was just a boy, he decided to learn to play the piano. Why do you think this was? Do you think that he wanted to learn to play the piano so that he could express his innermost feelings through the catharsis of musical projection? No, he wanted to play so that he would be admired and appreciated by his peers. Know this, as Scratch knows...nothing we do is for the intrinsic value of the action. What we do is for the outside acknowledgement of our peers. We do all for the love and affection of others. It is what validates us, and makes us whole.

This knowledge, this ability to tap into the mysteries of the universe for fun and profit, can only be gleaned through the constant repetition of ritual. One must be raised by the wolves of the Dodge Tribe to truly understand their practice, but for now, attempt this mantra at daily rise and daily rest until you feel your ability to transcend social mores and morays to grab that brass ring.

A Mantra To The Meat-Bearers So That We May Find It
HOT FAST AND NOW

B-B-B-B
B-B-B-B
B-B-B-B
Bur-Bur-Bur-Bur
Bur-Bur-Bur-Bur
Bur-Bur-Bur-Bur
Bur-Bur-Bur-Bur
Bur-Ger, Bur-Ger, Bur-Ger, Bur-Ger
Bur-Ger, Bur-Ger, Bur-Ger, Bur-Ger
Bur-Ger, Bur-Ger, Bur-Ger, Bur-Ger
Bur-Ger, Bur-Ger, Bur-Ger, Bur-Ger
Bur-Ger Big-Maak, Bur-Ger Big-Maak, Bur-Ger Big Maak, Bur-Ger
Bur-Ger Big-Maak, Bur-Ger Big-Maak, Bur-Ger Big Maak, Bur-Ger
Bur-Ger Big-Maak, Bur-Ger Big-Maak, Bur-Ger Big Maak, Bur-Ger
Bur-Ger Big-Maak, Bur-Ger Big-Maak, Bur-Ger Big Maak, Bur-Ger
My Way, My Way, My Way, My Way
My Way, My Way, My Way, My Way
My Way, My Way, My Way, My Way
My Way, My Way, My Way, My Way
Cold Side Cold, Hot Side Hot, Hot, Hot, Cold, Cold
Cold Side Cold, Hot Side Hot, Hot, Hot, Cold, Cold
Cold Side Cold, Hot Side Hot, Hot, Hot, Cold, Cold
Cold Side Cold, Hot Side Hot, Hot, Hot, Cold, Cold
Hot Fast Now, Hot Hot, Hot Fast Now, Fast Fast, Now Now
Hot Fast Now, Hot Hot, Hot Fast Now, Fast Fast, Now Now
Hot Fast Now, Hot Hot, Hot Fast Now, Fast Fast, Now Now
Hot Fast Now, Hot Hot, Hot Fast Now, Fast Fast, Now Now
Char-Grill, Fry Grill, Char-Grill, Fry Grill
Char-Grill, Fry Grill, Char-Grill, Fry Grill

Char-Grill, Fry Grill, Char-Grill, Fry Grill
Char-Grill, Fry Grill, Char-Grill, Fry Grill
Big, Boy, Beef, King, Mick, Food
Big, Boy, Beef, King, Mick, Food
Big, Boy, Beef, King, Mick, Food
Big, Boy, Beef, King, Mick, Food
Food, Fun, Food, Fun
Food, Fun, Food, Fun
Food, Fun, Food, Fun
Food, Fun, Food, Fun
Fun Time, Fun Meal
Fun Time, Fun Meal
Fun Time, Fun Meal
Fun Time, Fun Meal
Please Toy, Please Toy
Please Toy, Please Toy
Please Toy, Please Toy
Please Toy, Please Toy
Please Toy Inside

14. Sell, Sell, Sell

The mighty towers of the Sell Inc. Corporate Mall poked defiantly through the incoming clouds of acid rain. The sprawling, monstrous building seemed to be grabbing at the clouds as if to say, "I will take your chemically-ridden ass and drag it down to my earth."

This obscene temple of ownership was home to most of the executives of Sell Inc., along with offices for all its holdings. Made of vomit green glass and airbrushed steel, it had a true poker face facade, and revealed little of the hardcore evil that lived inside.

In a Bored-Room on the eighty-first floor of Tower D, an overweight man in an ill-fitting suit licked his finger and dipped it into the sugar powder donut fallout that sat at the bottom of a Dookey Donut (Sell Inc. Food Division) box. His eyes lingered on the bottom of the Gynofoam container, avoiding eye contact with his superiors who clearly wished to bury him and all of his kind. His boss, not knowing his old nickname, calls him Peter. Fat Fatty Ass Assy is what the kids in school used to call him until one day he grew tired of their vicious barbs and ate them. Three days later, he let out an enormous belch, took a big shit and enjoyed a non-filtered cigarette. Ah, catharsis through fine dining.

So Peter sat, stuffing his mouth one more time to cope with his belly-aching stress. The room was filled with white pudgy males over the age of 35, with thinning hair and shallow personalities. These piranha scum-sucking bastards were assembled once more in the name of Satan.

"Hey who ate all the fucking donuts?" asked one charming dark-haired gentleman.

"When is this god-damned meeting going to get going? I have a lot of shit to make people do," yelled another highly educated being.

"Do you know how many value propositions I have to process today? Let's get this shit going," declared another stately gentleman.

As these finely worded questions arose from Sell Inc.'s ranks, the main doors opened into the room and a distinguished man of approximately 64 years of age slowly walked in, slammed his artificial cow eye briefcase onto the table, ran his fingers past his greying temples and flashing implants and said, "Right now you useless pack of swinging dicks, I have great umbrage with you all. Your current numbers suck donkey dick. You see these cybernetic implants in my head? They aren't just for show. They give me constant updates on the market as well as vital insider info. I haven't been running this company for years on my good looks. But I could, you stupid fuckers."

The CEO had spoken. He cracked open his case and threw out a pile of thick collated pages that hit the table with an ominous thud.

"Listen up. You will all be handed a detailed quarterly report of the company's current figures. It was tallied by an independent firm, contracted by certain subsidiaries that we contacted through registered mail by work of legal consul and advice of a pack of rabid grandmothers up on 72nd Avenue. I, for one, am NOT pleased at the figures. I want breakdowns. I want our current ideas socialized in the public relations department.

Everything we discuss today will circle back around later. We need to know the hydraulics of the situation, net it out, and timebox our forecasts when needed."

The CEO took a pause. Peter and the rest of the gang scrambled for their own copies of the glorious report, feigning interest in the hopes of drawing attention away from their lack of ability. The pages were passed about the table until none remained.

Back to the CEO.

"Ok, you rat fucks. Here's the deal. According to our figures, there are actually over thirteen small businesses that we don't own. Unfortunately, we don't know the names of all of them. We are missing the names of two. I want to know what they are. Then, I want to own them, and none of you will rest until I do.

I want a full company barn-raising effort on this one, and you can expect a grueling 360-degree review. Don't mistake this for a day-two project. You can reconsign any thinking of that sort. Don't think you can throw this over the wall at some versatilist working in the office next to you."

The CEO paused to clear his phlegmy throat before continuing.

"If we have learned anything as a corporation over the past few months, it is that there is opportunity in devastation. Our paradigm is simple, boys -- maintain the bottom line and our allegiance is to profit above all. We are the new high priests, and we WILL own it all. I have divided you into pairs to help facilitate this plan. You can find your unit and assignment placed upon the wall."

Tired already, Peter raised a sagging eyebrow to the wall. Scribbled on bar napkins were pairings involving everyone in the board room. All but Peter. The CEO picked up on this and rattled off a quick commentary that he had been saving for him.

"That's right, Peter, you sorry sonuvabitch. Nobody wants to work with you. I don't even know why I promoted you. I guess I was just high on victory at the time. Everyone hates your fat ass. That's why you'll work alone. And don't you go and bite your lip and cry like all the other times I screwed you over. You'll do it solo and like it, you fat, rat fuck."

With the CEO's subtle commentary dancing delicately on his ears, Peter did his best not to flap his arms like a bird and sing the Star Spangled Banner. No, he took the news like a man. He pissed his pants.

Peter was used to the abuse in a trendy Stockholm Syndrome kind of way. His whole life had been filled with bullies and abusers. At his age, it was all he knew and a victim was all he knew how to be.

All the other boys had buddied up, grabbed their assignments and hauled ass. Peter just sat in his seat and fuddled about. Soon, the only two people left in the room were Peter and the CEO. The CEO looked over at Peter with a look of pity in his eye and said, "Did you eat all the goddamn donuts? For Red J's sake, you are one sorry shit. Look, I'm watching for you to screw this one up good, fat boy, and when you do, the credits will roll on your mediocre career. You hear me?"

All Peter could do was nod. He understood. He understood too well. He watched the CEO lift himself out of his seat, grab his briefcase, and strut out the door. It was at that moment that Peter realized how he could succeed at his job and change the CEO's mind. All that he needed was to make a stop at his friendly neighborhood megamall and pick up some books at B. Dolt Books. With his newfound epiphany, Peter rose from the molded plastic chair and waddled over to the assignment board. There was only one napkin left. It said:

For a good time, call Wanda TY-600

Peter flipped it over. On the other side, in a manic scrawl, was the cryptic name: The Limp Pigeon.

Peter considered the note before eating it.

The Limp Pigeon.

Hmmmm. Yes, Peter was going to get to the bottom of this one.

$

Fun fact: The Corporate World, as it is known in the Village is a decidedly incestuous one. It should come to the surprise of no one that the CEO took immense pleasure in cornholing a number of young male interns and older male executives. In fact, the 34th floor of the Sell Inc. World Headquarters contains the holding pens for the male concubines of the CEO. Filed away in posh-but-cramped concubicles, the men wait to pleasure their lord and master. This scenario was frightening to outsiders, but for the men of Sell Inc. it was better to know that they should walk in to work backwards with their pants down. Sell Inc. will fuck you in the ass, so you might as well get something out of it, like a paycheck.

$

Spontaneous Combustion (SC) was one of a million patents developed (or stolen) at Sell Inc. Someone thought it would be a hot seller. Peter had been on the development team for that particular project. It had been the first program that Peter worked on after being enlisted by the corporation. It was on the SC project that he realized that the name of the game was indeed, combustion. Well, actually, more like consumption. Victory Through Consumption was the lifestyle that ol' Fat Ass arrived at. He had taken that concept and ran with it until he ran out of breath. He made it down the hall, but was exhausted before he reached the elevator.

Peter understood this corporate thing and it was while he sat in an Auntie Nuke's Home Atomic Cookin' Kitchen (also owned by Sell Inc. -- the entire franchise) stuffing down five anchovy and feta cheese burritos that he figured out how to apply the education the SC project had given him.

It was about CONSUMPTION.

With grand agility, Peter wiped off the crumbs from his lower lip and stood with five deft movements. Upon achieving full, erect status, he gathered his now-dry pants and strutted out into the mall.

The Sell MegaMall, as it is named, is a horrific, human Habitrail complex that provides the first five floors of foundation for the Sell Inc. headquarter buildings. The 1000-plus stores (all owned by Sell Inc.) provide a necessary source of profit for the company, as well as creating a central area to employ and monitor the lower middle classes of the Village. It is in these slums that executives (those who fall out of grace in the eyes of the father CEO) crawl about in hopes of some deep-down-bargain-basement redemption. Or at least a nice pair of wipe-and-wear trousers.

Knowing that he would only have so much time to complete his mission, Peter decided to hoof it in hopes of discovering The Limp Pigeon. With 1,000 stores, it would take a while to sort through the piles of merchandise to search for clues. There would have to be some system that could bring it together. There had to be. A quick glance at his Red J wristwatch (when the hands are on the 3 and 9, look out kids!) told Peter he better haul ass if he wanted to get back to the cube on time....

$

Steadfast on the honkey tip, the CEO looked down at his daily planner.

In bold letters it said:

Let Somebody Else Do It. What Do You Pay These Idiots For?

The CEO smirked at his little joke. No, one could not just pass the buck when you have an operating budget of a trill-zillion dollars. You would need to hire a number of people just to pass those bucks. The CEO could not ignore the tens of thousands of people who kept the ball rolling for Sell Inc. but he tried.

The CEO was actually in good spirits. If you looked carefully at his array of cybernetic face implants, you could see that they blinked in a quiet harmony as if they were almost pleased. Early reports had come in leading to the takeovers of a small egg roll factory and a glass eye emporium, resulting in the number of small businesses loose in the Village down to single digits. News like that made it hard for him to wipe the bare-toothed smile off his face, so he didn't try. Instead, he fed some guppies to his oriental fighting fish and sighed knowing that he was getting closer to complete domination of the Village. The General may believe he was in power as he sat on the King's old throne in the palace, but the CEO was THE MAN who held the Village by the short hairs. Once the Village takeover was complete, he could look at attempting a merger with the Dodge Tribe and then expand beyond the borders of the Village.

$

Peter's fatness spilled over his cluttered cubicle located on the 87th floor, five rows back from Kitchenette Land and three columns over from the Assistant to the Assistant Associate Secretary. The floor map solidly placed his fat ass at E-5. As his stubby fingers plunked away at the keyboard, Peter began to run crosschecks on all stores that had anything to do with birds. He was so into it, as a matter of fact, that he didn't notice the footsteps of his immediate supervisor on the thick green shag carpeting. By the time he hit enter on the keyboard, the boss was upon him like a fly on shit.

"Hey big guy, I was wondering if you had made any progress on this limp wrist thing. It could get, uh, you the promotion we all deserve," said the thin, athletically built college grad who happened to suck the right appendage and get a pretty ok, entry level, middle-management position.

Peter turned his head and studied the young man for a moment. Ah, why the hell not, he thought.

"I'm making some serious headway."

The supervisor perked up and giggled like a pregnant Catholic schoolgirl. "Really?"

"Yeah. Why don't you come by my apartment for a power dinner and I'll show you what I've cooked up."

"Fantabulous. I'll be by about eight or so. Right after my workout."

Peter smiled as the supervisor power walked away. All he could think about was barbecue sauce.

$

Five o'clock came around and Peter was released from his desk. Like every day before it, and every day that would follow, Peter loaded onto an elevator which challenged weight restrictions, fire codes, and common decency. Crowded, smelly, and nearly non-operational, the elevator slowly took him thirty floors down to the singles section in the residential area of the Sell Inc. dormitories. Here, Sell Inc. kept their employees close to the teat. If you worked for the corporation, it was required that you live on campus.

Peter popped out of the elevator like a three-day zit. Waddling down the corridor, he couldn't help but notice the piles of used condoms and empty wine bottles that decorated the otherwise bland hallway. Holding back great feelings of jealousy, he managed to make it to the end of the hall ending his evening death walk at the steel door of his apartment. He entered his home and set up for the evening ahead. Even though he was as tired as a tribal armband tattoo, he knew that he had a dinner appointment to prepare for, and some art to create.

Peter had few pleasures, the main one was watching Network One. He grabbed a case of beer from his refrigerator. Sitting his sorry fat ass in an "Over-Sized chair," he turned on the TV and machine-gunned through the channels like a knife-that-had-just-cut-a-can-but-was-now-cutting-a-tomato-razor-thin. Since he was an unwashed bachelor type, he didn't have to care if anyone would suffer whiplash from his avant-garde channel flipping. He was free to fly without guilt.

He spent most nights in front of the cathode altar, but he would not like you to have the impression that he was a jellied brain housed in a mass of blubber. No, Peter was a keen artist housed in a mass of blubber. His canvas was the television, and the remote control was his brush. Like a guitar, Peter played solos on his remote. The channels were like chords, and the snippets and sound bites he raced between were like individual notes.

Like a symphony to the conductor, was the television to Peter. And so his performance began...

Click!

Channel 1: Footage of a military man on water skis doing inane tricks. Announcer: "And so the General proved himself able to launch..."

Click!

Channel 2: Abraham Lincoln on a lawn chair drinking a can of beer. Lincoln: "Brrrrapppp!"

Click!

Channel 3: A small insect curls on a tree branch. Narrator (with British accent): "The intrepid insect injects a heroin-like substance in his microscopic veins, mainly out of desperation but also because it..."

Click!

Channel 4: A bunch of pathetic loafs sitting around a bar. "Tastes Great!"

Click!

Channel 5: A pile of bones on a showcase. Announcer:"...was not the only thing said at the last supper! Now you can have the highly collectable bones of the disciples of the Big Red J for the low, low price of $100,000. What a conversation piece, whatta..."

If Peter had any children, he would have sent them to the refrigerator whenever he needed a fresh beer. Unfortunately, but understandably, Peter had no children, so he kept a case of beer between his legs for safekeeping. Having just finished another perfect, albeit short solo on his remote, he rewarded himself with a fresh cold brew. It was hard to be an artist. It was hard to understand the potential of something so powerful. How is it that so many just sit idly by and merely absorb it? Yes, while the TV was something for billions to consume, it was something for Peter to create with.

Today had been a productive day. After drinking three more beers he now had three top-notch solos recorded and ready for distribution. Peter was indeed a dedicated artist, but he was no starving artist. His fat ass was enough evidence of that fact. Peter fed his fat ass by selling his TV solo recordings to collectors around the Village who could appreciate his mastery over the remote control.

It was not the inevitable fame and fortune that comes with genius that kept it interesting for Peter. It wasn't the hordes of screaming young girls or the fancy parties that kept him going. It was something for Peter and his therapist to know, so stop getting so nosey.

After uploading his latest vids, Peter set up for his dinner guest. Scrounging through his kitchen unit, he sorted through various print-outs of recipes. There was one somewhere around that was perfect for tonight's engagement.

$

Recipe for: Upwardly Mobile Meatloaf

1 Whole (gutted) Career-minded Youngblood Idiot Hotshot
2 Cups Breadcrumbs
10 Oz. Crack Cocaine
1 Bar Deodorant Soap
5 Bars Baking Chocolate
1 Jar Gourmet Hot Sauce

Instructions: Preheat gas oven to 555 degrees. Grind flesh and bones of young executive. Mix with breadcrumbs. Form into loaves. Place into oven, bake until done. In the meantime, take brisk shower to wash the blood off of your body and smoke the crack to cleanse your mind. Lather, rinse, repeat. Return to oven, remove meatloaf. Douse thoroughly with hot sauce. Eat until stomach aches. Shove chocolate bars up your ass and stick head in oven. Hallucinate about promotions you'll never get and raises you'll never see. Serves as many as desperation will allow.

$

Peter considered the recipe that his great-grandmother had written. It had been passed down for generations.

Shit. Where in the world am I going to get chocolate bars at this hour? I guess it doesn't matter, I can't afford to kill myself anyway. It's just too damn expensive.

Regardless of the cost of chocolate bars or assisted suicide in the Village, Peter was definitely going to make a meal out of that asshole power-puss guest superior. In the middle of his gourmet thoughts, opportunity knocked. Actually, BZZZZZZZT went the Hi-tek Wonder Buzzer--*Not Just a Doorbell, but a Way of Life*, goes the jingle. The buzzer was one of the many glamorous products sold at the Handy Randy Hardware Stores – *For Your Total Testosterone Needs.* Peter zipped up his Sell Inc. Employee Leisure Smock and bumbled towards the door.

The buzzer went off a total of 5 times in the 30 seconds it took Fat Ass to walk to the door. Peter hit the button that triggered the ParaNoidVid Alert -- a nifty video camera/screen combo that allowed the customer the luxury of secretly viewing any impatient visitor at the door.

It was not the person Peter was expecting. It was a woman. Fat Ass nearly ripped the door off its hinges in his excitement.

"Ummm, hello," he said in his usual loser-esque manner.

"Hi, big boy."

She was beautiful. She must have been at least four feet tall with long, brown, stringy hair that thinned in large but fortunately sporadic patches. She was slightly scarred, but only about the face, arms, and hands. And, best of all, she had some teeth left. In another world, she may have been cast as the head leper in a straight-to-DVD horror flick, but in the Village (with all its environmental hazards), she was a good 9 out of 10.

Peter just couldn't believe the vision standing before him.

"My name is Marissa and I'm your new next-door neighbor. I work in mailroom number 33 on the West End of the 80th floor," she announced.

"I'm Peter, but all my friends and co-workers put me down and call me Fat Ass," said the main man with the cellulite infested buttocks hidden in his leisure smock. "And I work --"

"I know where you work, I've had my eyes on you for quite a while. Don't ask me why, that's my little secret. It's time that you met me. Here's my vidphone number. Let's get together soon!"

If Fat Ass had smacked the bit of paper from Marissa's hand any faster, she'd be nursing a nub.

"It's a date?" he said in quietly questioning voice.

Marissa smiled, her yellowed, cracked teeth gleaming in the low-wattage florescent light. She gave Fat Ass the thumbs up sign and skipped down the hall, chanting some twisted children's rhyme:

Six cornshafts and a chainbound freak
I'm cuckoo for corn nuts
And I'll slap the spit out of
Your beak
You cocksuckinq cartoon!

Ah! And she was cultured, too! Peter wet himself in happiness. What a stroke of luck! Smiling, he turned and headed back into his apartment.

$

Channel 1212: Announcer: Why The FUCK would we give you up to 50% off used snack food wrappers and old virtual reality Chinese finger traps? BECAUSE YOU'VE EARNED IT BABY!

Click!

Channel 1760:

Exterior (Night): CARNIVAL DEL RIO

Naked partiers smear various dessert toppings onto each other. Various daisy chains and other orgy-porgy configurations fill the screen.

Announcer: People are living it up and you poor schmucks sit on your asses at home, callousing you thumbs playing ridiculous vidgames and blowing bloody snot out of your noses. Face it, YOU'VE GOT A BREAK COMING!

Click!

Channel 0089: Long Shot: Hundreds of people run down hall of a ritzy hotel.

Cut to Announcer: Get down to the Sell Mall NOW. Hell, it's only a walk right down from your apartment in the same goddamn building. 50% sales are going on all over the place, just waiting for a hip-happening consumer such as yourself to take advantage of them. COME DOWNSTAIRS NOW, YOU MONKEYS!

Click!

Fat Ass turned his attention away from the DigiWall VidSkreenz and focused on his doorbell, which once again was buzzing like a white trash teenager. He opened the door without even checking to see who it was. Fortunately, it was Captain Kiss Ass (this is the name Peter had concocted for the young and willing (about to be dinner) executive.

"Hey, how the hell are ya!" Kiss Ass bellowed.

"Well, hello to you too," replied Fat Ass, gesturing for the Youngblood to enter the living space.

Kiss Ass jumped right in, briefcase in one hand, and a case of expensive, dark, chewy beer in the other.

"Nice digs," Kiss Ass said as he silently noticed how Peter's dorm room/apartment/nook had the same layout as his own.

"So talk to me," he continued with a wink. "What's the pigeon poop?"

"Hold on. Let's get settled first. What do you say -- let's crack a few of these beers open," offered Fat Ass.

"Crack? No, ahhhhh...I stopped doing that stuff. Bad for business. Had to give something up for Lint. I had to cut something loose."

Peter winced. "No. What I meant was, oh hell...GIMME A BREWHAUS DUDE!"

"DUDE!" the executive responded. "Incoming!" he said as he tossed a can of stout in Peter's general direction.

(NOTE: In case you might not understand what has just transpired, Peter recognized that he would be able to better communicate with his douchebag boss if he spoke in what is known colloquially as "Frat Greek." Realizing that this youthful player had probable kissed ass throughout school and most certainly had belonged to a social and/or business fraternity, Fat Ass deduced that he would know “Beer Talk.” Insights such as this allow the worker to forge better communication which is crucial for goal achievement. This is what is known as a SOUND BUSINESS PRACTICE. Live it.)

So the two men sat, drinking beers and playing an intricate game of peekaboo.

"HA HA," chuckled Kiss Ass. "I can see you!" The young man frowned. "Now really. Can we talk shop?"

Peter stalled. "Aren't you hungry? Those burritos I called for should be on their way any time now."

"Well, we can discuss the lame pigeon angle until then. I have info to share as well. Right in this briefcase," he said patting the bag.

Fat Ass began to feel antsy as he knew he had no data to offer.

"Why don't you play a game of Chronic the Blunthog on my home vidgame system while I go into the other room and get what I promised to show you," offered Peter.

"You've got the Chronic? Ohboyoboyoboyoboy!" cheered Kiss Ass.

Relieved, Peter set him up with the game. Its mesmerizing 1,000,000,000 bit graphics, swirling colors, and hypnotic sound would certainly buy Peter time. At least a minute or two.

He hurried into the kitchen as the beeps and boops of the Chronic echoed across the dorm room.

"I love this game -- my son plays it all the time! I just can't figure out how to get the Golden Joint that ends the game," the up-and-coming victim yelled from the other room.

Peter couldn't help but grin. *Oh what a fool.* Scrambling to get the things together, he hummed his favorite little ditty:

Come on down to Burger Butt! Eat our goods -- they'll bust your nut!

"Lyrical genius," he said aloud, as he wound his safety orange Power Garrote ™ (for those executive-style murders) around his pudgy palms. He was ready to get all *American Psycho* on Kiss Ass.

As he quietly walked up behind the soon-to-be meatloaf, his waddling steps were muffled by the video game's life-like Dolby surround sounds. If there was any chance at all that his movements might still be heard, his target's giggles of joy assured maximum din.

$

As with many things in life, the actual killing was rather anticlimactic, although Fat Ass did indeed get his pants wet in the process. The problem was the timing. He managed to choke the poor bastard just as he captured that elusive "Golden Joint." The young fuck was so taken by actually doing something that he could take credit for honestly, he was already short of breath. So, it was no trick when old Fat Ass took him from behind, wrapping the steel wire suddenly around the yuppie's neck. Yes, his eyes did bulge and eventually pop from pressure, blood spurting out, dripping down his face -- his puffy, swollen, bright red face. And he did kick about quite a bit, pleading for his life with a pathetic whine not unlike the noise lobsters make when they are boiled alive. The young victim clawed at Peter's arms, causing deep scratches and jamming the executive's neatly groomed fingernails with Fat Ass' upper epidermis, blood and thick arm hair. His tears were ignored and he eventually collapsed and died. This sort of violence is somewhat gratuitous and needs no more patronage.

What is infinitely more interesting is what happened after Fat Ass gutted and cleaned the corpse.

$

Ding-Dong.

Peter stood in front of Marissa'a apartment door.

Ding-Dong? Who the hell still has a doorbell that goes, Ding-Dong?

The door cracked open and Marissa looked through the narrow slot with her one good eye. Seeing Fat Ass, that one good eye opened wide and she ripped the door open with verve.

"So what brings you here, big boy?" flirted Marissa.

Peter extended his arms to reveal a slightly spiced tray of cooked beef.

"Why, meatloaf, of course," he said.

"MEATLOAF? WELL, SHIT! COME ON IN!"

Peter followed her limping form into the dark and cluttered shoebox apartment. Although her place had the same layout as his, he was impressed by her stylish sense of interior decoration. Careful piles of dirty rags and rotten carry-out containers gave the place a lived-in feel, while the inch of dust that coated everything in sight gave it a decided industrial/postmodern/depression-era attitude.

"Funky," said Peter, "with a decided Cindy Lauper avante-gardness."

"Why, thank you. Why don't you take off the silly corporate overall and relax a bit? I'll slide into the kitchen nook and find a couple of convenient canned beverages for us."

It was a good thing that Peter took Marissa's suggestion and began to take off his smock because in his cannibal lust, he had forgotten to check for blood stains. Sure enough, there were smears of blood all over his cotton-poly mix blend LifeSmock ™. Fat Ass quickly stripped off the uniform to reveal his global frame dressed flatteringly in a forgiving set of Scoobie Dubie UnderWearz.

"Oh well, no sense in hiding things," he thought.

Marissa returned to the living cubicle with two canisters of low-grade popular priced beer.

"You know Peter, I'm not the type of person to just say this but I would very much like to commit acts of fellatio upon your Zeus-sized body. I would then like to mount your pole in a sincere statement of my personal freedom."

"Well, far be it for me to deny someone their desires," he agreed with a grin.

"But I just can't do it," she complained.

"Is it because you don't even know me?" he asked.

She giggled, but soon formed a serious expression.

"Peter, sex isn't something for two people to share. It's intimate. I need to do it on stage with about 100 people whooping and screaming."

It was at this point that Peter knew he would never understand women.

"Fine. We can do it wherever you like. Wherever you feel comfortable."

"YAY! Now I know that I can take you to the Limp Pigeon!"

Now an offer for a blow job and a fuck is what Peter liked to hear, but an offer to visit the mysterious Limp Pigeon is what he wanted to hear. Stretching the limits of the imagination, he proceeded to play dumb.

"The Limp Pigeon?" he asked in a clever yet kind of dumb nervousness.

"Oh honey, it's a sex club. Now you just sit here and touch yourself while I get ready," Marissa twittered.

Peter could hardly believe his luck! Not only was he going to fulfill the plot of his story, but he was going to GET LAID! And it wasn't going to be that bland, plain old sex he was used to not getting, it was going to be some sort of public exhibition FREAK SEX! Hallelujah! Praise the Big Red J!

Marissa came out of the other room dressed elegantly in a spider web of thin black leather straps which crisscrossed her dwarven body in a sexy-yet-ready-for-shipping manner. Peter immediately got excited, but fortunately, no one has to describe his hard-on in detail.

Marissa looked Fat Ass over. He was definitely going to need a make-over. She released a small smirk across the terrain of her face as she yanked him by the arm and pulled him into the changing room.

(Had Marissa been interviewed by Network One's Main Celebrity Makeover Maven Phil McCracken she might have said: "Well, you see Phil, what we had to do was spruce him up a little bit with some lederhosen. Leather shorts really do make the man. Although his obesity doesn't really make for much of an appetite, Peter seems to carry his weight with a fair bit of confidence. Now, unfortunately there is nothing we can do about his lack of even moderately acceptable looks, and his hair is simply dreadful; therefore, we covered the whole mess up with a daring bondage mask. You will notice that the eyeholes and the mouth neatly zip up as necessary. You have got to admit, he's a helluva guy to be walkin' into a mess like the one fast approaching.")

Fat Ass put a long coat over his EasyWipin' PlaLeather Hot Pants and Brace™ combo. He stuffed the mask into his pocket. He and Marissa were going to have to play it cool as they were about to attend a highly illegal establishment. Of course, due to the importance of this mission, Peter was sure that any capture by the authorities would require the bare minimum paperwork to negate. This was an important piece of networking, and Red J was on his side. At least he was finger lickin' good y'all.

Marissa and Peter left the apartment and headed down the hall to the HydroLift Elevators. The hi-speed lifts were the backbone of the Sell Inc. complex. The anxious couple killed the wait by making cutesy faces at each other and moaning sporadically.

Once on the lift, Marissa hit the button that would send the elevator down to sub-basement 33. Peter raised an eyebrow. Marissa winked. He made a mental sticky note. It would be important to remember every detail.

Sub-basement 72, Peter noted.

The lift flew within current government speed parameters down its shaft to arrive quickly and efficiently. Peter was absolutely amazed at the fact that the lift did not stop at any previous floors. Marissa reassured him by mentioning that she had punched in a stealth code ("Hot Tuna," to be precise) in order to place the lift in express mode.

Hot Turkey, Peter noted.

The door of the elevator opened into a dusty, dark corridor. Mustard colored paint peeled from the ancient walls. Light bulbs flickered, fighting to maintain the appearance of operation.

"Where are we?" asked Peter.

"It's the old city, pal. Now if we are going to see the opening act, we need to hurry. Follow me," Marissa whispered.

The couple ran down the dirty hall, kicking up clouds of semi-noxious soot and sending dust bunnies to scatter for greener pastures. They passed rusted metal doors and sliding panels, old movie posters, and other artifacts of that other time. They ran under winking neon signs for products that no longer existed. Eventually they came to a wall-sized, corroded steel grate. Marissa motioned Peter to open it. After a brief but perspiration-inspiring exertion of physical force, Fat Ass managed to pry the fucker open.

Marissa darted into the opening, firing up her trusty flashlight, given to her courtesy of a cigarette company giveaway.

Peter followed. They scurried through some sort of service tunnel thick with low-flying pipes. Peter managed to hit his head twelve times. Hell, pain builds character.

The crazy quilt of halls, doors, tunnels, and nooks ended with a sharp right turn into a wide hallway which terminated with a set of 30 foot tall security doors, guarded by two large, naked, ex-professional athletes. The doors were beautiful gold inlaid panels with large mosaics of Limping Pigeons in rubies, diamonds, and emerald tiles.

"I have to warn you about something, Peter. From this point on, the evening is going to be extremely pornographic. If you don't care for pornography, this would be your last chance to duck out."

Peter didn't move.

"Now act like nothing special is going on."

Peter just stood and stared as she darted for the two guards. Before he could utter the words "Ron Jeremy," Marissa had blown both the muscular men in a way that made them pass out from squirting out too much manjuice.

"Come, there isn't much time!" Marissa shouted.

Fat Ass bolted for the doors.

"Couldn't you have just shown them your invitation?" he asked when he caught up with his date.

Marissa smirked once more as she opened one of the great doors.

He forgot his question when the view of the inside of the club reached his virgin eyes.

What a breath-taking sight! The doors opened into a massive ballroom where hundreds of people lay on large cushions fucking and sucking and making the sign of the double-backed beast as if it would all be gone tomorrow.

"At the Limp Pigeon, no orifice is safe," said Marissa sagely.

From their vantage point, Peter could see a multitude of doorways and rooms that led from the main chamber. Old men, young women, young men, old women, dogs, clowns, mules, mutants, soldiers, Martians, rock stars, executives, plumbers, shop owners and high government officials all frolicked while scantily clad waitrons and bartenders served wicked cocktails. Other sales-type people shucked their wares: Sexual devices all configurations, drugs of every flavor, party hats -- if you wanted it, they had it.

Peter was simply dazzled. For every tight-fisted fantasy that had ever ended in a perfumed box of tissue, there was an actuality taking place before his very eye, and he was invited to partake. Marissa turned and studied his befuddled face.

"I just want to get drunk on cock," she said innocently.

This jarred Peter back into reality. "Uh, where's the show?"

"You silly," she said giggling. "Everything is the show, although there are a number of rooms where people perform a variety of acts to drool over. Now let's play a game!"

"Ok. What do I do?"

"Just turn around and count to 100. I want you to find me and fuck me. And if anything happens along the way, knock yourself out."

Peter kind of liked the idea of this game so he turned around and counted to 100. Slowly. So she could get a big head start. It was going to take time to research the Limp Pigeon. He was going to have to search this place from butt cheek to butt cheek and leave no opening unchecked.

As he counted, he fished out the bondage mask that would allow him to move anonymously through the club. He pulled it over his head, zipping up the sides to reveal a perfect fit. And one might have seen his smile if Fat Ass had bothered to unzip the mouth.

"Woun Hunnnmmmddruuud," he tried to say.

Unzipping the eyes and mouth of the mask, he found it much easier to see and breath. He then turned around to face the room. There they were, the multitude of nameless faces writhing and pumping away in groups of every size and demographic. Bodily fluids flowed regularly in a bacchanal celebration of everyone's friend, The Orgasm. Still, the orgiastic sight did seem somewhat normal, as Peter didn't actually see any sort of position or grouping that he hadn't seen in over 20 years of porno consumption. Just like Lewis and Clark, so did Peter begin his great search.

$

"Would baby like a caramel apple?" asked the father figure of Peter's flashback.

"Yes, daddy. Where are we?" asked the seven year old version of Fat Ass.

"Why we're at the mall. You like the mall," said Daddy reassuringly.

"But we're lost. I can't find my way," said young Peter about to wail.

"Now son, don't bite your lip and cry. There is a simple way to remedy anytime you might feel lost in a mall. "

"What's that, Daddy?"

"Simply always turn right when given the opportunity to turn right. Eventually you'll come full circle."

"Gee dad, that's really smart."

"Yeah, now get lost."

$

Wading through a furious daisy chain involving a group of wilding cheerleaders and five off-duty deacons, Peter managed to make his way to the first door on the right. He was certain that Marissa would not have the time to clear the main chamber unless she had ducked into the closest door. And that would be the large green door that he now stood in front of, drawing up the courage to enter.

"By the POWER of the Mitchell Brothers, so let it be done!" Peter boomed as he swung the door open.

Inside was a large, oval shaped chamber lined with EaZyWype Pleather™ couches. Old business types were having their laps attended to by overweight eunuchs dressed as Harem dancers.

Some of these guys looked familiar. A eunuch turned to Peter.

"Hey Baby, have a seat and the next available operator will be on your line in just a moment," he said shooting off a toothless smile.

"Uh, I was just passing by," Fat Ass mumbled as he made his way to the door on the opposite wall. Boy, were those eunuchs going at it, grinding into the men's hard-ons like they were making bread. Some sort of annoying mariachi music was whining through shitty speakers, accentuating the whole mess to the point that Peter practically bolted for the other door.

"Heeyahhh!" Peter grunted as he barreled into the next room.

It was dark. Peter's eyes had to adjust. He seemed to be in some narrow corridor lit by a single red light bulb. There was a series of doors that lined the hall. Short men and women in party hats slid in and out of the doors, giggling and chanting some mantras. He put his hand out, feeling for a door knob. His finger brushed up against some sort of gently curving handle made of a soft, pliable plastic.

"Ahem," said a gravelly voice less than a foot away.

That was no handle.

"Uh, sorry," said Peter, embarrassed at his mistake.

"What's your name, Sailor?"

Peter scrambled, not wanting to give the man the wrong idea. He managed to find an actual doorknob, turn it, and jump into a cramped but safe place. It was a small booth with a 37" HDTV screen set in the wall opposite the door. There was a red plastic bucket flipped over. About a thousand wads of used tissue covered the floor. Peter took a seat on the bucket.

The TV screen suddenly flicked with life. Its aspects were filled with the likeness of a beautifully androgynous female. She smiled.

"Put a dollar in the slot!" she barked.

Startled, Peter reached his grubby hand into his pocket and pulled out a piece of green paper victory. He slid the bill into a slot marked "PUMP ME BABY."

The face smiled again.

"Ah, that's much better. So, what's your fantasy, stud?" she asked with a sultry vibe all her video own.

Peter had heard of interactive porn, but had never seen or used it. He was a little disoriented by her question, but he realized that this could actually be a good opportunity to learn a bit about the Limp Pigeon.

"Uh, actually I would like to get a little information."

"You don't want me to make my cocksucking face?"

"Well, that's ok, really. I just need to know --"

"I will tell you nothing unless I get to make my cocksucking face," she said licking her lips slightly.

"Fine," Peter said with a sigh. "Make your cocksucking face."

"Yay!," she blabbered. "Ok here goes."

She puckered her lips and sucked in her cheeks. And if she had a dick in her mouth, it would have definitely been a cocksucking face. Peter blushed, as he could feel a little blood pumping into his crotch. He tried to play it cool.

"Marrvy. Simply marrvy. Now can I ask you a question?"

"Shoot. Shoot it all over me."

Peter felt his rapidly advancing erection press against his tight, shiny pants.

"Right. Uhhhh, tell me about the Limp Pigeon."

"That's not a question."

He winced. "Ok. Can you tell me about the Limp Pigeon?"

"Yeah, but you gotta do something for me."

"What?"

"Make me whole again," she said, her lower lip turning outward.

"Hold up. Make you whole again?"

"I wasn't always just a face on an HDTV screen to get some asshole horny so he could whack off into a napkin while I watched in utter boredom. No, I was a whole, real person once. The bastards that run this place captured me with a DeLuxe Vid Scanner and downloaded me into this cum-stained closet. My body is on ice. You know, in storage. Get me out."

"I didn't know they could do that now."

"Son, you know how they grow talent for Network One. Everyone knows that. You never thought that they might be able to transfer consciousness? I mean, I am grateful to still be myself. It's not like my brain got stuffed into a vacuum cleaner or a messenger bot. I can still communicate."

"I can't make any promises. I'm a corporate boy. I can probably get you a new body much easier than springing your old one. This is new to me, but we can figure it out," offered Peter.

"You're a corporate, huh? Figures. There's a ton of corporate assholes leaving traces all over this joint. What makes you different from any of the others?"

Peter thought for a moment. "I have a mission to accomplish here. Number One is to see if I can strike a deal with the owner of the joint so that Sell Inc. can launch a takeover. Number Two is to find my date and fuck her."

"Lofty goals, running dog. Look, if I point out who the owner is, will you work out a plan for my safe escape?"

"Are you on an open circuit?"

"Yes it's an open circuit. I think."

"Look, when I get out of this club tonight, I will immediately get on the net and download you right off the circuit. You can stay on my terminal until we can find you a proper vessel."

Her face lit up. "That is a deal. Now all I can tell you about the owner is that they call him Merlin."

"Merlin?"

"It's because of his wand. Now listen. My online address is TY-600. Merlin can be located on the Lance-a-Lot Superfeed. Use my codename."

"Does your codename happen to be Wanda?"

She laughed. "Why, it just so happens to be. How'd ya know?"

"Just seemed right. Gotta keep your eyes peeled in this place. Now I have to catch up with my date. Hang tight," Peter said, rising from the bucket.

"I'll be waiting," she said with a smile.

$

"Tastes just like chicken," said Merlin with a magical grin as he lifted his dripping beard from the comforting warmth of Marissa's crotch.

"Have a cigar," she offered, holding out two fine tight Cubans.

"I don't smoke cigars. You do," he said, offering a light from the end of his finger.

Marissa stuck one of the thick, brown cigars in her mouth and sucked hard. The blunt fired up nicely. It had a smooth flavor.

As she took a deep drag she inadvertently hacked up some pubic hair and cum, a minor side effect from the evening's indulgences.

"Now who is this fellow that you brought down with you tonight?" Merlin asked.

Marissa smirked. "His name is Peter. He's in Takeovers."

"I think I know the boy. I imagine that Sell Inc. is looking into getting a piece of the pigeon," deduced Merlin.

"Yeah, you know a lot for a guy who models a pointy cap. I lost Fat Ass right away so that I could warn you. Besides, I don't really want to fuck him."

"But does anybody want to fuck anybody?" Merlin waxed philosophically. He looked to the ceiling in consternation. "I guess that is a stupid question."

"Now don't get deep on me, honey, only deep in me," she mused. "I just thought you might want to know that there was an active agent loose in the club. You might want to set him up."

Merlin stood up from the cushy mat the two had been sprawled out upon. His wand was quite prominent. "There could be much to gain from a merger. I am going to have to think about this one."

"Think about money while you fuck me," purred Marissa. "I might have to fuck this guy tonight, so I would like to have something I want inside me before something I don't."

Merlin began to work his magic with vigor.

$

In the meantime, Peter had managed to make his way through three more rooms. The first room consisted of three waterbeds on which dancing girls in seal costumes blew not horns, but lines of swollen members. Each man in the line had been chosen for a particular note in the range in which the "seals" played. As each man blew his wad, he would sing his designated note. The resulting tune sounded a lot like Yankee Doodle Dandy. No shit. Really.

The second room was set up theater-style. As each member of the club walked in, they were handed a luxurious diaper with a Reelsatyn Rayon mix lining. A heavy metal act of some sort wailed its aggressive tones on stage and everyone shit their pants in time to the music. Peter did not stay for the encore.

The third room proved to be a bit more on the safe side. It was done in a lovely cheetah-skin pattern. It was set up like a mini-cabaret. A number of respectable patrons, namely a few former presidents (kept alive with cybernetics and nanobots -- from the days before the King), a few old Rear Admirals, and ex-hosts of failed children's TV shows applauded loudly as two men of middle age slid up and down a double-dong on a small, rotating pedestal for their entertainment.

Peter took a seat at one of the back tables, hoping to just observe, but his tranquility balloon was popped by a skinny loser in a button down shirt who just had to ask:

"Is anybody sitting here?"

It was a crying shame that Fat Ass hadn't been better at thinking on his toes, because he said: "No."

The dork smiled and grabbed a chair.

"I'm Bill from Vancouver. And you are?" asked the scrawny lad.

"Peter's the name. What are you into, Bill?"

"Virtual sex. I just had a blast with a computer generated Marlene Dietrich. It was smooth like voodoo butter," the dork said with glee.

"Virtual sex? Is that like actual sex?"

"No, but it's virtually sex."

Peter winced. "You like the techno stuff, eh?"

"Oh yeah, and they have plenty of it here. There are at least eleven virtual stations in the club. You can fuck and suck celebrities, friends, family members, dead people, cereal mascots -- whatever you've always wanted to lay your pipe into but reality wouldn't give you the chance," proclaimed Bill.

"Why that's special," nodded Peter, "say Bill, you seem to know a lot about the Pigeon. Come here a lot?"

Bill scratched his head a little. "Well, Bruce introduced me to it about a year back. I don't get involved in anything except the computer wet dreams. And a little stage work here and there. Why?"

"Well, it's my first time, and I don't really know my way around here," Peter said shyly.

Bill chuckled. "A virgin, I never would have guessed! Ya know, you're a stand-up guy. I have a copy of a map I made when I was first starting to come here. Some of the rooms have changed, but it should help you get around," he said as he fished around in a small knapsack.

Bill produced a sleek UltraTek handheld notebook. He said a few private words to the computer and it began to burp out a nice little map.

"Now, I'll tell you right now, you'll want to leave this cabaret on the right-hand side, because looking at you, you would be better off skipping the next three rooms to the north," he said as he ripped off the map and handed it to Peter.

"Why is that?"

"The room directly north of here lets you dress up as a lounge singer. It is sort of like karaoke except they randomly shove fresh fruit up your ass. Then there's one of those 'dungeons' and although you're sporting a fine mask, your personality suggests that you might not be ready for the discipline that they offer. The third room is a studio for the creative use of snack cakes, and you look like you should be on a diet, anyway."

Peter got a little ticked off at that comment, but he kept his cool.

"God, you've been such a help. Can I buy you a drink or something?"

Bill shot a glance at the two men on stage. You couldn't even see the dildo.

"I can't. I'm about to go onstage, and I still have to put my Rooster costume on," he said glumly. "You're welcome to stay for the proceedings."

Peter watched Bill walk away and then began to study the map.

$

YOUR HANDY GUIDE TO THE LIMP PIGEON

Hey folks -- we're glad to have you here at the Pigeon. Whether this is your first time or you are a charter member, there are always plenty of surprises for you! As you will inevitably find out, LP services people of all genders, age groups, sexual orientations, and genital configurations.

We are techno-friendly with full Virtual Reality capabilities, cyborg-friendly and we have complete Artificial Intelligence accessibility. We have members from all parts of the world, including some from parallel dimensions. Our sprawling complex has over 500 pleasure rooms (which are constantly updated based on current technological and societal trends), several restaurants and bars, a research laboratory, saunas, bathhouses, massage parlors, a 32-screen movie theatre, 10 live theaters, 1000 video peep shows, 30 live peep shows, give and take playrooms, a casino, a 1,000,000 title video library, a 10 million title magazine/book library, our own cable news channel, a parking garage, our very own roller coaster, a gift shop, full medical staff, and many more features that we are continually working on!

We have an exclusive membership policy, so anybody can join! Just pay the one-time only membership fee and you are free to stop by anytime as we are open 24-7. On the second page of this glossy promo brochure you will find an extensive color coded map for you to begin your hunt for personal treasure.

Remember, there is nothing that can't happen here, that's why it's so great! Just don't tell anybody what we do here and we won't have to kill you!

A recent addition to the Pigeon is our Amber Lynn Tribute Exhibition which includes....

$

Somehow Peter had found himself being cornholed by a 500 pound transsexual named Bruno. It hurt, but he was still enjoying himself. He had also found himself dancing in the indoor waterfall with five Samoan Vibrator Jugglers doing a variation on the Hustle. And, stopped by a haughty-taughty cocktail party where nobody was wearing any pants. It really separated the men from the boys.

The outfit that Marissa gave Peter to wear to the club had removed him of a watch, and he had no idea how much time had actually passed. Being that there was no natural light in the Limp Pigeon, he could only gauge the amount of time he had spent in the club by how much his ass hurt. By the pulse of the throbs, Peter figured that it could have been at least 8 hours. This was truly a wonderful place. Peter had come in a virgin and whatever innocence he once possessed had been slaughtered. It was time to rest and consult the map. He found a quiet alcove to ponder the wonders of the Pigeon.

As Peter sat on his side to give his ass a break, he felt a contentment that junk food and cannibalism had never been able to deliver. For the first time in his miserable life, he actually felt happy. It would be hard to give the Pigeon up. Working out a deal with the owner and handing this jewel of place over to Sell Inc. would surely destroy it forever. The Company would come in and find a way to make it family friendly. It seemed almost impossible, but they had done the same with slaughterhouses and toxic waste dumps. They would probably put in better lighting, create a logo, and develop a cartoon with Network One. Yes, Sell Inc. could really ruin a good thing.

But what to do? Eventually Peter would have to go home and report to the CEO. This sucked, and not in the good way.

While Peter was considering living in the Pigeon for the rest of his life, he was too deep in thought to notice Marissa slide into the alcove. When she spoke, it made him jump a bit.

"Hey, did you get lost? How come you never came to fuck me?" she asked.

After clenching his chest, Peter felt a bit stunned.

"Hey Marissa. I didn't see you sneak in."

"That's the problem. You didn't see me. Do you know how many people I screwed while I waited for you to find me? You must have had something better to do."

"I'm sorry Marissa. I did get lost in the club. This place has been a real eye-opener. It opened some other things too."

"Well, I'm glad you solved your chocolate-frosted existential crisis. Now are you going to fuck me or what?"

"Yeah, sure. You want it here or what?"

"No," she said as she grabbed his hand. She stood up, and with all her might pulled Peter up as well.

Without another word, Marissa led Peter through a room that featured a choreographed fuckfest with ninjas and cheerleaders. At the far end of the room was a green door. She pushed it open and walked Peter inside.

The room was by far the most boring room Peter had seen in the whole club. He didn't even know if he would be able to get hard for her in such a bland surrounding.

"I just want some quiet time with you," she said as she laid down on a round velvet couch and pulled her legs behind her head.

Peter shrugged and started to touch himself. It would take some work, but as long as there weren't any interruptions, he would get hard enough to fuck her.

Just as he reached maximum stiffness, the door opened behind them.

"Ah there you are," said a booming voice.

"FUCK! Merlin, can't you see we're busy?" Marissa screamed as she still held her wanton position.

Peter turned and there stood Merlin. A tall man, even taller with his pointy cap, Merlin sported a large grey beard and matching robe. He held his hand out to Peter.

Peter took his hand off his prick and shook the magician's hand. "Hey. So you're Merlin."

"Hi Peter. Yes, I am Merlin. And I know many things. I know how many cocks Marissa has had for dinner tonight and I know plenty about you."

"Is that so?"

"Yes, Peter. I know that you aren't here to get your rocks off. At least, that's not why you came," Merlin said laughing at his own pun. "You are here on behalf of Sell Inc. and your beloved Department of Takeovers."

Peter was impressed. The man knew a lot about the situation. Peter was also impressed that Marissa still held her flying V sex pose. He glanced over at her. She motioned for him to continue to talk to Merlin.

"I'll be okay," she mumbled as she slowly undid her legs.

Merlin put a hand on Peter's shoulder and pulled him back to the conversation.

"Peter, have you enjoyed your evening here at the club?" he asked.

"Yeah, I would have to say I have never experienced anything quite like it."

That was an understatement. Peter had nothing in his life experience to compare to the Pigeon. But for all its flourish, the club was burning him out. Sure, he had just performed unique and downright wrong sex acts of the I-never-used-to-believe-your-letters variety, but the sum of his mood's equation was simple. His elusive target for his desires -- Marissa -- had not delivered her promise, so Peter was not completely sold on the club's value.

"Don't cloud your judgment, Peter. I think you might be able to visualize what this club would turn into if Sell Inc. got its hands on it, right?"

Peter nodded.

"Not good. It would not be good. I know that you have a job to do. I also know that you can't wait to fuck Marissa and you're pretty excited about downloading Wanda and keeping her as your concubine."

Peter was taken aback. Merlin knew a lot about him, but was it really so surprising? It was his club, after all, and he was the wizard. At least he dressed like one, and his wand was certainly impressive.

"You can have all those things Peter. You just need to keep quiet," said Merlin.

Peter sat quietly, balancing the pros and cons of the situation with the scales of his imagination.

"By your silence I can see that I have given you a lot to think about. You are probably wondering what might happen to you and the quality of your job if you don't deliver the club to your CEO. I am going to show you something, and I think that it will help you make a sound business decision," said the wizard as he stood up and walked over to a red door. He motioned for Peter to stand up and join him.

"But before I truly blow you mind, I think that you should know a little about me Peter. I wasn't always the massive stud that you see before you. I was once a loser like you."

Peter winced. He was a loser. No argument there.

"I even worked for Sell Inc., just like you. I spent my days in the corporate grind, trying to climb that ladder, but to no avail. I would spend my nights working out my frustrations by hanging out in public bathrooms and fucking strangers."

Peter felt a bit better about himself with that piece of information. At least he never trolled public bathrooms.

"Then I realized that I shouldn't be looking up. I should be looking down. There were a lot of people in those bathrooms, and that meant potential profit. I explored the bowels of the Sell Inc. mall until I found this place. You could say that business literally exploded over night," Merlin chuckled.

"I know you really wanted to fuck Marissa tonight. Believe me, she is worth obsessing about. However, I have something much better for you to fuck, and once you see it, I think you will realize how important it is to keep the club exactly where it is," said Merlin as he opened the door.

Peter stepped forward to see what was behind the door. A blinding wave of colored, flashing lights caused him to hesitate, but once his eyes adjusted, they opened wide with understanding. It was a large, theater-style room, not unlike others he had passed through on his mission to find Marissa. The door itself opened out to the stage, and beyond it, Peter could see the silhouettes of at least 100 people in the crowd. That wasn't what rang Peter's bell. It was what was on stage that really grabbed his attention.

On a slowly spinning dais -- center stage -- was the naked CEO of Sell Inc. positioned on all fours. He was clearly waiting to be mounted. Peter turned in amazement to Merlin.

"Peter, it is time for you to fuck your boss in the ass. Because you're wearing that bondage mask, he will never know it's you that's fucking him. But that's not even the best part. The best part is that he comes here all the time looking to be fucked in the ass. If this club gets bought out by Sell Inc., he probably won't be able to do this anymore. It will be too high profile for him."

Peter began to understand. He nodded at Merlin and walked out to the stage. Grabbing a conveniently placed bottle of lubricant, he began to massage his quickly stiffening member. Peter took a firm position behind the CEO and pushed his rock hard cock into his hated boss' ass. The CEO's asshole tightened at first, but then gave way to Peter's manhood.

With each thrust, Peter felt the years of abuse from the CEO disappear. With each thrust, Peter began to feel lighter. With each deep, hard, thrust, Peter began to understand how revenge could feel.

As he hammered away at the CEO's ass, Peter finally felt normal. He could get used to this.

15. Act Now and You Will Get a Second One Free

Interior: Office

You sit in front of a large desk. You are in a strange office. A man in a top hat sits behind the desk. He speaks to you.

Hey, I think you need to check your email. Did you get the auto response that I sent in regards to your application? The one that reads something like "thank you for applying, you have excellent qualifications, but unfortunately the position is filled." If you received this email, you can disregard it.

I was very impressed by your interview. You were well spoken, and you sold your skill set with panache. You have the hunger in your eyes, you're a straight shooter, and clearly, as you told me in the interview, you are a PEOPLE PERSON. A real TEAM PLAYER.

It's an incredibly tough market. It's hard to get a job, that's evident by the gaps of experience on your resume. Nice resume by the way. Love the parchment paper, and no one ever uses quill and ink anymore. Say, are you one of those steampunk cosplayers? Do you own goggles? Ah, never mind.

Your personal psych evaluation results proved very interesting. Never have I seen anyone so pliable and willing that was convinced they were smarter than 95% of the population. I love this answer about aliens being discovered. You say you would be fine with it, but you are worried what other people will do. Funny, that's what everyone says.

Your gratitude should really begin now.

Do you know how many people applied for this job? Yeah, I know your distant Uncle Earl has been working on the loading dock for 20 years, but surely you must know that he has no juice here. Think about it, he's still on the loading dock.

Your gratitude should really begin now.

All kinds of roaches came out of the woodwork on this one. There were kids fresh out of the educational mill, elderly fuckheads that would rather work than die, and then folks like you, folks taking a step back on the career ladder because the shit happened and now they can't keep up with the black card monthly payments. You just had to have it, didn't you? Hey, no judgment, I had to have it too. I am just doing a better job of keeping it, that's all.

But that's why you're here, and that's why you are so grateful. Remember that feeling when my subordinate called you and told you to come in and talk with me? Do you remember how the mere suggestion of opportunity caused you to squirt right in your pants? Never lose that appreciation. It will protect you.

Let's get the general agreement right out of the way. Don't expect me to take care of you. I will not look out for you. I will expect everything you have to offer each and every day. I will create policies for intangible reasons and demand you follow them. I will remove them just as quickly. And if it is a policy you don't care for, give it two weeks. If it sucks, no one will be following it then.

I will constantly bury you in emails, phone calls, documents, and website logins. I will have a new important resource for you to master each day, and the next day I will think you are an idiot for using it. I will create forms and surveys, demand you take them, then do nothing with the results. I will be pure chaos. You will love me for it.

Your gratitude should really begin now.

The paycheck you receive will be the exchange of your time and sanity for an unstable currency that is ultimately nothing but a number on a page. Remember, the name of the game is to get that number as high as possible. I am counting on your blind dragon chasing to complete this equation.

Now that we have all the official bullshit out of the way, let's take a good look at you. Ah, you are perfect. A true beauty. Has anyone told you how beautiful you are today? Well, let me be the first.

You want this job, don't you? You know that there are a lot of people out there who would love to trade places with you right now. Trade places with you in this very moment? Don't be nervous, it's okay to smile a little bit.

Now I can't just give you the job, you still need to prove that my instincts are right, and you are the perfect person for the job. That should make you feel confident as we move forward with your audition. And, as I have told you before, you really need to express your gratitude.

Your gratitude should really begin now.

I will extract my pound of flesh. If you want to travel this road, you will have to pay the toll. I will accept nothing less. Now, as you look about the office, you will notice a number of strange devices on my desk. These are my special testers, and they will help me determine if you are indeed the PERFECT FIT.

You had to know that I would expect a number of things today. I require a blood sample. A urine sample. A drug test. A hair follicle test. A personality inventory. A fingerprint. A retinal scan. And, I require a highly invasive process of finding the largest objects that your mouth and ass can physically handle. Before you walk out, just remember what it is like out there. Remember what the streets are like. Remember the creditor calls and the potential lawsuits. Now, tell yourself you can do this.

I believe in you. I believe you can handle all I have to offer. You will need to if you plan to survive with the company. We will not relent, and you can expect to take it in the ass on a daily basis. I will fuck you in the ass so hard that your soul will die a little more with each thrust, but it will pay the bills. So, bend over my desk, don't pay any attention to the video recording device in the corner, and brace yourself.

Your gratitude should really begin now.

16. Now New and Improved

Filled with rage, the Soldier slammed his custom wheelchair down the rubble-infested streets of the Village. The boy back at the hospital had been right; the chair had some balls to it. The Soldier found that he was able to zip in and out of traffic and around three vehicle fires. The best part was that he looked good while doing it. It was a sharp ride.

Ultimately, this was of little consolation. The reality was the Soldier was losing his faith in the rebellion, the General, and himself. As the chair bobbed and weaved itself through random obstacles such as handjob kiosks and download stations, the Soldier took advantage of the onboard computer to dictate a letter to his mother.

"Mom, I'm sitting in a high-speed wheel chair on my way to challenge the General. Now I know the first thing that you would want to know is why I haven't been writing to you much and why I am in a goddamn wheelchair. Well, I have been promoted several times since I joined the Rebel Army, and I found my way to the General's inner circle. That promptly led to a death assignment, and here I am, with torn up legs wondering what the hell got me to this place."

The Soldier paused just long enough to negotiate over a sleeping refugee.

"Anyway, I have changed a lot since first joining up and I can't truly say it was for the better. I find myself wanting to buy random expensive things to impress people so self-centered they often don't care. I have been watching outrageous amounts of porn, and I think I may have carpal tunnel syndrome as a result. I joined the rebellion because I thought the monarchy was a tragic joke, and change was needed. Now I'm wondering if it's a case of the 'devil you know.' I'm resigning today and plan to escape, so you should be seeing me soon. Love, your little doo-dah."

The Soldier pressed the send button and concentrated on circling around a marching band that filled the street. The gates of the royal palace were dead ahead.

$

Peter was not having a good day at Sell Inc. He was currently standing on the CEO's conference room table, having no idea how it could support his weight. He was trying to find a happy place, as he was facing a room full of sweaty salarymen who were attacking him with random office supplies, taunting him over his failure to secure the Limp Pigeon.

"Lolzers, fatty fat fatty. You can't close," said an account rep as he chomped into an Auntie Nuke's protein bar. "You're such a loser."

Security cameras would later provide a hot Internet clip that would make 5 different "Top Ten" lists by the end of the year. Peter was being severely abused.

The CEO calmly sat watching the industry stoning with quiet amusement. He waited until his minions had run out of missiles. His men settled down, and attempted to catch their breaths. He stood up to address the room.

Looking at Peter, he frowned.

"Do you know why we ridicule you?" he asked.

Peter looked at him long and hard. Ah, if he only knew who had fucked him in the ass the night before he might be offering him flowers, or maybe request a blood test.

"You're kidding, right? I mean they have been at this for almost two hours now. I think I have it figured out. You guys all think I suck," snapped Peter.

"I'd say that's pretty much the size of it. Now then, are you going to do something about it or are you just going to remain standing on that table, hoping somebody throws you some food and it magically falls into your mouth?

"Well, I am hungry. Getting abused burns calories."

The CEO looked away, clearly annoyed. He had had about enough. Also, his ass was a bit sore and every time he moved, he winced. It would probably be best not to let the boys in on that one.

He waved his hands at Peter. "All right guys, one more hour of this and then we have to move on."

The seething crowd of power ties and pressed pants moved to begin another brutal assault on Peter's character. Peter looked over at the CEO and smiled. He had found his happy place.

$

Father Everhard sat in his kitchen, munching on some piece of microwavable crap that actually tasted better with the plastic wrapper left on. It was kind of like melted no-fat cheese. He was working on his latest sermon entitled, "What the Hell Just Happened?"

He looked down at his notes. Strong title? Check. Funny joke about Red J and the Thirty Virgins of Solomon? Check. Long rant about how the rebellion had screwed everything up and he would probably end up in jail for talking about it? Check.

It was a dandy of a sermon. It was going to cause a lot of problems for Everhard, but he thought that it might be what the Red J would want. The rebellion was not a comfortable place for the clergy of the Red J. The Red J stood for order and justice, but most importantly, maintaining the status quo. The whole internal conflict had left him with precious time to shoot hoops and go cruising.

He read over the sermon again. How could he deliver such an incendiary message and not end up hanging from a light pole in the center of the Village?

Maybe a couple of jokes about boobies?

He still had a couple of days before Mass. Maybe a walk would clear his head, he thought as he put on a slick pair of sneakers and trotted for the front door.

Yeah, boobies. Not his favorite thing in the world, but most people seemed to love them.

Outside, the air was thick and heavy. Fires raged all over, and the Village looked worse than ever. The King's loyalists had picked up steam, and were causing considerable damage.

Everhard walked past several reconstruction projects that had been bombed. They had all been abandoned. One currently housed hundreds of refugees, whose dirty unfed children played games like "Who had Tetanus?" and "Could That be Food?" They were charming imps, and seemed to enjoy whacking each other with 2x4s and rocks. Cute kids, really.

As he was touring the devastation, Everhard couldn't help but wonder where the Big Red J was in all of it. Where was he? This was just the kind of thing that he lived for. At least, that's how every issue of the scripture read. The Red J was horribly, totally, conspicuously silent. Maybe he was out taking care of something bigger, something of galactic importance? Maybe he was captured and facing certain death at the hands of one of his arch enemies? Maybe he was just being lazy? Rather than have a crisis of faith, Everhard thought that maybe the Red J needed help. Maybe he was just the guy for the job.

$

The Soldier sat in frustrated silence as the palace guards ran him through their usual protocols. It was never fun, and very redundant.

Two guards, smartly dressed in decorative uniforms, each proudly displaying over fifty pieces of flair each, stood in front of the Soldier. The first guard passed the Soldier a wireless security key pad.

"Go ahead and swipe your card, sir."

The Soldier whipped the card out from one of the wheelchair's custom leather saddlebags. He ran the card through angrily.

"Very good, sir. Now if you could just enter your PIN."

The Soldier tapped the ultra-soft grip key pad, which made pleasant notes completely contrary to his mood.

The keypad unit blared loudly. It did not like his PIN.

The first guard grimaced. The second guard looked over and whispered something into his ear. The Soldier sighed. The second guard spoke. "Sir, try to enter it again, please."

The Soldier pounded the keys, beginning to sweat profusely. If his PIN did not go, the resulting protocols would be painful and generally unpleasant. The unit blared in protest a second time.

"Ok sir, I'm going to have to put you though the secondary protocols. This will go much easier if you agree to participate. Otherwise, I might have to shoot you or send you off to the Necro-krofts," said the second guard.

"Fine, then. Let's just get this shit over with," surrendered the Soldier.

"Glad to see that you're a player. Ok, let's go! Listen to my directions carefully, and respond on the keypad with the appropriate number. For directions in English, please press 1. Para direcciones en español, por favor apriete 2. Pour les directions dans le français, appuyez s'il vous plaît 3. Für Richtungen auf Deutsch, drücken Sie bitte 4. Para direções em alemão, por favor pressione 5. Для указаний на русском языке, пожалуйста нажмите 6. Voor routebeschrijvingen in het Nederlands, stuur dan een druk op 7. Dla Polski w kierunkach, proszę nacisnąć 8. Por direktoj En Esperanto, plaĉi (al) gazetaro 9. All others, please press 0."

The Soldier confidently pressed 1.

The first guard spoke. "Very well, English it is. Kinda boring, don't you think? Anyway, to enter your private security code, please enter the first 5 digits of your street address followed by #, then *, and finally @!$%&. Remember these must be in proper order, or the menu will reset to the beginning."

The Soldier gingerly typed in his street address, which thank the Red J, was exactly five numbers. He then pressed # and *.

What was that last bit again?" the Soldier asked.

The guards stood in silence.

The Soldier entered what he thought was the proper order of symbols. The guards stood in silence, their faces emotionless. The Soldier tensed up, waiting for the worst -- a reset.

"Ah, we're just fucking with you. Ok, now enter your 20 digit Village Identification Number," said the first guard chuckling.

$

Peter endured several more hours of humiliation before the CEO took him into a side room and told him that he was being moved to another department.

"I'm telling all the guys you were fired, but I have better plans for you," the CEO whispered as he scratched at one of his temple implants. "Go to your cube and clean it out. Go home and wait for further instructions."

Peter nodded briskly and his double chins flapped solemnly. He had been spared again. Seemed that no matter how much he fucked up, he was still able to keep his job. Hell, he had even been promoted.

Peter walked through the boardroom, keeping his eyes to the floor. It was actually more of a shuffle, but it did the job. His colleagues made mocking faces and noises, and were far too happy about the whole thing. Peter desperately wanted to yell at them and tell them that they would be next; that the axe swung on the regular at Sell Inc., but it wouldn't do any good. These guys were backstabbing bottom feeders, so self-centered that they would think that Peter was talking about the guy next to them instead.

Peter made his way to his desk before he even risked looking up. When he finally did, he was smiling. After hours of abuse, he could go home and work on his secret project, getting Wanda into a human form. But first he would have to clean his desk out.

That was no easy task. One might have a better chance of giving an elephant a bath with a toothbrush. Peter's cube was a mess, a monstrous collection of candy wrappers, gynofoam food containers, and crushed drink cans. A good anthropologist could determine a history of Peter's between meal snacks for the past few years merely with a quick glance. The cleaning crew had long stopped visiting Peter's cube, mainly because they had lost three good janitors just trying to maintain the piles of garbage Peter called his work station.

Peter took a quick glance around. He only needed two things and he could make an escape. Pulling the top drawer open, he found his 30 TB flash drive and a half-eaten Auntie Nuke's Chocolate Orgy bar. Ok, he was set. After a twenty minute mad dash for the elevator, Peter was on his way home -- to get Wanda on his flash drive and make some waffles.

$

Father Everhard was for the most part, a simple character. He vacillated between periods of great faith and an utter absence of conviction. When he had the faith, he was so motivated that he could probably fill ten workshops with "Gettin' Your Life Together" rhetoric. When the faith wasn't there, he was of no use to anyone.

Fortunately for Everhard and his nearly written sermon, he was full of it by the time he made it back to the church. It had not been easy, as Everhard spent the last ten blocks running full bore as the local albino gang chased him down, hoping to rob him of his wallet and make him generally uncomfortable as the presence of most albinos will do.

Sweaty yet driven, Everhard sat down at the kitchen table and blasted out a sermon that wouldn't leave a dry panty in the house. This would be the sermon to end all sermons, something some parishioners were sure to be happy about. This town loved rants and speeches, so it was about time for Everhard to make some lasting impressions.

Feeling like he had been productive, Everhard put on some sagging shorts and his favorite retro b-ball jersey, the defunct Hammington Hot Dogs. Red J, what a great team they were! There was something about their logo, a bright red wiener, sitting in yellow bun with a squirt of ketchup that spelled out Hammington, that excited Everhard in ways that he wouldn't understand until years later when he would attend a disco dance party down at the pier.

Everhard jumped out onto the court. It was truly a miracle of the Red J that the court had been spared by all the attacks and explosions of the past months. Besides a bit of ash and what might have been someone's right arm, the court was in fantastic shape. Everhard warmed up, doing a few jumping jacks and adjusting his cup. He was just about to practice his free throws when he heard a muffled cough come from the bushes that bordered the court.

Everhard froze up. Was it his old stalker who had finally figured out his new address? Was it one of the terrifying loyalist insurgents? He palmed the ball firmly and slowly scanned the bushes.

"Aw, don't be scared. I ain't gonna hurt you. I just wanna play," said an unknown voice.

"Well, come out of the bushes slowly. You're freaking me out right now," said Everhard.

"Fair enough," said the voice.

Everhard stood motionless as he watched a tan and toned demi-god of a man step through the greenery. He was wearing a stone-washed denim loincloth, and he had long, black, luxurious hair. His muscles were toned, and he looked like he might have a three percent maximum body fat. Everhard just stared as he walked up and smiled. The man looked deep into his eyes and said:

"My name is Carlos ConPollo of the Dodge Tribe. I have come to trounce your ass in a game of 'Horse' and then give you an offer you can't refuse."

Still in awe of this magnificent beast of a man, Everhard merely nodded and began dribbling the ball. "Okay ConPollo, we are going to make the first shot from here."

Everhard planted himself just to the right of the basket and banged one in off the backboard. He felt a rush of satisfaction and couldn't keep the smug look off his face.

"Okay. Your turn," he said coyly.

$

"And now, finally, please type in the first forty digits of Pi," said the second guard.

The Soldier had been typing numbers into the infernal keypad for several hours. This was how the security worked at the palace. The idea was not to keep the wrong people out, it was just to bore them to the point that they would no longer wish to enter the fortification.

And it would have worked once more if it weren't for the rage that fueled the Soldier. He managed to get all forty in proper sequence, and he watched with sick satisfaction as the two guards finally stepped aside for him. Firing the wheelchairs engine, the Soldier made his way inside. It was time to confront the General.

But first he would have to find him, as the court was empty. There wasn't even a single sore concubine to point him in the right direction. Where was everyone? Was there another truck pull? Was the rodeo in town? What the fuck?

The Soldier decided to snoop around while he had the chance. The former King's court was a mess of dirty dishes, piles of filthy underwear, and open porno magazines. The once regal and glorious room now looked like a frat house. In some ways, it was a shame. In the Soldier's eyes, the monarchy needed to fall. The people needed their freedom— freedom from consuming, freedom from fear, and so on. But, he didn't want to trade it for what was essentially a used condom philosophy: fuck anything that moves.

The General had never portrayed himself as a mascot for disheveled autocracy. When the rebellion had begun, he offered a diverse menu of options at prices anyone could afford. Now that the dinner rush of revolution was over, it was just a matter of time before the loyalists finished off the buffet and found a new lunch spot.

The random explosions that occurred throughout the day suggested otherwise. Could it be possible that the loyalists could take control and install their new mascot of power? Did they even have one? The King was most assuredly dead, or at least it fell that way. No one had heard from him since the day the crown fell.

The Solider whipped his wheelchair around the room, studying the frescoes that depicted the history of the King's reign. Many of them had been painted with whiteout, and it looked like someone (the General, perhaps) had sketched in crude stick figure drawings of the revolt and the events of the past few months. Although they looked like they had been drawn by a five year old, they were accurate. Sadly accurate.

The Soldier waited several hours in boiling silence before the General finally appeared. He stumbled into the court alone and clearly hammered. He clumsily made his way to the throne and slumped down into it.

"General!" the Soldier shouted.

The General didn't move.

The Soldier faked a cough to get his attention.

Again, no movement.

Finally, the Soldier put his chair in high gear and slammed into the throne, paraplegic rugby style, and managed to tip the whole damn thing over, dumping the General into a pile on the floor.

"What the fuck!?!" cried the General, rubbing his eyes. Soon though, he was able to focus on the Soldier. "Well if it isn't my two favorite advisers," he slurred.

The Soldier took a quick look around and thought about correcting him, but the General was so drunk it probably wasn't going to matter.

"General, take a good look at me, uh, us," he insisted.

The General appeared to gather his faculties and stared at the Soldier. The General was a wreck, his clown makeup smeared and worn. His red wig was askew, and it appeared that he had wet himself. Still, he somehow managed to radiate the confidence of a great leader and thinker.

"My boys, you've certainly looked better."

"General, take a look at me! I'm in a goddamn wheelchair!"

"Yes, yes, you both are. This is true. And what of it?"

"That's pretty much it. I'm in a goddamn wheelchair."

"I'm not making the connection."

"General, that's the thing— you aren't making a connection! You've lost sight of what's important...why we had the rebellion in the first place."

The General straightened up in a semi-sober stance. He was now clearly offended.

"Look son, I don't know where the fuck you think you are, but you will show respect! This part about you being in a wheelchair, what— do you think you deserve an apology? That's what happens in war."

"But we're not at war! You sent me to die for no reason! I'm lucky I'm still alive."

"Yes you are. But I didn't send you to die. I sent you to lead others to die. You fucked up."

"That's your answer to this? I fucked up? I followed your orders."

"I guess I thought too much of you. But still, there is something about you that I really like. I also think that you are a bit misguided about the rebellion, but I would rather have you work from ignorance anyway."

The Soldier was baffled by the General's unapologetic attitude. He could feel his hopes and ideals run for the exit, never to return.

The General stood up and went to a desk on the far side of the throne room. He pulled the top drawer open, and pulled out a strange looking gun.

"Son, this is for your own good. I wondered what this thing was doing in the desk, but now I can see an immediate application. Good night, kid."

The Soldier fired his wheelchair into reverse attempting to flip up and around. The last thing that he heard and felt was a strange hiss and a sharp bite on the neck.

$

With the waffle iron raging, Peter moved with a speed that he didn't even know he possessed. Since the previous night at the Pigeon, he had been obsessing about Wanda. Sure, the complete experience had been profound, and there had been much to reflect upon, but Peter found that his thoughts always returned to Wanda.

He had felt a connection with her, and even though she was disembodied, he thought he could love her. He wanted a chance to find out.

Shoving syrupy bits of waffle goodness into his mouth, Peter sat down at his computer and began hacking away, looking for the Pigeon's server. He waded through directory after directory, and could see that it would take some time. Peter decided to put the machine on auto-hack and watch some TV.

In the artistic style that the underground art nation was beginning to appreciate, Peter sat in his cushy chair and began to surf channels.

Channel 23:

Click!

Channel 54: Five scruffy children run through back alleys in the Village.

Kid #1: How much do you think we'll get for a whole arm?

Kid #2: Ah, three or four.

Kid #3: We'll be able to have all the candy we want!

Kid #1: If they still make candy.

Click!

Channel 79: 3 Trappist monks play basketball video games in a shadowy hall.

V/O: They had better hurry up with virtual reality, because regular reality is bad for your health.

Monks (in unison): Four out of five doctors don't leave the house anymore because of cancer!

Click!

Channel 118: Blank screen.

Unseen voice: Last but not least, nothing at all.

Click!

Channel 556: 10 gasping penguins counting their pocket change.

Penguin #1: What good are coins when plastic chips work so much better?

The other penguins nod in agreement.

Click!

Channel 888: A talk show host interviews a man with rotting flesh.

Host: So you had large cankers as a result of the flame-retardant sugarless bubblegum? Fascinating. Now what caused you to lose your jaw?

Click!

Channel 45: A complete pervert stands on a street corner exposing his penis to old ladies.

Man: Do you want fries with that?

Old Ladies: Fast food was never like this!

Click!

Channel 7856: A cowboy rides through a junkyard on a diseased and bruised horse with a compound fracture. His foam cowboy hat is on fire, a brown noxious smoke cloud forms over his head. He coughs and wheezes into a dirty red bandanna.

Cowboy: Ah, sweet land of liberty.

Soundtrack: "Home on the Range"

Click!

Channel 9134: George Washington sits amongst Rastafarians, cheerleaders, nuclear scientists, oversized cartoon characters, and the whole G.I. Jehosephat Commando Squad.

George (speaking into a megaphone): Listen up, rascals. We got a big day ahead of us. Weez gonna kick some limey butt and free ourselves from tyranny so that no one can learn from our history!

The crowd cheers. George puts on a large baby blue plastic construction helmet with a flashing red siren on top.

George: Grab your money-saving coupons and AK 47s and follow my lead!

The massive throng goes over the hill. Cut to Benjamin Franklin in Bermuda shorts reading a letter. Cut to close-up of letter:

Letter:

Dear Ben,

I am writing this to tell you that this is probably my last day on the planet. I fear for my life. I was engaging in a search and destroy investigative mission in deepest of darkest areas, Battle Creek. The natives surprised me and I was overwhelmed. They have taken my Stupid Soaker and impounded my Dodgem car. The natives all resemble the mascots of food products, predominantly those of breakfast cereals. Tomorrow I must duel with one of their leaders in a to-the-death cage match of Killem' Krushem' Robots. I am currently being held in a large glass bowl, neck high with milk and flakes of some sort that don't get soggy in milk. I AM IN DEEP! DEEP IN SOG-FREE SHIT!

Signed,

Jacob P. Smorely, Adventurer and Anthropologist, Esq.

Click!

DING! DING! DING!

Peter froze. The dinging could mean only one thing -- he had found Wanda's server. Grabbing his waffles, he jumped out of the chair with the energy of ten men and rushed over to his computer. His face fell, realizing that the glowing blue screen meant his computer had crashed, and he would have to reboot.

$

If there had been an Olympic team for "Horse," then ConPollo would have been a starter. He was really tough, and Everhard was working his balls off to keep in the game. Every time Everhard set up an impossible shot, Carlos was able to respond. They had been playing for hours, and the priest could feel all the electrolytes draining from his body. He would need a high-sugar energy drink soon, or it was going to be all over. He couldn't lose on home court. That would be an embarrassment.

Everhard brought all he could to the game. ConPollo was a hell of a trash talker and Everhard had heard everything from an inventory of his personal hygiene to a play-by-play account of how

ConPollo had fucked his mother. Apparently she was a major slut. Not being skilled in the ways of personal humiliation, Everhard decided to chat up the primitive warrior in the hopes of distracting him.

"So how are things with the Dodge Tribe these days?"

ConPollo had been in the middle of a jump shot, and Everhard's question threw him off just enough that he missed the shot. Everhard smiled.

"Business has been better, that's for sure. The economy of the Village is failing. The war cost too much. Real estate is at an all-time low. Inflation is high. Energy costs are through the roof. And, a lot of people are dead. We've lost half of our customer base. That hurts the most," said ConPollo.

Everhard set up the next shot, which involved a granny release and two bounces. Maybe he could make the Olympic team with this one. After a perfect release, Everhard finally felt that he could take the game.

"Sounds like you guys are seriously fucked."

ConPollo snagged the ball and looked at Everhard sternly.

"And not even a kiss. That's what brings me here. The market is collapsing, and being that the Dodge Tribe has always circled like vultures, we feel that there is no more meat on this carcass. We are getting ready to make a major move, and we could use a guy like you with us."

"I don't even know you people. What do you need me for?"

"The Church of the Red J is global. You know people. You could help us set up a solid business foundation when we reach our next rest area. We would reward you handsomely."

Now this was something to consider. Everhard was on the verge of a great sermon, a sermon that would change the lives of his congregation.

"Actually, I have some big plans as well. So what we are talking about is forming a mutual admiration society?"

ConPollo grabbed Everhard's hand and pumped it hard. "You got it buddy. That and a complete rebranding of the Tribe. What do you need to get out of here?"

"Merger it is. My sermon is this Sunday. I will join you immediately after."

$

It took several days for Peter to bypass the Pigeon server's intricate defense network. The server had bounced Peter from ghost network to network, routed him through phone lines and broadcast channels, and finally dumped him into someone's virtual media library where he had to endure three hours of polka music before finally running an encryption worm that burrowed itself into the Pigeon hub.

Peter had taken three sick days, ordered out for food thirty times, and used up every box in the pantry that had the word "batter" on it. Exhausted and frustrated, his face could barely manage to show the exhilaration he felt when he finally found the file folder set named "TY-600." It was time to rescue Wanda from her two-dimensional virtual life of faking blowjob faces and taking money shots directly on the monitor.

He slammed his flash drive into the machine and hit the large red download button on his desk. Soon it would be done.

Or not -- the download meter read 20 hours remaining. That was ok with Peter, because now that he had found Wanda, he would need a body to download her to. It would have to be a body that he could love. It would have to be a body he could look at for a long time to come. There was really only one body that he knew would work. He would need a plan.

Peter was actually talented at planning. He began to bounce around his apartment, gathering everything he would need to make Wanda real. He had the brain transfer hub, from a previous fetish that hadn't worked out well. He had the cables for the hub, and an extra power generator to handle the overload. Everything he would need to actually perform the download was in the apartment. All he really needed was sleeping pills and chocolate chip muffins.

An hour later, Peter had baked a fine batch of muffins with that something special that was sure to make his plan a success. He took a long shower and made sure to thoroughly scrub his entire body, especially the remote and typically untouched areas. When he got out of the shower, he took a long minute to inspect his decidedly non-Thor like physique. He had several contusions and scratches from his night at the Pigeon that were struggling to heal, but otherwise he was in one large piece.

He put on his finest plastic coverall and grabbed the basket of muffins. Not long after he found himself at Marissa's door, knocking as if he had to take a shit. He could hear her muffled voice telling him to wait, but he could not control himself and continued to pound away at her door.

After what seemed to Peter to be longer than preparing a microwave dinner, Marissa opened the door. She looked annoyed.

"Peter, what is it?"

His brain wanted him to speak, but Peter's mouth wouldn't cooperate. He stood in front of Marissa, jaw locked tight.

"Red J damn it, I am completely sore and tired from our trip the other day. I need my sleep. What the hell do you want?"

Peter's brain released word after word, but he couldn't speak. He looked at the muffins, hoping that he could find strength in their chocolate morsels.

"I'm closing the door, Peter."

As Marissa began to exit the scene, Peter's backed up thoughts exploded onto her face. "Ijustthoughtthat you mightwant some muffins."

"Theothernightwas spectacularand I washoping that youmightwant to spendsometime together, ah aha ah," Peter said eloquently.

She looked at him as if he was a puppy caught in a barbed wire fence.

"Oh pookey, I don't want to have a relationship with you. One man isn't enough for me. Even though you probably have the mass of five men, you don't have five cocks. You're sweet, and that isn't completely lost on me."

"But, I thought we had something special the other night," whined the fatty.

"My man, you had something special the other night. Your finale was god-like, and I am expecting really great feats of sexual depravity from you in the future. The club absolutely loved what you did to the CEO. But me and you— there is no me and you."

"Are you sure about that?"

"I gotta be. Peter, didn't your father ever teach you not to fall in love with a slut?"

Peter nodded in agreement. His father had taught him that right before he shipped out with the Marines. It was the only lesson he had taught him.

"Well, ok then. I have to go. Gotta soak the vag in some Epsom salts."

"Don't you want the muffins?"

"I can't Peter. Gifts build expectations. See you around."

She closed the door, leaving Peter and his plans out in the hallway to rot. It wasn't going to go down like this. He knocked on the door again.

This time she opened the door forcefully.

"Can't you take a hint, fat boy?"

Peter said nothing and wrapped his hands around her neck, using his weight to push her into the apartment. She struggled, but he was too much for her. His grip was strong, as he masturbated frequently, and always to completion.

$

Before he had even opened his eyes, the Soldier knew that something was very wrong. He wasn't feeling right, and not in the way that usually costs money. He could hear the beeping sounds of computers and the click-clack of keyboards. He could hear the sounds of sensible shoes circling his body. Where was he? Who were these people? Why did he feel so strange? Then he heard voices, and for once they weren't inside his head.

"Dude, this is going to be so sweet when he tries it out."

"I know! I've wanted to try something like this since I started watching anime."

"I hope he likes it."

"Yeah, it's gonna fuck his shit up."

The last voice was enough to concern the Soldier. It was time to let his presence be known.

He sat up violently and his eyes popped open to see four young men in lab coats standing over his body. He had surprised them, and two of them were now wading in piss puddles.

When the Soldier looked down at his legs, he wanted to piss as well, but he found out that he couldn't.

From the waist down, his body was gone. In its place was hard, unpolished steel. These fucking kids had given him cyborg legs. His groin was gone as well, and there was what looked to be a metal jockstrap.

"Ahhhh, fuck!" screamed the Soldier. "You guys took my legs. And my COCK! Oh, it's all over, it's FUCKING OVER!"

The Soldier pushed himself off table, and the sheer weight of his new legs forced him onto his feet. The wannabe mad scientists clung to their clipboards, excited for the moment but fearing that they might not make it home for dinner.

The Soldier began to stomp around the room, tipping over monitors and breaking any pane of glass in his vicinity. His eyes were on fire, and he was breathing smoke.

"Did somebody say malt liquor?" asked one of the mad scientists.

At this point, all the lab-coated assholes swarmed the Soldier, sticking various devices in his face as well as waving them frantically around his new legs. The devices felt like annoying mosquitoes, and the Soldier wanted nothing more than for them to stop.

So he started to stomp them. *Why not try out the new legs?*

So he stomped and stomped across the room, crushing the puny science nerds one by one. The brutal squishing deaths of their colleagues did nothing to persuade the others to flee, they just pushed the pulpy masses out of the way and kept coming for the Soldier's shiny new legs, wanting to collect as much data as possible.

After several cruel minutes, it was all over. Not a single lab coat remained. And the Soldier was somehow a bit less for it.

Nevertheless, this was not a time for introspection. The Soldier made a slow turn and began marching his cybernetic legs out of the room, finding that they were very responsive but so heavy that he felt that they were more of a vehicle he was piloting instead of augmented limbs.

The hallway rocked with vibration as his powered feet pounded downward at a high rate of speed. He was racing down the hall on his new legs, and would be back in the General's court soon.

$

It had taken the last few days, but Everhard had run around like a drunk monkey and managed to get his world in order. He had thought a lot about his time in the Village, from simple missionary to public figure to celebrity. His celebrity status could be argued, but hell, there were a lot of people in the Village who knew who he was and what he was capable of doing. Most of these people had their cases against him thrown out of court.

There was much to risk by leaving the Village. The priest could be excommunicated, or even worse, transferred to a villainous parish. As a priest, he could be forced to redeem himself in the eyes of the church and maybe even the Red J himself. That could be a very ugly consequence. There was always the chance that no one in the church front office would even realize he was missing.

Leaving the Village meant leaving it all, everything Everhard had worked to build. The basketball half-court behind the church was one of his great achievements, and it killed him to think that he might never get to play hoops again. And what of next year's Passion Play? Who would take over that future tradition? Who would take the time to market it properly to ensure a maximum audience?

There was too much to lose, and Everhard knew that. There was also the chance that the continued insurgent action would remove the church permanently with some variety of high explosive or rocket. The smartest thing. thought Everhard, would be to simply pack up the church for a while and simply head out with Carlos and the Dodge tribe for a vacation of sorts.

Let the Village sort itself out, and perhaps in a while he could return and continue his work. And if the Village didn't sort itself out but instead bombed itself into a parking lot, then Everhard wouldn't become a martyr. He would live to preach another day.

Everhard looked at his new Sunday watch. It sparkled with encrusted diamonds and rubies. It was some hardcore bling. The face of the watch featured a glittery version of the Red J logo, and the hands outstretched telling Everhard that it was primetime. It was time to open the church up for service.

He squirted the last of his breakfast into his mouth. Instead of the usual Auntie Nuke's breakfast burrito, he had opted for something lighter, one of Auntie's breakfast squeeze bagels. The bagel goo was thick and grainy and if you didn't drink enough coffee with it, it would turn into a paste and lock your jaws. Everhard had been drinking coffee constantly with the goo, but was now so wired he couldn't stand still.

He ran from the kitchen into the church, lighting candles, turning on the neon signs, and firing up all the plasma screens near the altar. He ran into his changing room and put on a fresh smock and cape. The cape, an accurate replica of the Red J's own cape, was practically the reason Everhard joined the priesthood in the first place. No other religion offered nearly as interesting a costume for their clergy.

Everhard quickly brushed his hair, checked his teeth, and ran up to the front doors. He could hear a fairly large crowd outside. Throughout all the nastiness in the Village, his congregation had remained roughly the same size aside from the collateral damage caused by the war. His people were loyal, and he would certainly miss them. His one consolation was that he knew he had a mighty fine sermon for them. One they could live off spiritually for weeks for come.

Everhard opened the doors and addressed his congregation. "Ok, have your IDs out and your cover charge ready. You're in for a great show today!"

$

Peter dragged Marissa's unconscious body down the hall and back into his apartment. There had been only a few eyewitnesses to his actions, but it was the Sell Inc. way to pretend that nothing had happened. He was confident that the people he had passed in the hall would stay out of his business. They would deem it unprofitable to do anything, and would most likely move on to whatever was next on their action lists.

Peter laid her body down on the couch. He didn't have the proper rigging for this kind of process, most people didn't. He had engineered something close to it, and it would have to do. He filled up a syringe with a mighty cocktail sure to keep Marissa under for several hours, and jammed the needle into her neck, making sure to empty it completely.

The ugliest part of his plan was complete, and to celebrate he made himself a heaping sandwich so artfully designed that it actually had the flesh of four dead animals and three of their milk products. It was sandwich godhead, and Fat Ass considered it for a moment before he began to devour it.

Brushing the crumbs off his face, Peter ran a virus scan on Wanda's file. It was clear, and it was time to bring Wanda into his apartment. His fingers twitched and twittered with excitement as he typed in the final code to place Wanda on his personal server.

It only took five computer crashes and two power surges before he was looking at her beautiful CGI face.

"Hey handsome, took ya long enough," she said.

Peter laughed, belched and nearly threw up his sandwich.

"I'm so glad this worked. I wasn't even sure that it would," he said.

"Sugar, I never had a doubt. She strained to look over his shoulder. "Is that my vessel? Is that my new body? She's not very cute."

Peter frowned. Oh lord, if she wasn't happy with Marissa, he didn't know what he could do. Men that were Peter's size often had a hard time attracting women.

"It'll do for now. I am sure that we will be able to get you something much nicer at some point later," said Peter.

"Maybe track down my original body? Fair enough. I'm just ready to get moving. It's been awhile."

Peter nodded to the screen and began setting up for the transfer. Pulling out a natty pile of wires and patch cables, Peter began to run around the room, as if he was building a bicycle with Chinese language directions. He felt as if the door could be kicked in at any moment, that someone or something would ruin his happiness plan. He rarely caught a break, so it was a deeply ingrained fear that he could lose everything at any given moment.

By the time Peter was ready to go, the room was a complete obstacle course and Wanda had gone to screen saver. It would probably be better this way, what with having both women unconscious. He carefully approached his computer keyboard and hit the "insert" key.

The power surge caused by the transfer caused five floors of the employee apartments to completely black out, and the brief riots that ensued were excellent cover for the celebration that exploded in Peter's apartment. It had been a successful transfer.

Marissa (now Wanda) jumped furiously while screaming various high quality, poly-syllabic profanities. Peter had put on his favorite hip-hop album, by an artist known only as MC Douche, stripped down to his jockstrap, and was now blasting pieces of cheap sheetrock out of his downstairs neighbor's ceiling by jumping with Wanda. Marissa's decrepit body and Peter's ridiculous mass mattered little to the two new friends-with-benefits. This was pure joy, and that was very difficult to find in the Village.

"That's it buddy," Wanda exclaimed. "We're going to get tattoos!"

$

"Back again, eh? You've come to thank me, I presume," said the General lounging in a most unattractive fashion on the former King's throne.

The Soldier laughed in a way that begs for medication. He had just spent the last 10 minutes stomping his way from the lab to the King's chamber. He had obliterated anything in his way, and that meant a concert of gore and flesh pulp that would take cleaning crews 5 days and 30 gallons of bleach to restore.

"No sir. I am not here to thank you. I am now a complete monstrosity," countered the Soldier.

The General displayed great disappointment and sat up in the royal chair.

"You're not happy? I thought you'd love getting back on your feet."

"Sir, they're not my feet. My feet are now in a jar being pickled. What I have now is obscene. I mean, where the fuck is my pecker? What am I supposed to do now?" demanded the Soldier.

"Son, don't you worry about that. My R&D team will have something even better than your little dick soon enough. What your problem is, it's that you don't see the up-side. You're a serious fucker to be dealt with now. My Necro-Krofts aren't going to go anywhere near you. You'll be able to crush the competition, literally, and you'll never need shoes again. The possibilities are endless."

The Soldier gritted his teeth. The General was the Lord of the Spin, and he had a way of selling you bullshit and convincing you to super-size it. The Soldier knew that the longer he stayed in the room, the greater the chance was that he might actually get mesmerized by the General, and who knows what piece of his humanity he would lose next? He should just stomp the General in the face and get it over with. He was thinking straight murder, and his mind was growing more unclear with each passing second.

The General's painted-on clown smile was the devil, and try as he might, the Soldier could not look away. There could be a special prize inside, some kind of perk the General was waiting to give him. He could even get promoted again! Maybe a pay raise was on the way. An extra quarter an hour, perhaps?

The General watched the Soldier's anger diminish. "Are you all done venting now? Are you ready to hear about what I have in store for you and your bright, shiny legs?" asked the General. The General had all his charm guns blazing, and the Soldier's rage gave way.

"Yes sir!"

"That's a much better attitude. You're a team leader all the way, and now with those legs, you're more than the average bear. I'm giving you a new assignment. I want you to lead the Necros on a special search-and-destroy mission. I want you to root out each and every insurgent. Go door to door, fuck up some families, see who's hiding who or what. Then, once you find them— step on their heads."

"Sir, that seems like a good plan. But the Necros? How do you organize them? They don't operate in that fashion. They are more like wild dogs."

"Or sharks with blood in the water. You'll figure it out."

The Soldier saluted, turned, and stomped his way out of the room. Part of him was still furious at the General for taking his legs and some of his humanity. Furious for taking a simple boy and turning him into a self-compromising yes man. Every time the Soldier would draw a line for himself, the General would find a way to get him to cross it. The man had serious charisma, and the Soldier would be victim to it for as long as he served him. This was the grim reality, but at least he knew where he stood.

$

Father Everhard stood at his pulpit, rolled up his sleeves, and let loose.

"Greetings my friends, campers, and mutants of all ages. I stand before you to purge myself of any and all transgressions towards you. Yes, I am a sinner.

A sinner in the eyes of the Red J and his superdisciples. My deeds cross every one of our faith's 'naughty' list. Standing here now, I can only expect coal in my stocking this Kristmas. But that is the least of my worries. I'm beyond a stay at Alcatraz and I'm on a trip straight to pain of death. Hello, I'm an entertainer.

I've presented countless drivel at this lectern. You've bought it. I have aided the manipulators that have packaged filmed lies to continue your subliminal worship of me, when you should have been praying to the Red J. My church, your temple, is an institution, and I have not been paying my tuition.

Many intellectuals would look to you when casting blame. But I know that it is I who is accountable. I contribute to the thought pollutions — the attacks of sight and sound that you could not escape with the most devious of plans. I have learned the language of our fetish culture and I know how to create celebrity.

Fame is a formula. It is a quality you can obtain to affect others like a drug. Like a spell, a better magician may cast stronger magic, enduring time and trend. A poor or novice spell weaver may summon the zeitgeist, and be successful, only to never practice the dark arts again.

I think I've got it. Between careful study, ass kissing, and luck, I've managed to bust open the initial door to the maze of fame. But where is the cheese?

The cheese is inside, man. But few really know where to look. The Village is like weather, unavoidable, and can only be dealt with. The rain might soak you, and you look to me to be your umbrella. I cannot be that umbrella, and don't stand in the open because the lightning could scramble your eggs.

How you plan for the weather is up to the individual. I can give you reports, but I cannot be accurate. Each time I address you I am simply pulling shit out of my ass. I piss on your head and tell you that it's raining. I shit on your head and tell you it's snowing. I ejaculate...you get the idea.

You might not be able to stop a blizzard, but you can wear a long coat. And maybe mittens.

Too many in the face of gold want jewels. Those holding diamonds, precious metals, and other agents of wealth merely want more and will tell you not to look the clouds, not to notice the sudden winds, not to close the windows.

It will not be a sprinkling rain. It will not pass over as a scattered shower with plenty of blue sky behind it. We are stuck way past the point of safety and are enduring the fiercest storm of our lives.

We've always said that it can't happen here, it can't happen to us, that's what happens to other people. We were wrong. I was wrong. The floods have come to claim our labors. It cannot be random or without prejudice. We are being punished for our race's disrespect. It could be an arch villain. It could be the Red J himself working from the shadows to punish us for not towing the line well enough. I have thought long and hard over this one, and I just gotta shrug my shoulders. It's one big W-T-F around here.

Paybacks are a bitch, and this mud ball we live on is a prick of a loan shark.

We are all guilty of doing and not doing, of conspiring and contradiction, of exploitation and obedience, of killing and dying, of stealing and buying, of rape and cowardice, of faith and apathy, of committal and betrayal, of spying and ignoring, of targeting and evading, of commanding and submission, of lying and believing, of demanding and sacrificing, of desire and refusal, of flesh and machine, of money and soul, of good and evil, of imperialism and salutation, of gluttony and starvation, of swimming and drowning, of guns and butter, of comedy and tragedy, of distraction and pettiness, of denial and the viciousness in maintaining the status quo.

Sins of all measure these are, never ending, faceless, and continually changing faces, evil in their normality and habitual behaviors. They are proponents of the common destruction of basic goodness. These continual acts of humanity assure our extinction. The bed we make will not let us sleep in it, so we sleep on the floor. What a corner we've painted ourselves into!

We are all sinners, using one another, selfish in our relations. We are unable to comprehend the ceiling of the universe above. We will crush each other like insects. We will devour each other. We, unlike the insects, cannot even see our own hive, nets or hill.

Please dear Red J, let your foot be swift and timely!

Yes, the foot is coming. We certainly deserve it. We have been forsaken, we have driven the Red J away. He hears our alarm of irresponsibility, and when he comes to answer it, it will not be to rescue us, but instead it is his vengeance that will come flying down from the sky. Do you get it, people? We are now villains, and every hero we know and worship will come to destroy us.

Unless we change our ways. Unless we get with it. Unless we stop snorting coke off our mirrors and instead look at our own reflection.

We can turn this death ride around.

I believe this to be true. I believe that we can find our sidekick ways, and return to the Red J's side before he even notices how much we've fucked up.

I am proposing a plan. I speak of action. The Village is war-torn and ragged. Attempts to rebuild have been as successful as Sisyphus and the rock. Each brick built is blown apart. I am going for help. I am going to find the Red J and beg for it.

What I need you all to do is straighten up and start flying right. Get your shit together and make this a moral town worth saving, because if you don't clean up your collective act, and I bring him back to this mess, he's just going to barbecue us with his heat vision.

Can I count on you?"

Father Everhard never heard the crowd's wildly positive response as with the final words of his rant, his eyes rolled back into his skull and he fell to the ground spent.

It wouldn't be until hours later that ConPollo was able to revive the priest.

17. But Wait, There's More

Exterior: Beach

You are walking along a beach with a man in a top hat. The water crashing along the shore comforts you. He says:

I know what you have been thinking.

We have gotten to that point, the point of no return. I can see the fear, or perhaps the disgust on your face. I can see that I could lose you.

Please don't go.

I think that maybe you don't want to go, that you want to throw yourself forward into something amazing, something life changing.

Something with...purpose.

Purpose is a funny thing. You can be given it. You can find it. If you don't have it, you're really just fucking around.

I can give you that purpose. That reason for being that you are so desperately craving. I see that massive hole in your chest. I know exactly how you feel.

I once had that hole. I was a walking hole.

Then I figured it out. And if you stick with me, I promise to share my secret with you. But I need to ask you something.

What would you do for love?

If you have been paying attention at all, love is something that we all have been telling you is the most wonderful thing in the world. It is the one thing that everyone needs to thrive. If you don't have it, you're a loser.

What do you love?

Do you love me? Do you think you could love me? Can I get your undying pledge? What can I do for your love?

If we are going to get anywhere with this, you are going to have to love me.

I demand your love.

I see that's not a stretch for you. You think of yourself as a person ready to give that love, at least that's what everyone has been telling you. You have heard what a wonderful gift your love is, and you want to give it away.

Well, God bless you. I think you're ready. I think you are ready to know.

But let me ask you this.

Can you be loyal?

I need loyalty from you in order to work. I need to know without a flicker of doubt that you will stand behind me at the ready. That you will not flinch in the face of the beasts that will be sure to set upon us. I need to know that when you sign your name on the dotted line, that you will fucking stand behind it.

Sure, your love is nice. There's no question. But beyond your love, what I really need is your loyalty. That loyalty is your ticket. I am about to hand you a magic shovel that will help you fill that hole, and make you a solid, real person.

I know that's what you want. I know that's what you have always wanted.

I am so smart. And you're smart for listening to me.

So let me ask you something.

What are you willing to sacrifice?

There's no free lunch. There's always a price. There's a ticket to buy. There are dues to pay. Anything that's worth anything is going to cost you.

Look at that hole in your chest. That hole in your soul, if you will grant me that. Tell me, can you do the time? Can you pay the price? What is it all worth to you?

How about this? How much have you paid already? I am talking lifetime here. How much have you spent – time, money, blood – in your lifetime trying to fill that big fucking, gaping hole that has never gone away?

I thought so.

This time is going to be different. This time what you pay for will do the job. You will fill that hole, and you will know that your sacrifice was worth it.

You have been lied to, time and time again. I get that. It is painful and confusing. You have the love, you will grant your loyalty, and you want a fucking solution. But at the same time, you have serious trust issues.

You don't want to get hurt. You don't want to get ganked. You don't want the same damn thing to happen one more time.

It probably isn't enough to me to tell you to trust me.

But that's where the sacrifice comes in.

We are going to fill that hole for you. It's going to be an epic moment in your life and I promise that if you listen to me and do what you're told, you will have everything you have ever thought you wanted. And that has got to sound pretty damn good.

What more could I possibly offer?

Now this sacrifice business...I am not sure how messy it's going to get. That's why I need your love and loyalty to pull this off. I need to know that you will run straight up a hill while facing intense machine gun fire. I need your obedience. I need you to follow ever order I give. Because if you don't, this is not going to work at all.

I want you to know that you have got me pretty excited. I have thrown some heavy shit down. I ask too much. You have not walked away. In fact, you look more interested than ever. I cannot tell you how beautiful this moment truly is. Can you feel it too? We are about to do something wonderful together.

It's rare that I find someone of your integrity. Someone who is willing to pay the price. Someone who knows what the meaning of sacrifice truly is. Someone like you.

You will be my model, the one that I hoist up above all others and proclaim my perfect subject. You will glow with the adoration of others, and you will inspire many to greatness.

We only have to take a bit more of this journey and then I can teach you everything I know. I will open the book of great secrets and pour them into your brain.

Just promise me that whatever happens, you will always love me.

Please don't go.

I don't know what I would do without you.

18. CTRL+ALT+DEL

It had certainly been an eventful morning for the Soldier and his Necro-kroft minions. After a nutritious breakfast of artificially colored Craptastic Corn Craters Cereal and fruit milk (at least for the Soldier, the Necro-krofts didn't appear to be hungry, in the traditional sense), the newly formed death squad began its door-to-door Village tour of unleashed and unfettered atrocity. The method was quite simple, and something that the Soldier was actually proud of, considering it was a quick improv of a strategy.

Of all the desperate dreams that the Villagers clung to, one of the most painfully fruitless was the Content Creators Media Warehouse Giveaway Sweepstakes. It was well known to all, as most Villagers had seen winners presented with oversized checks and balloons on Network One for years. No one had actually met a winner in person, but the video confirmation seemed to be enough to keep the cruel myth going.

What few knew was that to register for the bullshit lottery was to sign up for a lifetime of complete hounding – direct mailings, spam emails, text bombs, and a barrage of inappropriate late night phone calls. With each communication, there was yet another opportunity to sell off one more bit of your soul in the hopes of winning some life changing amount of cash. It wouldn't last long since it would most certainly be handed over to the greedy bastards at Sell Inc. who would be happy to convince you that Object A (made in China) was the one thing that would complete your life.

Knowing that there wouldn't be a citizen alive who wouldn't tear the door off the hinges for that oversized check, the Soldier put together a kit of balloons, streamers, and the like (can't forget the fake microphone). Simple plan: knock on door, wait for citizen to peek out the living room window or peep hole (the ones that used a glory hole were more entertaining, however). Once they saw that big crazy cardboard check, they would conveniently ignore the presence of the ridiculously inhuman Necros and the decidedly frightening squad of death troopers in gas masks. The fake check was better than a cloak of invisibility (+10 to saving roll). The citizen would open the door, with a massive smile plastered across their face.

This is when they would meet the steel boot of the Soldier, who had really gotten the hang of having massive romper stomper cyborg legs. Although at first he played nice, a few pesky resistors with straight razors convinced him he should just crush the door opener with a boot to the cranium. It doesn't take but a few gashes to the face — oh, that will leave a mark — to convince a man to get all preemptive on a bitch.

Once the perp was squished, the Soldier would call out to the squad, “Search the domicile for any signs of loyalist paraphernalia. T-shirts, mugs, guns — what the fuck ever!” If there was any sign of even a smidge of sensitivity for the King, it was stomping time. There was no room in the Hummer to take anyone back to base. This was a one stop stomp shop.

It was an effective squad. They could tear a place up in no time, although the Necros tended to get distracted easily, especially by children. The Necros were essentially retarded, and tended to default to thinking it was all fun and games. Of course, they had that rough touch, so a game for them was as good as a shotgun blast to the chest, but it took much longer.

Interestingly enough, for all the ruckus that their systematic extermination would generate, this didn't stop the Soldier's team from decimating a house and its occupants and then moving promptly to the house next door to repeat the process. Those dumb asses really wanted the oversized check. And the Soldier, boots dripping in blood, was less astounded by this fact with each skull he crushed under his metal feet.

$

Scratch was cranky. He was a cranky son of a bitch who had a policy of letting "God's alarm clock" wake him. The morning was not his friend so being violently shoved back into consciousness was not a particularly acceptable thing for him. Never mind the fact that he had been enjoying an outstanding wet dream featuring no less than 10 name brand porn stars...goddamn it!

Regardless, he was up now and standing over him was none other than his main man, Carlos ConPollo.

"Well, by the morning's glory, I can tell that you are happy to see me!" laughed ConPollo.

"Carlos, what the hell do you want?"

"We gotta break camp, it is time to leave for the next valley."

"Yeah, yeah. But we're basically set. Just get the people going. There's a lot of shit to take care of."

"Scratch, open your damn squinty eyes and take a look around. We're ready."

Scratch rubbed the sleep out of his eyes, sat up a bit on his elbows and took a gander. Sure enough, everyone was packed up and standing in a semi-circle surrounding him. Oh, the eyes on these people, they were issuing murderous assaults with their invisible lasers, it made his dreamy porno hard-on go soft.

"Yeah buddy, it's like three in the afternoon. You gotta lay off that cough syrup," said ConPollo with clear distain.

Scratch stood up, and arched his back in a way that truly accentuated his manly, muscular torso. He also scratched his balls a bit, but the previous part with the muscles was enough to melt the expectant crowd.

"Hey folks!" Scratched yelped as he waved to the venerating crowd that was his tribe.

"Hi Scratch!" they yelled back in unison.

"Are you folks ready to get the hell out and grab us some manifest destiny or what?"

The crowd only smiled. There was a bit of excitement building, but they kept quiet for the most part.

"I do believe that you are," Scratch assured. "Okay now, get to your vehicles. I have selected the hottest chick in the tribe to drop the flag. When you see her drop that flag, gun it bitches!"

The tribe responded without hesitation. Scratch ran to the bus, hopping on and happily finding the "King" (yeah, whatever), Andy, Fake Brad, and ConPollo ready to ride with him. Finally, the moment had arrived! ROADTRIP. DESTINY. REST AREAS. THE LONG AND WINDING ROAD.

Yep, greener pastures and all that shit. Load up the truck and move to Beverly.

$

Peter and Wanda enjoyed a honeymoon of sorts. Although the downloading process had been a bit awkward, the mere fact that Wanda had a body made for a non-stop fuckfest made it well worth it. By the time they finally passed out from exhaustion, they were both solidly chaffed.

They had covered all of the standard positions one might find in a typical holoporn: missionary, doggy, cowgirl, reverse cowgirl, inverted cowgirl, 69, 68, a double-back razor, rusty trumpet, bloomers away, and a few that they would have to document for future sexology. There had been lubes, battery operated devices, electrical devices, and a Halloween mask. They had used food, makeup, and a deck of cards at one point. In fact, there is no telling how long they had actually been at it. It was a complete loss of time.

But that's the cost of love, or lust, and for once Peter was ready to pay.

Lately, things had been quiet on Peter's floor. Of course it may have been the fact that he was lost balls deep inside Marissa – er, Wanda. The usual noise of foot traffic hustling through the hallway, especially during peak hours was unnerving. Peter cracked an eye open, awoken by the sound of nothing. In Peter's life, this was actually a Bigfoot-sighting rare event. He never turned the Entertainment Center off, there was always broadcast noise filling the apartment. He always slept better that way.

Taking a look around the apartment, Peter began to realize what was going on.

"Hmm, seems that the power is out."

"I wonder how long it's been like this?" Wanda asked.

Peter had no fucking idea. They had been lost in a sexual black hole. He shook his head and pulled on a cozy set of terry cloth coveralls.

"I think that maybe I should take a look around," he said.

"I want to come too," said Wanda as she dressed. She had chosen spandex hot pants and electrical tape Xs for her nipples. Decent walking around clothes.

Peter gingerly opened the door to the apartment and took a peek out into the hall. No power there as well. Near darkness. Not a sound.

"Ok— did the world end while we were fucking?" Peter asked.

Wanda smiled. "Sure felt like it big boy."

Peter liked hearing that. No one had ever wanted to be with him, and certainly, no one had ever been satisfied by him. This was a new way of life. He fought the urge to piss his pants from fear.

"Well, looks like we have another adventure ahead of us. Unless the Rapture just happened, everyone has pulled an Elvis on us. Maybe we didn't get the memo," Peter mused as he began to throw moderately useful items into a backpack.

Peter packed the bag with energy bars, trail mix, a couple rolls of toilet paper, and a box cutter. He took a flashlight and handed one to Wanda.

"You ready for this shit?" Peter asked, as the couple ventured out into the quiet madness.

$

By late afternoon, the Solider and his fun death squad/posse had covered most of the residences in the immediate vicinity of the palace. Although they had not found any evidence of loyalist terrorism, it had been decided that the most proactive policy was to simply stomp and break anyone that happened to be at home. Although they may have been innocent at the moment, it was just a matter of time before they would update their relationship status with the General. Best to just take care of things now, rather than dodge more bombs later.

The Solider was cleaning off the viscera from his metal legs and boots. The brain matter was tenacious and clingy stuff. It was hard to get the deep and sparkly clean that the Soldier had been trained to achieve back in the early days, when he had first signed up with the General. He was going to need a multipurpose cleaner to get into all the crevices amid the hydraulic tubing and such.

Cleaning was a meditative process for the Soldier. It was simple. Something was dirty, so you cleaned it. The state of the matter at hand is obvious, and it is clear when you are complete. There was nothing like that for the Soldier now. Scanning the rest area he had chosen for his squad, namely due to the high population of glory holes in the men's room, he took a quick inventory.

Twelve Necros still remained. They were tireless, their perma-grins displaying no useful information. They didn't seem to need to eat or rest. They only did so in a dark mimicry of their human masters. They were simple creatures, yet deadly and evil. Having command over them was no reassurance whatsoever. They could turn on you at any time. What made things different now was the Soldier knew he could stomp them down to fuzzy bits of foam and sponge whenever he felt like it. Although he had not been happy with the wheelchair and losing his legs (not to mention his fucking dick), the cyborg appendages had not only transformed him physically, but mentally, and maybe even spiritually as well.

He just didn't give a fuck anymore, and anyone that had a problem with that would eat boot.

Six death troopers still remained. They kept a good distance from the Necros, and they were smart enough to keep one man on watch while the others rested. There was no way the Necros would get a drop on them. They were confident, but clearly had a healthy nervousness about them. This was a good thing.

In short, the Soldier had only lost a couple Necros, and six troopers. Of course, this mattered not as the General could give a flip about losses. He could always find more bodies to arm and order. The Soldier didn't care. From the moment that he walked on his mechanical legs, what was left of his humanity began to pour down the back of his legs like a Blue Ribbon Beer fueled morning after.

The Soldier called up the local map on his wrist unit. He began to mark off the blocks they had covered. Three sectors purged by dinner time. Not bad. He took a look at the next zone, and paused. Amongst the winding streets (urban planning by way of hallucinogens) there was a familiar name. Zooming in, he could see it was still standing.

It was his parent's house.

$

Scratch's convoy rumbled along the highway, the ancient and cracked pavement gratefully accepting their journey. Looking at the copious amount of weeds and burnt out vehicles that decorated the road, it was clear it had been some time since anyone had traveled upon it.

Scratch had a grin from ear to fucking ear. Sure, losing regular business partners can be a discouraging thing, but the excitement of new trade, a new place to plant sticks, and being far from the madness of the King or the General— this was promising.

Father Everhard, brought to Scratch's bus by Carlos ConPollo, had taken the seat at the very back of the bus. He had chosen this spot so he could maintain a melancholy gaze out the back window, watching the Village shrink as it was eaten by the horizon. Everhard had known no other place his entire life, so this was certainly a BFD as far as he was concerned. ConPollo had asked Everhard to board Scratch's bus as his religious affiliation might help new members of the tribe (there had been a tremendous amount of refugees from the Village) feel more at home. Everhard had agreed but no one had approached him, either the night before or up until now. Everhard managed to combine a frown with a wince (a frince) as he continued to stare out the window.

The Big Red J, well he was supposed to save people when they couldn't save themselves. Everhard had been a true believer from the very beginning, from the first moment that he cracked open an Adventures of the Big Red J comic book. Issue #74, the one where Red J fought the Commission of Ethics (damn, what a twist ending on that one), placed the Red J in a highly ethical dilemma in which he created a causation loop that opened 5 alternate universes into one spot, collapsing reality upon the Commission and its minions. Of course, the Commission was too big to fail, so the Red J had to offer bonuses to the leaders of the Commission. The minions were torn to pieces.

It was a story that was sure to capture the imagination of any young child, and that had certainly been true for Everhard. As soon as he finished reading that comic, he stole a few bucks out of his mother's purse and promptly mailed in his Sidekick application. And seemingly overnight, the return mail offered the acceptance of his application and a bunch of goodies, such as a decoder ring and piles of sugary protein bars for bulking up. Everhard was in.

He had never looked back, not until now, as he was literally looking back. Everhard had quickly moved up the Sidekick ranks in the Village, he had always shown great promise, and was willing not to spread the secrets he shared with some of the priests. He read every Red J book he could obtain, including several shipped in from the church's archives. Everhard read with such passion that he wished he could climb inside those four-color panels and fight side by side with the Red J, or at least one the other J-Leaguers.

But that never happened. He never got to meet the Red J or any of his disciples. Met a guy in spandex once, but that really isn't something to go into now.

Everhard sighed. Had this all been for nothing? Had he invested balls deep into a belief system that only truly existed on the printed page? He looked at the receding skyline of the Village, with its now constant plumes of smoke and thundering explosions. Surely if the Red J were real, this would not have happened.

And with that, his crisis of faith had solidly taken root. It should come as no surprise to you that, in that very moment, Everhard noticed a flying red blur traveling somewhat parallel to the Dodge Tribe's column of vehicles.

$

Peter and Wanda walked out into the corridor. The usual truth-exposing painful florescent lighting had given way to dim emergency lamps.

"Peter, I just want you to know how great you look," commented Wanda.

Peter cracked a smile. He squinted to see the end of the hall, but just couldn't quite make it out. Turning on the flashlight, he began a slow creep in the direction of the elevators.

"This just doesn't make sense. Where the hell happened to the power? Where the hell is everyone?" Peter asked.

Wanda merely shook her head. It was still a Cyberfrankenstein miracle that she was able to even appreciate the physical realm, and odd or not, it was as puzzling as a 24 hour convenience store posting their hours on the front door.

The hall held an eerie stillness. Peter and Wanda began to slowly walk towards the elevator bay, noting open apartment doors, various dropped personal items, and the usual strewn trash. Peter had a thought, but decided not to share it. The silence was almost sacred. Without any sort of dramatic interruption, the pair made it to the elevators and quickly discovered that they were not working.

"I figured as much, but I suppose it was worth a try," Peter sighed.

"Well, honeyskillet, what's the plan?" asked Wanda.

"Hmm, at this point it's clear something is wrong. This is not the usual nonsense. I think we need to get out of here, if only because it looks like everyone else fucking did. We'll have to take the stairs, and that's going to suck, but once we get to the Mall levels, we can loot some supplies, a vehicle, and most importantly a portable TV. I think I'm having withdrawals."

Wanda nodded, and knew that Peter was serious about his TV withdrawals. They took to the stairs.

It was about a bazillion flights down to the mall level. It was a long flight. Wanda, fresh to her body, was ready to bound down level to level, simply enjoying the fact that she now had a pair of legs to spread, er, walk with. Peter, his girth a true detriment in any activity involving movement, required regular breaks fueled with energy bars and trail mix. The toilet paper had also come in handy.

However, the trip down had given Peter and Wanda some time to get to know each other. Up until now, it really had been just about the fucking. Now it was real. Wanda's almost childlike questioning of life and physical existence had initially been entertaining, but on question number 300, when Wanda wanted a comprehensive explanation of how a DVR worked, Peter found himself daydreaming about throwing her down the stairs, and when she began to suggest that he should drop a little weight, he was ready to choke the bitch.

It was only when they found themselves about 10 floors out from the first Mall level that Peter began to remember what life had been like before Wanda, really only days ago — what he had gone through to get her, and where he had found her. Annoying or not, she was his girl, and that was something he had never had been able to say about anyone.

He had to look over to her and smile. If he drew upon his deep and ingrained Sell Inc. training, he could find a way to mold her. She had no idea about the real world, all she had ever known was what was put in front of her at The Limp Pigeon, and that typically meant phallus. He had a real opportunity to create a woman that would see the world as he wished her to see it, and that was pure fucking gold.

They reached the first Mall level, there were too many to count, but each one pretty much had the same stores or the same kind of stores, and all of them had vehicle bays. Still not a soul. Was it possible that Peter had actually downloaded himself into an alternate world, and Wanda was tricking him?

It was a metaphysical knuckle sandwich, and Peter wasn't about to consider it, especially with an abandoned Crapplebee's with fried everything dead ahead.

"You like chicken fingers?' Peter asked with a sparkle in his eye and drool on his chin.

$

The Soldier had not been home since that fateful day when he decided to stand for change, pack his shit, and head out to work for the General. There had been the letters home, but as time had gone on, and the fact that he had never received any kind of reply from dear old mom and dad, well the motivation had just not been there. That and the fact that crosstown traffic was a real bitch, especially when commuting from the hills on the outskirts of the Village.

Boy, they were in for a shock. He was quite literally half the man he used to be. Now he was a cyberson. Wonder how that would go over?

He waved the boys over and motioned for them to hold back to the sidewalk while he approached the door. The Necros contented themselves by wandering over to the neighbor's yard and attempting to capture the little yap dog that barked bloody murder at their presence.

It was between the first and second knock on the door when the Soldier heard a sickening crack and then sweet silence. That dog hadn't lasted long, and he wasn't sure how long the Necros would be able to contain themselves before they wandered back. He was going to have to take quick inventory of the situation if the folks were home.

After a series of fist pounding, the door lock clicked and the Soldier's mother took a peek out of the crack.

"Sonny boy?" Mom asked.

The death squad chuckled, forcing the Soldier to give them a shut up wave.

"Hey, mom."

"Why my stars and stripes, I didn't know if I would ever see the day that you would return. I didn't think I would see you breathing, I can tell you that," Mom said with dimple-popping grin.

"You always were so positive," the Soldier remarked through his teeth.

"So what brings you home? Tired of the rebellion and all that?"

"Mom, are you going to invite me in or what?"

"Oh my, did I forget my manners! Yes, of course, come on in," Mom said with a dramatic gesture for him to walk in.

With a careful look to the left and right, the Solider took a step inside. Sure, his legs were half a ton of metal, but his feet felt even heavier. Why was this so hard?

Home had been a safe place. There had been little trauma in his early years, for the most part home life had always been quiet and free of drama. His parents had always gotten along, and there was little to report. It had been an abnormal life by Village standards. But from that, there had been growing discontent from within him. It may have been the youthful compunction to destroy the old and established, it may have been a constant diet of conspiracy theory and three chord anger rock, it may have been boredom. From an early age, the Soldier felt that he must destroy the status quo.

Looking around a house filled with collector spoons, thimbles, glass figurines, and his father's balls in a jar on the mantle, one would never have guessed that this cozy fortress of knick-knacks would be the vat that would distill the now right-hand man of the greatest rebel the Village had ever known. The new status quo, no less.

The Soldier's mother could see the air traffic level of consternation that furrowed the Soldier's brow.

"Oh, dear. What's wrong?" she asked.

"Nothing," He curtly responded.

"Hmm. Well, your father is in the garage working on something. Do you want to bring your friends in for cookies and milk?" She said with a smile.

"Not sure that's such a good idea, Mom. This is a bit of a business call. Official business."

"Oh my, whatever could bring you home ON BUSINESS?"

"The business, isn't here specifically, but you're on a list."

"Oh, this doesn't have to do with all that Socialist stuff your father dabbled in back when we were in college?"

The Soldier chuckled. "No, Mom. This is related to the current state of events, you know the revolution and all the knockback that's been going on."

His mother nodded sagely. "Yes, of course, dear. Please, invite your friends in and I will put some noshes out. It would be rude to do otherwise."

$

Scratch had pulled the convoy over at the third rest stop they had passed. The ritual demanded Union stops every third rest area. One could not anger the gods of the Union. You could end up wearing cement shoes. Scratch never understood what that meant.

The Tribe, as well as their new guests, moved quickly to make the rest stop comfortable. They brought their vehicles into a loose circle, and began to set up tents, prop up awnings, and set out the lawn chairs. Even in a rush, the Tribe traveled in style. Typically, rest stops would last a day or two anyway, so it was best to settle in a bit.

Scratch rubbed his stomach and looked back into the bus. Quietly sat his strong man ConPollo, along with the Andy, Fake Brad, "The King," and Father Everhard. Wow, what a motley bunch.

"Why are you guys so damn quiet? It's like I'm on this bus by myself or something." He asked.

The men looked at each other. No one said a word.

"Did somebody just fart? What the hell?"

ConPollo looked at Scratch with a sly grin. "I don't think any of them have ever been outside of the Village before. It's probably a hell of a shock."

"Carlos, you always nail it. Guys, man...it's gonna be ok. Yeah, it's true that all you have ever known is truly gone. It's also true that the future is unknown. I get it. You're worried."

The men nodded enthusiastically.

"Well, I want you to take a good look at me." Scratch stood up, the model of muscular maleness and perfect proportion in his loincloth, with just the right amount of tan to truly bring out his muscle tone.

"I have been many places beyond the Village. I have been the leader of a nomadic tribe for a good long time. I have seen kings and mayors and presidents come and go. Me? My tribe? We just keep on truckin'. We thrive in the chaos of change. It's the butter to our biscuit. You stick with me, you got it made in the shade. No shit. Just relax. It will work out nicely.

The men looked at each other once more. Andy decided to speak for what they were thinking. "Well, shit. There aren't any other options to speak of, and goddamn, this guy is pretty charismatic." They all nodded once more and began to exit the bus.

"That's it guys, go stretch your legs. Some of the babes might be up for a little manual stress relief, if you ask them nicely," Scratch offered.

That seemed to brighten up the crew, and they shuffled off into the makeshift camp. All but Everhard.

"Scratch?"

"Yeah, buddy. What's up?

"I don't think I am going to be able to continue on with you. Something has come up," uttered Everhard.

"You're not thinking about heading back, are you?" asked Scratch.

"Oh hell no. I have come to the conclusion that I have to take a separate path for now, but I am convinced you will not be hard to find. All I ask is for one of your motorcycles and some traveling rations," Everhard said with resolving sigh.

"Vision quest? Something along those lines? Get some answers? I dig it, man. Shit, that's what the Tribe is all about. I will get you the finest motocross bike I've got, some good grub, and some water. You gotta talk to a man about a horse? I got your back.

Everhard was impressed by Scratch's level of insight. It was clear why he was the man he was.

"Look, go grab some food or something. I just gotta confer with the Elders and I will get you on your way."

Everhard was happy for the first time in a long time. He now had a chance, a chance for what was yet to be determined.

$

Peter was in hog heaven. He had often fantasized about having access to a large industrial-sized fryer and an endlessly deep walk-in freezer filled with breaded appetizers of all varieties. Through the kitchen window, he could see his beauty, Wanda, sitting at the bar with her chin propped up by one arm, looking somewhat listlessly around the empty restaurant.

"You ok, honey?" Peter asked.

Wanda looked over at Peter, with tired eyes. "I know I haven't been in this world very long, but I did expect a few more people to be walking around. I dunno, seems a bit boring," she said.

Peter joyfully dropped breaded pig bits in the fryer bin as he simultaneously pulled the hot-and-ready fried cheese logs out of the frothing oil. "Well, my dear, I have no idea where everyone went, but I think we will find out soon enough. I find that fried cheese always gives me clarity," said Peter.

Wanda gave him an incredulous look. "If you say so," she replied.

Peter was beginning to feel anxious about Wanda. It was one thing to bring her into the world, and actually fulfill his goal of having a female companion before having his body dumped down a chute for recycling. It was another to bring someone into an apocalypse. Seriously, we're talking about having to explain everything twice. The before and now the after...what a pain in the ass this was turning out to be.

What was that quote? You don't pay the prostitute for sex, you pay her to leave?

"Well, sweets, truth is that most people suck. It's true that usually this place is full of people ordering all matters of processed food goodness, having trendy drinks, and wondering what dessert will complement their appetizer-entrée combo meal. If they aren't doing that, they are pondering the actual age of the fake antique bric-a-brac that adorns the walls. It's a bit of an authentic existential crisis over dipping sauces. One day, you'll be glad you never met these people," Peter declared, as he walked up to the bar bearing two heaping platters of fried randomness.

"They sound sad," said Wanda.

"Sad and pathetic. I was never a fan. And, before you get all misty about it, you should know that most of them treated me like shit. I doubt I will miss the Sell Inc. folk," Peter said as he began to test the stress limits of his cheek food storage pockets by stuffing in as many pork nubs he could.

"Sad and cruel. What world have I come to live in?" Wanda said with a frown.

"A better one now," Peter said. "One where we can write the rules. Now, have something to eat, we are going to jack a car in the parking garage and get the hell out of here."

$

Although it was against his better judgment – for all parties involved – the Soldier made his way to the front door and waved his men in. It was strange to be home. It was not a place that he ever expected to see again. Mom was far too friendly, and was Dad really in the garage? Was this a test? The General was pretty fucked in his skull, so that was a distinct possibility. His men met him at the door. The Soldier made a hand gesture to remind them to keep their eyes open for trouble, and to not be romanced by the Auntie Nuke's Pockets of Hot Food that were sure to be laid out.

It was a long set of gestures, and the Soldier was fairly convinced that he lost a few of them halfway through.

"Honey, are you going to stand at the door all day, or let your friends in?" asked Mom with a smile.

The Solider nodded in agreement, and guided his men in. Their eyes were wide open in amazement.

"You grew up here?" asked a trooper. "This place is crazy. What's the doily count here anyway? How does a man get to be as angry as you with all of the ceramic kitties on the mantle?

Before he began to explain the supplanting of parenting for the collecting of ceramic kitties, the Soldier notices the ball-busting smirk on his man's face.

Ok, no need to go down that path, he thought.

Mom put the platter of Auntie Nuke's on the table and motioned for the men of the Soldier's death squad to come over and eat. They obliged. The Soldier stood silently behind the group of men as they crowded the table, stuffing their mouths and crafting inappropriate jokes about heated pockets. Mom stood off the side, with a satisfied look on her face.

Upon deciding that the food wasn't poisoned, the Soldier took the opportunity to walk around the house a bit. It was amazingly unchanged from the moment he headed out the door to join the revolution. How could he change so much, and this place so little? Half his body was now auto parts, and the same damn spoon collection sat mounted on the wall. His humanity was slipping with every murder in the General's name, but there were the crystal ponies in the glass case as always. Where once he was kind, his cruelty was growing, then he noticed the "Hail the King" collector's plates.

Ummm. "Hail the King"?

"HEY SON!"

The Soldier's deep introspection was interrupted into panic. He turned around quickly to see his diminutive Father standing not two feet away, wiping off a wrench with a dirty rag.

"Getting a look at the place? Getting a good look? Does it bring back any memories?" Dad asked, looking the Soldier deep in the eyes.

"Jeezuz, Dad. You scared the crap out of me," the Soldier stammered. "There are a few things I don't remember being here before, but yeah, I guess."

"Well, that's good. Real good," said Dad. It would have been nice to hear from you. We were pretty sure you were dead. There's been a lot of death going around these days."

The Soldier nodded.

"You've changed quite a bit since we last saw you. What the hell are these?" asked Dad, rapping the Soldier's metal legs with his wrench.

"Umm, not sure how much I want to talk about that," the Soldier said.

"Funny, that's all I want to talk about," said Dad.

$

Scratch looked at the Whiney-bago and sighed. Red J fuck, he was going to have to speak with the Elders. What a pain in the ass. The smell of mold and cabbage and penny slots radiated from the RV, an early warning system that told anyone approaching that it was going to be unpleasant.

Scratch begrudgingly rapped on the door.

"What's the password?" a wheezy voice asked.

"I've fallen and I can't get up!" replied Scratch.

"You may enter," the voice wheezed back. A small set of electric stairs lowered, and Scratch pulled the sticky door open. It took a moment for his eyes to adjust, between the darkness and dust of the cabin it was hard to make out the details. Sadly, not long enough, as he was soon able to make out the wrinkled, naked forms of the Elders, who apparently were enjoying a round of bingo with unlimited prune juice for all.

Oh, that smell.

"What is your business, chop chop!" demanded the Main Elder, a fluffy fat man of an age undetermined by science.

"Elders, we are clear of the Village. We are currently at a rest area, as per tradition," announced Scratch.

"Excellent, excellent," the Main Elder replied.

"We have come to the point of Trip-tik, the establishment of future stops of interest and final destination," said Scratch.

"Yes, yes," the cabal of Elders intoned.

"What is your desire?" asked Scratch.

"Very good," responded the Main Elder. "We have spent some time discussing this and we have two major requirements. First, that it possesses a warm climate. It was too damn cold in the Village. Second, that it is both scooter and wheelchair accessible."

"Done," said Scratch. "As you know, I always plug in that consideration. We have others though...we will need to set up a new trade partner, to keep the supply of properly wrapped, sealed, and processed foods. Fuel, oil, salty and sweet snacks. Someplace with ample BOGO deals, someplace that will honor our coupons."

"Yes, yes," the cabal confirmed.

"It has been some time since I made a jog for the border, but I know how to smell a deal. It's my recommendation that we cut East, and set up just outside the Hive," Scratch suggested.

"Interesting," said the Main Elder. "Start dealing with the folks we blasted into the stone age two Kings ago. Besides what you have stated as a needs analysis, what drives you to latch onto the Hive? You know what they do."

"Yes, Main Elder. I do know what they do. I also know that they have been busy appropriating every product and method implemented in the Village and have worked to improve them. They have comics, costumes, and perversions that put the Village to shame. And, they are damn handy with touch screens and circuit boards, a market we have yet to even get into."

"Fine, fine. A new market it is. I have heard that their work in cryogenics is something we should be considering as well, " said the Main Elder.

Scratch cringed at the thought of sustaining the miserable lives of the Elders, but managed not to show it.

"Interesting, I will have to look into that," said Scratch. "Well then, after a day of prep, it will be 23-skeedo to the Hive. It'll be a blast."

"Yes, yes. Now don't let the door hit your ass on the way out," the cabal muttered in creepy unison.

Scratch gladly jumped for the door, neatly dodging it as it slammed shut, bouncing a few times in the door jamb thanks to a weakened spring. He had a smile on his face. It was rare that he was able to get what he wanted from the Elders. Usually he was forced to endure long, boring stories of how hard things used to be, about limited resources, and cardboard shoes. Oh, and that little chestnut about not having access to four-wheel excitement, and relying upon true one horse horsepower. It was incredibly easy today, and although Scratch was happy, it made him a bit nervous as well.

Nervous was good, Scratch thought. It would keep him on edge, keep him from getting too comfortable. Now to attend to Everhard's needs. A vision quest always got Scratch a bit giggly, it was just about the best thing a man could do. A quick stop to the biker pit, and all would be set.

$

Peter had settled on a cute minivan that offered a lot of storage and TV screens in every headrest. Who knew how long they would be on the road? As he stuffed the back with every possible box of non-perishable food he could find from the nearest mall food court, Wanda had gotten busy welding spikes and other protective ornaments to the vehicle, as they had no idea what apocalypse would greet them when they opened the garage doors.

The van was parked in a small sealed bay, and there was little to go on. All the video cameras wired to the outside showed nothing but static and snow, and there was little noise outside to suggest any kind of life at all. Rather than worry, Wanda continued to weld, and took short breaks getting familiar with the van's plethora of convenience electronics. It was jammed with every possible connection, from Internet, to GPS, to Instant Porn. She thought she recognized a few folks from the Pigeon as she flipped channels.

It was good to be free of that nonsense, and to have a body was simply beyond any hope or expectation she ever had as a digital hooker. It may not be her original body, but it was better than nothing. Looking over at Peter, she was a bit sad. He was not quite the man she thought he was. Far too preoccupied with stuffing his face. Far too eager to sit in front of a monitor and flip channels. His art, he had said. What a joke. And the weight, at first not so important. But now, he was too much man. Literally, there was too much of him. Still he did free her from a "life" of wadded Kleenex and "O" faces.

At that moment Peter stumbled into her stream of consciousness. "You look pretty deep in thought, sweetcakes. "Careful, too much of that will kill ya."

It was true, she was deep in thought. Peter had snuck up on her, and the interruption was a bit jarring. But, what was not jarring at this point?

"We're set here. All that's left is to open the garage door and head out in that big bad world. Was there anything you still need to grab? One last trip down to the Pigeon? Who even knows if anybody is down there?" Peter smiled.

"I hope the goddamn ceiling came down on that place," Wanda said with disgust.

"We don't need it anyway," said Peter. "The only two good things about it were meeting you and fucking my boss in the ass. Gotta admit, those are two wicked awesome things, but you're right. We don't need it."

Peter opened the door for Wanda, who slowly climbed into the van, pensively taking the passenger seat. Peter, still happy as a pig in shit, didn't notice her slight emotional removal from his story arc. He had no idea that deep inside, she was about to be done with him. Peter hopped into the driver's seat and pushed the big button on the automatic garage door opener.

The garage door opened slowly, inching up in a stuttered mechanical manifestation of anticipation.

$

The Soldier stared at his father, studying his face. Sure, the wrinkles, the hairline (receding), the mischievous glint in his eye—they were all there. However, there was a serious quality about his demeanor that he either didn't remember or didn't exist before.

Out of the corner of his eye, he could see his mother serving up various treats and noshes to his loyal death squad. Kicking down doors and casting judgment made a man hungry, and they devoured everything placed before them.

"So what's the deal with the Tin Man act?" his father asked.

"Ahh, the war has done the old give-and-take, Dad." replied the Soldier.

"So I see. I assume these bad boys augment your leg strength and speed? I have done a little reading on these sorts of enhancements, of course only the consumer quality ones. These are straight military. Jack boot grade A. Perfect for crushing the opposition, I imagine," said Dad.

"Yeah, they have had their uses. I didn't ask for them. They kinda just put them on me after I got my legs blown off," said the Soldier as he strained to get a view of the Necros out in the yard. Red J help us if they get inside the house, he thought.

"Didn't ask for 'em? Not like you, I think. Of course, war has a way of changing a man. With you, it's just a bit more externalized."

Okay, the Necros were nowhere to be found. Not even random sounds of hellacious torture in the distance.

"What are ya nervous about, son?"

"Fuck Dad, what is there not to be nervous about?" said the Soldier, slightly nodding in the direction of the King collector's plate.

"True Son, very true," said Dad, whipping out a small baton tipped with a menacing arc of electricity.

"FUCK!" exclaimed the Soldier as he spun to dodge his father's swing. Quickly looking to his men, his panic levels increased as he realized that they all sat slumped in their chairs, unconscious or maybe even dead.

The first blast from the baton stung like a bitch, but wasn't enough to stop the Soldier from moving. What kept him from moving was the damn metal legs. Great for forward and back, not so much for lateral. He could never play running back. He could hear his father chuckling. There was something odd about it.

The second blast from the baton was far more painful. Dad must have turned it up a few notches. One leg gave out as the Soldier was finally clearing the living room. He looked to his mother, stoic as she stood over the table of bodies.

"Sorry it has to be this way, honey," she said.

"Me too," said the Soldier, kicking the table to splinters. It was enough to get her to jump back, and the sheer force coming out of his leg was enough to blast his men's bodies to the far walls. A nice clear space to work with.

Dad came swinging in, moving faster than he should. The Soldier was able to dodge the first swing, then the next. He threw up an elbow, and tried to shove him away. There was no way he was going to strike, as it would probably kill him.

"Ah, you're such a fucking pussy!" yelled Dad. "Why don't you try to land one on me? Afraid you'll rip your dress? Why don't you hit me with your fucking purse?"

That was enough to flip the switch, and the Soldier took the offensive, crushing his father's left foot under his heavy steel boots.

"You didn't need that, did you? Whoops," said the Soldier.

His father hopped back on his good foot and took another swing. The ozone smell and the crackling of the electrical tip floated millimeters away from the Soldier's nose.

"Ah, hold fucking still, you know how this is going to end," said his father, gritting his teeth.

"Jury is out on that, mother fucker," replied the Soldier, crushing his other foot.

"Like son, like father, huh," his father said, beginning to sound out of breath and weakened.

"Hey man, I didn't want it this way," said the Soldier.

"Us either. You just had to go out that door and sign your ass up for the General's cause, without any real idea of what it meant, and what it was going to mean," said his father, bending over and rubbing his shins. His feet were pancakes, and whatever pain he was feeling, he hid it remarkably well.

It was at that moment that the Soldier heard the crackling noise of another baton. It was his mother, and she was driving the tip into the base of his skull. After that, it was lights out.

$

It didn't take Scratch long to find where his Biker Boys had settled. Between the loud, drunken roars and assless chaps, it was easy to find their small circle of special debauchery. They typically set up shop a bit off the proper campgrounds, to satisfy their outlaw, isolationist philosophies, and to spare the others of the smell.

The Dodge Tribe as a whole was iconoclastic, free spirited, and lived to stick it to the man. The Biker Boys were a more extreme subset of that attitude, keeping to themselves as much as possible.

Scratch, ever the savvy leader, let them be. It was rare that he would even acknowledge their existence.

Besides, they often stabbed outsiders for no reason. They did not like to be bothered. One had to approach them openly, waving your arms over your head so as not to surprise them.

When Scratch reached their enclave, he was relieved to see them engaging in the Wet T-shirt ritual. This was a good indication that spirits would be high, and that special requests would possibly be entertained. The Boys formed a tight circle around some delightful trollop who was doing her best to ape poses from various ancient heavy metal music videos. She was referencing the ancient high arts, and certainly was smarter than the total IQ of the mob surrounding her.

"Yeah!" yelled one of the Boys.

"Hell, yeah!" yelled another.

Scratch, still waving his arms, moved up to the circle. Before he could do anything, he was grabbed and pulled into the middle, and promptly blasted with a hose.

"Meh, this one is flat chested. I like the big tits," said a gruff voice.

With his dignity dripping off his face, Scratch lowered his arms. He knew that it was important in the early moments of the conversation to show strength.

"That's 'cause I'm not a chick, man," said Scratch.

"Oh, I'll make a woman out of you," replied the gruff voice.

The mob cackled and guffawed. Not Scratch's strongest opening with the Boys. However, they were familiar with Scratch, so the subsequent hazing was rather minor, and thankfully did not involve being pissed on. After a bit of roughhousing, Scratch sat down with the Sergeant of the Biker Boys, Frank Vincent.

Frank was a huge man, nearly seven feet tall. He had arms of steel, a pot belly, and a beard to his belt. He was known to be surly, but fair. He listened to Scratch's request.

"So if I'm hearing you right, you want one of our bike's so some Red J charlatan can solve his mid-life crisis of faith? Hrmmmm," grumbled Frank.

"Dude, I know. Seems like a waste of valuable resources, but the Dodge Tribe fully supports all vision quests. Typically, the ROI on such a venture is quite good. He might build some fantastic new networks and markets for us, depending on how far he travels, who he meets, and what he learns."

Frank nodded in agreement, and made a slight grunting noise. Frank was very much a man like Scratch, living off the land, and making his own trades to support the areas of his operation that Scratch and upper management could not. And with the Village being a done deal, case closed, and all that, new business relationships were important to foster.

"Fine, but he's not getting one of the good ones. I got a scooter out back here that should suffice, Frank answered, walking towards a small tent. Frank went into the tent, made a few noises of struggle, and wheeled out a silver scooter in relatively in good shape that had a plastic bin bungee strapped to the back fender.

"This sucker gets great mileage, and is well within the range of the newbie rider," he said with a smile.

Scratch took one look at the scooter, smiled, and shook Frank's hand vigorously.

"This will do just fine. In fact I think he's going to love it," smiled Scratch.

$

Peter and Wanda sat in disbelief. The garage door had opened, and what greeted them wasn't quite what they expected. Looking out the windshield, Peter saw nothing but an empty street, strewn with garbage, and rotting dead bodies covering most demographics.

"Nice place you brought me too," sneered Wanda.

Peter gasped for breath. What kind of devastation had occurred during his marathon sprint from virginity with Wanda? How long had they been isolated in carnal bliss? What the fuck had happened to the Village?

"For a guy who spends a lot of time in front of the TV, you seem remarkably out of touch," Wanda said with a biting tone.

Peter thought to protest, but deep down he had to admit that she was right. What world had he brought her into? What flavor of disaster was this? He began to feel the fear, the fear he hadn't felt since his visit to the Limp Pigeon. It was an all-encompassing fear of the future, not just that of the Village, not just the loss of the status quo, but also the fear that he could lose her. For the first time, that was truly real.

Peter gently put his foot on the gas pedal and eased the minivan out of the garage. Slowly cruising down the service road, Peter decided to circle the Sell Inc. Mall complex and get a general idea of the situation. Sweat began to form on his furrowed brow, and he began to experience a sense of discomfort in his lower intestine. As they began to wander through the spider web of cross streets and access alleys, it was apparent that there was no human life in the vicinity, aside from the homeless guy who insisted on cleaning the minivan's windshield at three different intersections. Peter was actually impressed at how fast the guy could change locations, and never be any less annoying in his approach.

The piles of bodies were massive. All forms of Village residents lay dead on the street: business drones, megaconsumers, tattooed street kids, banana vendors, electronic repair troops, uniformed traffic cops, uniformed King loyalists, steroid muscle monsters, fashion models, the General's guard. Dead, all of them, and not all that recently for some.

Peter stopped the minivan when he heard Wanda sobbing.

"I can't take this. What kind of bullshit place is this? I want to go back," she stammered.

Peter put a hand on her shoulder. The reassuring paw, he called it.

"I don't think there will be anything to go back to," he said in a very poor attempt to assuage Wanda's tears.

"Well, what the fuck are we going to do?" she wailed.

"I am going to get us out of town. We'll camp for a day and figure out a good plan of action."

Wanda looked at Peter hopefully, but there was a subtle expression of doubt.

"I guess that sounds good," she said weakly.

Peter put the minivan back in gear, and drove the van onto the expressway heading out of the Village, surprised that he even knew what road to take.

$

It was with a wince that the Soldier opened his eyes. The bright light of an exposed bulb burned deeply, and it's brightness made it difficult for him to understand his surroundings.

He did immediately recognize his parents standing over him with grim faces.

"Ah, the son rises," his father quipped.

"It's about time. I was thinking we might have to wake him so he didn't miss the big show," his mother remarked.

A bit groggy, and in a fair amount of pain, the Soldier began to assess his situation. Once again, he found himself strapped to a gurney, with a mass of vaguely menacing medical equipment surrounding him. His parents stood over him stoically, and several masked doctors flitted into the background. Beyond that, he spied his father's workbench, shelves filled with boxes labeled in scrawled handwriting, and a pile of his old childhood toys in the corner. He was in the basement of the house he grew up in. And quite possibly, the house he would die in.

"What's going on? What are you doing?" the Soldier demanded.

"We are going to see you through to you logical conclusion," his father stated dryly.

"What the fuck is that supposed to mean?" the Soldier asked.

"Take a look at you son. You are half the man you used to be. And that part, the part that walked out this door to sign up for the General's fucking slaphappy meal, well that part is gone forever. We have come to peace with that," his mother said.

His father cracked a slight smile. "You have turned out to be much different from we would have ever expected. And, you are a massive disappointment to us."

His father's comment stung worse than the taser baton.

"You always told me to make something of myself. Well, here it is," the Soldier retorted.

"Here it is indeed. You have certainly exceeded everyone's expectations. However, you clearly are no son of ours anymore. You are the General's son, through and through," his father said with a sigh. "And this is going to hurt you much more than it will hurt us, but being good parents we have talked about this, and we feel it's the best thing for all parties involved."

"So what, you love the King, you love being able to get it your own way. So what, are you going to kill your only son? Is this what this is, some kind of forcible suicide, homicide, death by needle thing? Is this what you would do to your flesh and blood?" the Soldier screamed in protest.

"Now son, we would never kill you, but I will remind you that you are half of our flesh and blood. The other half is gone now. The General killed that part of you for us. We are going to seal your fate by continuing the work of the good General. We will make you complete," his father said gravely.

"And what of my men?"

"They are all dead. That was easy. And your demonic pets? They have wandered off, making their way through the neighborhood. We will hunt them slowly and methodically until they have all been terminated. Of course, we might just have you do that," his father said with a chuckle.

"And why the hell would I do that?"

"Because when we are done with you, you will be gone. All that you know and believe will have disappeared. All you will know will be your prime directive. All you will know is the cold steel that encases you. All you will know is your programming. You, who you are, will cease to be. In its place, a glorious steel man with no mercy or moral barometer," his father said.

And with that his father motioned to the far left corner of the basement. There sat a large metal framework, not unlike a propped up suit of armor. It included a menacing skull-shaped torso, large arm plates covered in spikes, and a bucket shaped helm with a glowing red eye slit, the eye sliding from left to right.

"Yes son, we are going to turn you into a fucking cyclon," his father said matter-of-factly.

$

Father Everhard stood in front of the scooter that Scratch had proudly presented to him. In his mind's eye, Everhard had pictured an epic, screaming hog on which he could epically travel his vision quest. What sat in front of him left a bit to be desired. Yes, it was functional, not completely beat to hell, and had a fine airbrushed flaming skull on the side of the fuel tank. Still, it was only a scooter, and it was a pussy ass ride.

"So what do you think?" asked Scratch with a smile. "I had to do some serious bargaining to capture this little beauty."

Everhard had been raised to be polite, and as a member of the clergy, he always operated at some level of co-dependence.

"I am sure she will get some great gas mileage," was about all Everhard could muster. Inside, he was ready to explode. He wouldn't get five miles on the thing before it would probably crap out.

"No doubt, and that's a strong quality. Not a whole lot of gas stations out in this rugged terrain. It even has a solar panel, so you can run electric if things get tough," Scratch said with a salesman's polish.

Everhard took a walk around the scooter. Small tires. Worn out seat. Broken side mirrors. Pink helmet. Woot. Scratch sensed his apprehension.

"Look, I know it's not what you were hoping for, but if you are truly on a vision quest, then you can count on other means of travel coming your way. This scooter really just gets you started. I am sure that upgrades will come your way," Scratch said apologetically.

Everhard nodded. Rarely did a vision quest end in the manner it began. There was not much time as it was. The red flying blur he had seen had not appeared since, and he needed to get moving.

"I'll take it. What do I owe you?" asked Everhard.

Scratch shook his head. "Nothing, but should something really great go down, I would hope that you would bring some of that love back my way. I am not sure exactly where the tribe will end up, but just check your network feeds and you will find us, that much I am sure of."

Everhard slung his pack over his shoulders and mounted the scooter. His legs were quite long for it. Scratch tried hard not to laugh. The priest did look a bit ridiculous. Scratch reached out and shook Everhard's hand.

"I certainly hope that you find what you are looking for."

"Me too," said Everhard. "I have wanted answers for some time...I can wait no longer. I hope that he's ready for me." Everhard revved the scooter's engine. It was less than impressive.

Scratch smiled. "Whatever your vision quest brings, it will bring truth with it. Safe travels."

Everhard gave Scratch a quick salute and opened the throttle. As he slowly crept away, Scratch suddenly felt satisfied knowing that he had done at least one thing right this day. With Everhard on his way, it was now time to pack the Tribe up. They would begin to make their way to the Hive.

$

It had taken Peter a few hours to get them out of the Sell Inc. quadrant of the Village. Many of the roads had been blocked with debris and makeshift walls, which based on body count, had not helped many people survive the cataclysm at all. However, once they cleared the consumer mecca, Peter and Wanda both began to notice life on the streets, life that resembled how things used to be. The sidewalks were thick with pedestrians, and none seemed worse for the wear.

Peter pulled the minivan off to the side of the road, lowered his window, and motioned for a young boy that had been sitting on the curb to come speak to him. Annoyed, the boy removed his headphones and walked over to Peter.

"Yeah?" stated the eloquent young man.

"Hey buddy, just wondering...what the hell happened over at Sell Inc.?" asked Peter.

The boy laughed. "You don't know? Oh, that's rich."

Peter frowned. *Another fucking smartass. Just what he needed in his life.*

"Nope, that's why I am asking."

The boy seemed amused that he was irritating Peter. "What a noob. Why don't you check the forums?"

Peter began to unlock his seat belt, with the full intention of getting out of the minivan and squashing the kid. Wanda put a hand on his knee, which stopped him. Peter looked at Wanda, who was sporting a very disapproving look. He turned back to the boy.

The boy stared back at him. Peter stared at the boy. Neither made a move. After a long, pregnant pause, Wanda waved at the boy, who didn't react. That is, until she pulled up her shirt, revealing her supple breasts.

"GENERAL'S TROOPS ARE GOING CRAZY, KILLING EVERYONE THEY SUSPECT IS CLICKING 'LIKE' ON THE KING'S PAGE!" the boy blurted.

Having no idea that his new love had just exposed herself to a minor, Peter smugly thanked the boy and shooed him off. "Aren't you glad your man can take care of business?" Peter said to Wanda.

"Absolutely dear. Absolutely," she said with a slight roll of her eyes. "So now what?"

"We still need to get the hell out of town. I am going to download a new map to the GPS and plan the quickest route out of town. With any luck, we should be clear by nightfall.

"So that's it? You download me, promise me life in the big city and then promptly drive me out of town?" protested Wanda.

Peter began to feel the fear, yet again. The fear that he was inches from blowing it. "I would rather promise you life in the big country than death in the big city. I'm just trying to look out for your best interests," offered Peter.

"Peter, I know that your intentions are sincere, but I am not sure you realize how to take care of me. I have wants and desires that you may not fully understand. I will give you one day in the country, and then we will have to figure this thing out," said Wanda.

Peter didn't wait for the maps to download. He pointed the minivan due east and drove recklessly for the horizon.

$

The Soldier was now truly sentient. There was a level of clarity and logic that was present that he had never experienced before. His brain was flooded with sensory information. His eyes viewed an H.U.D. that provided him with layer upon layer of information. Auditory overflow overwhelmed him, and it took a moment for him to instinctively lower its volume. His mind seemed to move more quickly, its ability to analyze stimulus was far beyond its normal scope. In what would have taken minutes to sort out before, occurred in milliseconds for him now.

His status was simple. He was still in the basement. He was still on the gurney. His parents and the doctors surrounded him, smiles upon their faces. He heard numerous comments about the overall success his recovery, how much faster it was than thought, how all of his vitals were solid. There were crisp sounds of high fives and hands clapping. A quick scan of the room identified six human individuals, all with solid heat signatures.

With explosive speed, the Soldier jumped off the gurney and stood facing his targets. With brutal efficiency he analyzed each individual position and engaged. Two heads crushed together immediately. A long spike popped out from his left forearm, quickly stabbing a third in the throat. Three now dead, and the others were just beginning to react. They were allowed three steps to the door before the Soldier fired the chain gun mounted to his right shoulder, cutting them down instantly. His parents became a fine red mist.

The Soldier moved to the basement door, continuing to run a scan of the room for additional targets and to capture its interior to his memory banks. Moving with high efficiency, the Soldier made his way to the ground floor, running an archive recording as he systematically searched for evidence and destroyed that which was unneeded. Within five minutes, the house was completely destroyed, and the Soldier had a full record of the home and its inventory. Making his way outside, the Soldier located six Necro-krofts in the neighbor's yard, tossing a small child between them. His sensors told him that they were giggling, which was an appropriate response to their situation. The launching of a small antipersonnel grenade made quick work of them, the foam fur and purple viscera rising eight feet and in all directions.

The Soldier stood in the middle of the road in front of his childhood home. Shooting flames from his left arm, the home began to burn. There were two possible strategies now, and according to his H.U.D., option two would take an hour to complete, a full thirty minutes less than option one.

The choice was clear. The Soldier squatted low and launched himself in the direction of the General's palace.

$

Scratch was very pleased. Normally, the Tribe would lackadaisically gather up their belongings, pack up the cars, and leisurely begin the next leg of whatever their current journey might be. Perhaps it was just a sense of purpose that made them move more quickly. Perhaps it was the horrific sounds of destruction that they heard coming from the direction of the Village. Although they could no longer see it, the massive clouds of black smoke and the constant explosions were proof enough that something catastrophic was taking place behind them. All the more reason to move forward.

Scratch was back at the wheel of his wonderful bus, the true mystery machine. With Carlos at his side, Andy, Fake Brad, and the King, he felt ready to roll. He put the bus into gear, honked the horn three times for good luck, and pushed the beast onto the road. Looking in his rearview mirror, he watched as his glorious convoy took shape, forming a column of roaring horsepower and diesel fury. There was truly nothing like the road. Carlos looked to him, smiled, and made his way to the back of the bus, to begin looking over maps. The King quickly took his seat.

"Hey Boss," the King motioned with a smile.

"Aha, right back 'atcha. From the sounds of it, it's clear that you got the hell out just in time."

The King frowned slightly. "It's true. Those days are done, and by the size of those mushroom clouds on the horizon, I am guessing they are done for just about everyone back there," he solemnly replied.

Scratch gave the King a pat on the shoulder. "Hey man, fresh slate and all that."

"Maybe, maybe. Maybe not. I'm thinking that I might need a break today. No wait, I think I just want to live my way." The King shook his head. "I don't think I am making much sense."

"Nah, Daddy-o. I pick up what you are laying down. Heavy is the head that wears the crown. Well, don't worry. Where we are going, it will take you some work to find any kind of leadership position."

The King began to open his mouth to respond when the bus lurched violently. There had been nothing in front of them, and there had been no indication of attack.

Scratch fought the wheel. "What the FUCK was that!?!"

He looked in the mirrors, and the entire convoy seemed to sway a bit, but no damage was apparent. However, the road ahead was a different story, something very strange was on the horizon. The road itself shot straight ahead through a flat plain. Aside from some small brown shrubs sprinkled here and there, there was hardly any natural landscape. That is what made the large black obelisk to the left so very obvious. As they drove past it, Scratch could feel its vibrations rattle the bus.

"Carlos!" Scratch yelled. "Get on your walkie and let everyone know there is some weird shit ahead."

Carlos managed to get the order out just as a large vaginal rift of purple energy opened up in front of the bus. Scratch had no time to react, and the bus plunged into it. Then there was nothing.

$

Peter was deep into his nervous eating. As he navigated the demolished streets of the Village, looking for a way out, he crammed his mouth with all varieties of salty starches and frosted whatevers. Although it helped him focus, it did not relieve his stress in any way. Wanda had tried to help with a handy, but all he could produce was a limp noodle. Her disgust was clear. This did not make the situation any easier.

Explosions could be heard in the distance, and the streets were filled with panicked mobs running who knew where. They ran screaming, arms flailing in every direction. Some were clearly injured, bleeding profusely. Others clenched missing limbs. Perhaps what Peter did not see was the most telling. There was not a single Rebel soldier on the street. There was no order, and no one seemed to even be trying.

Peter suddenly felt a sadness, a longing for the comfortable constants that used to fill his days. The shitty job. The shitty apartment. Being bullied and berated on a daily basis. The usual warm and fuzzies.

His TV. *Oh Red J, when would he get to watch his TV again?* What a terrible realization. The headset monitors in the minivan would simply not do.

His microwave. *Oh fuck, what about the microwave?*

All gone. Peter looked at Wanda, whose lack of enthusiasm for the current situation was broadcasting off her at industrial strength levels.

Fuck.

Peter weaved the car around two large piles of debris and a pack of blue suits that seemed to be engaged in some kind of gladiatorial combat featuring tridents. Clearing the pack, an explosion flipped the car, slamming it into a storefront. Peter's large girth proved to be better than airbags, but Wanda was thrown from the vehicle. Throwing down a bag of Auntie Nuke's Corn Hide Bits, Peter climbed from the wreckage. He screamed for Wanda, looking in all directions.

All he had to do was look forward. There, standing a good eight feet tall was a monstrous robot looking thing, silver shining metal, with strange logos painted on its limbs. The skull-like helm featured orange horns that grew horizontally out of the sides, and an uncomfortably amusing red nose capped its face. The steel technobeast held an unconscious Wanda in his arms.

"Put her down!" Peter screamed.

The robot turned its head slightly as if to consider Peter's request. It responded by grabbing him by the shirt and tossing him into the air.

$

The Soldier landed violently on the steps of the palace. The General's guards, a mixture of highly efficient ninja-like clowns and mutated Necro-krofts moved in to engage him. His enhanced senses quickly identified a kill order, and the Soldier systematically disemboweled the troops, using his spear appendage for close targets and the blazing mini-gun for ranged ones. The guards quickly died where they stood, and the Necros became frivolous piles of foam and poison ichor.

The Soldier walked through the main doors, into the heart of the keep. With the alarm bellowing, his entrance was met by waves of obedient rebels, who quickly disappeared in explosions of blood and bile, but their tenacity was admirable. A few minutes and several hundred corpses later, and the Soldier reached his objective -- the inner chamber.

The General sat on the former King's throne, a bong sitting in his lap and a remote control in his right hand.

"My oh my, have you changed," said the General dryly.

The Soldier stood silently, with various responses scrolling on his display. Silence remained the best option, and the Soldier selected it.

"What, nothing?" asked the General, taking a deep pull from his bong.

The Soldier took a step forward, beginning to analyze the most brutal and painful end to the General's existence.

"Well, I suppose it had to end like this, I can't imagine how else it could go. Just remember what you were and what you have become. And remember who got you there," the General said, cracking a sad smile underneath his smeared clown makeup.

The Soldier began walking towards the General. The General pointed the remote at the Soldier, jamming its buttons. The Soldier continued to move forward, gears whirling, building up energy. The increasing whine of his motors increased, as did the panic on the General's face as he realized his remote was not working.

"This is a fucking failsafe. Goddamn engineers! They said this would work!" screamed the General as he slammed the remote to the floor, jumping from the throne. He attempted a run for the door, but was interrupted as the Soldier moved to his position and grabbed his neck with a vise-like grip.

A sensation of pleasure worked deep inside the Soldier's processors as he began to crush the General's windpipe. His gurgling sounds of desperation echoed throughout the chamber, as his body flailed uncontrollably. There were several snaps, a crack, and a pop. Moments later, the General was dead. It had been an amazingly quick death.

The Soldier ensured the General's departure as he threw his body to the ground repeatedly, until it was nothing but a pile of oozing viscera with a clown nose. Concluding that the General was permanently incapacitated, the Soldier moved to the banks of computer servers on the far edge of the room. Plugging in through a small, finger-like appendage that issued from his wrist, the Soldier joined with the massive network that maintained the Village's infrastructure.

Systematically, he shut down Network One, the water system, traffic lights, and the wireless communication web. The Village was dark. The Soldier then moved quickly from the inner chamber, crushing any remaining resistance within the palace, until he made his way to the street. Offline recordings would show the Soldier systematically moving throughout the Village destroying all life in his path. Of all the carnage, of all the death, there was only one strange moment where the Soldier stopped a moving vehicle, grabbed its female passenger, and threw its morbidly overweight driver clear of the area.

The last remaining footage of the one man cyborg apocalypse shows the Soldier standing on the roof of the burning Sell Inc. Headquarters. The unidentified woman stood next to him smiling.

$

Scratch sat on the side of the road dazed. His bus, his convoy lay on the road, vehicles overturned as if an angry child had thrown his toys. Bodies lay everywhere. It took several minutes to gather his senses. The fucking ringing in his ears, well that took days to clear.

Slowly his tribe began to move, gathering themselves, and eventually wandering about.

Carlos limped towards Scratch, attempting to pull an arrow from deep in his thigh.

"What the fuck, boss?" Carlos muttered.

Scratch didn't know what to tell him. He could not remember.

A large, morbidly obese man came flying into the camp, landing with an unceremonious thud. Carlos and Scratch looked at the crater.

"Seriously. What the fuck, boss?"

Scratch had had no idea what the fuck was going on. Looking back at the road behind them, the entire Village was in flames, massive clouds of dark smoke squatting above its skyline, and they were growing quickly. Scratch pointed at the devastation.

"I don't know, but I know this. We are putting as much fucking distance between us and *that* as quickly as possible. Get everyone's shit together and let's get the fuck out of here!"

Carlos nodded in agreement and limped off to make things happen.

19. Stand By...We Are Experiencing Technical Difficulties

Exterior: The same bleak, trashy, field you were standing in before.

There are less people that you recognize in the crowd. Most are in tears. The man in the top hat raises his megaphone. You feel an incredible amount of dread.

It's now that time on the show when we turn to our personal hand-tooled leather bound copy of the Book of Revelations and Traditional Wok Cooking the Old School Way.

Turn to Page 3.

The Book Of Revelations is your handy guide to the obvious signs that the sky is falling, Chicken Littles. The low priests in the high office and the high-on priests in the front office have convened over beers and burritos, sacrificed two small barnyard animals and have DINED AND DASHED. They have scoped out the scenery and it does not bode well.

The dark shadow trail of Armageddon looms over us, and shit, do you know how much a movie costs these days? It's like they make popcorn out of solid gold. They want you to stay home.

It is said that a lone figure, distant and unclear, will step to the plate and call out the downward spiral of life on this miserable speck of a speck on the Demigod of the Month's sorry, omnipotent, pimply ass. This figure brandishes a trumpet to punctuate every end-of-life-as-we-know-it photo opportunity.

And when that dark Big Band Sound starts to wail, baby, and get ready to dig the bitter end.

The trumpet blows once, and your Ed McMahon sealed envelope with your possible winnings arrives via registered mail to your El Rancho Villa style home. This envelope, along with all of its contents spells (when the first letter of every sentence in the Free

Truck Early-Bird Offer is selected), the word Babylon, which of course is an anagram for DEVILED HAM IS COMING. This is also known as the opening of the First Seal act, or the falling of the tower of Potted Meat Product.

The 'What's On Second Seal' is all that typical stuff: the sea turns to fire, the moon becomes the color of money, no smoking signs go up everywhere, the animals finally admit they can talk, and hailstones the size of volleyballs fall to Earth causing irreparable damage to Gulf Coast homes with no hurricane insurance. After the opening of the Second Seal, clothing decorated with professional athletic team logos is suddenly affordable.

The First Stage of the Apocalypse, consisting of the opening of the First and Second Seals will last approximately six months, to begin on a Monday and end on a Monday, with one long weekend off so that everyone can get to know the Antichrist on a private junket to Barbados. Be sure to pack your sunscreen people!

Speaking of the Antichrist, he will make himself known initially through a series of Top 10 Hit Records in the popular alternative music market. Capitalizing on current consumer trends, he will sell his mark through mass merchandising, home shopping, social networking, micro-blogging, direct mail, infomercials, and classic cold-call telemarketing.

He'll go right to the top, baby.

The Third Seal involves the arrival of the four dreaded Horsemen of the Apocalypso: War, Death, Famine, and Cheney. Each harbinger brings (hence the term harbinger) their own thematic style of awfulness. This is immediately a disappointment to three of the four horsemen as War, Death, and Famine have all been present on the planet for some time. Cheney, however, would have to run for office, and his chances aren't that great.

At this point, our trumpeter blows one fine solo – but is he appreciated? No. Rather that listen to a neat jazz groove, people will stand around, ridicule Christians, drink beer, and buy souvenir T-shirts. Cable TV rates skyrocket (again).

There will also be these pain-in-the-ass people who insist that you stream your media, and upload all your personal data to the cloud. These fuckers are to be shot on sight. Trust me, you will be very happy you did.

The Fourth Seal, when broken, will result in the issuing of fetish leather wear (similar in style to the outfit Mel Gibson wore in *The*

Road Warrior) to each and every citizen. This was not in the original script, but the art director thought it would give it a nice feel or something like that. He mumbles, so who knows what magazine he's ripping off?

As soon as all the costumes are handed out, the beheadings shall continue!

The Fifth Seal, also known as Double Coupon day, and in some mythologies, BOGO day, is when, to a world that seemingly could take no more punishment, rock-bottom prices begin to skyrocket, then hit bottom again. At this point even those hardcore individuals who still had hope in humanity will simply shrug, shake their heads, and hold out their hands as a gesture of futility.

And on an even larger scale, all the plain-belly Sneetches will want to be star-bellied Sneetches, and this guy appears and he happens to have a machine that allows them get stars on their bellies and vice versa. The Sneetches will get worked into a frenzy and eventually nobody will know who's who – kind of like buying clothes at the Fruity Republic.

The Sixth and final Seal is the big doozy, the ultimate kick in the pants: The Take-Me-Away-Born-Again Rapture Fiesta. At this point nothing matters— steal a TV, send your food back because it was cold when you got it, have unprotected sex, jaywalk, trout fish clearly over the limit, have five drinks too many, call your mother, sign up for classes whose times overlap, return your movies late, screw your sister, eat fatty foods, forget your homework, lie, cheat, steal, see evil, hear evil, speak evil, stop making sense, reveal your nefarious/villainous plot because the hero of your story is facing certain death, act like Scott Baio in the morning. In short, do everything you do anyway. If there's something you always wanted to regret doing, do it because big nasties will be coming out of the Earth and crush every trailer park still standing. The clock is ticking, bitches.

And if this wasn't enough for you, a terrible contagion that will literally cause your flesh to explode off of your body will become popular with the late-night set, who will discover infection right around the fourth meal of the day. This lines up nicely with a TV broadcast where the President will announce full disclosure, yes there are aliens and all that shit, but guess what, there is a freaking meteor about to hit Earth and life expectancy has gone from 74.5 years to roughly ten minutes or so.

The broadcast is then interrupted by agents of the Illuminati, who admit, yeah we pretty much made up everything in your history books. Why? Because, they will explain, they were very, very bored and people are stupid. Then, for that last nine minutes of ridiculous life, every perpetrating mofo on the planet from the Lizard People to the schmuck who designed pill bottles to be hard to open, grab the mic and admit their sins.

This is of course, too little, too late.

My friends, this is the final checkout time. All keys must be at the front desk and any calls made will be charged to your room, X-rated movies will be charged as well. Nothing will be left, this is the end of our long and tedious going out of business sale. Somebody has just asked God how many licks does it take to get to the center of this mud ball and he has responded: Press 3 to delete!

Well, it's been nice knowing you, happy trails and all that crap! Don't let the door hit ya in the ass on the way out! See ya suckers, thank you Cleveland, goodnight!

RUMORS & LIES

Tom Lucas was born in Detroit, on the tail end of the '60s. Throughout his childhood, Tom found solace in comic books, Star Wars action figures, and the supreme baby sitter, the television set.

In his teen years, Tom lived in a central Detroit neighborhood featuring a predominantly Polish population. Tom was faced with a choice. Go to some post-apocalyptic plaguehaus inner-city public high school, or to attend a Ukrainian Catholic high school. Not wanting to stab or be stabbed, Tom went with the private school. However, being neither Ukrainian nor Catholic (baptized yes, practicing NO), Tom struggled while earning quality teen angst credibility. To make money, Tom flipped pizzas. To save money, he drank really cheap beer.

In college, Tom changed majors several times before deciding that an English degree would be a sound choice. (To this day, he is not sure why he wasn't the target of an intervention.) Never one for consuming great literature, but rather a copious consumer of media, Tom worked his way onto his college's daily newspaper, reviewing films and eventually becoming the Entertainment Editor. This led to pounds of free tickets to movies, and a stack of promo CDs. But during those years, Tom was more satisfied by spoken word performance, which led to many appearances on local radio, as well as a hosting gig at Lollapalooza III. Tom also self-published several comic books, which were well received and presented in a comic book art show in Portugal, of all places.

Tom was not content to follow this path, and felt that a solid decade of bad choices would make life much more interesting. Some highlight-reel decisions included being a bartender in a blind pig for three years, working in the world of automotive sales training, and moving to LA in 1998.

LA was Tom's deal with the devil, and if this were an episode of True Hollywood Story, these were the years of darkness and drug use you typically find around the 25-minute mark. Tom lived in Venice Beach, made PowerPoint slides for car salesmen, and created a massive screw-up portfolio for himself. Its diversity was quite impressive.

But what great story filled with mistakes doesn't feature redemption? In 2003, he finally figured things out and made an incredibly desperate decision to move to Florida. There, in the plastic land of Boca Raton, he reinvented himself.

With years of clarity finally improving his mental function, Tom remembered his passion for writing and began work on Leather to the Corinthians, his first full-length novel...his response to a lifetime of media over saturation. As a writer he currently participates in the high art of blogging and building a modest social network that provides him with the ability to write snappy comments and register his approval with only a click. You can find and stalk the mystical Mr. Lucas @:

Blog: www.readtomlucas.com
Twitter: @readtomlucas
Facebook: Tom Lucas (author)

C'mon, become a part of his mad, mad, world! You know you want to.

A FEW MOMENTS OF QUALITY TIME WITH THE MAN BEHIND THE MADNESS

Who is Tom Lucas? Well, if you just read his bio, you'd know he's a badass. Some might consider his musings the love child of Kurt Vonnegut and Philip K. Dick. If Tom was an animal he'd be a Liger. Have we piqued your interest? Good. Read on to learn more about this evil genius and his words that burn.

Q: Tom, How do you define yourself as a writer? Who do you speak to through your words?

I'm not typically a word-sketcher. I don't take my notebook and sit in the back corner of a coffeehouse, looking cool, writing down random nonsense. If I were though, I know I would rock it.
I write. I write all kinds of things. At my core, I am a major smart-ass and somewhat surly, but you will find that my mind creates all kinds of material that doesn't seem to line up with that. Yep, I'm complicated.

I am a writer that works best when I have purpose... a mission... a quest... a deadline. I need to be organized, and I need to work my thoughts out in advance before I sit down at the keyboard.
I love comic books, Sci-fi movies, and video games. I read books too, all kinds of books. However, you won't find an ounce of pretension. I don't believe that words will save me or anyone else. I don't walk in parks with a notebook searching my heart. I will never write a touching tale of father-son bonding.

Here's the thing...I don't write nice genre pieces. It's a slippery thing that I've got going on. So, who would enjoy it? Let's see: Gamers, Comic book readers, Humorous Sci-fi peeps, Literary, I'm-cooler-than-you kids (SLAM DUNK WITH THESE FOLKS),People who like pop culture references, People sitting in waiting rooms for a long time, The disenfranchised, The 99%, Old Punk Rockers (the DIY crowd), and anyone else who likes to read a good mindbender.

Lately, I have been putting it out there doing some spoken word and recording my work. You'll find downloads on my site: **www.readtomlucas.com**

Q: When and how did Leather come into existence? What's the message all about, man?

Leather to the Corinthians is a book that took some time to write. Pieces here and pieces there, put together on my summers off (I taught high school during that time). Some elements in the book are from scrawlings I made in undergrad, a million years ago. There have been times when I hated every word of it. Times when I couldn't believe the genius of it. Nervous moments when handing it over to someone else. Joy from praise by those who read it.

My purpose for writing this book is that I want to burn the palaces down. My goal for the book is to give everyone that is as frustrated as me a chance to laugh a bit. I think much of the world sucks, that people and human nature have ruined so much of it. As I am not a member of the Star Chamber, my only option is to satirize it to the ground.

It's not a neatly placed genre book. Leather to the Corinthians could become a major cult book (that's the dream) or it could be considered pure garbage. Being a writer means being brave in a way that those who do not write will never truly understand. It's a white knuckle experience. It carries considerable emotional risk. I'm rolling the dice on it. I'm always up for a challenge.

There are a few different ways I like to pitch the novel:

1. My novel is a high concept satire, along the lines of *Gulliver's Travels* or perhaps *Alice in Wonderland.* It centers on a kingdom broken by civil war and an ensemble of characters that represent various aspects of society, such as big business, organized religion, the military-industrial complex, fast food, and so on. It's an excuse for me to sarcastically tear down the "pillars" of society.
2. It has a distinctive non-chronological style where events are described from different characters' points of view and out of sequence so that the time line develops along with the plot.

3. Or maybe: A blend of satire, gallows humor, the scatological, working blue, science fiction, comic books, Saturday morning Kroftian nightmare.
4. Then there's this: An absurd and apocalyptic genre mash-up postmodern fuck you to the world.

Q: You mention that you love comics and we learn in your bio that you've successfully published a few...Tell us about that and do you plan on either putting out more or somehow incorporating those elements into your novels?

I have loved comics all of my life. My very first reads were Dennis the Menace and Richie Rich. I always thought Archie could fuck right off, though. Don't know why, but I always hated that ginger bastard. Soon I discovered Mad and Cracked magazines, and superheroes were not far behind. Indie comics would follow that. I will read comics until the day I die, but I am certain that my tastes will change. Comics are a perfect blend of film and literature, and I would love to take *Leather to the Corinthians* and turn it into a graphic novel. Based on reader interest, I can definitely see that happen.
Besides writing future books featuring our Villagers, I would also like to publish a collector's edition of Leather to the Corinthians filled with professional and fan art. The Village is a visual place, and there are endless opportunities to capture it. It pretty much demands it.

Q: In Leather, are there any characters that do you personally identify with? Who are your favorites? Who do you hate and want to punch in the face?

There's a bit of me in most of the characters in the book. At times I have been the doubt-ridden soldier, the desperate corporate drone, and the cavalier tribal leader. It's hard to nail down my favorites, as each character will be explored in much greater depth in future books. I am perhaps most excited to explore Father Everhard's vision quest and explaining where Scratch and the gang traveled to at the end of the book. Where the hell did they go? How long were they gone? And what the fuck really happened?

The two most deserving of a punch in the face would be the CEO of Sell, Inc. and Peter. And I think we will all see that happen in the future.

Q: Who is the beguiling side-show barker that leads us into your intriguing interludes? It seems like he epitomizes "THE MAN". Will you tell us more about our mysterious narrator?

The barker represents those things in life that are beyond our control, those things that make us feel powerless and angry. As this is different for each of us, it's my hope that readers will put their own unique imprint on the barker and truly personalize the experience.

Q: What is the "Hive", we're intrigued. Will they be featured in your next epistle?

The Village is a chaotic place, filled with many unique characters. It serves those with power well, and all others must suffer the exploitation. The "Hive" on the other hand, runs like a machine, and every denizen of it has a particular role to play. It's the complete opposite of where the characters have run from. We'll see how well it works out for them; I'm not making any promises.

Q: Speaking of which, when can we expect more? Will our heroes be back? Where will we find them? What new town, adventures and interesting folk will they encounter?

I have already begun working on the next book, and I expect to have it out in the fall of 2013 – provided that the world has not ended. Your favorite characters will be back, and we'll spend some quality time with all of them. The Village has been conquered by techno-apocalypse and the struggle to return it to what it once was will be a priority. We will explore the Church of the Red J, live in the "Hive" and also have some fun attacking everything that is fucked up about the world today. There will be some fun new characters entering the mix, and if I have a bad day, I just might kill one or two as well. Either way, it's going to be a party.

K
K

www.ingramcontent.com/pod-product-compliance
Lightning Source LLC
LaVergne TN
LVHW020706110826
845149LV00012B/2127

* 9 7 8 0 9 8 8 5 2 6 1 0 5 *